THE AUTHOR

Herbert George Wells was born in Bromley, Kent in 1866, the third son of an unsuccessful shopkeeper. At eighteen he broke his indentures as a draper's apprentice and became a pupil teacher at Midhurst Grammar School, from where he won a scholarship to the Normal School of Science, South Kensington and studied biology under T. H. Huxley. Although distracted by politics, writing and teaching he obtained a B.Sc. in 1890 and then lectured for the University Tutorial College until the success of his short stories allowed him to become a full-time writer. Idealistic and impatient, he flung himself into contemporary issues – free love, Fabianism, progressive education, scientific theory, 'world government', human rights. His personal life was equally restless; after an early marriage to his cousin Isabel in 1890 ended in divorce, he married a pupil, Amy Catherine Robbins, in 1895, and was later involved with a series of remarkable women including Amber Reeves, Rebecca West, Elizabeth von Arnim and Moura Budberg. He died in London in 1946.

H. G. Wells wrote over a hundred books, achieving unparalleled international fame for a British writer. His work ranged from the famous scientific fantasies like *The Time Machine* (1895) and realistic comedies like *Kipps* (1905) to provocative topical novels such as *Marriage* (1912), *Mr Britling Sees It Through* (1916), *The Autocracy of Mr Parham* (1932) as well as *Christina Alberta's Father*, and controversial or encyclopedic works like *A Modern Utopia* (1905) or *The Outline of History* (1920). He describes his own life in the two-volume *Experiment in Autobiography* (1934) and *H. G. Wells in Love*, unpublished until 1984.

CHRISTINA ALBERTA'S FATHER

H. G. Wells

New Introduction by
Christopher Priest

THE HOGARTH PRESS
LONDON

Published in 1985 by
The Hogarth Press
40 William IV Street, London WC2N 4DF

First published in Great Britain by Jonathan Cape 1925
Hogarth edition offset from the original British edition
Copyright the Executors of the Estate of H. G. Wells
Introduction copyright © Christopher Priest 1985

British Library Cataloguing in Publication Data
Wells, H. G.
Christina Alberta's father
I. Title
823'.912[F]P R5774.C4
ISBN 0 7012 0579 2

Printed in Great Britain by
Cox & Wyman Ltd
Reading, Berkshire

INTRODUCTION

Christina Alberta's Father was first published by Jonathan Cape Ltd in 1925. Attracting H. G. Wells to the list had been something of a coup for Cape, as it was then still a young firm. The first of Wells's novels for Cape had been *The Dream*, a year before, and according to the Cape biographer, Michael S. Howard, they had been prepared to invest an immense proportion of the company's resources in this one author. It is not difficult to see why: Wells was at the height of his fame, and commanded a huge audience.

But ten years later, Wells himself was dismissive of the novels he wrote in the mid-1920s. 'I have to admit,' he said in *Experiment in Autobiography*, 'that the larger part of my fiction was written lightly and with a certain haste.' In the same passage he went on to exonerate *Christina Alberta's Father* to some degree, because he believed that the central character was a 'caricature–individual' of whom he was not ashamed. Wells's defensiveness about his fiction from this period is probably caused by the fact that his preoccupation, and also his greatest success, was with journalism. *The Outline of History* (1920) had absorbed him, and was a runaway success. His mind was not fully on his novels, and he fitted them into the interstices of his non-fiction writing.

The omens are not good for *Christina Alberta's Father*. When you learn that the serial version was called *Sargon, King of Kings*, and that it deals with a middle-aged Englishman deluded into believing he is the reincarnation of an ancient Sumerian king, the heart can be forgiven for sinking a little.

However, this hastily produced novel, with its deluded caricature at its heart, and written by an author with his mind on weightier matters, turns out to be a pleasant surprise. Sixty years after its first appearance, *Christina Alberta's Father* looks altogether more substantial and achieved than even the author was prepared to believe. Partly this is because of our hindsight – as with so many novels by Wells, this one was ahead of its time – but partly through our surprise: it is a forgotten book, obscured by the prolificity of its author, one more novel lost amongst so many others that he wrote.

The novels of H. G. Wells draw on two great inspirations, and they are to be found in everything he wrote.

He was first of all persistently and consistently auto-biographical, whether he was drawing on his memories, his relationships, or the people and places around him. In his lifetime he published more than fifty novels, and every single one draws directly or indirectly on his life; indeed, it is hard to think of any other writer who has so ruthlessly plundered his own experiences for his fiction, at least over so long a period of time. Secondly, Wells was a novelist of idea: he had an impatient, agile, visionary mind, uniquely capable of both the long view and the small insight. His novels brim with ideas, and with the urgency of idea-finding, and always with the sheer exhilaration of a superior intellect working in public.

Autobiography and ideas: these are both revelatory forms of writing, external manifestations of personal discoveries in the writer's life.

They are clearest in his early work. Wells's childhood is well recorded, and we know that he was a late developer: his youngest years were often marred by ill-health, and always by poverty, but he grew up in a world of self-discovered ideas, reading voraciously to supplement the poor formal education he was receiving. After abortive entries into trade – drapery, pharmacy, drapery again, then a little teaching – he won a scholarship to the Kensington Normal School of Science, where he studied biology under T. H. Huxley. He was in his late twenties when he wrote his first novels: by some standards a young age for a novelist, but Wells was impatient for the off.

There is a rawness to H. G. Wells's early novels, but it is this that gives them their durability. His head was spinning with the discoveries he was making about himself, and about the world of ideas, and he wrote with an energy and directness of purpose that found an audience almost at once. Most of his scientific romances were written in the first ten years of his career, and it is surely no accident that these are the books that have remained among his most popular. Successive generations of readers have discovered for themselves *The Invisible Man, The War of the Worlds, The Time Machine*, many others; these books have been in print in one form or another since they were published, and they have a particular appeal to the young. The same popularity has been true of novels like *Love and Mr Lewisham, Kipps* and *Tono-Bungay*: these were his first forays into fictionalized autobiography, and they too have worn the years well.

But Wells did not of course stay raw, and his impatience was assuaged. With success came acceptance and a degree of financial security; he met other writers – Shaw, Gissing, Bennett, James – and was admitted to whatever it is that constitutes the literary world; his second marriage, to Amy Catherine Robbins, was a success at least insofar as it gave him domestic security, a sound business partner and manager, and a loving friend whom he trusted absolutely. Most of all, with the beginning of the new century, Wells underwent a change in his approach to writing that almost proved disastrous. It came with the publication in 1901 of a book of speculative essays called, with cumbersome portentousness, *Anticipations of the Reaction of Mechanical and Scientific Progress upon Human Life and Thought*.

Wells was restless with his reputation as a scientific romancer, and since 1896 he had been working fitfully on the novel that was to become *Love and Mr Lewisham*. In letters written at this time he spoke repeatedly of his wish to establish himself as a serious writer of social novels, and as a commentator on current affairs. The turn of the century gave him the idea of a series of essays looking forward to society as it might be a hundred years later, and these, after first appearing in a magazine called *Fortnightly Review*, became *Anticipations*. The impact of this book was spectacular: it was a bestseller (eight printings in the first year alone), and was published in America and throughout Europe. Praise for it was extravagant, and its author was hailed as a prophet and a seer.

H. G. Wells was never the same again. Until *Anticipations* he had been merely popular, and earning a reliable income; after *Anticipations* he was important, influential and, with occasional lapses, extremely well off.

Anticipations, and other books that followed in the same vein, profoundly affected Wells's approach to his fiction. He developed confidence in his ideas, and brought them more overtly into his stories. It is probably overstating it to say that his head was turned, but none the less there is a discernable difference in the novels he wrote thereafter. His prolific output continued, and amongst the novels he was to write were some of his best: *Ann Veronica, The History of Mr Polly, Mr Britling Sees It Through*, and others. But also among them were some of his worst, and these were often didactic, padded, unstructured, talky; in other words, they were thinly disguised vehicles for his obsessions. He attacked the Catholic church, wished for a world state, urged the creation of an 'open conspiracy', quarreled with other writers, ranted about the failures of the educational system, and so on. Perhaps the clearest example of how seriously he took the importance of his fictional warnings and prophecies is in the introduction he wrote to a later edition of *The War in the Air*. This novel, first published in 1908 (when aircraft could barely manage to stay aloft), accurately forecast the threat of aerial warfare. In 1941, towards the end of his life, Wells wrote with heavy emphasis that he would like his epitaph to read: 'I told you so. You *damned* fools.'

A novelist's insistent belief in the accuracy of his predictions does not guarantee the imaginative value of those ideas. When Wells became didactic his fiction was unpersuasive, but when his imagination was given free rein his beliefs were eloquent. A fine example of this can be found in *The War of the Worlds* (1898). In the final chapter, reflecting on the long-term effects of the Martian invasion, the narrator observes:

It may be that in the larger design of the universe this invasion from Mars is not without its ultimate benefit for men; it has robbed us of that serene confidence in the future which is the most fruitful source of decadence, the gifts to human science it has brought are enormous, and it has done much to promote the conception of the commonweal of mankind.

Coming as it does at the climax of one of Wells's greatest descriptive passages, this early precursor of his obsession with the world state has all the passion and resonance that is lacking in some of his later novels, when his ideas as such had more confidence. In his early work the ideas gave shape to the metaphors that put the muscle and energy into his stories; later, Wells abandoned the metaphor and took up the stance of a lecturer.

But not so in *Christina Alberta's Father*, because although it is a novel of ideas, the book has a structured narrative and the didactic elements are well assimilated. In *The Outline of History*, Wells had recorded the story of Sargon of Sumeria with some approval, and as the unfortunate Mr Preemby's delusion overtakes him his conception of a better world is pure Wellsiana. Against expectations, these scenes are written with considerable sensitivity, and Preemby-as-Sargon turns out to be much more sympathetic and complex than Preemby-as-Preemby. One of the most moving scenes in the book takes place shortly after Mr Preemby's incarceration, when the awfulness of his fate comes home to him. Briefly, Sargon recedes and Mr Preemby resurfaces: he recognizes that conventional sanity is an option, but in the end declines it. Wells wrote this novel many years before clinical research into people with multiple personalities, yet Mr Preemby's case is an almost classical example. It seems likely that Wells's intention with Mr Preemby's delusion was essentially didactic, yet his treatment was instinctive and imaginative, and in this long central passage we glimpse once again a pure Wellsian vision, a startling return to the directness of his first novels.

In spite of the author's assertions within the story, the focus of interest is actually Christina Alberta herself, one of Wells's feisty young women, Ann Veronica as she might have been in the 1920s. Arms akimbo (on several occasions) she dominates the novel, especially in the early scenes. Her frustrations in the Petunia Boarding House, her relationships with the young men attracted to her, and her flight into the bohemian world, are all described with wit and precision. When Mr Preemby is with her, some of Wells's best comic scenes appear, in particular the portrait of this dry old stick trying to maintain appearances while his daughter's arty friends debauch through his newly acquired bedsitting room.

As in all of Wells's novels, autobiographical sketches appear. There must be something of the author in Mr Preemby, but more of him in Sargon. Christina Alberta herself is Amber Reeves as she might have reacted to the 1920s, and some of her attitudes are close to those of Odette Keun, Wells's companion at the time this novel was written. We see perhaps another side of Wells himself in the character of Paul Lambone, and Udimore, Lambone's house in Kent where the story ends, is obviously Spade House shifted a few miles down the coast. But these are only sketches: the body of the novel is its story, hinted at in the wilfully misleading title, and narrated with all the relish of a great storyteller. *Christina Alberta's Father* is one of the best of H. G. Wells's late novels, undeservedly neglected for years, and a pleasure to rediscover.

Christopher Priest, Harrow 1984

Contents

BOOK THE FIRST
The Coming of Sargon, King of Kings

PAGE

CHAPTER THE FIRST

THE EARLY LIFE OF MR. PREEMBY   11

CHAPTER THE SECOND

CHRISTINA ALBERTA   28

CHAPTER THE THIRD

IN LONSDALE MEWS   50

CHAPTER THE FOURTH

THE PETUNIA BOARDING HOUSE   86

CHAPTER THE FIFTH

THE SCALES FALL FROM MR. PREEMBY'S EYES   116

CHAPTER THE SIXTH

CHRISTINA ALBERTA CONSULTS A WISE MAN   134

BOOK THE SECOND
The World Rejects Sargon, King of Kings

CHAPTER THE FIRST

INCOGNITO   165

CONTENTS

PAGE

CHAPTER THE SECOND
THE CALLING OF THE DISCIPLES   198

CHAPTER THE THIRD
THE JOURNEY OF SARGON UNDERNEATH THE WORLD   221

BOOK THE THIRD
The Resurrection of Sargon, King of Kings

CHAPTER THE FIRST
CHRISTINA ALBERTA IN SEARCH OF A FATHER   249

CHAPTER THE SECOND
HOW BOBBY STOLE A LUNATIC   305

CHAPTER THE THIRD
THE LAST PHASE   350

CHAPTER THE FOURTH
MAY AT UDIMORE   377

Book the First

THE COMING OF SARGON, KING
OF KINGS

CHAPTER THE FIRST

The Early Life of Mr. Preemby

§ 1

THIS is the story of a certain Mr. Preemby, a retired laundryman and widower, who abandoned his active interest in the Limpid Stream Laundry, in the parish of Saint Simon Unawares, near Woodford Wells, upon the death of his wife in the year of grace 1920. Some very remarkable experiences came to him. The story is essentially a contemporary story: it is a story of London in the age of Sir Arthur Conan Doyle, broadcasting, and the first Labour peers. The historical element in it is insignificant and partly erroneous, and the future, though implicitly present, is substantially ignored.

Since washing in London, like the milk trade and baking and the linendrapery and various other branches of commerce, is something rather specialized and hereditary and a little difficult towards outsiders, it is necessary to explain that Mr. Preemby was not a laundryman born. He had little of the spirit and go of a true London laundryman. He married into laundrying. He met a Miss Hossett at Sheringham in 1899, an heiress and a young lady of great decision of character; he wooed and won her and married her, as you will be told, almost without realizing what he was doing. The Hossetts are big people in the laundry world, and the Limpid Stream concern which presently fell into the capable hands of Mrs. Preemby, was only one of a series of related and sympathetic businesses in the north, north-east and south-west districts of London.

Mr. Preemby, as Miss Hossett's family came to recognize quite frankly and explicitly at a very early stage, derived from a less practical strain than his wife. His father had been an artist of considerable charm and unpunctuality, a

photographic artist, who resided at Sheringham and made
what were called in the eighteen-eighties, 'gem' photographs of the summer visitors to that place. In the
eighteen-eighties he was a well-known Sheringham figure,
dark and handsome and sometimes a little unkempt, wearing a brown velvet jacket and a large grey soft-felt hat. He
would fall into conversation with the visitors upon the
beach, and a certain air of distinction about him would
bring a sufficient proportion to his studio to maintain him.
His wife, our Mr. Preemby's mother, was a patient, under-
developed personality, the daughter of a farmer near Diss.
When presently Mr. Preemby senior passed out of his
son's life – he became romantically entangled with a small
variety entertainment in the summer of 1887 and vanished
away with it in the autumn with as little fuss as possible,
never to return to Sheringham – Mrs. Preemby senior
became the working partner in a small lodging-house and
died in a year or so's time, leaving her furniture, her
interest in the lodging-house and her only son to her
cousin and partner, Mrs. Witcherly.

Young Albert Edward Preemby was then a good-looking,
slender youth of sixteen, with his father's curliness and
his mother's fair hair and eyes of horizon blue, dreamy and
indisposed for regular employment. Even as a child he
had been given to reverie; at school he would sit with sums
or book neglected before him, looking beyond them at unknown things; his early experiences in business were disappointing by reason of this abstraction. After a number
of unsuccessful attempts to exploit his gifts at some favourable point in the complex machinery of our civilization, he
came to rest for several years in the office of a house-agent
and coal-merchant in Norwich to whom his mother was
distantly related.

Some ancient, remembered, sentimental tie helped
Albert Edward to this appointment and shielded any im-

perfections in his performance from too urgent a criticism. He did much better at it than anyone could have expected. The calling of a house-agent differs from most other callings in the fact that the necessary driving energy is supplied entirely by the clientele, and there was something about the letting of the larger houses that touched the dormant imagination of young Preemby. He revealed a natural gift for attractive description and was duly entrusted with the work of collecting particulars from prospective lessors. He had a quite useful hopefulness. And even the coal proved unexpectedly interesting so soon as he found that none of it had to be carried about by him. He could never believe that all the golden scales one finds in it were pyrites. He cherished a secret dream of a great commercial enterprise to work cinder heaps for residual gold. He told no one of this project, he took no steps to realize it, but it warmed his daily routines with its promise of release and wealth. And when things were slack in the office in the early afternoon and he was left in charge, he would go and sit on the coal counter and pick out the coal samples for the little trays and turn them over and over and view them from various angles and weigh them in his hand and lapse into the most splendid visions.

And if inquirers after houses came in, he would receive them with a manner almost regal.

In Norwich he became a member of the Y.M.C.A., but he was interested in its literary rather than its religious side, and he attended any political debates available. He never spoke in these debates, but he sat at the back reflecting that politicians are, after all, no more than puppets in the hands of the silent rich men who sit behind the scenes. It was in Norwich, too, that he was able to buy his first tailor-made suit, of a most becoming grey. When he went to stay with Mrs. Witcherly at Sheringham for his summer holiday of a fortnight, she was delighted by the improvement in his appearance and much impressed by the active hopefulness that had replaced his former lethargy. Upon the sea front in the afternoon in his grey suit, to anyone who did not know about him, he might have been almost any sort of prosperous summer visitor.

It seems a yesterday, and yet it seems ages ago, that our plump and short Mr. Preemby was that small blonde young man twirling his stick and glancing furtively but desirously at the lady bathers in their vast petticoated bathing dresses and oilskin caps, as he strolled along the Sheringham front. That was in the days when motor cars were still rather a joke, a smell, and a noise and wayside repairs, and flying was understood to be impossible. Queen Victoria had had her Diamond Jubilee and nobody thought Albert Edward, Prince of Wales, would ever survive to be King. The War in South Africa was being arranged for that summer, to last six months and employ forty thousand men. And it was on the third day of his grey suit holiday at Sheringham that Mr. Preemby was run into by his future wife, Miss Hossett, riding on a bicycle, and thrown against and almost run over by her friend Miss Meeta Pinkey.

Because, incredible as it may seem to the modern reader, people did succeed in those distant nineties, before the coming of the more suitable automobile, in knocking down and running over other people with the sluggish apparatus, bicycles, horse-drawn vehicles and so forth, then available.

§ 2

Miss Meeta Pinkey was an emotional blonde girl, and she fell off her machine gracefully and naturally into Mr. Preemby's arms as he was hurled against her. It would seem to have been the original intention of Destiny to have made this the beginning of a permanent relationship, but in this matter Destiny had reckoned without Miss Hossett. Miss Meeta Pinkey was as ripe for love just then as dry gunpowder is for a bang, and she was already deeply in love with Mr. Preemby before she had been replaced securely on her feet. She stood flushed and round-eyed and breathless, and Mr. Preemby looked quite manly and handsome after picking up her bicycle with an air of rescue.

Miss Hossett, after butting against Mr. Preemby, had swerved, dismounted, and stood now prepared for a dispute. The collision had further loosened the already loose handlebar of the entirely untrustworthy hired machine she had been riding. It was this looseness had caused the accident. Her attention seemed divided equally between this and the possible grievance of Mr. Preemby. 'I rang my bell,' she said.

She was flushed and erect. She was a round-faced girl with a long, thin neck, a good bright complexion, glasses on her thin nose and a resolute thin-lipped mouth.

'I did all I could to avoid you,' she said.

'Awkward of me,' said Mr. Preemby disarmingly. 'I was lost in a day-dream.'

'You aren't hurt – ?' asked Meeta.

'Startled,' said Mr. Preemby, 'especially where the wheel got me. This place is full of corners.'

'I'd've been over,' said Meeta, 'if you hadn't caught me.'

Miss Hossett was reassured about any possible conflict with Mr. Preemby. Evidently he was going to be quite nice about the accident. 'This handlebar was as loose as could be,' she said. 'Look at it! You can twist it about like on a swivel. They ought to be punished for letting out such machines. Some of these days one of 'em'll get let in for Damages. Then they'll be a bit more careful. Scandalous I call it.'

'You can't ride it at all now,' said Mr. Preemby.

'No,' she agreed. 'Have to take it back to them.'

It seemed only right and proper for Mr. Preemby to wheel the machine for her back through the town to the hiring place, where Miss Hossett reproved the hirer, refused to pay anything, and secured the return of her deposit in a few well-chosen words. Miss Pinkey paid the hire of her bicycle for a First Hour. It seemed natural after that for the little party of three to keep together. They kept together with a faint sense of adventure, and Mr. Preemby behaved as nothing less than a normal lodger at Mrs Witcherly's establishment and summer visitor to the seaside. His new-found friends were Londoners, and he referred himself to Norwich and the management of house property. He was quite amusing about Sheringham. He said it was 'a dear little backward-forward place,' that it was a real treat to come to for a breath of sea air.

'I don't like regular smart places,' said Mr. Preemby. 'I'm too absent-minded.'

§ 3

In after years Mr. Preemby would often try to recall the various stages that led to his marrying Miss Hossett, but there was always a vague sense that he missed out something, though he knew not what it was nor where it ought to have come in.

At first things did not look in the least like his marrying Miss Hossett. Indeed they did not look like his marrying anyone, and if the word marriage had been whispered in his ears as the possible consequence of this encounter he would have been terrified. He perceived that he was acceptable company to these girls, but it seemed to him that it was Meeta who formed the link between them and himself. A fourth person presently joined their company who answered to the name of Wilfred, and it seemed to Mr. Preemby that the air of mutual proprietorship between Wilfred and Miss Hossett was unchallengeable.

The young people wandered in a little party along the sea front until the sea front came to an end, and there they found a sheltered and comparatively secluded niche in the brow of the low cliffs and gave themselves up to the delights of Spooning; and it was Meeta who Spooned with Mr. Preemby that afternoon and Wilfred who Spooned with Miss Hossett. Across the gulf of a quarter of a century the memory of Mr. Preemby was still certain that this was so.

The fashions of life change from age to age. Knowledge has spread and refinement increased; and a generation of young people, more restrained, more sophisticated, or more decisive than their predecessors has taken possession of the world. This Spooning was an artless, clumsy dalliance in great favour in those vanished days, a dalliance that was kept within the bounds of strict decorum – if ever that became necessary – by cries of 'Starp it' or 'Starpit, I tell you,' on the part of the lady. They embraced, they kissed, and put their silly young heads together and so whiled away the long waiting-time before love had its way with them. The summer resorts of England were littered with young people indulging in these poor, silly, undignified anticipations of love. Mr. Preemby, it became manifest, was a natural born Spooner.

'It's lovely,' said Miss Meeta, 'the way you squeeze me.'

Mr. Preemby squeezed some more and ventured to kiss a hot ear.

'Go On with you!' said Miss Meeta, in a voice thick with delight. 'That little moustache of yours – it *tickles*.'

Flushed with encouragement and preoccupied with ideas

for further enterprises, Mr. Preemby did not remark that the affairs of Miss Hossett and her Wilfred followed a more troubled and less satisfactory course. Wilfred was not a type that appealed to Mr. Preemby. In spite of the fact that he was much less neat in his dress than Mr. Preemby – he had grey flannel trousers, an old fancy vest, a tweed Norfolk jacket, and low brown shoes with light-coloured socks – he impressed Mr. Preemby as being consciously a social superior. He was young – the youngest of the party – and yet dominant. He had large red hands and big feet, much untidy hair, ill-regulated features that might later be handsome, and a hoarse guffaw. He viewed Mr. Preemby as though he knew all about him and thought the worse of him for it, but did not intend to make any positive trouble for the present about his existence. He was, Meeta whispered, a medical student at Cambridge, and his father was a Harley Street physician who had been knighted. He did not Spoon with any abandonment; he seemed weary of Spooning, he had perhaps been Spooning for some days, and his conversation with Miss Hossett went on in subdued contentious tones. He sat a little apart from her amidst the sand and coarse bluish grass, and her face was flushed. What they said was inaudible to our intertwined couple.

'Chris and Wilfred don't get on together as we do,' Meeta said in a low voice. 'They're sillies.

'He's like all the men,' said Meeta, ''Sept one perhaps. Want everything they do and give nothing.

'He won't even say they're engaged,' she said. 'Dodged seeing her father.'

There was a pause for reflection and then a renewal of endearments.

'I'm gorne on you,' said Meeta. 'I *am* fair gorne on you. You've got the bluest eyes I've ever seen. China blue they are.'

18

§ 4

So detachedly it was that Mr. Preemby and his future wife passed their first afternoon together. He remembered it, as he remembered most actual things, indistinctly, in a setting of hot sand and sunshine, blue-grey grass and a line of poppies nodding against an intense blue sky. And then across these opening memories Chris Hossett seemed to leap at him with flushed cheeks and glowing eyes, magnified by her glasses.

Two or three days intervened before that passionate pounce. Mr. Preemby, in his character of an incidental visitor to Sheringham, was under no obligation to produce a social background, but Miss Pinkey introduced him to two large, kindly aunts of a sedentary sort, as a young man related to Miss Hossett who had saved her from a nasty fall off a bicycle, and he and she both went to tea with Chris Hossett's 'people.' Old Mr. Hossett was a very ailing man, excessively fat and irritable; he had never been the same, whatever the same was, after his only son had died; and Mrs. Hossett, an energetic lean threat of what her daughter might become, had to wait on Mr. Hossett hand and foot. She had spectacles instead of Chris's glasses, her eyes were careworn and her complexion was leaden and her neck lean. There were also a married cousin and his wife, a Mr. and Mrs. Widgery, who seemed to be under the impression that Mr. Preemby was a relation of Miss Pinkey's. Mr. Widgery had a long pockmarked face and the dullest brown eyes Mr. Preemby had ever seen. There was nothing difficult to eat at tea and Mr. Preemby got on very well listening to an explanation of the precariousness of Mr. Hossett's existence, due to heart trouble, from Mrs. Hossett and of just how unsatisfactory and distressing it was to come away and leave the laundry in the hands of a manager. Wilfred did not come to the tea. He had been asked but he did not come.

The next day Mr. Preemby met Wilfred on the sea front watching the girls bathing from a bathing machine. Afterwards all four went for a walk in search of privacy, and it became evident that Miss Hossett declined to Spoon further with Wilfred. It was evident that there was profound trouble between Chris and Wilfred. They scarcely spoke as they returned towards the town; and before the sea front was reached Wilfred said 'So Long,' quite suddenly, and turned away and vanished up a road running inland. Thereupon Wilfred passed out of Mr. Preemby's world; Mr. Preemby never knew what became of him and never wanted to know; and the next day he became aware for the first time of Miss Hossett's magnified eyes, regarding him with an interest and a challenge that made him feel almost uncomfortable.

Miss Hossett became a serious obstacle to the Spooning of Meeta. The quartette was now reduced to a trio; and Mr. Preemby found himself the apex, so to speak, of a triangle, the eternal triangle in an exceptionally acute form. Whenever Meeta was on the one hand, Chris was on the other. She called him 'Our Teddy'; she pressed upon him; she went so far as to stroke his hair. Meeta's endearments faded to some extent in the presence of this competition, but she made no explicit objection.

Deep in the nature of the human male is a fount of polygamous pride. Mr. Preemby in these novel circumstances was proud and disingenuous. He believed himself 'carrying on' with two girls at once, and it seemed to him to be a very splendid situation. But indeed it was not so much a case of carrying on as of being carried off. In the American world of emotional imaginations there is an ideal called the Cave Man, much cherished by quiet, unaggressive women because its realization would involve so little trouble on their own part. The Cave Man is supposed to seize and grip and carry off and adore. In this simple love story of Mr. Preemby's Miss Hossett played the Cave Man's rôle, up to the carrying-off point at any rate. On the first occasion of their being alone together she drew him to her and kissed him on the mouth with a warmth and an intensity and thoroughness that astonished and overwhelmed Mr. Preemby. It was quite different from Meeta's coy achievements, or anything he had ever met around Norwich. He had not known that there was such kissing.

And in the warm summer twilight Mr. Preemby found himself being carried off to a lonely piece of beach to Spoon with Chris Hossett. The light of a rising full moon mingled with the afterglow; pebbles shone out like gems and stars. He carried himself bravely but he was all atremble. He knew that this time the enterprises would not come from him. And the Spooning of Chris Hossett was no more like the Spooning of Meeta than a furnace glow is like the light of the moon.

'I love you,' said Chris as though that justified anything, and as they stumbled homeward at an hour that Mr. Preemby called 'feefully late,' she said: 'You're going to marry me aren't you? You've *got* to marry me now. And then we can *really* make love. 'Soften as we like.'

'I can't rightly say that I'm exactly in a position to keep a wife just at present,' said Mr. Preemby.

'I don't see that there's any necessity for me to ask a man to keep me,' said Miss Hossett. 'You're a wonder, Teddy, anyhow, and I'm going to marry you. It's got to be, and there you are.'

'But '*ow* can I marry you?' asked Mr. Preemby almost peevishly – for he was really very tired.

'One would think to hear you that no one had ever

married before,' said Chris Hossett. 'And besides – after this – you *must*.'

'Mind you I've got to go back to Norwich next Tuesday,' said Mr. Preemby.

'You ought to have thought of that before,' she said.

'But I'll lose my situation.'

'Naturally father will find you something better. We aren't poor people, Teddy. There's no need to be scared about it. . . .'

In such terms was Chris Hossett wooed and won by Mr. Preemby. He was scared, dreadfully scared, but also he was tremendously roused. It impressed him as being a wildly romantic affair and very terrifying and a little hard on Meeta Pinkey. But he was bustled along too fast to think very much about Meeta Pinkey. He was introduced over again to the Hossett parents next day as their daughter's affianced husband, and in secret she gave him three golden sovereigns to buy her an engagement ring as a surprise. Mrs. Hossett behaved at first as though she approved of Mr. Preemby and disapproved of the marriage, and then after what was clearly a stormy scene upstairs with her daughter, she behaved as though she approved highly of the marriage and thought Mr. Preemby a very objectionable person. Mr. Hossett would not speak to Mr. Preemby directly, but he spoke of him to his wife and to imaginary auditors in Mr. Preemby's presence as a 'scoundrel' who had 'got hold' of his girl. Yet he, too, seemed to regard the marriage as desirable, and no one made any reply to his *obiter dicta*.

It was all very puzzling and exalting to Mr. Preemby. He did little except what he was told to do. He was carried over his marriage as a man might be carried over a weir. He left any explanation to Mrs. Witcherly of what was happening for some more favourable occasion. He went off on Tuesday with his little valise as though he was going back to Norwich. He wrote a simple letter of regret to the house-agent and coal-merchant. Private affairs, he said, of an urgent nature prevented his return to his duties. Mrs. and Miss Hossett went up to London with him. They all took rooms at a temperance hotel in Bloomsbury, and Mr. Preemby was married by special licence at St. Martin's by Trafalgar Square.

Then he went down to the Limpid Stream Laundry to live with his parents-in-law and master the duties of assistant manager, canvasser, and publicity agent. Mr. Hossett never spoke to him and sometimes talked rather unpleasantly about him when he was in the room, making accusations that were better ignored, but Mrs. Hossett gradually became cordial again. And presently Mr. Hossett had a heart seizure and died, and in the course of a few months Mr. Preemby found himself a father. When he was first confronted with his daughter and, as it proved, his only child, he thought her an extremely ugly little red object. He had never seen a baby at so early a stage before. She had a lot of very fine moist dark hair which subsequently gave place to a later crop; she had large indeterminate features and remarkably large feet and hands. Mr. Preemby had an absurd impression that he had seen her somewhere before and hadn't liked her. Then in a day or so she became a quite ordinary pink baby and wonder gave place to affection.

She was christened Christina Alberta after her mother and Mr. Preemby.

§ 5

In time all these experiences mellowed in Mr. Preemby's memory into a vague, glorious, romantic, adventurous past. He continued to be rather dreamy and distraught, but on the whole he made a dutiful, faithful husband, and he got on very well with his masterful and capable wife.

She was, he had discovered on his marriage, three years his senior, and she continued to be in every respect his senior to the day of her death. But she treated him with proprietary affection; she chose all his clothes for him, she cultivated his manners and bearing and upheld him against all other people. She dressed him rather more like a golf champion than he would have done himself if he had had any say in the matter. She would not let him have a bicycle for many years, she was a little exacting about his ways of keeping the laundry accounts, she fixed his pocket-money at ten shillings a week, and she was disposed to restrict his opportunities for conversation with feminine members of the laundry staff. But he made no marked protest against these slight deviations from the customary obedience of a wife. A tendency to plumpness manifested itself, and he grew considerable quantities of blonde moustache without apparent effort.

Their home was an agreeable one, the more so after Mrs. Hossett had followed her husband to his resting place, under a marble crucifix with a dove and olive branch in relievo at the intersection of the arms, at Woodford Wells. Mr. Preemby became a great reader, reading not only romantic novels – he had a great distaste for 'realism' in any form – but ancient history, astronomy, astrology, and mystical works. He became deeply interested in the problem of the pyramids and in the probable history of the lost continent of Atlantis. Mental science also attracted him, and the possibility of increasing will-power very greatly. He would sometimes practise will-power before the looking-glass in his bedroom when Mrs. Preemby was not about. At nights he would sometimes will himself to sleep instead of going to sleep in the usual fashion. He gave a considerable amount of attention to prophecy and eschatology. He developed views of his own about the Day of Judgment that might have led to a breach with the Established Church if Mrs. Preemby had not thought that such a breach would react unfavourably upon the Laundry. As time went on he accumulated a library of upwards of a thousand volumes and a very considerable vocabulary.

His wife viewed these intellectual preoccupations with friendly sympathy, at times even with pride, but she took little part in them herself. The Laundry was good enough for her. She loved the Laundry more and more; loved its piled clean and starched shirts and collars and its folded and stacked sheets, loved the creak of its machinery and the suddy bustle of the washing room. She loved to have it all going on, orderly and right; to feel everything going through the tubs and washers and wringers, sure and safe; nothing astray, nothing missing at the end. When she walked about the place voices were hushed and scrubbing became respectfully assiduous. And she liked making things pay.

On Sunday afternoons and on days when the laundry had no need of his services, Mr. Preemby took long walks. In fine weather he would walk into Epping Forest or to Ongar or even into the rustic peace of the Roothings, but in dull weather he would go Londonward. After a while the trams were extended as far as the present terminus at Woodford and it became possible to ride very pleasantly right into the heart of London by way of Seven Sisters Road and Camden Town or, with a little bit of extra walking, by the Lea Bridge Road and the Angel and Holborn.

The greatness and multitudinous activities of London stirred slumbering strands of Mr. Preemby's imagination. He would go in and lunch at an Aërated Bread Shop on a scone and butter, with a cup of cocoa and perhaps a jam-puff, and he would spend hours looking into shop windows and sometimes even making small purchases. He loved Charing Cross Road with its book-shops, Tottenham Court Road, Holborn, Clerkenwell, and the Whitechapel Road, but Piccadilly and Bond Street and Regent Street seemed costly and lacking in true intellectual interest, and he felt his baggy tweed knickerbockers and cap a little out of tune in these smart places. Sometimes he would go to the British Museum and look very hard at objects connected with the pyramids. Great public events always drew him to London. If there was a great murder or a great fire or a Royal Wedding or a Royal Funeral, Mr. Preemby would be sure to be looking at it where the crowd was thickest, often with a neat packet of provisions, a sandwich, an orange, or so forth, that Mrs. Preemby had provided. But he never saw illuminations and fireworks because Mrs. Preemby liked to have him at home when the day's work was over. He enjoyed the Great War of 1914–18 gravely and profoundly. Once he passed a man whom he thought afterwards was almost certainly a German spy. The thought thrilled him for days. He had given him a good look anyhow. He attended air raids in plenty, and he saw the Potters Bar Zeppelin shot down. He was a good four years too old for compulsory military service when the time came, and Mrs. Preemby would not let him be a special constable because she thought he might catch cold.

Mr. Preemby's work in the counting-house was not very onerous, but he also gave thought and attention to the extension of the business outside. He invented several attractive circulars. His experience as a house-agent had trained him to note the existence of large comfortable-looking houses that might otherwise have escaped his observation and to ascertain whether they were occupied; he would then find out whether the Limpid Stream Laundry got the washing from such establishments, and if not

26

he would send a circular and even follow it up with a personal letter. He was vaguely observant about the premises. He would go sometimes and look for quite a long time at the furnaces or the delivery-vans or any new piece of machinery like the new calendering machine until he got used to it. But if he stood about where there were girls working, Mrs. Preemby would make some excuse to get him back into the office because, as she explained, she thought a man standing about affected the girls' work unfavourably. He took in and sometimes read the *British Laundryman* and the *Dyers' and Cleaners' Gazette.*

Occasionally he had happy ideas. It was his idea to paint the delivery vans bright blue and decorate them with a swastika, and to paint exactly the same colour and design on the front of the laundry and put it on the bills. But when he wanted to put the van drivers into swastika caps and blue the clothes baskets, Mrs. Preemby said she thought the thing had gone far enough. It was also Mr. Preemby who suggested Ford cars instead of horse vans as early as 1913. This change was made in 1915.

And at home with her peaceful interested father and her busy, occasionally rather astringent, mother, Christina Alberta grew to girlhood and womanhood.

CHAPTER THE SECOND

Christina Alberta

§ I

THIS story, it was clearly explained in the first paragraph of the first section of the first chapter, is a story about Mr. Preemby in the later years, the widower years, of his life. That statement has all the value of an ordinary commercial guarantee, and on no account shall we ever wander far from Mr. Preemby. But the life of his daughter was so closely interwoven with his own during that time that it is necessary to tell many things about her distinctly and explicitly before we get our real story properly begun. And even after it has begun, and while it goes on, and right up to the end, Christina Alberta will continue to intrude.

Intrusion was in her nature. She was never what is called an engaging child. But she always had a great liking for her daddy and he had the greatest affection and respect for her.

She had little or no tact, and there was always something remote and detached, something of the fairy changeling about her. Even her personal appearance was tactless. She had a prominent nose which tended to grow larger, whereas Mrs. Preemby's nose was small and bright and pinched between her glasses, and her father's delicately chiselled and like some brave little boat shooting a great cascade of moustache; she was dark and both her parents were fair. As she grew up the magic forces of adolescence assembled her features into a handsome effect, but she was never really pretty. Her eyes were brown and bright and hard. She had her mother's thin-lipped, resolute mouth and modestly determined chin. And she had her mother's clear firm skin and bright colour. She was a humming,

28

shouting, throwing, punching child with a tendency not to hear admonitions and an almost instinctive dexterity in avoiding sudden slaps. She flitted about. She might be up the drying-ground or she might be under your bed. The only thing to do was to down and look.

She danced. Neither Mr. Preemby nor Mrs. Preemby danced, and this continual jiggeting about perplexed and worried them. A piano or a distant band would set her dancing or she would dance to her own humming; she danced to hymn-tunes and on a Sunday. There was a standing offer from Mr. Preemby of sixpence if ever she sat quiet for five minutes, but it was never taken up.

At her first school, a mixed day-school in Buckhurst Hill, she was first of all extremely unpopular and then extremely popular and then she was expelled. Afterwards she did fairly well at the Taverners' Girls' School at Woodford, where she was recognized from the first as a humorist. There was always a difficulty in calling her any other name than Christina Alberta. People tried all sorts of names but none of them stuck but 'Christina Alberta.' 'Babs' and 'Baby' and 'Bertie' and 'Buss' she was called at home and 'Ally' and 'Tina,' and at school they tried 'Nosey' and 'Suds' and 'Feet' and 'Preemy' and 'Prim.' Also 'Golli-wog' because of her hair at hockey. These all came off again, and left the original name exposed.

She was quick at her lessons and particularly at history, geography, and drawing, but disrespectful to her teachers; at school hockey she played forward right with marked success. She could run like the wind, and she never seemed blown. Her pinch was simply frightful. She could make sudden grimaces with her nose that gave the weaker sort hysterics. She was particularly disposed to do this at school prayers.

Between her mother and herself there was a streak of

animosity. It was not a very broad streak, but it was there. Her mother seemed to cherish some incommunicable grievance against her. It didn't prevent Mrs. Preemby from doing her duty by the child, but it restrained any real warmth of affection between them. From an early age it was Daddy got the kisses and got climbed over and pulled about. He returned this affection. He called her 'my own little girl' and would even say at times that she was a Wonder. He took her for walks with him and told her many secret things that were in his mind, about the Lost Atlantis and the Lamas of Tibet and the fundamentals of Astrology preserved indecipherably in the proportions of the pyramids. He'd often wished, he said, to have a good look at the pyramids. Sometimes one man saw things that others didn't. She would listen intently, although not always in quite the right spirit.

He would tell her of the virtue and science of Atlantis. 'They walked about in long white robes,' he said. 'More like Bible characters than human beings.'

'Good for the laundries, Daddy,' said Christina Alberta.

'All we know of astrology is just fragments of what they knew. They knew the past and future.'

'Pity they were all drowned,' she remarked without apparent irony.

'Maybe they weren't all drowned,' he said darkly.

'You don't mean there's Atlantics about nowadays.'

'Some may have escaped. Descendants may be nearer than you suppose. Why you and me, Christina, we may have Atlantic blood!'

His manner conveyed his conviction.

'It doesn't seem to help much,' she said.

'Helps more than you think. Hidden gifts. Insight. Things like that. *We* aren't common persons, Christina Alberta.'

30

For some moments the two of them pursued independent reveries.

'Still we don't *know* we're Atlantics,' said Christina Alberta.

§ 2

After she had fought her way to the sixth form in the Taverners' School the educational outlook of Christina Alberta was troubled by dissensions both within the school and without. The staff was divided about her; her discipline was bad, her class work rank or vile, but she passed examinations, and particularly external examinations by independent examiners, with conspicuous success. There was a general desire to get her out of the school; but whether that was to be done by a university scholarship or a simple request to her parents to take her away, was a question under dispute. The games mistress was inclined to regard murder as a third possible course because of the girl's utter disregard for style in games, her unsportsmanlike trick of winning them in irregular and unexpected ways, and her tendency to make drill and gymnastics an occasion for a low facetiousness far more suitable for the ordinary class-room. The English and Literature mistress concurred – although Christina Alberta would spend hours over her essays working in sentences and paragraphs from Pater and Ruskin and Hazlitt so that they might pass as her own original constructions. It was not Christina Alberta's fault if ever and again these threads of literary gold were marked in red ink, 'Clumsy' or 'Might be better expressed' or 'Too flowery.' Only the head-mistress had a really good word for Christina Alberta. But then the head-mistress, as became her position, made a speciality of understanding difficult cases.

And Christina Alberta was always quietly respectful to the head-mistress, and could produce a better side to her nature with the most disconcerting alacrity whenever the head-mistress was called in.

Christina Alberta, as soon as the issue became clear to her, decided for the scholarship. She reformed almost obtrusively; she became tidy, she ceased to be humorous, she lost sets of tennis to the games-mistress like a little sportswoman, and she stopped arguing and became the sedulous ape of Stevenson for the estranged English mistress. But it was up-hill work even in the school. There was a little too much elegant surrender in her reformed tennis and a little too much parody about her English in velveteen. The possibility that she would ever join that happy class of girls who go in from the suburbs to classes in London and lead the higher life beyond parental inspection and sometimes until quite late in the evening in studios, laboratories, and college lecture-rooms, seemed a very insecure one, even without reckoning with the quiet but determined opposition of her mother.

For Mrs. Preemby was not the woman to like a daughter educated above her parentage and station. She came to lament her weakness in not bringing Christina Alberta into the laundry as she herself had been brought in at the age of fourteen. Then she would have learnt the business from the ground up, and have qualified herself to help and at last succeed her mother, even as Mrs. Preemby had helped and succeeded Mrs. Hossett. But the school with its tennis and music and French and so forth had turned the girl against this clean and cleansing life. She was rising seventeen now, and the sooner she abandoned these things which lead straight to school-teaching, spinsterhood, Italian holidays, 'art' clothes, and stuck-up incapacity, the better for her and every one.

She made a campaign against Christina Alberta's habit of

32

sitting about in unladylike attitudes and reading; and when
Mr. Preemby took the unusual and daring course of saying that it was a bit hard on the girl, and that he didn't
see any harm in a book or so now and then, Mrs. Preemby
took him up to Christina Alberta's own little room to see
what came of it, and more particularly to see the sort of
pictures she'd stuck up there. Even when he was confronted with a large photographic reproduction of Michael
Angelo's creation of Adam as the master had painted that
event on the roof of the Sistine Chapel in Rome, he still
made a feeble show of resistance, and said that it was 'Art.'

'You'd stand anything she did, I believe,' said Mrs.
Preemby. 'Look at it. Art! Look at these books! Darwin's
Origin of Species! That's a nice book for a girl to be prying
into.'

'Very likely she doesn't see the harm of it,' said Mr.
Preemby.

'*Her*!' said Mrs. Preemby compactly. 'And look at this!'

'This,' was Howe's *Atlas of Biology*. She opened it to display its large pages crowded with pictures of the detailed
dissection of a frog.

'Reely, my dear!' said Mr. Preemby. 'It's one of her
schoolbooks. There reely isn't nothing what I should call
improper in that. It's Science. And, after all, it's only a
frog.'

'Pretty things they teach at school nowadays. What with
your Art and your Science. Doesn't leave much to the
imagination. Why, when I was a girl if I'd asked Ma
what was inside *any* animal, she'd have slapped me and
slapped me hard. And rightly. There's things rightly hid
from us – and hid they ought to be. God shows us as
much as is good for us. More. No need to *open* animals.
And here – here's a book *in French*!'

'H'm,' said Mr. Preemby, yielding a little. He took up the
lemon-yellow volume and turned it over in his hand.

33

'All this reading!' said Mrs. Preemby and indicated three shelves of books.

Mr. Preemby assembled his courage. 'You mustn't expect me to go against reading, Chris,' he said. 'It's a pleasure and a light. There's things in books . . . Reely, Chris, I believe you'd be happier if you read a bit. Christina Alberta is a born reader, whether you like it or not. She gets it from me, I suppose.'

Mrs. Preemby started and regarded his flushed opposition; the anger in her eyes was magnified through her glasses. 'It's wonderful,' she said after a little pause; 'it's truly wonderful how Christina Alberta manages to get everything she wants.'

§ 3

Miss Maltby-Neverson, the head-mistress of the Taverners' School, called upon Mrs. Preemby and shook her resolution a good deal. She was obviously a lady, and the school washing ran in term-time to twenty pounds a week. She was taken to see the scandalous picture and she said: 'Very beautiful, I'm sure. One of the really Great Paintings in the world. Pro-foundly religious. It's the very words of the Bible made into a picture. What do you find in it to object to, Mrs. Preemby?'

Whereupon, as if by a trick, the picture ceased to be scandalous and Mrs. Preemby was ashamed of herself. She saw now there never had been anything wrong about that picture.

Miss Maltby-Neverson said that Christina Alberta was a difficult type but a thoroughly interesting personality, a *real* personality. She had a great capacity for affection.

'I haven't found that,' said Mrs. Preemby.

34

'It is a type I have studied,' said Miss Maltby-Neverson, simply but conclusively.

She explained that Christina Alberta was an *active* type. Left to herself without employment to *stretch* her faculties she might easily get into almost any sort of mischief. Almost any sort. Not that there was anything wrong in her essentially. It was just energy. Given good hard work and a scope for ambition, she might become a very satisfactory woman indeed – possibly even a distinguished woman.

'I've no use for distinguished women,' said Mrs. Preemby shortly.

'The world has,' said Miss Maltby-Neverson gently.

'I'm afraid I'm one of the old-fashioned sort,' said Mrs. Preemby.

'Christina Alberta isn't.'

'Let the man be distinguished abroad and the woman distinguished at home,' said Mrs. Preemby. 'I'm sorry to differ from you, Miss Maltby-Neverson; but one cannot help one's opinions.'

'It depends upon ourselves,' said Miss Maltby-Neverson.

'I'm afraid I like men to rule,' said Mrs. Preemby. 'Woman has her place in the world, and it isn't man's.'

'But I thought Mr. Preemby rather favoured the scholarship idea.'

Mrs. Preemby was baffled. 'He *did*,' she said as though she did not see clearly what that had to do with the matter.

'Give the thing a trial,' said Miss Maltby-Neverson. 'After all, she may not win this scholarship.'

But Christina Alberta won it with marks to spare. She took no risks. It was a biennial scholarship which had been established by a benefactor of advanced views. It was tenable at the London School of Economics. As soon as Christina Alberta knew she had secured it she went,

35

without consulting her mother or anyone, to a hairdresser's and had her hair bobbed. To Mrs. Preemby this was almost a worse blow than the scholarship. She surveyed her shock-headed, handsome-nosed daughter in her short gymnastic skirts with a qualm of sincere hatred.

She wished she could make her daughter feel about herself as she felt about her. 'I wish you could only see yourself,' she said with concentrated bitterness.

'Oh, *I* know,' said Christina Alberta.

'I suppose you're a judgment on me,' said Mrs. Preemby.

§ 4

But Christina Alberta had only studied in the London School of Economics for a year, she was beginning her second year when her mother obliged her to resign her scholarship. Christina Alberta had stayed late in London one evening without telling her mother she was going to do so, she had gone to a discussion of the Population Question at the New Hope Club in Fitzgerald Street, and she had come home smelling so strongly of tobacco that her mother had repented of and revoked all her concessions to modernity there and then.

She had been waiting for that moment for many months. 'This ends it,' she said as she let her daughter in.

Christina Alberta found there was no immediate way round or through that decision. She worked her father and Miss Maltby-Neverson in vain. But instead of resigning her scholarship right out as she had been told to do, she played for time and explained her absence by a vague reference to family trouble.

Mrs. Preemby in those days was already in very bad health, but this fact was completely overshadowed in the minds of both her daughter and her husband by the far more urgent fact that she was now constantly in a very bad temper. Everything was conspiring to worry her – except Mr. Preemby, who knew better than to do anything of the sort.

The closing years of the Great War, and still more so the opening year of the Disappointing Peace, were years of very great difficulty for the laundry business. The munitions business put laundry girls above themselves and there was no doing anything with them. Coal, soap, everything was at unheard-of prices, and it was impossible to get back on the customers by raising the charges. People, even the best sort of people, were giving up cleanliness. Gentlemen of position would wear their dress-shirts three or four times and make their undervests and under-pants last a fortnight. Household linen was correspondingly eked out. People moved about; the new army officers' wives came and went, here to-day and gone to-morrow, leaving unpaid bills. Never had Mrs. Preemby known so many bad debts. Van men came back from the army so shell-shocked and militarized that they embezzled out of pure nervousness and habit. Income tax became a nightmare. Outside as within, Mrs. Preemby's life was a conflict. She kept the Limpid Stream Laundry paying all through that awful time because she was a wonder at management, but she did it at a terrible loss of vitality.

She became bitterly critical of the unhelpfulness of Mr. Preemby and her daughter. When they tried to be helpful she criticized their incapacity. They did more harm than good.

Meal times were awful. She would sit flushed and glowering through her glasses, obviously afflicted by a passionate realization of the world's injustice and eating very little. Mr. Preemby's attempts to start a cheerful conversation were rarely successful. Even Christina Alberta was overawed.

'Things going a little better this morning?' Mr. Preemby would try.

'Can't I get rest from business even at my meals?' the poor lady would complain.

Or, 'Looks like pleasant weather for the Derby.'

'Pity you can't go there for all the help you are in the place. I suppose you haven't heard what's happened to van number two.'

'No!' said Mr. Preemby.

'You wouldn't. Hind mudguard smashed. Been done for weeks. And nobody knows who did it. One would think that that was a man's business anyhow. But it's left for me to find out. And pay for. Like everything else in the place.'

'I'd better make inquiries.'

'I know those inquiries of yours. Better leave the whole thing alone now. Grin and bear it. . . .'

The silence of the meal would be restored.

She seemed to set a high value upon these awful silences. She even complained that he ate his cheese biscuits audibly. But how else can one eat cheese biscuits? Christina Alberta was made of sterner stuff and became controversial. Then her mother would flare out at her insolence and declare that 'one or the other of us' leaves the table. 'I'll read upstairs,' said Christina Alberta. 'It isn't *my* wish to be lunching here.'

Before the abrupt ending of Christina Alberta's university career she was present only at breakfast and supper; supper wasn't nearly as awful in quality as breakfast, and breakfast could easily be bolted and got away from; but after the New Hope Club catastrophe, she was present at all the meals, a sort of lightning conductor for her father and something of a restraint upon, and an added exasperation to, her mother. She took the line of agreeing that if her university career was to end, then she must go into the laundry business; but she argued very stoutly that to do that with any hope of success under modern conditions meant a 'proper business training.' If she could not go to the London School of Economics then she ought to go to Tomlinson's Commercial Training School in Chancery Lane and learn book-keeping, shorthand, typing, business correspondence, précis, commercial French, and so forth. And after three weeks of painful midday meals this proposal was adopted under stringent conditions and her season-ticket to London was renewed. She worked her way very passably through another winter with Tomlinson's as her school and most of London as her playground. She learnt all sorts of things. She added a new set of friends and acquaintances, some with bobbed hair and some without, of the most various social origins and associations, to the circle she had already acquired at the London School of Economics.

When presently Mrs. Preemby began to speak of a gnawing pain that oppressed her, both her husband and daughter took it at first as a new development of her general grievance against them and felt no particular apprehension about it. Mr. Preemby said he thought she ought to take advice or see some one about it, but for some days she treated the suggestion with scorn. If once she got in a doctor, she said, they'd have to find some one else to look after the laundry. Doctors put you to bed and give you things to keep you there. Otherwise how could they get a living?

Then suddenly she changed. One morning she confessed she felt 'dreadful.' She went back to bed and Mr. Preemby, with strange premonitions that the world was coming to an end, trotted off for a doctor. The clinical thermometer showed a temperature mounting above one hundred and one. 'It hurts. My side hurts,' said Mrs. Preemby. 'I've had it once before, but not like this.'

Christina Alberta came home that evening to discover herself capable of fear, remorse, and tenderness.

She had some strange moments with her mother in between phases of weak delirium and insensibility. Mrs. Preemby's face seemed to have become smaller and prettier; the feverish flush in her cheeks simulated youth. She was no longer hard or angry, but rather pathetically friendly. And Christina Alberta hadn't seen her in bed for years.

'Take care of your Daddy,' said Mrs. Preemby. 'You owe more to him – and less to him – than you think. I had to do all I've done. Take care of him. He's gentle and good and easily persuaded and not to be trusted alone in the world. . . .

'I've never been quite all a mother should be to you. But you've been *difficult*, Christina. . . . I've had a great respect for you. . . .

'I'm glad you haven't my eyes. Glasses are a Curse . . .'

Anxiety about the laundry occupied a large part of her thoughts.

'That woman Smithers in the washing room is a thief, and I'd get rid of the new man Baxandale. I don't know why I've kept Mrs. Smithers on so long. . . . Weakness . . . I'm not sure about *him*, there's nothing positive yet, but I feel he's not straight. . . . I'm very much afraid we've let Lady Badger's account run too long. Nowadays titles – want watching. I've been misled by her. She promised a cheque . . . But I doubt about you two in the laundry altogether. He can't and you won't. *You* might have done it . . . Never mind that now.

'Sell it as a going concern? The Widgerys might come in. He's hard, but he's straight. Straight enough. They might like to come in . . .

'It's never entered my head I wasn't good for twenty

years yet. . . . I wish the doctor wouldn't think of operating. It won't do any good.'

She repeated many of her phrases.

'I hate the thought of being opened,' she said. 'I suppose –. Like those frogs in your book. . . .

'Packed like a bag. . . . Never get it back again. Loose bits. . . .

'Washing-basket or something to keep it together.'

Then her mind went off at a tangent to things beyond Christina Alberta's understanding.

'Sneaked off and left me to it. . . . I wonder what he's doing now. . . . Suppose . . . Fancy, if it should be him that had to operate. . . . Operate . . .

'Children we were.'

She seemed to recollect herself and regarded her daughter with a hard inquiring eye. Some instinct in Christina Alberta told her to assume an incurious expression. But these words struck upon her mind and stayed there and germinated like a seed. Children they were, and he had sneaked off? Queer and yet according with all sorts of other imponderables.

§ 5

Mr. Preemby looked unusually small but unusually dignified in his full mourning. Christina Alberta was also extremely black and shiny. Her skirts reached for the first time in her life to her ankles; a sacrifice that she felt would be particularly acceptable to the spirit of the departed.

A new thing had come into Christina Alberta's life – responsibility. She perceived that for unfathomable reasons she was responsible for Mr. Preemby.

It was clear that the sudden death of his wife under the surgeon's knife had been a very great blow to him. He did not break down or weep or give way to paroxysms of grief, but he was enormously still and sad. His round china-blue eyes and his moustache looked at the world with a mournful solemnity. The undertaker had rarely met so satisfactory a widower. 'Everything of the best,' said Mr. Preemby. 'Whatever she can have, she must have.' Under the circumstances, the undertaker, who was a friend of the family, having met both Mr. and Mrs. Preemby at whist-drives quite frequently, showed commendable moderation.

'You can't imagine what all this means to me,' said Mr. Preemby to Christina Alberta, quite a number of times.

'It was a pure love match,' he said; 'pure romance. She had nothing to gain by marrying me. But neither of us thought of sordid things.' He was silent for a little while, struggling with intractable memories. He subdued them. 'We just met,' he said smiling faintly; 'and it seemed that it *had* to be.'

'Sneaked off and left me'; came a faint whisper in Christina Alberta's memory.

§ 6

There was much to see to in those days of mourning. Christina Alberta did her best to help, watch, and guide Mr. Preemby even as her mother had desired, but she was surprised to find in him certain entirely unexpected decisions that had apparently leapt into existence within a few hours of her mother's death. One was a clear resolve that he and she must part company with the laundry either by selling it or letting it, or, if no means of disposing of it offered, by burning it down or blowing it up as speedily as possible. He did not discuss this; he treated it as an unavoidable necessity. He expressed no animosity for the laundry, he made no hostile criticism of the life he had led there, but every thought betrayed his fundamental aversion. And also they were to go away – right away – from Woodford Wells and never return thither. She had come to much the same decisions on her own account, but she had not expected to find them in such quiet strength in him.

He became explicit about the future as they sat at supper on the evening of the funeral.

'Your mother's cousin, Sam Widgery,' he said, 'was talking to me.'

He munched for a moment; his moustache went up and down and his eyes of china-blue stared out of the window at the sunset sky. 'He wants to take it over.'

'The laundry?'

'As a going concern. And he being our nearest relation, so to speak, I'd as soon he had it as anybody else. Other things being equal. . . . Wish I knew what to ask him for it. I don't want to ask him too little. So I said I didn't care to discuss things at a funeral. Said he'd better come along to-morrow. Their place isn't doing well. It's got sort of embedded in Walthamstow. It would pay him to get out and let the land go for building. He hasn't got very much money. . . . But he wants this place. He reely wants this place.'

His blue eyes were the eyes of one who sees visions.

'I don't know if they taught you about making companies at the School of Economics. I'm a child at all that sort of thing. He talks about partnership or a mortgage or something like that, but what we want – what we want is a limited company. And what we want is something like debentures only rather more like preference shares. We want it so that whatever he draws out of the business we've got to draw out more. Otherwise the company can cut away the security for your debentures by paying too much

43

dividend on the ordinary shares. *He*'ll have the ordinary shares. Him and his wife. I don't say he'd do such a thing deliberately, but he might very easily be led into doing it. He's got to be looked after. We want to fix it so that if he pays more on his shares than we get on our shares we'd get our interest levelled up. It's all very difficult and complicated, Christina Alberta.'

Christina Alberta regarded Mr. Preemby with a new and deepening respect. She had never heard him make such a speech before at meals, but then he had never before been free from interruption and correction.

'We'll have to have it fixed up properly by our solicitors,' said Mr. Preemby.

'We shan't be badly off,' he continued, helping himself to cheese.

'There's a mortgage or so we've got and some houses at Buckhurst Hill. It's a curious thing, but your poor dear mother had a sort of faith in my eye for house property. She often let me guide her. And I always had a feeling for making some sort of reserve *out* of the business. . . . Very likely Sam Widgery will take over most of the furniture of this house. It's a bigger house than his . . .'

'Where do you think of going to live, Daddy?' asked Christina Alberta.

'I don't rightly know,' said Mr. Preemby after a moment or so of introspection. 'I keep thinking of different places.'

'London,' she said. 'If I could go back to study – before it is too late.'

'London,' he said, 'it might be.'

He hesitated over his next suggestion with the hesitation that had become a habit, so accustomed was he to see his suggestions crumpled up and flung aside. 'Have you ever heard of Boarding Houses, Christina Alberta?' he asked with an unreal carelessness. 'Have you ever thought it might be possible for us to go and live in Boarding Houses?'

'In London?'

'All over the world – almost, there are Boarding Houses. You see, Christina Alberta, we might get rid of our furniture here, except for my books and a few little things, and we might put most of that away for a time – Taylor's Repository would take care of that for us – and we might go and live sometimes in a Boarding House here, and sometimes in a Boarding House there. Then you could study and needn't keep house, and I could read and look at things and make memorandums about some Theories I've thought of, and talk to people and hear people talking. All sorts of people go to Boarding Houses – all sorts of interesting people. These last nights I've been thinking no end about living in Boarding Houses. I keep on thinking of it, turning it over in my mind. It would be a new life for me – like beginning again. Life's been so regular here. All very well while your poor dear mother was alive, but now I feel I want distraction, I want to move about and see all sorts of things and different kinds of people. I want to forget. Why! in some of these Boarding Houses there's Chinese and Indians and Russian princesses, and professors and actors and all sorts of people. Just to hear them!'

'There's Boarding Houses full of students in Bloomsbury.'

'Every sort,' said Mr. Preemby.

'One place that attracts me,' said Mr. Preemby, pouring out what remained of the beer, 'is Tumbridge Wells.'

'Isn't that sometimes called Tunbridge, Daddy?'

'Formerly. But now it is always spoken of as Tumbridge Wells. At this Tumbridge Wells, Christina Alberta, there are hills with names that point directly to some connection with the ancient Israelites, Mount Ephraim and Mount Gilboa and so on, and there are a number of curiously

45

shaped rocks, shaped in the likeness of great toads and prehistoric monsters and mystical forms and nobody knows whether they are the work of God's hand or man's. I am very anxious to see these things for myself. They may have a deeper and closer significance for us than is commonly supposed. There are plenty of Boarding Houses at Tumbridge Wells – I was told only the other day by a man I met in the Assyrian room in the British Museum – and some of them are said to be very comfortable and reasonable indeed.'

'We might go there for the holidays,' said Christina Alberta, 'before the London session begins.'

Outside was the summer afterglow, and a dusky peace filled the room. Father and daughter followed divergent trains of thought. Mr. Preemby was the first to break the silence.

'Now that I shall be in mourning, or half mourning, for some time I have decided to give away all those Harris tweed knickerbocker suits and stockings of mine. Some poor man might feel the comfort of them – in winter. I have never really liked those *very* baggy knickerbockers, but of course while your poor dear mother was alive her taste was Law to me. And those caps; they get over your eyes when you're hot. That tweed stuff . . . It is overrated. When you ride a bicycle or anything it ravels out with the friction of the seat. Makes you look ridiculous. . . . And I think that quite soon I shall get myself one of those soft grey felt hats – with a black band.'

'I have always wanted to see you wear one, Daddy,' said Christina Alberta.

'It would count as mourning?'

'Oh! yes, Daddy.'

Mr. Preemby meditated pleasantly. The girl had common sense. Her advice was worth having. 'As for putting the swastika on your poor dear mother's tombstone,

perhaps you are right in thinking it is not what she herself
would have chosen. It may be better after all to do as
you suggest and erect a simple cross. After all – it is *her*
tombstone.'

Whereupon Christina Alberta got up from her chair and
went round the table – almost at a prance, until she remembered things – and kissed him. For some obscure reason
she hated the swastika almost as much as she loved her
Daddy. For her it had become the symbol of silliness, and
she did not like to think of him as silly. Particularly now
when for some obscure reason she was beginning to think
of him as ill-used.

§ 7

There was much to see to before the Preembys could go
to Tunbridge Wells. There had to be quite a number of
interviews with Mr. Sam Widgery at Woodford Wells
and afterwards in the dingy offices of Messrs. Payne and
Punter in Lincoln's Inn. It was clear from the first to these
men of affairs that Mr. Preemby was a child at business,
but as they went on with him they realized that he was an
extremely greedy and intractable child. It was six weeks
before Mr. and Mrs. Sam Widgery could move in,
sullenly and resentfully, to the Limpid Stream premises,
and Mr. Preemby and his daughter could go on after a day
or so in London to select a Boarding House at Tunbridge
Wells.

Christina Alberta spent her early days as an orphan struggling against an unseasonable cheerfulness and a profound
sense of release. She found her father ready to accept
almost any explanation of her need to run up to London
for a day and even disposed to be tolerant when she came
home late. She had quite a little world of miscellaneous

acquaintances in London; fellow-students and their friends, fellow-students from the London School of Economics and fellow-students at Tomlinson's School and art students they knew and medical students they knew and girls from the provinces who had chucked their families and got typing jobs, and so on to models and chorus girls and vaguely employed rather older young men of the intellectual class. She met them in and about the class-rooms and in A.B.C.'s and suchlike places and in the New Hope Club, where there were even Labour politicians and men who claimed to be Bolsheviks, and she went to parties and duologues in studios in high, remote, extraordinary flats. It was tremendous fun, although a lot of it had to be snatched from the insistent claims and inquiries of Woodford Wells. And people liked her, they liked Christina Alberta, laughed at her jokes they did and admired her thundering cheek and never said anything about her nose. It was much more her natural world than the Taverners' School people had ever been. Nobody seemed to mind that she came out of a laundry; for all they seemed to care about that sort of thing, she might have come out of a gaol. In between the excitements of student life she even did some reading.

In her first grief for her mother she tried not to feel a sense of new unstinted freedom in regard to all these adventures and experiences. Her Daddy in his grief, bless him! was smoking much more than he had ever done before; he was even trying cigars; he had no nose for tobacco reek in his daughter – or for anything of that sort. He asked few questions and they were easily answered. Long years of exercise had made him almost constitutionally acquiescent. Christina Alberta realized that within very wide limits indeed now she might do anything she pleased whenever she liked. She realized also that there was no particular hurry to do anything at all. All the others seemed to be running about in pairs like knives and forks. It suited her humour to stay detached.

And the world had altered. This break-up of the old home, the death of her mother, the disappearance of every control except her credulous, inattentive Daddy, had jerked her forward from childhood to maturity. Hitherto home had seemed an eternal, indestructible thing, from which you started out for adventures, to which, whatever happened, you returned like a sea-rover to rest and where you went to bed and slept as you had been wont to sleep, secure, unthreatened. Now here the two of them, Daddy and herself, were in the open; no bolting place at all for them; anything might happen to them and might insist upon going on happening. She could now do just anything she pleased, it was true, but also she realized that now she had to take the unlimited consequences.

So that in spite of her sense of novel, unbounded freedoms, Christina Alberta found she did not go up to London any more than she would have done during her mother's lifetime. Many of her most attractive friends, it is true, were away upon their holidays. And she found her father's company unusually interesting. Every time she came back to him he seemed to be slightly enlarged and of a firmer colour and consistency. He reminded her of Practical Biology (Botanical Section) in the Taverners' School, when you take a dried-up bean out of its package and put it in a jar with water and observe it under the influence of warmth and moisture. It germinates. And he was germinating.

Mother had kept him dried up for nearly twenty years, but now he was germinating and nobody could tell what sort of thing he might become.

CHAPTER THE THIRD

In Lonsdale Mews

§ 1

AFTER a month of deep mourning, Christina Alberta
put aside her long skirts and returned to the more
kilt-like garments to which she was accustomed. She had
not been inactive while her father had conducted his business settlement with Mr. Sam Widgery, and she had
worked out a scheme of living that seemed to promise
quite a happy life for her father and herself. She fell in
with the Boarding House idea and with the project of
beginning at Tunbridge Wells. She ceased to struggle
with the fact that he continued to call it quietly but insis-
tently *Tum*bridge Wells; it seemed to her upon reflection
that *Tum*bridge was really the place he, at any rate, was
going to live at. That gentle departure from exactitude
was quite of a piece with his general habit of living a little
askew from actual things.

But she impressed upon him the view that since their
lives were to be migratory henceforth, and since there were
a certain number of books, unsaleable articles of furniture
that Mrs. Widgery would not take over at a valuation, a
number of curiosities – for example, a piece of shell which
he believed to be a fragment of a Great Auk's Egg, a Rosi-
crucian regalia, and a mummified hawk from Egypt which
had prophetic qualities – to consider, there must be a sort
of permanent headquarters in London, at which these
objects could be stored and to which he and she could
return from the various Boarding Houses round and about
the earth. And, pursuant to this suggestion, she made
inquiries and worked out an admirable project for sharing
some accommodation with two little friends of hers who
practised art, literature, and picturesque economies in a

50

converted mews in Chelsea. In fact, she made arrangements with them. She told Mr. Preemby she had made these arrangements according to his instructions, and after a time it did come to seem to him that he had given her the instructions upon which she acted.

Lonsdale Mews opens out of Lonsdale Road, Chelsea; and there is quite a noble entrance with large stucco pillars on either side and an arch over, on which is a design in relievo of Neptune and sea-horses and the words 'Lonsdale Mews.' Inside there had once been stables and coach-houses, and over each a bedroom and a sitting-room, which was also in the more prolific past, generally used as a bedroom, and a cupboard and a landing and so forth, the little home of the coachman (and his wife and family) attached to the genteel carriage and horses below. But the advancement of science and the progress of invention have abolished gentility, and so reduced the number of coachmen and carriages in the world that Lonsdale Mews has had to accept other tenants; and being too narrow down the centre for the coming and going of automobiles without a great deal of bashing of mudguards and radiators, has had to paint itself up attractively and fall back upon art and the intelligenzia.

Christina Alberta's two young friends were in possession of one of these perverted coachmen's homes, and as they were very inadequately prepared to pay the rent – it was a quite aristocratic rent – they were extremely glad to welcome Mr. Preemby and particularly Christina Alberta as co-tenants. Mr. Preemby was to have the big room downstairs and there he was to arrange his books and his surplus furnishings and ornaments and curious objects, and have a sofa that could be made into an apparent bed when he wanted to sleep in London. And Christina Alberta was to have a little bedroom for herself behind this wherein a breezy decorative scheme of orange and bright blue more than made up for a certain absence of daylight and fresh air. But when the two young friends had a party or when Mr. Preemby was away they were to have the use of the big downstairs room, and in the case of a party Christina Alberta's room was to be a ladies' cloak-room.

The lessors were to retain the use of the upstairs rooms and in the matter of the kitchen all things therein were to be held in common. None of this agreement was put into writing and many issues were left over frankly for future controversy. 'We are to be the pigs that pay the rent,' said Christina Alberta; that was the general idea. 'Much we'll work out,' said Mr. Harold Crumb. 'Much will work it-self out. It's no good being too definite.' What was definite was that Mr. Preemby was to pay the rent.

Mr. Harold Crumb was a red-haired young man, a shock-headed young man with a rampant profile, dressed in a blue overall, frayed grey trousers and slippers. He had large freckled hands and he did Black and White, which Mr. Preemby had supposed to be a whisky but discovered was an art. Harold lived by attempting to sell drawings for advertisements and pictured jokes for the weekly papers. His expression was lofty and his voice constrained and it seemed to Mr. Preemby that he was suffered rather than met by Mr. Crumb. With Christina Alberta Mr. Crumb seemed to be on terms of tacit friendship and no word passed between them. He lifted his hand and twiddled his fingers at her – with a kind of melancholy.

Mrs. Crumb was more effusive. She embraced Christina Alberta warmly and answered to the name of 'Fay.' Then she turned to Mr. Preemby and shook hands with him quite normally. She was a slender young lady with care-lessly bobbed corn-coloured hair, pale-grey eyes and an absent-minded face. She also was dressed in a blue over-all, she wore oyster-coloured stockings and slippers and possibly other things, and her business in life, Mr. Preemby learnt, was to review books for various newspapers and write romantic fiction for bookstall magazines. Her right forefinger had that indelible inkiness which only the habitual use of an incontinent fountain-pen can give. There was a big screen in the downstairs room Mr. Preemby was to have that Mr. Crumb had made and Mrs. Crumb had covered with the bright mendacious wrappers of the books she had reviewed. This exercised Mr. Preemby the more because several of the wrappers were manifestly upside down, and he could not understand whether this was due to art, carelessness or some serious mental lapse.

'We'll have something to eat,' she told Mr. Preemby, and then they could settle up things. But she had a surprisingly rapid articulation and it sounded like, 'We'll 'f sum t'eat 'n' then we'll set lup thins.' It took ten or twelve seconds to come through to Mr. Preemby's understanding.

Meanwhile she had turned to Christina Alberta. ' 'Dabit 'f work to do,' she explained. 'Bres no' clear' d'way. Late las' ni'. You be'r loo' roun' he' while Nolly gessomeat an' Ikn do 'p stairs fore you see't.'

'Right-o,' said Christina Alberta, understanding perfectly. Mr. Preemby was left stunned, with his lips moving slowly. 'So long,' said Harold, and took some money out of a black Wedgwood tea-pot and went and fell over things in the passage, and presently went out into the wide world while Fay vanished upstairs.

'She's gone upstairs,' said Mr. Preemby interpreting slowly, 'to do their rooms. And *he's* gone to get some meat. It's a nice large room, Christina Alberta – and quite well lit. Quite.

'I don't think I've ever been in a Mew before,' said Mr. Preemby, approaching a group of attractive drawings on the wall.

'In a *what*, Daddy?'

'In a Mew. Or in a *Studjo* . . . I suppose these are Originals.'

Christina Alberta awaited his reaction to the drawings with a slight anxiety.

'Looks like a lot of fruit and human legs and things,' said Mr. Preemby. 'Wonder what they mean? *Summer Night* it says, and that's *Passion in Solitude*. Don't quite see it, but I suppose it's symbolical or something.' He turned his round blue eyes to the room generally. 'I could get a mahogany cabinet for my Curiosities and have it against the wall *there* – I'd like the sort with glass doors so that people could see the things – and if there was some shelves put across that place, it would hold most of my books. There'll have to be a bed somewhere, Christina Alberta.'

'They've got a sofa upstairs,' said Christina Alberta, 'with an end that pulls down.'

'Might go there.'

'Or under the window.'

'Of course there's my clothes,' said Mr. Preemby. 'I almost wish I hadn't practically promised Sam Widgery your mother's wardrobe. Rosewood it is. It has a lot of room in it and it might have gone against that bit of wall there. The trunk will make a sort of seat if we get the corners mended. Wonder how that screen would look the other way up. Books might go behind it. These easels and things I suppose they'll take upstairs. . . . We'll get things settled all right.'

Christina Alberta turned about with arms akimbo to follow his proposals. She perceived that they threatened a considerable disturbance of the æsthetic balance of the studio. She'd just thought of a little bed-sofa affair with a bright rug over it. Silly of her to forget the baggage. But in the end perhaps it might be possible to arrest a lot of his

gear in the passage. The passage was so choked already
that a little more in it hardly seemed to matter. He could
go out and get what things he wanted when he wanted
them. She had a momentary anticipation of him in his
shirt and braces, routing in trunks.

'Of course,' said Mr. Preemby, 'when you said you'd got
two little friends in a *Studjo*, I thought they were two
girls. I didn't think they were a married couple.'

'They aren't so *fearfully* married,' said Christina Alberta.

'No,' said Mr. Preemby, and was restrained by modesty
from further speech for some seconds. 'Of course,' he
said, 'if presently a Family came along – well, we'd have
to move out, Christina Alberta.'

'Never meet families half way,' said Christina Alberta.
'It isn't very likely anyhow. You trust Fay.'

'You never know,' said Mr. Preemby rather weakly, and
showed a tendency to drift back to those ambiguous
drawings.

'About time we had a look at the upstairs rooms, Daddy,'
said Christina Alberta, and went out into the passage to
call 'Fay!'

The answer came remotely. "Lo?'

'Read-*dee*?'

'Not yet.'

Christina Alberta found her Daddy back in the illustrated
corner with his head on one side like an inquiring sparrow.
For some time nothing was said. 'Of course,' he remarked
at last; 'it's Art.' He turned away with his face pursed up
beneath the moustache humming faintly. She perceived
it was just as much Art as he could stand.

He ran his hand over the wall and turned intelligent eyes
to Christina Alberta. 'It's just canvas,' he said; 'what you
pack things in. With sort of dabs of gold paint. I don't
think I've ever seen walls that wasn't either done with
paper or distemper before. I suppose really one might

put all sorts of things on walls, cloth, bed-ticking, tarpaulin. Odd how one doesn't think of things.'

§ 2

Presently 'upstairs' was 'read-ee'; Mrs. Harold Crumb was free to answer questions and make explanations and Mr. Preemby could learn more of Christina Alberta's plans for his comfort. Upstairs was more various but less spacious than downstairs; the beds were dressed-up rather than disguised as divans and there was more vaguely improper but highly decorative Art. Like Christina Alberta, Mrs. Crumb had not fully considered Mr. Preemby's possibilities in the way of luggage, but she rose to the occasion very well. When Mr. Preemby spoke of the mahogany cabinet and the wardrobe, she said that it would be quite easy for Harold to 'camouflage' them with very, very bright coloured paint, and she thought a lot might be done for Mr. Preemby's trunks and clothes by making a curtained alcove in a corner. 'Trouble with clothes,' said Mrs. Crumb, 'is when somebody starts charades or dressing up. Nothing is sacred. Last week, somebody tore my only pyjamas limb from limb.'

'We'd have to arrange,' said Mr. Preemby, a little uneasily.

'We'll have to arrange somehow,' said Mrs. Crumb.

But before anything could be arranged definitely Harold returned from his shopping with a large piece of purple beefsteak in a mere loin cloth of newspaper, and a lettuce and a bundle of small onions in his hand and two large bottles of beer under his arm, and everybody's attention was directed to the preparation of the midday meal.

'Generally,' said Harold, 'we go Out for a meal. There's quite a decent aufschnittery and a little Italian place and so forth not five minutes away in the King's Road. It's more fun feeding Out. But we thought you'd like to see the studio put through its paces.'

Mr. Preemby in the course of his life had rarely seen meals prepared; somebody else had always laid a table and said 'Dinner's ready, Daddy,' or 'Supper's ready, Daddy' as the case might be, and he had just sat down, and it was with real interest that he obeyed Mr. Crumb's invitation to 'come and see how we do it,' and assisted under direction in the operations. Mr. Crumb, in a few well chosen words, introduced the cooking apparatus that clustered round the gas-stove; the gas-stove was lit explosively, Mr. Preemby handed things and held things under direction and got in the way a good deal. Christina Alberta, who seemed used to the job, chopped the onions and dressed a salad at a small kitchen table close at hand, and the steak got itself grilled fiercely and flaringly.

Meanwhile Mrs. Crumb laid a blue painted table in what was to be Mr. Preemby's room with an orange-coloured cloth and a selection of plates and parts of plates, yellow-glazed mugs with rudely painted inscriptions in some rustic dialect, 'Here's t' absent frens' and the like, several knives and forks, a pewter mug full of cigarettes and a bunch of sunflowers in a brown-glazed bowl. And at this table Mr. Preemby presently found himself seated very hot in the face and liberally splashed with fat from the grilled steak. Nobody said grace, and the meal began.

There was a general assumption that Mr. Preemby's tenancy was settled, though there were many points upon which he would have liked a clearer definition. He was particularly anxious to exclude as tactfully as possible his garments and his specimens from promiscuous use as properties when these charades occurred, but he did not know quite how to reopen the subject. And he was preoccupied by a doubt whether his long nightgowns of Saxony flannel, if they were publicly exposed, might not be considered old-fashioned by these artistic young people. But their talk jumped about so that it was difficult to lead up to what he had to say. He was accustomed, especially when company was present, to clear his throat 'h'rrmp' and waggle his moustache up and down a little before he spoke, and by the time he was ready to deliver what he had to say one of the others was away with something else. So that he hardly said anything but an occasional 'h'rrmp' all through the meal.

The two young ladies did most of the talking. Harold seemed moody, making an occasional correction or comment upon his wife's remarks and eating most of the steak with the pained expression of one who has tender teeth and is used to better food. Once he asked Mr. Preemby if he really cared for Good Music, and once if he had been to see the Iberian dancers last year, but neither of these inquiries led to a sustained conversation. 'Hrrmp. No-oh,' said Mr. Preemby. 'Not exactly. Not particularly,' and in the second case, 'No-oh I didn't.'

Mrs. Crumb talked brightly of various newspaper jobs she had got and how she had been asked to do a children's corner in the *Patriotic News* and whether she would accept the offer – Mr. Preemby thought the editors and newspaper proprietors she mentioned seemed a depraved lot – but mainly the talk concerned the movements and readjustments of a large circle of friends. After the meal there was coffee, and Harold, with an air of resignation, went and washed up.

There were many little things awaiting attention at the laundry, and after two or three cigarettes Mr. Preemby decided, 'It's time for us to be going, Christina Alberta.' 'We'll work it out all right,' said Harold on their departure.

There were intervals of meditation as Mr. Preemby and

Christina Alberta returned in the train from Liverpool Street to Woodford Wells. 'It's not what I've been accustomed to,' said Mr. Preemby. 'It's all very different from the way your mother used to manage things. . . . Less orderly. . . . Of course I could keep my clothes locked up in my trunk.'

'You'll do all right. They're perfect Dears. *She* loves you tremendously already,' said Christina Alberta.

§ 3

But before she went to sleep that night Christina Alberta experienced compunction. She felt compunction about these arrangements she was making for her Daddy. She doubted whether he would be truly comfortable and happy in that studio in Lonsdale Mews, and able to lead the life of steadfast curiosity he anticipated with so much quiet pleasure – ever humming to himself about it and working his moustache and saying 'h'rrmp,' when he was not otherwise engaged.

This story, it cannot be too often reiterated, is the story of Mr. Preemby who became, as we shall tell in due course, Sargon, King of Kings. But Christina Alberta has got herself hatched into this story very much like a young cuckoo in a wagtail's nest and it is impossible to ignore her. She was virtually in control of him and she had the egotism of her sex and age.

She had also a pitiless conscience. It was almost the only thing she could not manage in her life. It managed her. It was a large crystalline conscience with no foundations and no relationships; it just floated by itself in her being; it was her gravitational centre and the rest of her could not get away from it.

When Christina Alberta went up for examination and

judgment before Christina Alberta there was no nonsense in the proceedings, a fearful frankness; it was cards on the table, everything in evidence, no etiquette, not a stitch on, X rays if necessary. These examinations were all the more terrible because they were done in what was practically an empty room, without screens, curtains, standards or general beliefs of any sort. It is appalling to think of the drapery and function that was absent from Christina Alberta's court of conscience. In the first place Christina Alberta was completely and explicitly irreligious. In the next she was theoretically anti-social and amoral. She did not believe in respectability, Christian morality, the institution of the family, the capitalist system, or the British Empire. She would say so with extreme plainness and considerable detail except when her parent was about. Prevalent winds of sentiment did not stir her. She did not find the Prince of Wales ravishing nor *Punch* funny. She thought modern dancing tiresome, though she did it very well, and Wimbledon tennis and tennis-talk an intolerable bore. She favoured Bolshevism because everybody she disliked abused it and she hoped for a world-wide social revolution of an entirely destructive and cleansing type. What was to follow this revolution Christina Alberta, with the happy confidence of youth, did not seem to mind.

It is not for us to speculate here why a young woman born and bred between Woodford Wells and central London in the opening years of the twentieth century should confront the world with a mind so entirely swept and void of positive and restraining convictions; we put the fact on record. And if she had been sustained by all the beliefs in Christendom and a sure and certain respect for every detail of the social code, whatever that code may be, she could not have confronted the world with a more cheerful confidence, nor with a stronger persuasion that Christina Alberta had to behave, in some undefined fashion, well.

Christina Alberta had to be Christina Alberta, clear and sound, or the court of conscience made things plain and hard for her.

'Christina Alberta,' the court would say, 'you are the dirtiest, filthiest little thing that ever streaked the dust of life. How do you propose to get clean again?'

Or, 'Christina Alberta, you have been lying again. You'll lie to *me* next. First it was laziness made you lie and now it is cowardice. What are you going to make of yourself, Christina Alberta?'

There came a time when the court had to address Christina Alberta in this fashion; 'Your nose, Christina Alberta, is large beyond comparison. It will probably go on growing all your life – as noses often do. Yet you are setting yourself out to charm and fascinate Teddy Winterton. You go to places where you think you will meet him. You fuss and preen yourself like any female idiot. You dream all sorts of things about him, disgraceful things. You are soppy on this young man in spite of the fact that you know he is – no sort of good. You like him to touch you. You sit and look at him foolishly and you gloat. Does he gloat on you? Isn't it time you considered where you are going, Christina Alberta?'

And now the court was in full session and the charge, the charge for which there was no defence, was that she was going to take her absurd, unprotected Daddy and entrust him and his foolishness and his silly books and his ridiculous treasures and all his dreams and desires, to the insecure and unsympathetic studio of the Crumbs, not because of any vague and general hunger for London, though that was in the background, but because that studio was frequented by the all too seductive Teddy, because there she had met him and danced wildly with him and been suddenly and astonishingly kissed by him and kissed him. And then he had beguiled her to learn a dance with him and had got her to come to tea with him at his studio to meet his sister – who hadn't turned up. And there had been other meetings. He was impudent and provocative and evasive. All her being was in a state of high excitement about him. Coldly and exactly now the court unfolded the operations of her mind to her; showed how the thought of Teddy, always present and never admitted, had guided her decision to harbour with the Crumbs. Only now did she come to confession and clear vision. 'You have lied to yourself, Christina Alberta,' said the court; 'and that is the worst sort of lie. What are you going to do about it?'

'I can't let the Crumbs down now. They count upon us.'

'You are in a mess, Christina Alberta. You are in a worse mess than we thought you were. *Soppy* you are about Teddy Winterton. Why not call things by their right names? You are in love. Perhaps something frightful has happened to you. Little rabbits run about the hedges and every day is like every other day for them; they waggle their little noses and wiggle their little tails and do what they like with their paws. Until one day there is a ping and the snare snaps on the little furry foot and everything you try to do after that is different. The snare holds your movements and you must just dance round it and squeal if you like, till the man comes along. Is that what has happened to you? And for Teddy! Teddy, with that open, lying face!'

'No,' said Christina Alberta, 'I don't love him. I don't love him. I've been silly and soppy and adrift. I am no more worthy to be called Christina Alberta. But it hasn't got me yet and it shan't get me. I'll pull Daddy out of it and myself out of it; I vow and swear. . . .'

'H'm,' said the court.

62

§ 4

It seemed to Mr. Preemby that the first evening he spent in his new quarters in Lonsdale Mews was the most eventful evening in his life. Impressions crowded upon each other. Insomnia was not among his habits, but when at last he lay upon his shake-up bed he was kept awake for most of what was left of the night (it was the frayed piece with the bleak dawn in the middle of it) trying to get these same impressions sorted out, impressions about his new surroundings, impressions about Christina Alberta, impressions of new and unprecedented personalities, a marmalade of impressions.

Mr. Preemby and Christina Alberta arrived at the studio according to plan about half-past three, but the Picton van which had started that morning with Mr. Preemby's bags and trunks and the crates of books and curiosities and the late Mrs. Preemby's roomy wardrobe, which had after all been rescued from the clutches of Sam Widgery, did not arrive until it was nearly six. Unfortunately the furniture dealer in Brompton Road from whom Mr. Preemby had purchased a specimen-cabinet and a long low walnut bookcase had delivered these articles the day before, and all the animosity of the modern artist towards self-assertive wood had been aroused in Harold. He and Fay and a friend or so who had dropped in, had sat up quite late painting these new pieces a deep ultramarine blue with stars and splashes of gold like the paper they put round the necks of Ayala, Tsarist and suchlike champagnes. When Mr. Preemby saw their handiwork he could scarcely believe it was the same specimen-cabinet and bookcase.

'I suppose one could get it off again,' said Mr. Preemby.
'But see how they are assimilated by the room,' said Harold in high expostulation.

'I mean if we moved at any time,' said Mr. Preemby. 'I know it's art, and it goes with the things here very nicely, but there's neighbourhoods I wouldn't like to move into – not with these things as they are. You don't know what people's imaginations are like.'

Matters went a little tediously until the arrival of the Picton van. The sofa-bed was arranged and rearranged. The bed things, blankets, sheets and pillow-cases were to be put in a bundle on the top of Mr. Preemby's flat trunk behind the book-wrapper screen. 'We shall have to find some other place for the bottled beer,' said Harold. 'It's too hot in the kitchen and too dangerous in the passage. But I've an idea we might have it in the scullery under the sink, with a cloth over it and water dripping on the cloth. Evaporation. I'll see about it.'

Mr. Preemby was surprised by a yawn. 'I suppose you'd like to have some tea,' said Fay suddenly, and she and Christina Alberta prepared some.

Harold was obviously in a strained and nervous state. Mr. Preemby's patient little figure, sitting about, hands on knees, waiting for Picton's van, looking at things with innocent eyes and saying 'h'rrmp,' had much the same effect of nervous dislocation upon Harold that the mild and patient camel has on a horse. Harold chafed and pranced. He walked about and went upstairs and out and returned; he smoked endless cigarettes and pressed endless cigarettes upon Mr. Preemby; he made recondite remarks in a strained voice. 'All this is like something out of Dostoievsky,' he said to Mr. Preemby. 'In a different scheme of colouring of course. Different, but the same. Don't you think so, Mr. Preemby?'

Mr. Preemby nodded his head in a sympathetic, humorous, not too explicit manner. 'H'rrmp,' he said. 'It *is* a bit like that.'

'Things will work themselves out,' said Harold. 'Things

64

will work themselves out. You know that poem of Ruby Parham's.' He cleared his throat. 'It is called "Waiting",' he said. 'It goes like this –'

His eyes became fixed and glazed; his voice gathered volume, so that the words seemed more than life-sized.

> 'After every minute
> 'Comes another minute
> 'And then, rest assured,
> 'Another.
> 'Like drops from a ledge in the rain.
> 'You may not want to go on;
> 'But *they* will,
> 'Oh! endlessly
> 'Taking your life away, death, not final and complete,
> 'But death in the midst of life,
> 'Particles of death,
> 'Death by attrition.
> 'Drip on Old Death – in life!
> 'Slow, dull, implacable, unendurable!
> 'Drip on.'

'That "Drip on" is great. But perhaps you don't like modern poetry?'

'I don't *mind* it,' said Mr. Preemby genially.

'Of course, nothing of a really destructive nature *can* have happened to that van,' said Mr. Crumb in a pessimistic tone.

When Picton's van arrived and the roomy wardrobe began its destructive march through the passage, Mr. Crumb called suddenly upon his maker in a loud distressful voice and vanished for the better part of an hour.

Christina Alberta was torn between a sympathetic understanding of Harold's state of mind and the fear that her Daddy might perceive the unfavourable reaction he produced in Harold and be hurt by it. She and Fay became brightly helpful with the unpacking. 'If I might have one of those blue pinafores of Mr. Crumb's to put on,' said

Mr. Preemby, 'I'd be glad. These black things of mine show every mark.'

Mr. Crumb's overall reached far below Mr. Preemby's knees and somehow justified his calling it a pinafore. It brought out something endearingly infantile in his appearance that appealed to the maternal instinct lurking in Mrs. Crumb. She struggled with a persuasion that he was really a little boy of nine who had been naughty and grown a big moustache and that she had to take care of him and restrain him and generally tell him not to. The books were put in the bookshelves as Mr. Preemby said, 'just anyhow'; they could be sorted up later, but the curiosities and specimens took longer and had to be 'put out' more or less in the cabinet. There were not only real curiosities and specimens but many little things that Mr. Preemby had accumulated because they looked like curiosities and specimens. There was, for instance, a piece of one of the laundry delivery van mudguards so bent by a collision as to resemble a human torso in the most striking fashion; there was the almost complete skull of an unknown mammal, probably a fallow deer, picked up in Epping Forest, there was a potato, now rather shrivelled, in which it was possible to detect thirty-seven distinct human faces and – specimen of an entirely different quality – a large flint in which there were no less than fifty-five. Ages ago some primordial Preemby had discovered and loved that very same flint and had brought out the likenesses by chipping an eye here or a nostril there; but Mr. Preemby did not suspect the help of that remote and perhaps ancestral hand. Even in waking life Mr. Preemby saw faces in everything. What he would have been like with a high temperature it is impossible to imagine.

Christina Alberta's anxiety about her father's reception by the Crumbs diminished as she saw his virtual conquest of Fay. Fay treated him firmly but indulgently, and they

66

lost a good deal of time while she tried to see all the fifty-five faces of the wonderful flint. They had to start and start again, but always they lost count about 'Twen-tee' or 'Twen-tee-one.' The question would arise whether they were counting one of the faces over again.

Harold returned in a moody state and could be heard, all too distinctly, kicking Mr. Preemby's packing cases in the hall, but Fay went out to him with a lofty sleep-walking expression in her pale eyes, and the concussions ceased, and presently Harold came downstairs again looking almost handsome in nankeen trousers, a blue jacket with big silver buttons, and a voluminous black tie, and was quite nice to Mr. Preemby.

'You won't mind my touching that wardrobe of yours up a bit?' he said. 'It damps us off, as it is. Kind of reproaches us. One of us has to be altered, you see, it or me, and either I paint it or else I get a silk hat with a deep mourning band and a gold-handled umbrella – which would cost no end of money. Whereas I *have* the paint.'

'If you can get the paint off again,' said Mr. Preemby. 'You see if I was to move – *back*. . . . It's all right to have all this paint in a Mew. But out of a Mew . . .'

'Exactly,' said Harold. 'My idea is to make a little pink house of it with windows and so on. Something very simple. Rather like the scenery of a Russian Sketch. *Chauve Souris* sort of stuff. Conventional to the nth. And we might put up placards at the corner of it according to what is going on. Make a bit of an institution of it.'

'So long as it makes things agreeable,' said Mr. Preemby.

He found his hair being ruffled affectionately. 'Dear little Daddy!' said Christina Alberta.

§ 5

But now appeared a new-comer and life was made uncomfortable and complicated for Christina Alberta again by the presence of Mr. Teddy Winterton's candid insincerity. His graceful body, his movements, his voice, stirred her senses as she hated them to be stirred; his quiet impudence invaded her sense of humour; he wounded her pride and she longed to be even with him. She had no power over him and he behaved as if he owned her. She was always letting him go just a little too far. When he was about her nose cast a shadow that reached to her horizon. He stood now in the doorway – trousers of one pattern of tweed, waistcoat of another, Norfolk jacket of a third extensively unbuttoned in the accepted student style, and he watched Mr. Preemby carry his collection of roc's bones, found near Staines, across the studio on a tea-tray. His eyes were round with surprise and amusement; his mouth said noiselessly; 'What is it?'

Christina Alberta was not going to have her Daddy laughed at by any Teddy Winterton. 'Mr. Winterton,' she said. 'This is my father.'

'I'll just get rid of my bones,' said Mr. Preemby, 'and then I'll shake hands.'

'We'll just finish up Mr. Preemby's things and then we'll all go round to Poppinetti's to get some dinner,' said Fay. 'There's hardly anything left to unpack now.'

'Just one or two Antediluvium bones,' said Mr. Preemby.

Teddy seized upon one. 'This,' he said, inspecting it, 'is a fossil rhinoceros thigh-bone from the Crag.'

'It's an Antediluvium horse,' said Mr. Preemby.

'Forgive me! It's a rhinoceros bone!'

'Horses had rhinoceros bones in those days,' said Mr.

68

Preemby. 'And the rhinoceroses – ! They were incredible. If I had one I shouldn't have anywhere to put it.'

Mr. Preemby was extracted from his overall and restored to the black coat and the grey felt hat with the black band. He became one of a straggling party that went out of Lonsdale Mews to a little Italian restaurant in the King's Road. Three neighbours of the Crumbs mixed themselves up with the party, a very quiet man with silver hair and a young man and a dusky girl.

Mr. Preemby was much impressed by the novelty of thus going out for dinner, and expatiated on its advantages to the silver-haired man who seemed to be the quiet sort of listening man that Mr. Preemby liked to meet. 'You see you don't have to *cook* the meal and you don't have to lay the table and afterwards naturally there isn't any washing up. But I expect it comes more expensive.'

The silver-haired man nodded intelligently. 'Exactly,' he said.

Harold Crumb overheard this. 'Expensive,' he said, 'it isn't. No. Every other crime Poppinetti can commit, but that is barred by the circumstances of his clientele. He feeds us on stolen pigeons, his *dinde* is guinea-pig, his beef, *a l'omnibus*: what he minces God knows; what he puts into his ravioli makes even the Lord God repent of his extreme creativeness. But you see, you don't *think* about his ravioli, you eat 'em, and they're damned good. There are always flowers on the table and an effect of inexpensive refinement. You will see. You will see.'

Mr. Preemby saw. Poppinetti was a small man but carefully modelled on Caruso, and he received his large party with the deference of a diplomatist and the effusion of a geyser. He was particularly gracious to Mr. Preemby, bowing profoundly to him, and saluting him with great richness subsequently whenever he caught his eye. He seemed to Mr. Preemby to spend the rest of their time together going to remoter and remoter parts of the restaurant in order to catch Mr. Preemby's eye and bow and smile to him from greater and greater distances. Mr. Preemby had curious doubts whether he wasn't being mistaken for somebody else.

Signor Poppinetti, with an air of peculiar favour, guided the party to a long unattractive table near the centre of the restaurant and took their conflicting orders with the gestures of a conductor guiding an orchestra through a difficult passage. Mr. Preemby was passive but observant; he presently found himself eating macaroni and drinking a rough red wine with a name that sounded to his London tuned ears like a challenge. Chianti.

Harold Crumb showed great earnestness in the matter of macaroni. 'In order to taste macaroni,' he assured Mr. Preemby, 'it is necessary to fill the mouth absolutely full, good measure, pressed in and running over. To cut up macaroni with your fork as you are doing, is as awful as to cut an oyster. It – it devitalizes it.'

'I like it cut up,' said Mr. Preemby with unexpected firmness. And he cut up some more.

'Otherwise,' he said in a confidential aside to the silver-haired man, ' I can't help thinking it's earthworms.'

'Exactly. Exactly,' said the silver-haired man.

Harold exemplified generously. His rampant face riding over a squirming mouthful of macaroni was like St. George and the Dragon on an English sovereign. He whistled as he ate. Long snakes of macaroni hung thoughtful for a moment and then, drawn by some incomprehensible fascination, fled into him. Teddy Winterton and one of the new-comers from the studio next door emulated him. Christina Alberta and Fay showed the furtive dexterity of the female. But Mr. Preemby was glad when macaroni

70

was over, even though it raised the problem of eating an egg on spinach with a fork.

But he was not really troubled in his mind as a younger man might have been. He had the *savoir-faire* of middle-age. This restaurant dinner was on the whole a bright and agreeable experience for him. He liked even the corrosive taste of the Chianti. This Chianti you drank out of quite largish tumblers because it was almost as cheap and light as beer. It did not intoxicate but it warmed the mind, and it cast a pleasant and convincing indistinctness over the universe so that the Tunbridges all became Tumbridges without any question, and the secret dreams and convictions of the heart became certain knowledge. Presently Mr. Preemby found himself able and willing to tell things and hint much more important things about his collections to the white-haired man and also to the dark untidy girl who was sitting on his other side, and who came from the other studio and about whose name he had no idea, and presently to others; and when the bird came – it was a bird new to Mr. Preemby, and called, he gathered, *rabbkey* or *turkit* – most of the party was talking in the loud confused explosive way these young people affected about the lost *Atlantis*.

He had never spoken so freely before upon this topic. At home he had always been restrained by the late Mrs. Preemby's genuine lack of interest. And even now he was not prepared for positive statements or for an encounter with sceptical arguments about that great lost continent of the Golden Age. Atlantis had been the scene and substance of his secret reveries for many years; he knew his knowledge of it was of a different order from common knowledge, more intuitive, mystical, profound. From the outset his manner was defensive, discreet and obscure, as of one willing but not permitted to speak.

How did he know that there had been this lost continent?

'H'rrmp,' he said with the faint smile of peculiar knowledge; 'studied it for years.'

'What is the evidence?' asked the untidy young lady.

'So abundant. Impossible to retail it. Convincing. Of
various sorts. Plato has much about it. Unfinished fragment. Many books have been written. Many inscriptions in Egypt.'

'What sort of people were they?' asked the untidy girl.

'Very wonderful people, young lady,' said Mr. Preemby.
'H'rrmp. Very wonderful people.'

'Philosophy, no end I suppose?' asked the young man
from the next studio with his mouth full.

'What we know – a mere remnant,' said Mr. Preemby.
'Mere remnant.'

'How did they dress?'

'H'rrmp. Robes. White   robes – extremely   dignified.
Blue – azure – when justice was administered. Plato tells
us that much.'

'Could they fly?'

'They understood it. It was not made a practice of.'

'Motor-cars? All that sort of thing?'

'If they wanted to. There was less motoring – more
meditation. We live – age of transition. H'rrmp.'

'And then it all went phut?' said the young man from
the next studio. 'Submerged and all that. What a lesson!'

'That need not have happened,' said Mr. Preemby darkly.

Mr. Preemby became dimly aware of scepticism.
'There's not an atom of evidence that there ever was a
continent in the Atlantic,' Mr. Teddy Winterton was
saying to Christina Alberta; 'within thirty million years
of anything human. The ocean troughs go right back to
the Mesozoic age.'

Mr. Preemby would have noticed this remark but the
untidy girl asked him suddenly if he did not think that
the swastika was a symbol derived from Atlantis. He said

72

he was quite certain it was. She asked what it meant exactly; she had always been curious about its significance: and he became guarded and mysterious. She wanted moreover to know things about the costume of that lost world, about its social customs, about its religion. Were women citizens? She was certainly the most intelligent about it of all the company. The silver-haired man seemed to be faintly amused.

The rest of the company wandered off into a discussion of the possibility of going to the Chelsea Arts Ball in the character of a party from the Lost Atlantis. Many of their ideas Mr. Preemby thought trivial and undignified. 'Leaves us unlimited scope,' said Harold Crumb. 'We could invent weapons – have wings if we liked. Magic carbuncles on our shields – illuminated. Mysterious books and tablets. And a sort of peculiar wailing, drumming music; Mya, mya, mya.'

He pursed up his face and made a curious mooing noise with it to convey his intention, twiddling his fingers to assist the effect.

It was no good protesting against such imaginative ignorance. But to the dark untidy girl and to the acquiescent man with silvery hair Mr. Preemby continued to be quietly oracular and communicative from behind his moustache.

'But how are these things known?' the dark girl persisted. 'There is nothing in the British Museum.'

'You forget,' said Mr. Preemby. 'H'rrmp, the Freemasons. There are Inner Groups – traditions. Thank you. Just half a glass more. Oh! you've filled it! Thank you.'

As he talked he was aware of something going on between Christina Alberta and Winterton. At first it seemed not to matter in the slightest degree, but to be just part of the general unusualness of the gathering, and then it seemed

73

to matter a great deal. He saw Christina Alberta's little fist resting on the table, and suddenly Winterton's hand enveloped it. She snatched her hand away. Then something was whispered and her hand came back. In another moment the hands were five inches apart and it was as if nothing had ever happened between them.

He would probably have forgotten the momentary invasion of his attention by Christina Alberta if something else had not occurred at the phase of dessert. Poppinetti's idea of dessert was a sort of lottery of walnuts – if you found a sound one you won – masses of compressed and damaged dates and a few defiant apples. There was a great crackling. The company was littering the table with walnut shells, and the green, black and yellow corruption they had contained, when this second incident caught Mr. Preemby's eye. He saw Teddy Winterton run his hand very softly along Christina Alberta's forearm. And her arm was not withdrawn.

Every one was talking just then and for a moment it seemed to Mr. Preemby that he alone had seen, and then he caught an observant expression on the face of the silver-haired man. It was all very confusing, and this Chianti – though it was really not intoxicating – made everything swimmy, but Mr. Preemby knew somehow that the silver-haired man had also seen that furtive familiarity, and that he too didn't quite approve of it.

Ought one to take notice? Ought one to say anything? Perhaps afterwards. Perhaps when they were alone together, he might ask her quietly, 'Are you and that young man Winterton engaged?'

'A bit too much,' said Mr. Preemby quietly, meeting the eye of the silver-haired man. 'I don't like that sort of thing.'

'Quite,' said the silver-haired man.

'I shall speak to her.'

'You're right there,' said the silver-haired man warmly. A very sensible fellow.

A great rustle and a scraping of chairs. Poppinetti figuring upon an accounts-pad, came to collect the money.

'I'll pay for us, Daddy,' said Christina Alberta, 'and we'll settle up afterwards.'

Poppinetti bowing. Poppinetti on Mr. Preemby's right and on Mr. Preemby's left; several Poppinettis bowing. A great activity of Poppinettis handing hats and so forth. Poppinettis whichever way you turned. The restaurant rotating slightly. Was this Chianti perhaps stronger than Mr. Preemby had been led to believe? A number of Poppinettis opening a number of doors and saying polite things. Difficult to choose a door. Right the first time. Out into the street. People going by. Taxis. No more Poppinettis. But a girl ought not to let a young man stroke her arm at dinner, when anyone might see it happen. It wasn't correct. Something had to be said. Something tactful.

Mr. Preemby became aware that he was walking next to Mrs. Crumb. 'It was lovely to hear you talking about the New Atlantis,' she said. 'I wish I had been sitting nearer.'

'H'rrmp,' said Mr. Preemby.

Something very nice about Mrs. Crumb. What was it? Not so *fearfully* married, but married quite enough.

§ 6

Mr. Preemby thought they were going back for coffee and a little talk and then bed; he had no idea of the immense amount of evening still before him. He knew nothing as yet of the capacity for sitting up late and getting lively in the small hours possessed by this new world of young people into which Christina Alberta had led him.

And in a sort of hectic discontinuous way they were lively for hours. It became vaguely evident to Mr. Preemby that there was a periodic 'day' set apart by Mrs. Crumb for evening gatherings in the studio, and that this evening he had chosen for his settling down was such an evening. Fresh people dropped in. One it seemed was a portentous arrival, he came in quite soon after the return from Poppinetti's; he was very fat and broad, a white-faced man of forty or so, rather short of breath, with exceedingly intelligent eyes under a broad forehead and a rather loose peevish mouth. He carried himself with the involuntary self-consciousness of a man who thinks he is pointed out. His name it seemed was Paul Lambone, and he had written all sorts of things. Everybody treated him with a faint deference. He greeted Christina Alberta with great warmth.

'How's the newest Van?' he said, shaking her hand as though he liked it, and speaking with a singularly small voice for so ample a person. 'How's the last step in Advance?'

'You've got to meet my father,' said Christina Alberta.

'Has it got a father? I thought it just growed like Topsy – out of Nietzsche and Bernard Shaw and all the rest of them.'

'H'rrmp,' said Mr. Preemby.

Mr. Lambone turned to him. 'What a Handful a daughter is!' he said, and bowed slightly towards Christina Alberta, 'even the best of them.'

Mr. Preemby replied after the manner of the parents in Woodford Wells. 'She's a good daughter to me, sir.'

'Yes, but they aren't like sons.'

'You have sons, sir, I presume.'

'Only dream children. I've not had your courage to realize things. I've married a hundred times in theory and here I am just a sort of bachelor uncle to everybody. Poking in among the younger people and observing their behaviour with ' – his intelligent eyes looked quietly over his garrulous mouth at Christina Alberta – 'terror and admiration.'

Two other visitors appeared in the doorway and Mr. Lambone turned from Mr. Preemby to greet them as soon as Fay had done her welcome, a fierce-looking young man with an immense head of black hair and a little lady like a china doll dressed to remind one of Watteau.

Conversation became general and Mr. Preemby receded into the background of events.

He found himself side by side with his friend with the silver hair, against his bookcase. 'I didn't expect a party,' he said.

'I thought so too.'

'I only got here this afternoon. The vans came late and lots of my things are still to be unpacked.'

The silver-haired man nodded sympathetically. 'Often the case,' he murmured.

Every one was talking loudly. It was difficult to hear. It was confused sort of talking, and whenever two or three seemed to be interested in what they were saying, Fay Crumb went and interrupted them as a good hostess should. Other people, only vaguely apprehended by Mr. Preemby, got into the studio somehow. There was a red-haired young lady with a tremendous decolletage; behind you could see almost to her waist. He h'rrmp'd at it and thought of saying something about it, something cold and quiet, to the silver-haired man. But he didn't. He couldn't think of anything sufficiently cold and quiet to say.

Fay Crumb came and asked whether he would like some

77

whisky or beer. 'Not on the top of that nice Chianti, thank you,' said Mr. Preemby.

The conversation seemed to get noisier and noisier. In one corner Harold Crumb could be heard quoting the poems of Vachell Lindsay. Then Mr. Lambone came up and seemed to want to talk about the Lost Atlantis, but Mr. Preemby was shy of talking about the Lost Atlantis with Mr. Lambone. 'Getting on alright, Daddy?' said Christina Alberta, drifting by and not waiting for any answer but an 'h'rrmp.'

There appeared three young people with a gramophone they explained they had just bought, and Fay discovered that the beer had been forgotten and sent Harold out to borrow some from a neighbour. These new-comers made no very profound impression on Mr. Preemby's now jaded mind, except that one of them, the owner of the gramophone, a very fair young man with a long intelligent nose, was wearing the big horn of the gramophone as a head-dress, and that he meant to have that gramophone going whatever else might occur.

The music was dance-music, jazz for the most part and a few waltzes, and it revived Mr. Preemby considerably. He sat up and beat time with the leg-bones of a roc, and presently two or three couples were dancing on the studio floor. Curious dancing, Mr. Preemby thought; almost like walking – jiggety walking with sudden terrific back-swipes of the legs. There was an interruption when Harold returned with the borrowed beer – bringing its lenders with it. Then there was a general clamour for Christina Alberta and Teddy to 'do' their dance. Teddy was quite willing but Christina Alberta seemed reluctant, and when Mr. Preemby saw the dance he was not surprised.

'H'rrmp,' he said, and stroked his moustache and looked at the silver-haired man.

It really was too familiar altogether; for some moments the principals vanished upstairs, and came back altered. For some reason Teddy had adopted a cloth cap and a red neck-wrap; he was, in fact, being an Apache, and the bearing of Christina Alberta had become very proud and spirited with her arms akimbo.

Every one backed against the walls to clear a dancing floor. At the beginning it wasn't so bad. But presently this Mr. Teddy was pitching Christina Alberta about, throwing her over his shoulder, taking hold of her, bending her backward, holding her almost upside down, both legs in the air and her hands dragging on the ground. And she was red and excited and seemed to like these violent familiarities. There was a kind of undesirable suitability between them for such purposes. She and Teddy looked into each other's eyes with a sort of intimacy and yet with a sort of fierce defiance. At one point in the extraordinary dance she had to smack his face, a good hard smack, nicely timed. She did it with a spirit that made every one applaud. Whereupon he smiled and took her nice little neck in his hands and strangled her with great realism.

Then the gramophone had its death rattle and the dance was over.

Mr. Preemby's throat had not troubled him much since dinner, but now he said 'hrrmp' repeatedly.

They wanted Christina Alberta, bright and panting and shockheaded, to repeat the performance, but she wouldn't. She had had a glimpse of the solemn dismay and perplexity upon her Daddy's face.

The people from the studio next door were the next to give a display: they obliged with an imitation of a Russian imitation of a peasant dance from Saratoff. There was a gramophone record that was not quite the proper music, but it would do. That dance really amused Mr. Preemby.

The young man went down quite close to the floor and kicked out his feet with the greatest agility and the girl was as wooden as a doll. Every one clapped hands in time to the music, and so did Mr. Preemby.

And then came a further irruption. Five people in fancy dress demanding beer. They impressed Mr. Preemby as strange and bright-coloured, but totally uninteresting. One wore a red coxcomb and was dressed as a jester in cap and bells. The others just wore tights and bright things that signified nothing at all. They had been at some party given by somebody or other for the 'Young people.' They announced with shouts, 'They shut down at midnight. Yes, they shut down at midnight. When the young people go to bed.'

It was only too manifest that No. 8 Lonsdale Mews meant to do nothing of the sort.

Beer. Mr. Preemby declined. The last of the beer. Cigarettes. Much smoke. The last of the whisky. More gramophone, more dancing and Harold Crumb's voice loose again in recitation. Beer or whisky had thickened it. But there were countervailing noises. Movement. A circle was cleared. Not more dancing! No. Feats of strength and dexterity with chairs, performed chiefly by Teddy Winterton, the gramophone owner, and Harold. This stunting stopped presently and the company flowed back towards the middle of the room. Talk Mr. Preemby could not follow; phrases he could not understand. Nobody taking the slightest notice of him.

A sense of weariness and futility and desolation came upon him. How differently were the evenings of the past spent by the good wise people of the lost Atlantis! Philosophical discourse they had, the lute, the lyre. Elevated thoughts.

He caught sight of Mrs. Crumb yawning furtively. Suddenly, stupendously he yawned. And yawned again.

'Yaaw,' he said to Paul Lambone who was at his side.
'Proyawaw – Prolly thiswe sitting on my beawawd.'
'You live here?' said Mr. Lambone.
'Come to-day. Christina Albyawawawter arranged it.'
'The devil she did!' said Mr. Lambone, and looked across
the studio at her. For some moments he seemed lost in
thought.
'Very remarkable young woman that daughter of yours,'
he said. 'Makes me feel old-fashioned.'
He looked at the wrist-watch he wore. 'Half-past
one,' he said. 'I'll start the Go. . . .'

§ 7

Mr. Preemby heard a few sentences of the parting
between Teddy Winterton and Christina Alberta. 'Yes
or no?' said Teddy.
'*No*,' said Christina Alberta with emphasis.
'Not a bit of it,' said Teddy.
'I don't want to,' she said.
'But you *do*.'
'Oh, go to the devil!'
'Not as if there were risks.'
'I shan't come. It's preposterous.'
'I shall wait all the same.'
'You may wait.'
'Little Chrissy Hesitation. Anything to please you.'

§ 8

It took until past two o'clock for the Go Paul Lambone
had started to remove the last of the company.
'All hands to the bedmaking,' cried Fay. 'It isn't always
like this, Mr. Preemby.'

'Confess I feel tired,' said Mr. Preemby. 'Had a long day of it.'

Christina Alberta regarded him with belated compunction. 'It just happened like this,' she said.

'Not used to such late hours,' said Mr. Preemby, sitting on his bed when at last it was made, and he did a yawn that almost dislocated his jaw.

'Night,' said Fay, yawning also.

'We'll turn in,' said Harold. 'So long, Mr. Preemby.' The yawning seized upon Harold also. What a face he had!

'Goo-i.'

'Gawooi-i.'

The door closed upon them.

There was much to say to Christina Alberta, but it was too late and Mr. Preemby was too weary to say it now. And also he had no idea what it was he ought to say.

A casual remark fell out. 'I liked that man with the white hair,' he said.

'Did you?' said Christina Alberta absently.

'He was intelligent. He took a great interest in the Lost Atlantis.'

'He's stone deaf,' said Christina Alberta, 'and he's ashamed of it – poor dear.'

'Oh!' said Mr. Preemby.

'All this is going to be rather noisy for you, Daddy,' she said, coming to what she had in mind.

'It *is* a bit ramshackle,' said Mr. Preemby.

'We ought to go to Tunbridge Wells quite soon and look round there.'

'To-morrow,' said Mr. Preemby.

'Not to-morrow.'

'Why not?'

'The next day,' said Christina Alberta. 'I'm not quite sure about to-morrow. I'd sort of half promised to go somewhere else –. But it doesn't matter very much really.'

'I'd like to go to Tunbridge Wells to-morrow,' said Mr. Preemby.

'Why not?' said Christina Alberta as if to herself, and hesitated.

She walked to the door and came back. 'Good night, little Daddy,' she said.

'Are we going then? To-morrow?'

'No. . . . Yes. . . . I don't know. I *had* planned to do something to-morrow. Important in a kind of way. . . . We'll go to-morrow, Daddy.'

She walked away from him with her arms akimbo and stared at those queer pictures.

She spun round on her feet. 'I can't go to-morrow,' she said.

'Yes I will,' she contradicted.

'Oh hell!' she cried, in the most unaccountable and unladylike way. 'I don't know what to *do*!'

Mr. Preemby looked at her with grave and weary eyes. This was a new Christina Alberta to him. She ought not to swear. She did *not* ought to swear. She'd caught it up from these people. She didn't know what it meant. He must talk to her – to-morrow. About that and one or two other things. But Heavens! how tired he was!

'You –' He yawned. 'You must take care of yourself, Christina Alberta,' he said.

'I'll do that all right, Daddy. Trust me.'

She came and sat down beside him on his little half-fictitious bed. 'We can't decide to-night, Daddy. We're too tired. We'll settle to-morrow. Have to see what the weather's like for one thing. Wouldn't do to walk about Tunbridge if it was wet. We'll decide about everything to-morrow – when our heads are cool. Why! you dear little Daddy! It's just upon half-past two.'

She put her arm round his shoulders and kissed him on the top of his head and the lobe of his ear. He loved her to touch him and kiss him. He did not understand in the least how much he loved her to kiss him.

'Dear *tired* little Daddy,' she said in her softest voice: 'You are ever so kind to me. Good night.'

She had gone.

For some time Mr. Preemby sat quite motionless in a state of almost immobile thought.

The floor of the studio was littered with burnt matches and cigarette ends and the air smelt of stale smoke and beer. On the blue-painted table stood an empty beer-bottle and two or three glasses containing dregs of beer and cigarette ash.

It was all very different from Woodford Wells, – very different indeed.

But it was Experience.

Mr. Preemby bestirred himself to undress.

That night-shirt of Saxony flannel had still to be unpacked.

§ 9

In the morning Christina Alberta was still restless and quite undecided about going to Tunbridge Wells, though the weather was perfectly fine. About half-past eleven she disappeared, and after a light lunch with Fay – Harold was out also – it became evident to Mr. Preemby that the visit to Tunbridge Wells was postponed for the day. So he went to South Kensington to look at the Museums there. He did not go into them actually, he just looked at them and at the colleges and buildings generally. It was a preliminary reconnaissance.

The Museums were quite good to look at. Larger, more

extensive, than the British Museum. Probably they contained – all sorts of things.

Christina Alberta reappeared in the studio about half-past six looking very bright and exalted. There was something about her subtly triumphant.

She offered no explanation of her disappearance. She was full of the visit to Tunbridge on the morrow. They must catch a train soon after nine and have a good long day. She was unusually affectionate to her Daddy.

Harold was out for the evening and Fay had some reviewing to do, so they had quite a quiet and domestic evening. Mr. Preemby read with a varying attention a nice deep confusing book he had found in the room upstairs called *Fantasia of the Unconscious* about the Lost Atlantis and similar things.

CHAPTER THE FOURTH

The Petunia Boarding House

§ I

MOST places in the world have sister cities and twins and parallels, but Tunbridge Wells is Tunbridge Wells, and there is nothing really like it upon our planet. Not that it is in any way strange or fantastic, but because of its brightly delicate distinction. It is clean and open, and just pleasantly absurd. It is not more than thirty miles from London, as the crow flies, but the North Downs six miles away dismiss with a serene and gracious gesture all thoughts of London from the mind. It is away from the main line out of London, inconvenient for season-ticket holders; there is no direct route for the hurrying motorist over those saving Downs; to Dover and Kent generally he goes to the east of it, and to Brighton he goes to the west – if he survive the hills of Westerham and Sevenoaks. Rich men's estates encircle it with accessible parks. Eridge, Bayham, Penshurst Park, Knole and the like, protect it from overmuch breeding of little villa residences. There it lies, on a rare piece of rocky soil, dry underfoot, airy and wholesome, with its friendly Common in the midst of it; its Spa of evil-tasting beneficent waters as the Stuart princesses drank them, its Pantiles and its Pump Room, much as Dr. Johnson knew the place. Mount Sion and Mount Ephraim, Beulah Road and something evangelical in the air, remind the light-minded visitor that London in the past was a Puritan city. Many a serious liver has been touched and found grace at Tunbridge Wells. Many a light liver has found fresh strength there. And thither came Mr. Preemby and Christina Alberta seeking a boarding-house – and they could have sought it in no more favourable locality.

86

They set about the search in a systematic way as became a couple, one of whom had been partially trained for sociological research at the London School of Economics and partially trained for business at the Tomlinson School. Mr. Preemby had been for beginning with a general lookround, just walking round and looking quietly at things for a bit, but Christina Alberta consulted all the agents in order, and bought a map and guide to the town and sat down on a seat on the Common and planned the operations that led quite readily and easily to the Petunia Boarding House.

In the guide Mr. Preemby read with approval some very promising words. 'Listen to this my dear,' he said. 'H'rrmp. "General Characteristics. Emphasis might very well be laid on the character enjoyed by Tunbridge Wells as a magnet for high-class residents and visitors. The town is never overrun with trippers, nor are its streets ever defiled by the vulgar or the inane. Its inhabitants are composed, for the most part, of well-to-do people who naturally create a social atmosphere tinged by culture and refinement." '

'*Tinged* is a jolly good word for it I expect,' said Christina Alberta.

'I think my instinct has guided me aright to this place,' said Mr. Preemby.

The Petunia Boarding House looks obliquely upon the Common from where Petunia Road runs into the quaint and pleasant High Street. It has not the towering magnificence of the Wellington, the Royal Mount Ephraim, the Marlborough, or their fellows, which face the sun so bravely from the hill-crest above the Common, but it is a house of dignified comfort. The steps, the portico, the ample hall, the name in letters of gold on black, made Mr. Preemby say h'rrmp several times. An excessively chubby maid in a very, very tight black dress and a cap and

87

apron, came and looked at Mr. and Miss Preemby with a
distraught evasive expression, answered some preliminary
questions incoherently, and said she would call Miss Emily
Rewster – Miss Margaret was out. Thereupon Miss Emily
Rewster, who had been hovering attentively behind a bead
curtain, thrust it aside and came ingratiatingly into the
foreground. She was a little high-coloured old lady, with
an air of genteel *savoir-faire*; she had a lace cap and wore
a great deal of lace and several flounces, and she had the
most frankly dyed chestnut hair that Christina Alberta
had ever seen. 'Was it just for a week or so Mr. Preemby
wanted to come, or something – perheps – more permanent?'

Explanations were exchanged. Mr. Preemby was to be
'more permanent'; Christina Alberta intermittent – and
rather a difficulty. The existence of head-quarters in
Chelsea was revealed discreetly, but not the fact that they
were in a Mews.

Miss Emily Rewster thought Christina Alberta could
be fitted in if she wasn't too particular about having
the same room, or exactly the same sort of room every
time she came. 'We have to menage,' said Miss Emily
Rewster.

'So long as the window opens,' said Christina Alberta.

The rooms exhibited were very satisfactory, (h'rrmp)
very satisfactory. A glimpse of a bathroom was given.
'You say when you want one,' said Miss Emily Rewster.
There was a dining-room with separate tables, and there
were flowers on every table, very refined and pleasant, and
there was a large drawing-room with a piano and a great
number of arm-chairs and sofas wearing flounces so like
the flounces of Miss Emily Rewster, and antimacassars so
like her cap, and with so entirely her air of accommoda-
ting receptiveness that it seemed as though they must be at
least her cousins who had joined her in the enterprise.

The piano wore a sort of lace bed-spread, and there were polished tables bearing majolica pots of aspidistra on mats and little less serious tables for use, and there was a low book-case with books in it and a great heap of illustrated papers on the top. The hall expanded at the back into a rather modernish lounge where two ladies were having tea; and there was also a smoking-room, where, said Miss Emily Rewster to Christina Alberta rather coyly, 'the gentlemen smoke.'

'We've been very full this season,' said Miss Emily Rewster, 'very full. We've had nearly thirty sitting at dinner. But of course the season is drawing in now. Just at present we're down to nine at breakfast and seven at dinner; two gentlemen in business here. But people come and people go. I've had two inquiries by post to-day. One an invalid lady and her sister. They think of drinking the waters. And there are Birds of Passage as well as Regulars. Just for a night or so. Motor families. They take us *en route*. That's where we have an advantage in being so close to the shops.'

She beamed intimately at Mr. Preemby. 'Often my sister or I pop out at the last moment and get in things ourselves. When every one else is busy. We don't mind any little trouble if it makes people comfortable.'

'We've been on the separate table system ever since the war,' said Miss Emily Rewster. 'So much more pleasant. You can keep yourself Quate to yourself if you wish, or you can be Friendly. People often Speak in the Drawing-room or in the Smoking-room. And they bow. Sometimes people get Quate friendly. Play Games. Get up Excursions together. Quate Pleasant.'

Christina Alberta asked an obvious question.

'Very pleasant people indeed,' said Miss Emily. 'Very pleasant people. A retired gentleman and his wife and her stepdaughter and two retired maiden ladies and a gentleman and his lady who has been in a forest in Burmah and so on.'

Christina Alberta restrained a ribald impulse to ask what a 'retired gentleman' or a 'retired maiden lady' really meant.

'I've always been attracted to Tumbridge Wells,' said Mr. Preemby.

'*Royal* Tunbridge Wells *if* you please,' said Miss Emily radiantly. 'The "Royal" was added in nineteen nine you know, by gracious command of his Majesty.'

'I didn't know,' said Mr. Preemby with profound respect, and tried it over; '*Royal* Tumbridge Wells.'

'Makes it rather a mouthful,' said Christina Alberta.

'A very pleasant mouthful for Us, I can assure you,' said Miss Emily loyally.

The Petunia Boarding House seemed so satisfactory to Mr. Preemby that it was arranged that he should return the next day but one, bringing with him some clothes and other luggage, and that Christina Alberta was to come and stay with him for a few days – there was a little room upstairs she could have – and then she would go back to London and her studies and take her chance of coming again when there was a room for her.

§ 2

In the train back to London Mr. Preemby rehearsed these arrangements and made his plans.

'I shall come down here the day after to-morrow, after I have put my collections in order at the Mew. I shall put the best things so that they can be seen through the glass of the cabinet, but I think I shall lock them up, and I shall bring down a few necessary books, and then when I have quite settled in I shall go and have a good look at these celebrated Rocks here.'

'We could come down in the morning,' said Christina Alberta, 'and go and look at them in the afternoon.'

'Not the same afternoon,' said Mr. Preemby. 'No. I want my mind to be quite fresh and open when I look at the Rocks. I think it will be best to see them quite early – after a night's sleep. When there are no other visitors. I think – I think, Christina Alberta, that for the first time I'd better go to them quite alone. Without you. Sometimes you say things, Christina Alberta – you don't mean to say them of course – but they put me out. . . .'

Christina Alberta reflected. 'What do you expect to find at these Rocks, Daddy?'

Mr. Preemby waved his moustache and the rest of his face slowly from side to side. 'I go with an Open Mind,' he said. 'Perhaps all of Atlantis was not lost. Some of it may be hidden. There are legends preserved by the philosopher Plato. Partly in cipher. Who knows? It may be here. It may be in Africa. A plan. A sign. The toad rock must be most singular. In the British Museum there is a toad rock from Central America. . . .'

He mused pleasantly for a time.

'I shall take a note-book,' he said, 'and several coloured pencils.'

He continued to meditate. His next remark came after an interval of three or four minutes, and was a surprise for Christina Alberta.

'I hope, my dear,' said Mr. Preemby, 'that among all these artists and people you are not getting Ram Shackle.

'I should be sorry to think you were getting Ram Shackle,' said Mr. Preemby.

'But Daddy, what makes you think I may be getting – Ram Shackle?' asked Christina Alberta.

'One or two little things I saw at the Mew,' said Mr. Preemby. 'Just one or two little things. You've got to be careful, Christina Alberta. A girl has to take care of herself. And your friends – decidedly Ram Shackle. Don't mind my making a remark about them, Christina Alberta. Just a word in season.'

Christina Alberta's answer came after a little interval, and without her usual confident ring. 'Don't you worry about me, Daddy,' she said. 'I'm all right.'

Mr. Preemby seemed about to change the subject. Then he remarked, 'I don't like that feller, Teddy Winterton. He's too familiar.'

'I don't like him either,' said Christina Alberta. 'He *is* too familiar.'

'That's all right,' said Mr. Preemby. 'I thought you didn't notice,' and relapsed into meditation.

But this sudden and unprecedented intervention in her personal affairs made Christina Alberta thoughtful for all the rest of the way to London. Ever and again she glanced furtively at her Daddy.

He seemed to have forgotten her.

But it was dreadfully true. Teddy Winterton had become – altogether – too familiar.

§ 3

In all ages competent observers have noted the erratic unexpectedness of destiny, and now Christina Alberta was to add her own small experience to this ever accumulating testimony. It seemed to her that in planting him out in the wholesome quiet of Royal Tunbridge Wells she was securing for her Daddy the very best possible conditions for a happy and harmless life. There had, indeed, been a notable change in the little man since her mother's death, a release of will, a new freedom of expression, a disposition to comment and even form judgments upon things about him. She had herself likened it to the germination of a seed brought out of a suppressing aridity into moisture and the light, but she had not followed up that comparison so far as to speculate what efflorescences might arise out of this belated unfolding of his initiatives. That here, of all places, he would meet just the stimulus that was needed for the most fantastic expansions of his imaginative life, that for him Tunbridge Wells should prove the way out of this everyday world of ours into what was to be for him an altogether more wonderful and satisfactory existence, never entered her head.

For three days, until a fretting urgency for events carried her back to London, she stayed in the Petunia Boarding House, and for all those three days there was no intimation of the great change in his mind that impended. On the whole he seemed unusually dull and quiet during those three days. He liked Tunbridge Wells very much, he said, but he was greatly disappointed by the High Rocks and by the Toad Rock when he came to examine them. He even doubted whether they were not 'simply natural.' This was a terrible concession. He tried hard to believe that the Toad Rock was like one of the big Maya carvings of a toad from Yucatan, a cast of which he had seen in the British Museum, but it was evident that with all the will possible he could not manage so great an act of faith. All the decoration, he declared, all the inscription had been obliterated, and then, making the great blonde moustache bristle like a clothes-brush: 'There never were any decorations or inscriptions. Never.'

It was clear to Christina Alberta that he must have evolved very extraordinary expectations indeed, to be so much cast down. She found herself very interested in the riddle of what was fermenting in his mind. It seemed to her as if he had regarded Tunbridge Wells as a sort of Poste Restante at which some letter of supreme importance had awaited him. And there was no letter.

'But what did you expect, little Daddy?' said Christina Alberta, when on the afternoon of the first day he took her to the Toad Rock to see for herself how ordinary and insignificant a rock it was. 'Did you expect some wonderful carvings?'

'I expected – something for me. Something significant.'

'For you?'

'Yes, for me. And every one. About Life and the Mysteries. I had grown a sort of feeling there would be something there. *Now* – I don't know where to turn.'

'But what sort of thing, what significance did you expect?'

'Isn't Life a Riddle, Christina Alberta? Haven't you noticed that ? Do you think it is just nothing but studios and dances and excursions and char-à-bancs and meal-times and harvest?' he said. 'Obviously there is something more in it than that. Obviously. All that is just a Veil. Outward Showing. H'rrmp. And I don't know what is behind it, and I am just a plain boarder – in a boarding-house – and my life is passing away. Very difficult. H'rrmp. Almost impossible. It worries me exceedingly. Somewhere there must be a clue.'

'But that's how we *all* feel, Daddy,' cried Christina Alberta.

'Things can't be what they seem,' said Mr. Preemby, waving his hand with a gesture of contemptuous dismissal towards Rusthall Village, public house, lamp-posts, a policeman, a dog, a grocer's delivery-van and three passing automobiles. 'That at any rate is obvious. It would be too absurd. Infinite space; stars and so forth. Just for running about in – between meals. . . .'

Now who would have thought, Christina Alberta re-

flected, that this sort of thing was going on in his head?
Who would have thought it?

'Either I am a Reincarnation,' said Mr. Preemby, 'or I
am not. And if I am not, then I want to know what all
this business of the world is about. Symbolical it *must* be,
Christina Alberta. But of what?

'All those years at the Laundry I knew that that life
wasn't real. A period of rest and preparation. Your dear
mother thought differently – we never discussed it,
h'rrmp, but it was so.'

Christina Alberta could find no adequate comment and
they went on in silence for some time. When they spoke
again it was to discuss how they could get round to the
High Rocks Hotel for tea.

§ 4

Mr. Preemby was evidently depressed and more than a
little aggrieved, but he had none of the comprehensive
despondency of your melancholic type. Concurrently he
was quite actively interested in the boarding house, and
the fellow boarders he encountered there. It was a novel
experience for him to be in a boarding house. During his
married life he had always spent his holidays with Mrs.
Preemby in seaside apartments, so that she could super-
vise the provisioning properly, and detect, expose and
rectify errors and extortion. They had taken drives inland
during these vacations, or camped on the beach while
Mr. Preemby and Christina Alberta had made sand-
castles or pottered among rocks, and Mrs. Preemby had sat
in a folding-chair and pined for the Laundry. If the
weather was bad they kept in their apartments, where
Mr. Preemby and Christina Alberta could read books
while Mrs. Preemby could pine for the Laundry almost as

95

well as she could on the beach. But deep in Mr. Preemby's heart there had always been a craving for such a collective, promiscuous life as a boarding house affords.

They had made the acquaintance of the second Miss Rewster, Miss Margaret Rewster, on their arrival with the luggage. She was a taller, more anxious and less richly belaced variation of her sister. They both, Mr. Preemby discovered, had a peculiar hovering quality. They seemed always hovering behind bead curtains or down passages, or looking over from staircase landings or peeping round doors; poor dears! they were dreadfully anxious not to interfere with their guests, but they were equally anxious that everything should be all right. At meal times they operated with the joints and dishes behind a screen, and the chubby maid carried round the plates and vegetables. And whenever Mr. Preemby looked at the screen he found either Miss Margaret Rewster peeping over the top of it at him or Miss Emily Rewster peeping round the end. It made him quite nervous with his forks and spoons. When he dropped his serviette he hoped that would pass un-observed, but Miss Emily noted it at once and sent the chubby maid to pick it up for him.

Mr. Preemby and Christina Alberta came down to dinner as soon as Miss Margaret had sounded the second gong, and so they were the first to be seated and could survey their fellow guests at an advantage. Christina Alberta was quietly observant, but Mr. Preemby said 'h'rrmp' at each fresh arrival. The next to appear were two Birds of Pas-sage, a young man in Hudibrastic golfing knickerbockers, and a lady, presumably his wife, in a bright yellow sporting jumper, who were motoring about Kent; they made strenuous attempts to seize a table in the window which was already reserved for Petunia Regulars and were sub-dued with difficulty, but perfect dignity, by Miss Emily. They then consulted loudly about wine – the young man called the lady 'Old Thing,' and 'Old Top,' forms of expression new and interesting to Mr. Preemby, and she called him 'Badger' – and the chubby maid produced a card of wines that could be sent out for. The young man read out the names and prices of wines and made his selection almost as though he were a curate officiating in a very large cathedral. His wife, to follow out that comparison, made the responses. 'Chablis such as we should get here might be too sweet,'' he proclaimed.

'It might be too sweet?'

'What of a Pommard, Old Top?'

'Why *not* a Pommard, Badger?'

'The Beaune is a shilling cheaper and just as likely to be good – or bad.'

'Just as likely.'

The chubby maid flew out of the room, list in hand, with her thumb on the wine he had chosen.

Meanwhile under cover of this hubbub the two ladies Mr. Preemby had seen at tea in the lounge on the occasion of his first visit, percolated unobtrusively to a table near the window. They were obviously sisters, both rather slender and tall with small, round, bright-coloured faces on stalk-like necks; they had sharp little noses, and one of them wore tortoiseshell spectacles. A gentleman with a white moustache, larger and nobler even than Mr. Preemby's, accompanied by a small alert-looking wife, was the next to appear. Possibly this was the gentleman who had been in a forest in Burmah. The small alert-looking wife bowed to the slender ladies, who became agitated like reeds in a wind. The gentleman took no notice of them, grunted as he sat down, produced glasses and read the menu.

'Tomato soup *again*!' he said.

'It's usually very nice tomato soup,' said his wife.

'But Three Times Running!' he said. 'It favours acidity. I don't *like* tomato soup.'

97

The table in the bow window was occupied by three people who drifted in separately. First came a little thin dark lady in grey, carrying a bead work-bag, then a little dark bald man with large side-whiskers whom she addressed as father, and then a plump healthy-looking wife with a radiant manner who swept in and distributed greetings.

'Did you get your walk, Major Bone?' she said to the gentleman from the Burmese forest.

'Just to Rusthall Common and back,' said Major Bone, speaking thickly through his moustache and soup. 'Just to Rusthall Common.'

'And you got a char-à-banc to Crohamhurst, Miss Solbé?' The two sisters answered in unison. 'Oh! we had a *lovely* ride.'

'So picturesque,' said the one with spectacles.

'So open and pleasant,' said the one without spectacles. 'Did you see the sea?'

'Oh plainly!' said the one with spectacles.

'Ever so far away,' said the one without.

'Just as if the sky had a steel edge,' said the one with spectacles.

'Exactly like a leetle silver line,' said the one without.

'H'rrmp,' said Mr. Preemby.

Small portions of fish followed the tomato soup, and were consumed in comparative silence. There was a little burst of scarcely audible conversation at the window table. 'Now is *this* the same fish as we had yesterday?' asked the wife.

'It is a very similar fish,' said the gentleman with whiskers.

'The menu simply says, "Fish," ' said the stepdaughter.

'H'rrmp,' said Mr. Preemby.

'I think our back tyres were too tight to-day, Old Top,' said the man in plus fours, in a very loud, clear voice. 'I felt the road dreadfully.'

'I felt the road dreadfully,' said the lady in the yellow jumper.

'I must let them down a little to-morrow morning.'

'It would be better.'

'To-morrow morning will do. I won't trouble to-night.'

'Much better to-morrow morning, Badger. You're tired to-night after all that bumping. You'd make your hands dirty.'

Silence and active business with knives and forks.

'Porruck hasn't written about that,' said the Major from the forest.

'Very likely he's busy,' said his wife.

Silence.

'H'rrmp,' said Mr. Preemby.

Christina Alberta searched her mind for some conversational opening that would give her father a reasonable opportunity to make an acceptable reply, but she could think of nothing that was neither too disconcerting nor too dangerous. She met his eye and he had the expression of one who holds out against a strain.

Fish gave place to lamb.

'I thought that road from Sittingbourne was just awful,' said the motoring gentleman.

'It *was* just awful,' responded his wife.

Christina Alberta saw her father's face working. He was going to say something. 'H'rrmp. To-morrow, if it is fine, I think we will go for a walk in the morning.'

The knives and forks were hushed. Everybody was listening.

'I'd love a walk to-morrow, Daddy,' said Christina Alberta. 'I should think there were some jolly walks about this place.'

'Exactly,' said Mr. Preemby. 'Very probably. The Guide Book is very reassuring. H'rrmp.'

He had the dignified expression of a man who has carried off a difficult duty.

Resumption of activity with knives and forks.

'Hard to tell this lamb from mutton,' said Major Bone, 'if it wasn't for the mint sauce.'

'Peas are never so nice as they are from your own garden,' said the wife of the whiskered gentleman to her step-daughter.

'It's late for peas,' said the stepdaughter.

The two Miss Solbés and the motoring gentleman began talking at the same time. Mrs. Bone expressed the idea that it was hard to get good lamb nowadays. Taking courage from this sudden swirl of conversation Mr. Preemby was emboldened to remark to Christina Alberta that he had always been attracted to Tumbridge Wells. He felt the air was a strong air. It gave him an appetite.

'You must be careful not to get fat,' said Christina Alberta.

The outburst of active human exchanges came to an end. Baked apple and custard were consumed in comparative silence. The chubby maid came to ask Mr. Preemby whether he would like his coffee in the lounge or the smoking-room. 'The lounge I think,' said Mr. Preemby. 'H'rrmp. The lounge.'

The Misses Solbé, bearing glasses containing sugar and lemon juice, flitted from the room. The people from the window table followed. The function of dinner was completed. They found themselves alone in the lounge. Most of the people seemed to have drifted into the sitting-room. The gentleman from the forests of Burmah went by towards the smoking-room, carrying a large cigar which had an air of also coming from the forests of Burmah. It did not look like a cigar that had been rolled or filled; it looked like a cigar of old gnarled wood that had been hewn from a branching tree. A straw came out of the end of it. . . .

Christina Alberta stood and contemplated a vast void of time, two hours it might be, before she could decently go to bed. 'Oh! this is the Life!' she said.

'Extremely comfortable,' said Mr. Preemby, sitting down with much creaking in a basket arm-chair.

Christina Alberta sat on a glass-topped table and lit a cigarette. She saw those two hours stretching before her, and she wanted to scream.

The chubby maid brought coffee and seemed gently surprised at Christina Alberta's cigarette. Whisperings off stage. Then Miss Emily became dimly visible through the bead curtain at the end of the passage, hovering. She vanished again and Christina Alberta finished her cigarette in peace. Mr. Preemby drank up his coffee. Pause. Christina Alberta swung her legs rhythmically. Then she slid off the table to her feet.

'Daddy,' she said, 'let's go into the sitting-room and see if anything is happening there.'

§ 5

In the Boarding Houses of the past the common dining-table was the social centre where people met and mind clashed upon and polished mind. But the spirit of aloofness, the separate table system, has changed all that, and now it is in the smoking-room or the sitting-room that the vestiges of social intercourse, advances, retreats, coquettings, exchanges, games and jests are to be found. But the company of the Petunia Boarding House was not in a state of social fusion. The only coalescence was a conversation. The wife of the gentleman from the Burmese forests had secured an arm-chair by the side of the fire-place, and she was describing in a low whisper the numerous servants she had had in Burmah, to the cheerful wife and the younger

Miss Solbé who was knitting. The Miss Solbé with the spectacles had fortified herself behind a table on the other side of the fire and was engaged meticulously with a very elaborate Patience. The gentleman with the side-whiskers sat rigidly on one of the sofas, behind a copy of the *Times*, while his daughter sat at a table close at hand and also threaded her way through a Patience. The Birds of Passage, after inquiries about movies and music-halls, had gone out.

Nobody took the slightest notice of Mr. Preemby and Christina Alberta. The two stood for some moments in the middle of the room, and then panic came upon Mr. Preemby. A dishonourable panic so that he threw his daughter to these silent, motionless wolves.

'H'rrmp,' he said. 'I think my dear, I will go to the smoking-room. I think I will go and smoke. There are some illustrated papers over there on the book-case for you if you care to look at them.'

Christina Alberta walked over to the low book-case and Mr. Preemby departed, h'rrmping.

She stood pretending an interest in the illustrated jokes and in the portraits of actresses and society people in the *Sketch* and *Tatler*. Out of the tail of her eye she surveyed those fellow guests of hers, and with a negligent ear she collected the gist of Mrs. Bone's dissertation upon the servant question in Burmah. 'They will plant the whole family upon you if they can – uncles and cousins even. Before you know where you are. . . .

'Of course a white woman is a Little Queen out there. . . .

'The chief fault of the cooking from my point of view, was the way it upset Major Bone. His stomach . . . far more delicate than a woman's.'

'He looks so stout and strong,' said Miss Solbé.

'In everything but that. In everything. But the Curries they used to make –'

She sank her voice, and the heads of the younger Miss Solbé and the pleasant mannered lady closed in upon her for the rich particulars.

What a Lot they were! Christina Alberta reflected. And they were living beings! The astonishing thing to Christina Alberta was that they were alive. And being alive and having presumably been a cause of considerable trouble, distress, emotion and hope to various people before they were got alive, they were now all in the most resolute way avoiding anything that with the extremest stretch of civility could be spoken of as living. Their hours, their days were passing; a few thousand days more perhaps for each of them, a few score thousand hours. Then there would be no more chance of living for ever. And instead of filling up this scanty allowance of hours and days with every possible sensation and every possible effort and accomplishment, here they were, gathered into a sort of magic box of atmosphere in which nothing could possibly be done. By anyone. . . .

Christina Alberta felt like a moth caught under a glass. Well, for a day or so, she had an excuse; little Daddy must be settled. But then? Nothing could be done here. Neither joy nor sorrow nor sin nor creative effort – because even Miss Solbé's knitting was being knitted to a prescription on a dirty cutting of printed paper. Everything they were employed upon was an evasion, everything. Even the whispered delicate hints of the diuretic, dyspeptic, infuriating and wildly aphrodisiac effects of Burmah Curry upon Major Bone in his younger days that were being handed out by his good lady to her intent hearers, were just a substitution of second-hand knowledge for realities.

And this Patience! Would she, Christina Alberta asked herself, would she ever come to play Patiences in Boarding Houses? Was it credible that some day she also would come to sit voluntarily in such an atmosphere?

'Rather sell matches in a gutter,' whispered Christina Alberta.

What a marvellous thing is Man! What ingenuities he has! what powers and capabilities! He invents paper and perfects printing. He develops the most beautiful methods of colour printing. He makes cardboard like silk and ivory out of rags and vegetable pulp. And all it would seem, that human beings, hanging for a little while in life between the nothingness before death and the nothingness after death, should fiddle away long hours in a feeble fuddled conflict with the permutations of duplicate sets of four differently coloured thirteens! Cards! The marvel of cards! All over the world millions of people drawing nearer to death and nothingness were pursuing the chances of the four thirteens: bridge, whist, nap, skat, a hundred forms of it. Directly they could get in out of the wet and dark, they sat down to that sort of thing, to the cards shining under the still lamps, to being endlessly surprised, delighted, indignant and despondent by chances that any-one who chose to sit down to it could work out and tabu-late in a week!

'Getting it out, dear?' said the younger Miss Solbé.

'The spades are *Wicked* to-night,' said the Miss Solbé with the glasses.

'Mine is going rather well,' said the daughter of the gentleman with the whiskers.

'Does your daughter play *Miss Milligan*?' asked the younger Solbé sister.

'*Eight-eights*,' said the comfortable wife. '*Miss Milligan* is too much for her.'

'Well, it *is* a Beast you know,' said the stepdaughter. 'You never know where you are with it.'

'Patience is Patience,' said the elder Miss Solbé. 'Nowa-days I often get it out. But not when the spades come as they've done to-night, both twos in the top row, and no aces till the last round but one.'

Christina Alberta thought it was time to change from the *Sketch* to the *Tatler*. She tried to do this with careless ease and flopped a dozen papers on the floor. 'Oh *Damn!*' said Christina Alberta to a great stillness. She struggled to pick up and replace the disordered sheets. For a time every one seemed to be regarding her. Then Mrs. Bone took up her discourse again.

'And you can't imagine their obstinacy,' she said. 'They are *wilfully* ignorant. When you show them, *then* they won't do it. I took my cook-boy in hand for a time – boy I call him, but he was quite a middle-aged man – and I said to him, "just let me show you some plain English cookery, a boiled fowl with nice white sauce, a few plain potatoes and vegetables – quite plain with the natural flavour left in – the sort of food that builds up these brave young Englishmen you see." Of course I'm not a good cook myself, but anyhow I knew more of English cooking than he did. But we never got further than the plain boiled fowl. He expressed the most violent disapproval – really violent I mean – of the whole proceedings. As I took hold of the things and got to work he began to behave in the most extraordinary way. He tried *not* to follow what I was doing. Tried not to. He said that if he cooked a fowl like that he would lose caste, lose his position in the local guild of cooks, be perpetually defiled and outcast. *Why*, he would not say. When I persisted he rushed up and down pulling at his black hair – a black madman, his eyes rolling frightfully. I could never make out what there was in a plain boiled fowl to cause such excitement. "This in my kitchen," he said. "This in *my* kitchen!"

'There I stood quietly boiling my fowl while all this pother went on. He hovered about me. He talked – fortunately in his own language. I even caught him pretending to be sick behind my back. Then he came and implored me to desist – with tears in his great brown eyes. He tried to say things in English. The Major always says that he was simply swearing, but I believe the wretched man really did believe that if he was to boil a fowl in the plain, whole-some, simple way nice people in England do it daily, he would be hung in the air, and the great jays of Burmah would come and peck – ahem!'

She cast a side glance at Christina Alberta, apparently lost in the *Sketch*, and lowered her voice.

'Peck at his *entrails*, just his insides you know, for a Thousand, Thousand Years.'

Sensation.

'You never know What Ideas Easterners will get into their Heads,' said the younger Miss Solbé. 'East is East, and West is West.'

But now Christina Alberta's attention was distracted by another set of phenomena. She had discovered that the thin, bald gentleman with side-whiskers, rigid behind his *Times*, was not really reading that interesting vestige of the British constitution at all. His gaze was not directed to the edge of his paper, but beyond it. He was staring from behind that ambush and round the corner of his glasses in a strange, hard-eyed way, without passion or admiration, at the upper part of Christina Alberta's black-stockinged legs as they delivered their last challenge to human censure before disappearing beneath her all too exiguous but extremely comfortable skirt. And also she was realizing that a furtive but intense scrutiny of her bobbed hair was disorganizing the Patience of the whiskered gentleman's daughter very seriously, and that it was also interfering with the proper laying out of a second and different sort of Patience by the elder Miss Solbé. And suddenly, to her extreme annoyance, Christina Alberta found a flush of indignation mantling her cheek, and a combative tingle

passing down the backbone of her straight little body.
'Why the devil,' Miss Preemby asked herself, 'why the
devil shouldn't a girl cut her hair to save trouble and
bother, and wear clothes in which she can walk about?
Anyhow, a mop of well-washed hair was ten times better
than those feeble, aimless interweavings of pigtails and
fringes and scraps and ends. And as for showing one's legs
and body; why shouldn't one show one's legs and body?
It was just a part of the universal evasion of life by these
people that had got most of their bodies hidden away, tied
up in a sort of bundle. Do they ever venture to look at
themselves? Those Solbé girls, once upon a time, they
must have been jolly little girls with an amused interest in
their stalky little legs, before they said Shush! and put
them away.'

Christina Alberta's speculative vein took charge for a
time. What becomes of legs that are put away and never
looked at and encouraged? Do they get etiolated and
queer, dead-white and funny-shaped and afraid of the
light? And after you've really packed your body away and
forgotten it, nothing is left of you but a head sticking out
and hands that wave about and feet with hidden and dis-
torted toes; and you go about between meal-times and take
trips in chars-à-bancs to see what every one sees and feel
what every one feels, and you play games by rule and
example according to your age and energy, and become
more and more addicted to Patience until you are ready
to cover yourself up in bed for the last time of all and die.
Evasion! And the fuss they had caused getting born! The
fuss, the morality and marriages and everything that was
necessary before these vacuous lives were begotten!

But it was all evasion, and the life shown in these *Tatlers*
and *Sketches* was evasion just as much. Just as much. All
these photographs of the pushful pretty, the actresses for
sale and the daughters who had to be sold, looked at you

with just your own question in their eyes: 'Is this the Life?'
The unending photographs of Lady Diana This, and Lady
Marjorie That, and Mr. So-and-So and a Friend of the
Duke of York or the Duchess of Shonts, at dog-shows, at
horse-shows, at race meetings, at royal inaugurations and
the like, were inevitably suggestive of obstinate doubts
that were in need of a perennial reassurance. The photographs of people playing tennis and such-like games were
livelier, but there, too, if you care to look at it, were
evasions. Evasions. Evasions.

Christina Alberta turned over the back numbers of the
Sketch without looking at the pictures before her eyes.

What was this Life she and these people and every one by
games and jokes and meetings and ceremonies and elaborate disregards and concealments were all evading? What
was this great thing outside, this something like a huge,
terrible, attractive and compelling black monster, beyond
the lights, beyond the movements and appearances, that
called to her and challenged her to come?

One might evade the call of it by playing Patience and
games perhaps. One might evade it by living by rule or
custom. People seemed to do so. A time might come when
that call to Christina Alberta to be Christina Alberta to
the uttermost and fulfil her mysterious mission to that
immense being beyond the lights might no longer distress
her life. She had thought that in a certain recklessness and
violence with herself she might fight her way out to the
call. She had made love now. Anyhow, she hadn't evaded
that. But – was it going to matter as much as she had
thought it would matter? She and her little friends were
playing desperate games with the material of love in a
world where Dr. Marie Stopes and Mr. D. H. Lawrence
were twin stars, and it was just something you went
through – and came out much as you had been before.
More restless, perhaps, but no further on. It left you just

where you had been, face to face with the unsolved darkness and that mysterious distressing unanswerable call to come out of it all and really live and die.

She had made love. . . . Queer it had been. . . .

These furtive people were watching and watching her, reading her thoughts perhaps, penetrating her. . . .

Christina Alberta shut her copy of the *Sketch* with something of a snap, and walked out of the drawing-room with a serene expression. She shut the door behind her and went downstairs to find what had happened to her father in the smoking-room.

'I'm leaving the best part of the talk behind me,' reflected Christina Alberta.

§ 6

She found that her father and the gentleman from the forests of Burmah, after a very prolonged and brilliant 'h'rrmping' match, had settled down to conversation. But unhappily the conversation was unsuitable for her.

'Siam, Cambodia, Tonquin, the country is full of such temples. They take you there and show you them.'

'Wonderful,' said Mr. Preemby. 'Wonderful. And you do not think the carvings you speak of –? Some high symbolism?'

Both gentlemen became aware of Christina Alberta, attentive and hovering.

'Symbolism,' said the arboreal gentleman, 'Symbolism,' and had complicated pharyngeal difficulties. 'Heathenish indecency. Difficult to discuss. . . . Presence of young lady. . . . H'rrmp.'

'H'rrmp,' said Mr. Preemby. 'Had you come down to say good night, my dear? We are having a rather – rather technical talk.'

'Sounds like it, Daddy,' said Christina Alberta, and went round and sat on the arm of his chair for a moment. 'Good night, little Daddy,' she said.

Reflective moment.

'I think this Tumbridge is going to suit me,' said Mr. Preemby.

'I hope it will, little Daddy. Good night.'

§ 7

Christina Alberta's first evening at the Petunia Boarding House has been described with some particularity because it is a sample of all the still and uneventful evenings that seemed to lie before Mr. Preemby there. It impressed her as an unfathomable enormity of uneventfulness in which nothing harmful or disturbing could conceivably occur to him. The last remote possibility of imaginative disturbance seemed to remove itself next day when Mrs. Bone announced to the whiskered gentleman's wife that she and her husband were off to Bath on the morrow: they were in luck it seemed; they had got the exact rooms for the winter in the exact boarding house they had always had their eyes on. 'Tunbridge seems so bleak,' she said. 'After Burmah.'

The dinner was like the previous dinner; the Birds of Passage had gone and Mr. Preemby astonished himself, Christina Alberta, the chubby maid and the assembled company by demanding whether it was possible to send out (h'rrmp) for a bottle or flask of Chianti. 'It's an Italian wine,' said Mr. Preemby to inform and help the chubby maid in her inquiries. But there was no Chianti on the wine-list supplied, and after a conversation markedly reminiscent of that of the Birds of Passage overnight, the Preemby table was stocked with a bottle of Australian

Burgundy and, at Christina Alberta's request, a bottle of mineral water.

After this display of initiative, self-assertion and social derring-do, Mr. Preemby did little but h'rrmp throughout the rest of the meal.

The subsequent life of the drawing-room was also vacantly similar to the previous evening. Christina Alberta got her possibly illegal cigarette in the lounge, indeed she smoked two, and Miss Margaret Rewster looked at her through the bead-curtain near the office and Miss Emily had a sniff from the landing upstairs, though nothing was said. And then Mr. Preemby followed Major Bone into the smoking-room to gather whatever further information he could about the temple decorations and religious customs of the peoples of Further India. He was inclined to think Major Bone rather biased by evangelical prejudice. But Major Bone was not even indignant about Eastern religions that night. He wanted to talk about Bath, and he talked about Bath. He told Mr. Preemby in very great detail about a remarkable occurrence at Bath. He had met a gentleman named Bone, a gentleman much of his own age and appearance, a Captain Bone who had also once been in Burmah. He detailed various extremely dramatic conversations between himself and the other Bone, occasionally going back and correcting himself. They had made the most elaborate comparison of their genealogies, and it did not appear that they were even remotely related. 'Most curious coincidence that has ever occurred to me,' said Major Bone. 'In Bath. In nineteen-oh-nine.'

In the drawing-room Patience prevailed and Mrs. Bone was talking about Bath. The cheerful wife of the whiskered gentleman said 'Deavning' to Christina Alberta quite suddenly.

'Oh! Good evening,' said Christina Alberta.

'You had a walk to-day?'

'We've been to see the Toad Rock and the High Rock and Eridge Park.'

'Quite a nice walk,' said the cheerful lady, and restored her attention to Mrs. Bone. Christina Alberta gathered she was to be noticed, but not made a pet of.

There was nothing for it but to go through the *Tatlers* and *Sketches* again. This time the pictures were exhausted, but there were reviews of books and one or two short stories. Christina Alberta read them all.

When she went to say good night to her Daddy she had come to a decision. 'Daddy,' she said, 'on Thursday, that's the day after to-morrow, I must go back to London. There are some lectures beginning.'

Mr. Preemby made no effective opposition.

The third evening was in countenance like the second except that the Bones had gone and that Christina Alberta was sustained by the thought that next day she would pass from the vacuities of Tunbridge to the tangled riddles of London. And there was a Bird of Passage present, an untidy young man of the student type with a lot of hair imperfectly controlled by unguents whose motor-bicycle had broken down just outside Tunbridge Wells. He lived somewhere away in the north, it seemed, in Northumberland; he would have to wait in Tunbridge for two or three days while some broken part of his machine was replaced from Coventry; he had taken refuge in the Petunia Boarding House and it was jolly hard luck on him. He couldn't budget for a trip to London; he would just have to sit down in Tunbridge. He was a Cambridge undergraduate and a geologist; he had a bag of specimens on his machine. These facts he conveyed across the width of the room to Mr. Preemby in the course of a rather one-sided conversation.

From the first Christina Alberta did not like this young

gentleman from Cambridge. He was like a younger, cruder Teddy Winterton, with impudent bad manners instead of impudent good manners, and with neither bodily grace nor good looks. And while he spoke to Mr. Preemby he glanced at her. But she had no inkling of the part he might play in the life of her Daddy and herself.

When she and her Daddy went into the lounge for coffee and her cigarette, the young man came and placed himself at an adjacent table and initiated some more conversation. Was Tunbridge Wells an amusing place? Was there any chance of his getting any golf or tennis?

'There are a number of delightful walks,' said Mr. Preemby.

'Not much fun alone,' said the young man.

'There are the pleasures of observation,' said Mr. Preemby.

'All this country has been pretty well worked over,' said the young man of science. 'Is there a Museum here?'

Mr. Preemby did not know.

'There ought to be a Museum in every town.'

Presently the coffee and the cigarette were finished. This evening Mr. Preemby was for the drawing-room. Major Bone had gone, the smoking-room had no attractions, and Mr. Preemby had exchanged a few amiable words with the gentleman with whiskers and hoped to follow them up. Christina Alberta went with him. At the sight of the old *Tatlers* and *Sketches* she remembered she had bought a book in the High Street that day, a second-hand copy of Rousseau's *Confessions*. She went off to get it. She found the young gentleman from Cambridge still sitting in the lounge smoking cigarettes.

'Pretty gloomy here,' he said.

'Oh! *I* don't know,' said Christina Alberta with an open mind, pausing before him.

'Nothing much doing – what?'

'It's not a Gala Night.'

'I'm stranded.'

'You must bear up.'

'S'pose you wouldn't be disposed to come out for a bit and forage around for some fun?' said the young man from Cambridge, taking his courage in both hands.

'Sorry,' said Christina Alberta conclusively, and turned to go on.

'No offence?' said the young man from Cambridge.

'Nice of you to think of me,' said Christina Alberta, who would rather have been thought utterly shameless than the least bit prudish. 'Good hunting.'

And the young man from Cambridge perceived that he was dismissed.

Christina Alberta went into the drawing-room for another tremendous bout of nothingness. But anyhow she had got Rousseau to read, and to-morrow she would be in London.

About the Rousseau –? She had always wanted to know how she stood towards Rousseau.

He carried her on to ten o'clock. But she didn't think much of Rousseau. He ought to have known a few of the New Hope Club girls. They'd have shown him.

§ 8

For three weeks Christina Alberta did not return to Tunbridge Wells, and when she returned she had passed through a variety of experiences that will have their due effect upon the course of this story. This story is the story of Mr. Preemby, and we have little sympathy with that modern sort of novel which will not let a girl alone but must follow her up into the most private and intimate affairs. Christina Alberta was perplexed and worried and would have hated the pursuit of such a searchlight. Suffice it that events had crowded so closely upon her that for whole days together she thought scarcely at all of her possibly quite lonely little Daddy at Tunbridge Wells. Then came a letter that brought her bustling down.

'I think it only right to tell you,' said the letter, 'that Very Important Communications indeed have been made to me *of the Utmost Importance*, and that I ought to tell you about them. They seem to alter all our lives. I know you are immearced in your studies, but these Communications are so Important that I want to talk them over with you soon. I would come up to the Studio to tell you about it all, but very likely Mr. Crumb might be in and I would much prefer to tell you here on the Common amid more congenial surroundings. Some of it you will find almost unbeleavable.'

'Communications?' said Christina Alberta, re-reading the letter. 'Communications?'

She went down to Tunbridge Wells that afternoon.

CHAPTER THE FIFTH

The Scales Fall from Mr. Preemby's Eyes

§ 1

'THE scales,' said Mr. Preemby, 'have fallen from my
eyes.'

He had chosen a seat upon the Common which commanded an extensive view of the town, the town crowned
by the green cupolas of the Opera House and lying as
though the houses had been shot out of a cart down the
long incline to the Pantiles. Beyond were the wide distances of the Kentish hill country, blue and remote.

Christina Alberta waited for more.

'This experience,' said Mr. Preemby, speaking with an
occasional h'rrmp; 'all these experiences – difficult to
relate. Naturally I think you are of a sceptical disposition
– taking after your dear mother. She was very sceptical.
Of psychic phenomena in particular. She said it was
Nonsense. And when your dear mother said a thing was
Nonsense, then it was Nonsense. It only made things
disagreeable if you argued it was anything else. As for
myself – always the open mind. No dogma either way. I
just refrained.'

'But Daddy, have you been having psychic experiences? How could you have psychic experiences down
here?'

'Let me tell you the story in due order. I want you to see
it as I saw it – in due order.'

'How did it begin?'

Mr. Preemby held up a propitiatory hand. 'Please! In
my own way,' he said.

Christina Alberta bit her lips and scrutinized the tranquil
resolution of his profile. There was no hurrying him; he
had to tell his tale as he had prepared it.

'I do not think,' said Mr. Preemby, 'that mine is a very credulous sort of mind. It is true I am not given to argument. I do not *say* very much. But I think and observe. I think and observe and I have a kind of gift for judging people. I do not think I am a very easy man to deceive. 'And it is to be noted that I started the whole affair. It began at my suggestion. I do not know what put it into my head, but I do know that it was me started the whole thing going.

'You know, after your departure our little band at the Petunia Boarding House was reduced to just six persons, not counting the young gentleman from Cambridge who was, as Miss Rewster says, a Bird of Passage. Naturally the six of us felt rather drawn together. There were the two Miss Solbés, both very intelligent young ladies, and there were Mr. Hockleby and Mrs. Hockleby, and Miss Hockleby, and there was me. We were drawn together at lunch after you had gone off – it was a little showery and we had a fire in the drawing-room and Miss Solbé, the one with the glasses, tried to show me one of her Patiences. We got into quite an interesting argument about whether it was possible to *will* which card would turn up next. I have always inclined to the view that for certain people, people with the necessary gift, it was possible to do so, but Mr. Hockleby showed himself extremely sceptical in the matter. He said that if there was a card on the top of the pack ready to turn up, and if one willed that a different card should turn up, then that meant that one had really by sheer will force to re-manufacture two of the cards in the pack, make them over again, each into the other, make them blank, reprint them and everything. But I tried to explain to him that this is not philosophically sound because of predestination. If you were predestined to will that such a card should be on the top of the pack, then that card was also predestined to be there. He argued –'

'But is it necessary to tell me all this, Daddy, before we get to your psychic experience?'

'It is just to illustrate the fact that Mr. Hockleby was an extremely sceptical person.'

'Was that young man from Cambridge present at the discussions?'

'No-oh. No. He was not. He had probably gone down to the Garage to see if his Spare Part had come. He was always going down to the Garage to see about his Spare Part.'

§ 2

Mr. Preemby h'rrmped and began a new section of his narrative.

'It was in the evening after dinner,' he said, 'that things really began. I went into the smoking-room – to smoke – and afterwards I went into the drawing-room, and when I went into the drawing-room I had no more thought of occult phenomena, Christina Alberta, than I had of flying over the moon. But as I came into the drawing-room I saw Miss Solbé looking at her Patience cards which she had just put out, and the way she was holding her hands on the table reminded me of the way I had read that people put their hands together on the table when they were trying experiments in table-turning. And almost without thinking I said: "Why, Miss Solbé, the way you are holding your hands is just the way they do when they are going to do table-turning!" I said it just like that.

'Mr. Hockleby was reading his paper at the time – the *Times*, I think, but it may have been the *Morning Post* – but he put it down when he heard me say that and he looked over his glasses at me and said, "You don't believe in that sort of thing, Mr. Preemby, surely?"'

'His wife was sitting with her back to me and from the way she spoke I think she must have been eating some sort of sweet or lozenge at the time. "*I* do," she said. "We did it at home dozens of times before I was married."

'And I don't know what put it into my head, Christina Alberta; it seemed almost as though it was something behind myself that did it, or it may have been a sort of antagonism I have always felt about that man Hockleby; but anyhow, I said, "I'd really like to try some of this table-turning."

'The younger Miss Solbé, she's really quite a charming young lady when you get to know her, and it seems she has been reading a little occult literature lately –'

'How old is she, Daddy?' asked Christina Alberta regarding him with a look of novel suspicion.

'I don't think she can be very much more than thirty-two or three. Thirty-four at the outside. And really quite well-read, quite well-read. Well, anyhow, she said she would like to try it. And Miss Hockleby, evidently she had been brought up on strictly sceptical lines by her father, she was curious too. So to cut a long story short, we tried it. Only Mr. Hockleby objected and Mrs. Hockleby overruled that. She was the only one among us who had ever seen anything of the sort before, and so it was she who arranged things and told us what to do. We chose a very solid table, the one that usually has the big aspidistra on it, and while we were turning out the lights –'

'But why did you do that, Daddy?'

'One always does that,' said Mr. Preemby. 'It makes the atmosphere more favourable. We lit a candle which Miss Margaret Rewster got for us and turned out all the electric lights; and while we were doing this, in came young Mr. Charles Fenton and said – *What* did he say? A peculiar expression. Ah yes! "Gollys," he said, "what's up?" '

'Was that the young man with the motor-bicycle?'

'Yes. The young man from Cambridge. We explained what we were doing and asked him to join us. He declared he knew nothing of psychic phenomena, had never experimented with it at all and seemed very doubtful about taking part in the trial. "I don't think there's anything in it," he said. "We shall just waste our time." Indeed, I remember now that he did go out intending to visit a music-hall, and then he came back and said it was raining. It's very important to note that he was not at all eager to join us and that he was quite uninformed about occult things because, you see, as I will tell you, we found out presently that he was a person of exceptional psychic gifts, much greater psychic gifts than anyone else among us.

'Well, we arranged ourselves about the table in the usual manner, thumbs and little fingers touching, and for a time nothing seemed to happen at all. We found Miss Emily Rewster was peeping in through the slightly open door, and perhaps that may have had an unfavourable influence. I suppose she wondered what we were doing and why we had asked her sister for a candle. Then Mr. Fenton got very restive and grumbled to himself and said it was the silliest way of passing an evening he had ever tried. It was a little difficult to persuade him to keep silence and persevere. "*All* right," said he, with a kind of resentment. "Have it your own way." And then suddenly came two violent raps, raps like little pistol shots, not immediately under the table it was, but as if it was in the air a foot or so under the table. And then the table began to move. Slowly at first, shifting along the floor, and then quite strongly twisting and pushing up against our hands. It was very weird and impressive, Christina Alberta, very weird and impressive indeed. It rose nearly two feet I should think and then Mr. Hockleby broke the circle and it fell rather heavily, I fancy, and the leg hit his shin. He uttered an exclamation and stooped to rub his leg, and in the indistinct light he hit his head on the edge of the table. It seemed almost a judgment on his scepticism I thought. We turned up one or two of the lights to attend to him. "I don't like this," said Mr. Fenton. "This is a bit too rum for me."

'I asked him to try just once more.

' "I don't like this table riding up like this," he said. "It's such a bad example for the chairs. Suppose some of them start playing cup and ball with us! You might get a nasty toss from a buck-jumping chair. And besides, it's a lot too like a Channel crossing for my taste."

'I think we were all a good deal excited by what had happened, and all the others, even Mr. Hockleby, were eager to continue.

' "Next time I shall *press* down," he said. I think he was a little suspicious that either his wife or me had something to do with the phenomena. Evidently spiritualism was a long-standing dispute between him and his wife. His wife said she had seen tables move before, but none so actively as this one had done.

'Down we sat again. We had hardly waited a minute before the table began rocking about in the most extraordinary fashion, and then absolutely flew up so violently that the elder Miss Solbé was thrown back over that Ottoman there is there, and I was bumped under my chin. At the same time there was a perfect volley of cracks, like somebody cracking his fingers, but ever so much louder. It was quite a comfort to have the lights up again and see Mr. Hockleby holding the table down firmly in its proper place. "Damn you," he said – quite loudly. "Damn you. Keep down." Miss Hockleby and her father picked up Miss Solbé, who was on the floor in a sort of hysterical fit of laughter, with her feet waving about.

' "I don't like this," said Mr. Fenton. "It goes through one like an electric shock."

'He spoke quite simply.

'The only one of us who had had any experience with occult phenomena was Mrs. Hockleby, and she had not done anything of the sort since her marriage to Mr. Hockleby five or six years before, because of his scepticism. She said now that it was very evident that some very strong and resolute spirit was present and was trying to communicate with us, and she explained a simple and safe method of getting into communication. We were to reform the circle round the table and we were to call over the alphabet, and when we came to the letter the spirit wanted there would be a rap and so we should be able to arrive at something definite. There is a sort of code quite well understood it seems in the spirit world, in which you convey "No" by one rap and "Yes" by two, and so on.

'We set to work at this,' said Mr. Preemby. 'We asked if the spirit would like to spell out anything and it answered with two very loud raps, and then Mr. Hockleby read out the letters: A B C and so on. When it got to S the spirit gave a rap so loud it made me jump.'

'And what did you spell out, Daddy?'

'A name quite unknown to me then – SARGON, and then KING OF KINGS. We asked: was the spirit that was communicating with us Sargon? The answer came No. Was Sargon present? Yes. Then who was our communicant? OUJAH. Who was Oujah? WISE MAN. It was a very slow process spelling out the words in this way, and by the time we had got so far we were all very tired. Mr. Fenton in particular was very tired. He yawned and seemed greatly exhausted, and said at last he felt so weary and muzzy that he *must* go to bed. That was really very natural, because though none of us realized it at the time he was the actual medium under Oujah's control. He went to bed and we tried to go on without him, but the magic had departed and we could not get so much as a rap. So we sat for a time talking all this over; Mr. Hockleby in particular was greatly flabbergasted, and then the rest of us went to bed.'

'Evidently Mr. Fenton made the raps,' said Christina Alberta.

'Evidently his presence was necessary for the raps to be made,' corrected Mr. Preemby. 'Quite unconsciously he was a Mejum.'

There was a pause.

'Go on with the story,' said Christina Alberta.

§ 3

'The next evening was wet again, and as his Spare Part hadn't come Mr. Fenton was able to join us once more. He made some little objection at first because he said he and his people were all Particular Baptists, and he was doubtful whether this sort of thing was not Necromancy and forbidden in the Bible. But I persuaded him out of that. And this time we spelt out a quite singular message. It was AWAKE, SARGON! ARISE OR BE FOR EVER FALLEN!

'Even from the first I had had a feeling that those messages from Sargon had something to do with me. Now suddenly conviction came upon me. I asked "Is Sargon present?" "*Yes.*" I knew it would be so. "Is it anyone in the circle?" "*Yes.*" "Is it this gentleman?" – pointing to Mr. Hockleby. A very loud *No.* "Is it me?" "*Yes.*"

'Mr. Hockleby I noted at the time looked annoyed – as though he felt it was he who ought to be Sargon.

'Then young Mr. Fenton stood up suddenly. "Oh! I can't stand any more of this," he said. "My head feels quite muzzy. I'm sure this sort of thing is harmful." He walked across the room and sat down suddenly with his hands hanging over the arms of the chair – it was one of the big arm-chairs covered in cretonne. We all felt very much concerned, but as for myself I was all in a daze at the thought of being this Sargon and being called upon so openly to rouse myself to action. I did not understand fully as yet all that it meant to me, but I did realize that it meant a very great deal.'

'But what did you think it meant?' said Christina Alberta sharply, and her perplexed gaze searched his profile. His blue eyes stared at things far away beyond the distant hills, strange things, fantastic empires, secret cities, mystical traditions, and his brows were knit in the effort to keep his story together.

'All in good time,' said Mr. Preemby. 'Let me tell my story in my own way. I was telling you, I think, that young Mr. Fenton said he felt heavy and strange. Mrs. Hockleby happily was quite equal to that situation. She had seen the same thing before. "Don't struggle against it," she said. "Let yourself go. Just lean back in your chair. If you want to lie quiet, do. If you want to say anything, do. Let the influence work." And she turned to me and whispered "trance."

' "What is a trance?" said Mr. Fenton – just like that. "What is a trance?"

'She began moving her hands in front of his face, "making passes," I think they call it. He shut his eyes, gave a sort of sigh and his head lolled back. We all sat round him waiting, and presently he began to mutter.

'At first it was just nonsense. "Oodjah Woojer Boojer," words like that. Then more distinctly, "Oujah the Wise Man, Sargon's servant. Oujah comes to serve Sargon. To awaken him." After that he seemed to wander off into sheer rubbish. "Why is a mouse when it spins?" he whispered in his own voice and then, "That damned Spare Part."

'Mrs. Hockleby said that was quite characteristic of this sort of trance, and then Mr. Hockleby got a writing-pad and a pencil to take down anything more that was said.

'And presently when Mr. Fenton spoke again, he did not speak in his own voice but in a kind of hoarse whisper quite different from his usual voice. It was the voice of this Oujah speaking – Oujah the control. With a slight accent – Sumerian I suppose.

'Well, the things he said were very astonishing indeed. I think that this Oujah was anxious to secure my attention by convincing me that he knew of things, intimate things that nobody else could know. At the same time he did not wish the others to know too clearly what he was aiming at. How did it go? What can I remember? Mr. Hockleby has a lot of it written down, but so far I have not had time to make a copy. "Child of the sea and the desert," he said, "the blue waters and the desert sand." Is it too fanciful to find an allusion to Sheringham in that? "Cascades and great waters and a thing like a wheel on a blue shield." That is more puzzling. But "cascades and great waters" set me thinking of our big washers. And you remember the swastika on our blue delivery vans, Christina Alberta? Is not that oddly suggestive of a thing like a wheel on a blue shield? The Norse peoples called the swastika the fire-wheel. "Armies with their white garments fluttering, the long lines drawn out – armies of delivery." That again is queer. One is reminded of armies and also – don't think me absurd! of the drying ground and the vans. It is like one thing becoming transparent and your seeing the other behind it.'

'Are you sure of the exact phrases, Daddy?'

'Mr. Hockleby has them written down. If I have not got them quite right you will be able to read his notes.'

'The swastika may be a coincidence,' said Christina Alberta. 'Or you may have been drawing it on the edges of the newspaper. You do sometimes. And he may have seen it.'

'That does not account for the blue ground. He laid great stress on the blue ground. And there were other things; matters known only to me and your dear mother. I could not tell you them without telling you everything. And small things, entirely private to me. The name of my late grandfather at Diss. Munday his name was. It is sometimes difficult to argue about things although one may be absolutely convinced. And all this was mixed up with broken sentences about a great city and the two daughters of the western King and the Wise Man. And also he called me Belshazzar. Belshazzar seemed to drift in and out of his thoughts. "Come again to a world that has fallen into disorder." These are remarkable words. And then "Beware of women; they take the sceptre out of the hands of the king. But do they know how to rule? Ask Tutankhamen. Ask the ruins in the desert." '

'Pah,' said Christina Alberta. 'As though women have ever had a fair chance!'

'Well, anyhow, Mr. Hockleby has that written down. . . . And it seemed to me that this too applied to me, for because of my great fondness for your mother I had let so many years of my life slip away. He said many other things, Christina Alberta, richly suggestive things. But I have told you enough for you to understand what has happened. In the end Mr. Fenton came-to quite suddenly, much more suddenly than is usual in such cases, Mrs. Hockleby said. He sat up and yawned and rubbed his eyes. "Oh Lord!" he said, "what nonsense all this is! I'm going to bed."

'We asked him if he felt exhausted. He said he was. "Absolutely fed up," were his actual words.

'We asked him if that was the end of his message.

' "What message?" he said. He had absolutely no memory of his communications at all. "Have I been talking?" he asked. "This isn't the sort of thing one ought to get up to. What sort of things have I been saying? Nothing objectionable I hope. If so I apologize. I mustn't do any more of this sort of thing."

'Mrs. Hockleby told him she had never met anyone with such a promise of great psychic power as he had, before. He said he was really very sorry to hear it. She said he owed it to himself to cultivate so rare and strange a gift, but he said That wouldn't do for his people at all. The rain had stopped and he said he thought he would take a walk down to the Pantiles and back before turning in. Perfectly simple and natural he was from first to last, and rather unwilling. And he really did look tired out.'

'Didn't he laugh once?' asked Christina Alberta.

'Why should he? he seemed a little afraid of what he had transmitted. The next day his Spare Part came. Mrs. Hockleby did her utmost to try to get him once more in the afternoon and develop his Communication, but he would not do so. He was full of questions about the ferry at Tilbury and the time of high tide. He would not even give us his name and address. When I spoke of sending Mr. Hockleby's notes to the *Occult Review* he was suddenly quite alarmed. He said that if his name appeared in connection with them it might mean a very serious row with his family. He would not even allow us to put a Mr. F. from Cambridge. "Put quite another name," he said, "quite a different name. Put anything you like that does not point to me, a Mr. Walker, say, from London. Or something of that sort." '

'Of course there was nothing for us to do but agree.'

§ 4

'And that was the whole of your communication, Daddy?'

'It was only the beginning. Because after that I began to remember. I began to remember more and more.'

'Remember?'

'Things from my other lives. Memories stored up. This young Mr. Fenton was, so to speak, no more than the first cut in the curtain of forgetfulness that hung between this present life and all my previous existences. Now it was rent and torn open so that I could see things through it at a dozen points. Now I begin to realize what I really was and what I can really be. . . .

'You know, Christina Alberta, I have never actually believed I was myself – not even as a schoolboy. And now it is interesting, I know and understand clearly that I *am* somebody else. I have always been somebody else.'

'But who do you believe you are, Daddy?'

'So far as I can gather I was first a chief called Porg in a city called Kleb in the very beginning of the world, æons and æons ago, and I tamed my people and taught them many things. Then afterwards I was this Sargon – Sargon the King of Kings. There is very little about him here in the Public Library, in the *Encyclopædia Britannica;* an upstart who took his name, *my* name, three thousand years later, an Assyrian fellow is the Sargon they tell about – he got mixed up with the Jews and he besieged Samaria – but I was the original Sargon long before there were Jews or anything of the sort, long before Abraham and Isaac and Jacob. And afterwards I was Belshazzar, the last crown prince of the Babylonians, but that is not very clear. That remains obscure. Only one part of the record is lit – as yet. And possibly I have been other people. But the figure that stands out in my memory now is Sargon. It is his memories have been returning to me. It is he who has returned in me.'

'But Daddy, you don't really believe all this?'

'Believe! – I *know*. Long before this Communication came to me I had had those intimations, – that assurance that I was somebody else. *Now* I see clearly. I can remember days in Akkadia now just as clearly as I can remember days in Woodford Wells. I could almost doubt whether I have ever lived at Woodford Wells; it seems so far away now. It was when I was in bed the night after Mr. Fenton had gone that these memories began to come. I was in bed, and then suddenly I was not in bed – I was reclining on a couch under a canopy, a canopy of pure white wool very finely woven and embroidered with emblems and symbols and suchlike things in golden thread, and I was upon my state barge upon the Euphrates. Two King's daughters, sisters, with slender necks, not unlike the two Miss Solbés except that they were fairer – and decidedly younger – *much* younger – and clad rather more in accordance with the requirements of a warm climate, chiefly in woven gold – sat and fanned me with fans of eagles' feathers dyed a royal purple. And at my feet sat my councillor Prewm, who was oddly enough extremely like Mr. Hockleby – just the same iron-grey whiskers and with the same little tufts of hair over his ears. He was wearing an extremely tall cap of some black woollen substance, and he was making memoranda with a wooden style on a tablet of wet clay. It was like writing on a mud pie. And beyond him were the officers of the boat on a kind of bridge – they were wearing leather helmets studded with brass – and then one saw the rowers below, chained to their oars, and then on either side spread the broad brown river just crinkled by the breeze.

The little boats fled to make way for us. They had coarse, square sails, and they lowered them and turned them about all in precisely the same way at precisely the same time. It was very pretty to see. Along the banks were little villages of mud-brick houses and clumps and lines of palm trees; and everywhere there were primitive contrivances, great bent poles of wood like giant fishing-rods, for raising water out of the river for the cultivation of the land. And the people were all crowded along the water's edge and bowing with their hands and foreheads in the water and crying, "Sargon the Conqueror, Sargon King of Kings!" '

'But Daddy, this was a dream?'

'How could I dream of things I had never seen nor heard of before?'

'One does.'

'One does *not*,' he replied with a quiet invincible obstinacy. 'I remember I was coming back from the South where I had given peace to a multitude of warring tribes, Elamites and Perrizites and Jebusites and people of that sort, and I was returning to my capital. I remember distinctly many details of the campaign and I know that with an effort I could recall more in the proper order. In dreams absurd things happen, dreams when you think them over afterwards are all at sixes and sevens, but this is all sane and orderly. One might think, Christina Alberta, that I had never dreamt dreams and that all these memories of that previous existence which crowd upon me now were a deception of my imagination! But I can go right back as if it was yesterday, and I am surer by far that I am Sargon than that I am Albert Edward Preemby your father. The former is my true self, the latter is just a very simple, unpretending wrapping that for some purpose, at present inexplicable to me, has hidden me from the world.'

130

He waved his hand with a bolder gesture than was habitual to him. He sat with his eyes wide open, looking at unseen things.

The girl regarded him for some seconds in silence. She was trying to grasp the full import of this amazing speech.

'And *this* was your Communication?' she said at last.

'You have to know,' he said. 'You have to serve and help me.'

(Help him! How could she help him or herself? How far was this thing going? What was she to do?)

'Have you told anyone else of this, Daddy?' she asked abruptly. 'Have you told anyone else?'

He turned his solemn little face towards her.

'Ah *there*,' he said, 'we have to be very discreet and careful – very careful indeed. Here and now is not the time to proclaim that Sargon, King of Kings, has come back to the civilization he did so much to found. One has to be careful, Christina Alberta. There is a spirit of opposition.

'For instance, I have told something of my first vision – dream you may call it if you like – to Mr. Hockleby. I described the resemblance between himself and Prewm. He was by no means pleased. His is a seditious, insubordinate nature. And besides – since then – I have recalled what happened – on the advice of Oujah – to Prewm. . . .

'And I have realized since then that, though one may be convinced oneself, it does not follow that one will convince other people. It is true that Miss Hockleby and the two Miss Solbés have asked me to tell them more of my dreams – they too call them dreams. But their manner was curious rather than respectful and I have been extremely reserved with them.'

'That's my wise Daddy,' said Christina Alberta. 'You have to think of your dignity.'

'I have to think of my dignity certainly. Nevertheless –'
His hands went out in a new amplitude of gesture.
'Here I am and this is my world. My world! I nursed it
in its infancy. I taught it law and obedience. Here I am,
the most ancient of monarchs. Rameses and Nebuchad-
nezzar, Greece and Rome, the Kingdoms and Empires,
things of yesterday – interludes while I have been sleeping. And clearly I have been sleeping. And clearly I
have not been sent back to the world without a mission.
This is a great and crowded world now, Christina Alberta,
but it is in a sad state of disorder. Even the newspapers
remark upon it. People are not happy now. They are
not happy as they were under my rule in Sumeria
thousands of years ago. In the sunshine and abundance of
Sumeria.'

'But what can you *do*, Daddy?'

'Dear Princess, my child, that I have to think out. Nothing hastily; nothing rashly.'

'No,' said Christina Alberta.

There came a pause. 'One person only seems to have
any belief in me. The younger Miss Solbé – Did you
say anything, dear?'

'No. Go on.'

'I have asked her if she too has had any dreams, any
vague memories of a previous existence. She seems to
have had something confirmatory in a shadowy sort of
way. Very vague intimations. She tells them timidly,
when her sister is not about. But she is under a mis-
apprehension that her relationship to me was a particularly
close and special one. She was not my Queen. There she
is wrong. It is perhaps natural for her to think so, but I
remember quite distinctly how it was. She was one of the
Twenty Principal Concubines who carried the Eagle
fans.'

'Have you told her that?'

'Not yet,' said Mr. Preemby. 'Not yet. One has to go discreetly in all these things.'

Another pause followed. Christina Alberta looked at her wrist-watch. 'My word!' she cried. 'We shall be late for lunch!'

She noted as they walked back towards the Petunia Boarding House that his bearing and manner had undergone a subtle change. He seemed larger and taller and his face was serener and he held his head higher. He did not h'rrmp once. He seemed to expect people and things to get out of his way, and it was as if the path was a carpet that was being unrolled before his advance. Had she been able to see herself she would have remarked an equal change in her own carriage. The dance had gone out of her paces. She walked like one upon whose shoulders the responsibilities of life might easily become overwhelming.

They were late for lunch, and all the other boarders were in their places, beginning. Every one turned to look at Mr. Preemby's face as they came in, and then they glanced at one another. 'So you've come back to us,' said Mrs. Hockleby to Christina Alberta, meeting her eye.

'It's jolly to be back,' said Christina Alberta.

CHAPTER THE SIXTH

Christina Alberta Consults a Wise Man

§ 1

CHRISTINA ALBERTA and Paul Lambone had been great friends for nearly a year. He liked her and admired her, and as became his literary line of work, he studied her. And she liked him and trusted him, and showed off a good lot when she was with him.

Paul Lambone wrote novels and short stories and books of good advice, and he was particularly celebrated for the pervading wisdom of his novels and the excellence of his advice. It was his pervading wisdom that had picked him up out of the general poverty of writers and placed him in a position of comparative prosperity. Not that his conduct of his affairs was wise, but that the quality of his wisdom was extremely saleable. Some writers prosper by reason of their distinctive passion, some by reason of their austerity and truth, some by their excellent invention, and some even by simple good writing, but Paul Lambone prospered because of his kindness and wisdom. When you read the stories you always felt that he was really sorry for the misfortunes and misbehaviour of his characters and anxious to help them as much as he could. And when they blundered or sinned he would as often as not tell you what was the better course they might have chosen. His book of advice, and particularly his *Book of Everyday Wisdom* and his *What To Do on a Hundred and One Occasions* sold largely and continually.

But like that James, King of England, to whom the Bible was dedicated, Paul Lambone was far wiser in his thoughts and counsels than in his acts. In small matters and most of the time his proceedings were foolish or selfish or indecisive or all of those things. His wisdom did not reach below the level of his eyes, and his face and body and arms and legs were given over to the unhappiest tendencies which were restrained by his general indolence rather than by any real self-control. He was very well off chiefly because he was lazy; he asked the highest possible prices for everything he wrote because that was just as easy as asking the lowest, and there was always a chance that the bargain would not come off and then he would be saved the trouble of correcting his proofs. He accumulated money because he was too unenterprising to buy things or incur the responsibility of possessions, and so he just let a trust invest it for him. His literary reputation was high because a literary reputation in England and America depends almost entirely upon apparent reluctance of output. The terse beauty of his style was mainly due to his sedulous indisposition to write two words where one would suffice. And in the comfort and leisure his indolence accumulated for him, he sat about and talked and was genially wise and got fatter than was becoming. He tried to eat less as a preferable alternative to taking exercise, but in the presence of drink and nourishment his indolence flagged and failed him. He went about a good deal, and was always eager for new things because they saved him from boredom, the malign parent of much needless activity. He had an expensive little cottage near Rye in Kent to which he could motor without needless trouble whenever London bored him, and directly his cottage bored him he would come back to London. And he visited people's houses a lot because it was too troublesome to resist invitations.

There were, it must be admitted, limits to the wisdom of Paul Lambone. It is often more difficult to see what is near us than what is far away; many a stout fellow who looks with a clear discerning eye upon the universe sees little of his toes, and ignores the intervening difficulty;

and something sub-conscious in Paul Lambone's mind obstinately refused to recognize the defective nature of many of his private acts. He knew he was indolent, but he would not allow himself to admit that his indolence was fundamental and vicious. He thought there was a Paul Lambone in reserve of very great energy. He liked to think of himself as a man of swift and accurate decisions who, once aroused, was capable of demoniac energy. He had spent many an hour in arm-chairs, on garden seats, and on Downland turf, thinking out his course of action on various possible occasions of war, business, criminal attempt or domestic crisis. His favourite heroes in real life were Napoleon, Julius Cæsar, Lord Kitchener, Lord Northcliffe, Mr. Ford, and suchlike heroic ants.

He liked Christina Alberta because of her tremendous go. She was always up to something; she preferred standing to sitting, and she kicked her legs about while she talked to you. He idealized her go; he attributed to her much more go than she really had. He was secretly persuaded that her blood must be like a bird's, a degree or so above normal. He felt that in imagination she had much in common with him. He called her the Last Thing, the Van, the Ultimate Modern Girl, and the Life Force. He openly professed pity for the unaided single-handed man who would in accordance with our social laws presently have to marry her and go her pace and try to keep her in order.

She had been to tea with him once or twice. She perceived his admiration and suspected a certain affection, and she basked in admiration and affection. She liked his books and thought he was very like what he thought he was himself. She told him all sorts of things about herself just to lift his eyebrows.

And he was wise all over her and round and about her, tremendously wise.

§ 2

It was quite interesting to be rung up by Christina Alberta and asked if she might come for tea and advice. 'Come along now,' he said. 'I'm probably all alone for tea.'

And as he replaced the instrument he said: 'Now I wonder what the young woman has been up to! And what she wants me to do for her.'

He went back to his sitting-room and spread himself on his very nice Persian hearthrug, and regarded the pretty silver kettle that swung over his spirit lamp. 'It won't be money,' he considered. 'She isn't the sort that tries to get money . . .

'She's barked her shins on something. . . .

'Girls nowadays are a lot too plucky – they're a lot too plucky altogether. . . . I hope it's nothing serious. . . . She's just a kid.'

Christina Alberta appeared in due course. Erect as ever, but nevertheless looking a little dashed and subdued. 'Uncle,' she said – for that was her theory of their relationship – 'I'm in trouble. You've got to give me all sorts of advice.'

'Take off that brigand's cloak,' he said, ' and sit down there and make me some tea. I've been watching your love affair out of the corner of my eye for some time. I'm not surprised.'

Christina Alberta paused with her cloak in her hand and stared at him. 'That's nothing,' she said. 'I can manage that little affair all right. Such as it is. Don't you worry about *me*, in that respect. Don't imagine things. But there is something – something different.' She threw the cloak over a chair back and came and stood by the silver tea-tray.

'You know my Daddy,' she said, arms akimbo.

'I never saw a more dissimilar parent.'

'Well – ' She considered how she should put it. 'He's behaving queerly. So that people may think – people who don't know him – that he's going out of his mind.'

Mr. Lambone reflected. 'Was it ever such a very serious mind to go out of?'

'Oh! don't make jokes. His mind was good enough to keep him out of trouble, and now something's happened and it isn't. People will think – some of them think already – he is mad. They may take him away. And there's just him and me. It's serious, Uncle. And I don't know what I ought to do. I don't know enough to know. I'm scared. I've got no friends that I can talk to about it. None. You'd think I'd have women friends. I haven't. I don't get on with older women. They want to boss me. Or I think they do. And I irritate them. They know, they feel – the proper ones – that I don't – oh! respect their standards. And the other sort just hate me. Because I'm young. The girls I know – no good for what I want just now.'

'But isn't there a man,' said Lambone, 'on whom you have a sort of claim?'

'You know who it is, I suppose?'

He was frank. 'Things rather show.'

'If you know him – ' She left the sentence unfinished.

'I know the young man only very incidentally,' he said.

'I go to Teddy,' said Christina Alberta without any further reservations. 'I went to him as a matter of fact before I telephoned to you. He hardly listened to what I had to say. He didn't bother.' She winced. Suddenly tears stood in her eyes. 'He was just loafing about in his studio. He kissed me and tried to excite me. He would hardly listen to what I had to tell him. . . . That I suppose is what one gets from a lover.'

'So it's got to that,' Paul Lambone reflected with hidden dismay, and then remarked a little belatedly: 'Not every lover.'

'Mine – anyhow.'

'And you came away?'

'*Well!* What do *you* think?'

'H'm,' said Lambone. 'You *have* barked your shins, Christina Alberta! More than I thought.'

'Oh, Hell take Teddy!' said Christina Alberta, putting it on a bit and helping herself by being noisy. 'What does that matter now? I've done with Teddy. I was a fool. Never mind that. The thing is my Daddy. What am I to do about my Daddy?'

'Well, first you've got to tell me all about it,' said Lambone. 'Because at present, you know, I've hardly got the hang of the trouble. And before you do that you sit down in that easy chair and I make the tea. No, not you. Your nerves are on edge and you'll upset something. You've been having your first dose of adult worry. Sit down there and don't say anything for a minute. I'm glad you came along to me. Very glad. . . . I liked that Daddy of yours really. Little innocent-eyed man he was. Blue eyes. And he was talking – what nonsense *was* he talking? About the Lost Atlantis. But it was quite nice nonsense. . . . No, don't interrupt. Just let me recall my own impression of him until you've had your tea.'

§ 3

When the tea was made and Christina Alberta had sipped a cup and looked more comfortable, Lambone, who felt he was managing things beautifully, told her she might begin.

'He's getting queer in his mind, but you know that he isn't really going out of his mind,' said Lambone. 'That's it, isn't it?'

'That *is* it,' said Christina Alberta. 'You see – ' She paused.

Lambone sat down in a second arm-chair and sipped his tea in a leisurely manner. 'It's a little difficult,' he said.

'You see,' said Christina Alberta, knitting her brows at the fire, 'he's a person of peculiar imaginativeness. He always has been. Always. He's always lived half in a dream. We've been very much together ever since I was born almost, and from the earliest times I remember his talks, rambling talks, about the Lost Atlantis, and about the secrets of the pyramids and Yogis and the Lamas of Tibet. And astrology. All such wonderful, impossible, far-off things. The further off the better. Why! – he almost got me into a dream too. I was a Princess of Far Atlantis lost in the world. I used to play at that, and sometimes my play came very near to believing. I could Princess it for a whole afternoon. Lots of children day-dream like that.'

'I did,' said Lambone. 'For days together I would be a great Indian chief, sentenced to death again and again – disguised as a small preparatory schoolboy. The incongruity didn't matter a rap. Everybody does it more or less for a time.'

'But he's gone on doing it all his life. And he's doing it now more than ever. He's lost the last trace of any sense that it is a dream. And some one played a trick upon him at Tunbridge Wells. Not realizing what it might mean for him. They seem to have muddled about with spiritualism in the evenings while I was in London, table-rapping and so forth, and a man who had nothing better to do pretended to have a trance. He told Daddy he was Sargon the First, Sargon King of Kings he called

him, who was Lord of Akkadia and Sumeria – you know –
ages ago, before Babylon was born or thought of. The
man who did it couldn't have hit on anything more
mischievous so far as Daddy was concerned. You see he
was exactly ready for it; leaving Woodford Wells where
he had spent half his life in one routine had cut him off,
even more than he was usually cut off, from reality.
He was uprooted already before this idea came to him.
And now it's just swamping him. It suited him exactly.
It – fixed him. Always before one could get him back – by
talking about my mother or the laundry vans, or something familiar like that. But now I can't get him back.
I can't. He's Sargon incognito, come back as Lord of
the World, and he believes that just as firmly as I believe
that I am his daughter Christina Alberta Preemby talking
to you now. It's a reverie no longer. He's got his evidence
and he believes.'

'And what does he want to do about it?'

'All sorts of things. He wants to declare himself Lord of
the World. He says things are in a bad way and he wants
to save them.'

'They *are* in a bad way,' said Lambone. 'People don't
begin to know half how bad they are. Still – I suppose
having a delusion about who one is, isn't Insanity. Does
he want to make some sort of fuss?'

'I'm afraid, yes.'

'Soon?'

'That's what worries me.'

'You see,' she went on, 'I'm afraid he's going to strike
most people as queer. He's back at Lonsdale Mews.
We had to come up from Tunbridge Wells yesterday.
On a few hours' notice. It's that has upset me. For a
couple of days things went on all right. Practically we were
turned out of the boarding-house. There was a frightfully disagreeable man there, a Mr. Hockleby, and he

seemed to take a violent dislike to Daddy. You know those unreasonable dislikes people take at times?'

'A very disagreeable side of human nature. *I* know. Why, people have taken dislikes to *me*! . . . But go on.'

'He and his daughter got upset about Daddy's queerness. They frightened the Miss Rewsters, the sisters who run the place. They said he might break out at any moment, and either he would have to leave or they would. There they were all whispering on the stairs and talking of sending for a policeman and having him taken away. What could I do? We had to clear out. You see Daddy had a sort of idea that when he was Sargon Mr. Hockleby had been alive too and had had to be impaled for seditious behaviour; and instead of letting bygones be bygones as one ought to do in such cases, he said something about it to him, and Mr. Hockleby construed it as a threat. It's all so difficult, you see.'

'He didn't try to impale him over again, or anything?'

'No. He doesn't do things like that. It's only his imagination that is doing tremendous things. He isn't.'

'And now he's in London?'

'He has a sort of idea he's overlord of the King, and he wants to go to the King at Buckingham Palace and tell him about it. He says the King is a thoroughly good man, thoroughly good; and directly he hears how things are, he will acknowledge Dadda as his feudal superior and place him on the throne. Of course if he tries to do anything of that sort he will be locked up for a certainty. And he's written letters to the Prime Minister and the Lord Chancellor and the President of the United States and Lenin, and so forth, directing them to wait upon him for his instructions. But I've persuaded him not to post them till he can have a proper seal made.'

'Rather like Muhammad's letters to the potentates,' said Lambone.

'He's thinking, too, of a banner or something of that sort, but all that's quite vague. He's just got the phrase "raise my banner." I don't think that matters much yet. But the Buckingham Palace idea, – something may come of that.'

'This is no end interesting,' said Lambone, and walked across his room and back, and then half sat on the arm of his easy chair with his hands deep in his pockets. 'Tell me; is he distraught to look at?'

'Not a bit of it.'

'Untidy in his dress?'

'Neat as ever.'

'I remember when I saw him how neat he was. Is he – at all – incoherent? Or does it all hold together?'

'Absolutely. He's perfectly logical and coherent. He talks I think rather better and more clearly than usual.'

'It's just one simple delusion? He has no illusions about having great physical strength or beauty or anything of that sort?'

'None. He's not a bit crazy. He's just possessed by this one grand impossible idea.'

'He's not throwing away money or anything of that sort?'

'Not a bit of it. He's always been – careful with money.'

'And he is now?'

'Yes.'

'Let's hope that lasts. I don't see that a man is insane because he believes he is a King or an Emperor – if some one tells him he is. After all, George V has no other grounds for imagining he is a King. The only difference is that rather more people have told him so. Fancying yourself a King isn't lunacy, and behaving in accordance with that idea isn't lunacy either. It may be some day, but it isn't so yet. No.'

'But I'm afraid that people will think that it is. . . .

You see it's only in the last few days I've realized how fond I am of my father and how horrible it would be for me if anyone attempted to take him away. I'm afraid of asylums. Restraint for those who can least understand restraint. He particularly would go mad in a week, really mad, if he got into one. That Mr. Hockleby has frightened me – he's frightened me. He was so intent and cruel. He was *evil* about Daddy – malignant. A nasty man.'

'Yes, I know,' said Lambone. 'Hate.'

'Yes,' she said. 'Hate.'

She jumped to her feet and took possession of the hearthrug, looking with her bobbed hair and short skirts and manly pose and serious face the most ridiculous and attractive mixture of fresh youth and mature responsibility conceivable.

'You see, I don't know what they can do with him – whether they can take him away from me. I've never been much afraid of what might happen before, but I am now. I don't know how to take hold of all this. I thought life was just a lark and people were fools to be afraid of doing anything. But now I see *life's dangerous*. I've never been much afraid of what happened to myself. But this is different. He's walking about in a dream of glory – with absolute wretchedness hanging over him. Think of it! People getting hold of him! Perhaps hitting him! An asylum!'

'About the law on these matters I know very little,' Lambone reflected. 'I doubt if they can do very much to him without your consent. But I agree about asylums. From their very nature they must be horrible places, haunted places. Most of the attendants – hardened. Even if they start well. Every day at it . . . too much for anyone. . . . I don't know how a lunatic is made, a legal lunatic I mean, or who has a right to take him. Somebody – I think two doctors – have to certify him or something of that sort. But, anyhow, I don't think your father is a lunatic.'

'Nor I. But that may not save him.'

'Something else may. He's as you say an imaginative – a super-imaginative man, possessed by a fantastic idea. Well, isn't that a case perhaps for a psycho-analyst?'

'Possibly. Who'd talk him back – to something like he used to be.'

'Yes. If such a man as Wilfred Devizes, for example, could talk to him – '

'I don't know much about these people. I've read some Freud of course – and a little Jung.'

'I know Devizes slightly. We talked at lunch. And I liked his wife. And if perhaps you could get your father away into a country cottage. By the by – have you got any money?'

'He's got the cheque-book, but he makes me an allowance. So far there's been no money trouble. He signs his cheques all right.'

'But he may not presently.'

'Oh! Of course at any time he may begin putting a swastika or a royal cipher in the place of his signature, and then the fat *would* be in the fire. I shouldn't know where to turn. I hadn't thought of that.'

'No,' said Lambone.

For some seconds – it seemed quite a long time to Christina Alberta – he said nothing more. He sat half leaning upon the arm of his chair and looked past her at the fire. She had said what she wanted to say, and now stood waiting for him to speak. His wisdom told him that things had to be done in this matter very soon; his temperament inclined him just to stay in that pleasant room and say things. Meanwhile she looked about the room and realized how comfortable a wise man could be.

It was the best furnished room she had ever been in. The chairs were jolly; there were bound books in the bookcase, a delightful old Chinese horse on the top of it; all his tea-things were silver or fine china; there was a great writing-desk with silver candlesticks; the windows that gave on Half Moon Street were curtained with a rich, subtly folding material very pleasing to the eye. Her eyes came back to his big fat face and his peevish mouth and fine, meditative eyes.

'Something,' he said and sighed, 'ought to be done at once. It isn't a matter to leave about. He might commit some indiscretion. And get into trouble.'

'I'm afraid of that.'

'Exactly. He's safe – where you left him?'

'There's somebody with him.'

'Who won't let anything happen?'

'Yes.'

'So far, good.'

'But what am I to do?'

'What are you to do?' he echoed and said no more for some seconds.

'Well?' she said.

'What in fact are *we* to do. I ought to see him. Decidedly. Yes, I ought to see him.'

'Then come and see him.'

'I ought to come and see him. Now.'

'Then let's.'

He nodded. He seemed to be making an intense internal effort. 'Why not?' he asked.

'Well?'

'And then – then we can broach a visit to Wilfred Devizes. Generally fix that up. Then our subsequent action will be determined by what Wilfred Devizes says. The sooner he sees Devizes the better. It's a question whether it wouldn't be better for you or both of us to see Devizes

first. No. Father first. Then when I'm properly instructed – as a lawyer would say – Devizes.'

A great tranquillity descended upon him.

She could not restrain a faint exclamation of impatience.

He looked up as if he awakened from profound medita-
tion. 'I'll come along now,' he said, 'to Lonsdale Mews.
I'll have a talk to your father and then I'll try to get at
Devizes and fix up some sort of a meeting between them.
That's what I ought to do. I'll go along with you now – at
once.'

'Right-o,' said Christina Alberta, '*come* along.' She
threw on her cloak and clapped her hat upon her head
in a dozen seconds and stood waiting.

'I'm ready,' she said.

'I'll just change this jacket,' said Lambone; and kept
her waiting a full ten minutes.

§ 4

The taxi dropped them at the entrance of the Mews.
'I suppose it won't matter our arriving together?' said
Lambone. 'He won't think it's something preconcerted?'

'He doesn't have suspicions of that sort.'

But when they reached the studio a little surprise awaited
them. Fay Crumb opened the door to them and her eyes
looked paler and her neck longer and her face more absent-
minded than ever.

'I'm so glad you've come at last,' she said in a flat, distraught voice. 'You see – he's gone!'

'Gone!'

'Completely. He's been away since three. He went out
alone.'

'But Fay, you promised!'

'I know. I could see he was restless and I kept telling

him you'd be back soon. It wasn't so easy keeping him. He walked up and down and talked. "I must go out to my people," he said. "I feel they need me. I must be about my proper business." I didn't know what to do. I just hid his hat. I never dreamt he'd go out without his hat – prim as he is. I just went upstairs for a moment to get something – I forget what now – but, anyhow, it wasn't there, and I may have spent five minutes looking for it – and meanwhile he slipped out. He left the door open and I never heard him go. As soon as I knew he'd gone I ran up the Mews right up into Lonsdale Road and stood about there. . . . He'd vanished. I've been hoping he'd come back every moment since. Before you returned. But! He hasn't come back.'

Her conviction was all too manifest that he would never come back.

'I'd have done anything – ' she said.

Christina Alberta and Paul Lambone looked at one another. 'This rather puts the lid on,' said Christina Alberta. 'What are we going to do now?'

§ 5

Lambone followed Christina Alberta into the studio and sat down at once on the simple couch that became Mr. Preemby's bed at night. The couch squeaked and submitted. He stared at the floor and reflected. 'I've got no engagements this evening,' he said. 'None.'

'It won't be much good waiting here for him,' said Christina Alberta.

'I feel in my bones he won't head back here for hours and hours,' he said.

'And meanwhile he may be up to anything!' said Christina Alberta.

148

'Any old lark,' said Lambone.

'Anything,' said Christina Alberta.

'Three,' said Lambone and consulted his watch: 'it's now nearly five. Do you think there is any particular place, Christina Alberta, more than any other place, where we might go and look for him? Where, in fact, we ought to look for him?'

'But will you come and look for him?'

'I'm at your service.'

'It wasn't in the bond.'

'I want to. If you won't walk too fast. I feel I ought to.'

Christina Alberta stood before him with her arms akimbo. 'I would bet five to one,' she said slowly, 'that he heads for Buckingham Palace and demands an audience – No, that isn't how he puts it – offers to give an audience to his Vassal, the King. He was full of that this morning. And then – Then I suppose they will lock him up and have an inquiry into his mental condition.'

'H'm,' said Lambone, and then, rising to the occasion: 'Let's go to Buckingham Palace.

'We'll go there at once,' he said, and moved slowly doorward. 'We'll get a taxi.'

They found a taxi in the King's Road. Christina Alberta did not belong to the taxi-ing class, and she was impressed by a sudden realization that Lambone had all these thousands of taxi-cabs upon the streets alert to do his bidding. The taxi dropped them according to instructions at the foot of the Victoria Memorial which gesticulates in front of Buckingham Palace, and they stood side by side surveying that building. 'It looks much as usual,' said Lambone.

'You didn't expect him to bend it?' said Christina Alberta.

'If he made a disturbance they've cleared him up very completely. That flag I suppose means G.R. is at home. . . . I wonder – what do we do next?'

He was rather at a loss. The emotional atmosphere of this wide-open place was quite different from the emotional atmosphere of his flat or the Lonsdale Mews. In the flat and in the Mews the appeal had been for him to act; the appeal here was not to make himself conspicuous. He was a man of decorous instincts. A car passed, a beautiful, big, shining Napier, and he thought the occupants looked at him as though they recognized him. Lots of people knew him nowadays and might recognize him. In his flat, in the studio at Lonsdale Mews, he could foregather with Christina Alberta without compunction; but now, in this very conspicuous place, this most conspicuous place, he had a momentary realization that he and she didn't exactly match, he with his finished effect of being a man about town, a large, distinguished, mature man about town, and she with her air of excessive youthfulness, her very short skirts and her hat, like the calyptra of a black mushroom, pulled over her bobbed hair. People might think them an incongruous couple. People might wonder what had brought them together and what he was up to with her.

'I suppose we ought to ask some one,' she said.

'Who?'

'Oh! – one of those sentinels.'

'May one speak to the sentinels at the gate? Frankly, I'm afraid of those tremendous chaps in the busbies. I'd as soon speak to the Horse Guard in Whitehall. He'd probably look right over our heads and say nothing. And we should just dither away from beneath him. I couldn't stand that. . . .'

'But what are we to do?'

'Nothing rash.'

'We *must* ask some one.'

'Away there on the left towards Victoria there's what looks like the real business way in. There's two police-

men. I'm not afraid of policemen. No. And of course
that man at the corner is a plain-clothes man.'

'Then let's ask *him*!'

Lambone made no move. 'Suppose he hasn't come here
at all!'

'I know he meant to do so.'

'I suppose if he hasn't come,' said Lambone, 'we ought to
wait about here on the chance of his coming.' He felt
extremely like flight at that instant. 'There ought to be
seats here.

'Come along,' he said, with a sudden return to manly
decision, 'let's ask one of those bobbies at the far gate.'

§ 6

The policeman at the gate to whom they addressed themselves listened gravely to their inquiries, making no instant
reply. He belonged to that great majority of English
speakers who are engaged upon the improvement of the
word 'yes.' His particular idea was to make it long and
purry.

'Yurrss,' he said breaking presently into speech: 'Yurrss.
There was a small gentleman without a 'at on. Yurrss.
He 'ad blue eyes. And a moustache? Yurrss, come to
think of it there *was* a moustache. A rather considerable
moustache. Well, 'e said he wanted to speak to King
George on a rather urgent matter. It always is a rather
urgent matter. Never "quite." Always "rather." We
replied, according to formula, 'e'd 'ave to write for'n
'pointment. "Perhaps," 'e says, "You don't know who I
am?" They all say that. "I guess it's something important," I says. "Not the Ormighty, by any chance," I says.
But 'e was 'ere last week and 'e wouldn' go away and they
'ad to take 'im off in a taxi-cab. You know there *was* a

chap 'ere, sir – Thursday last or Friday, I forget which –
with a long white beard and 'air all down 'is back. Very
like 'im I should think. Well any'ow this sort of dashed
your gentleman. He kind of mumbled a name.'

'Not Sargon?' asked Christina Alberta.

'It might 'ave been. Any'ow, "There is no exceptions," I
says. "Not even if you was a close relation. We got no
option here. We're just machines." He stood sort of looking baffled for a time. "All this must be altered," he said
in a sort of low, earnest voice. "It's the duty of every king
to give audience to every one, every day." I says, "Very
likely it is, sir. But we policemen aren't in any position to
'elp it," I says, "much less alter it." So off 'e goes. I kind
of tipped the wink to the detective at the corner and 'e
watched 'im go along the front and then cross over to the
monument and stand looking up at the windows. And
then 'e shrugged 'is shoulders and took 'imself off. And
that's the last I see of 'im.'

Lambone asked a superfluous question.

'It might be Piccadilly way,' said the policeman, 'it might
be down towards Trafalgar Square. Fact is, sir, I didn't
notice.'

It was clear that the conversation was drawing to an end.

§ 7

So that's that,' said Lambone. 'So far, good. He's still
at large.'

He expressed his thanks to the policeman.

'And now,' he said with an air of bringing out the solution
of a difficult problem very successfully, 'all we have to do
is to find him.'

'But where?'

'That's the essence of the problem.'

He led the way back to the Victoria Memorial and stood
side by side with Christina Alberta beneath that perfect
symbol of the British Empire, the statue of Queen Victoria.
They stared down the Mall to the distant Admiralty Arch,
and for a moment neither of them said a word. It was a
warm and serene October afternoon; the cupolas of Whitehall and Westminster's two towers and a brown pile of
mansions were just visible over the trees on the right,
transfigured to beauty by the afternoon glow; the two tall
columns of the Duke of York and Nelson rose over the
trees and buildings to the left; it was in the pause before
the dinner and theatre traffic begins, and only a few
taxicabs and a car or so emphasized the breadth of
the processional roadway. Half a dozen windows in
the Admiralty had taken fire already from the sinking
sun.

'I suppose,' said Lambone, 'he's gone down there.'

Christina Alberta stood with her arms akimbo and her
feet a little apart. 'I suppose he has.'

The wide road ran straight to the distant Admiralty Arch.
And through that remote little opening was Trafalgar
Square and Charing Cross and a radiating tangle of roads
and streets spreading out and beyond and further into the
twilight blue.

'What will he make for now?'

'Heaven knows. I'm bankrupt. I haven't an idea.'

Neither spoke for a little while.

'He's gone,' she said, 'just gone,' and that simple and
desolating thought filled her mind.

But the thoughts of Paul Lambone were more complex
and intricate.

He perceived that a serious adventure was happening to
him and that he was called upon to exert himself. He had
suddenly been called away from his tea and hot tea-cake to
hunt a slightly demented comparative stranger about

London. He wanted to do it, and he wanted to do it properly and in a way to impress Christina Alberta. And his intelligence told him that the best thing he could do would be to follow upon the probable track of his quarry and come up with him before he got into mischief. Or while he was getting into mischief – and interfere and carry him off. And meanwhile his more exercised lower nature was exhorting him to leave Christina Alberta to do the pursuing alone, and go back as straightly as possible to his ample arm-chair and sit down and think things out. And then go to his best club to dinner. And in fact quietly and neatly get out of this unexpected and tiresome business altogether.

And then he looked at Christina Alberta and realized that he could do nothing of the sort. He couldn't leave her. He looked at her profile, the profile of a grave child, and an almost maternal emotion was aroused in him. She looked with anxious and perplexed eyes at the blue and limitless city that had swallowed up her Daddy. The scene was still warm with the evening sun-glow, but the blue twilight gathered in the lower eastern sky. Here and there a yellow pin-point showed that London was beginning to light itself up. She couldn't go down that road alone. Absurdly, preposterously they were linked. The impulse to disentangle himself was the impulse of a selfish discretion that was rapidly taking all the happiness out of his life and leaving security and luxuries in its place. This was a call to that latent Paul Lambone to *act*. Even supposing she was a common, queer little flapper that his imagination had made into a friend and heroine, was that any reason whatever why he shouldn't see her through this trouble that had come upon her?

He made his decision.

'He won't go back for ages,' he said, following up the problem. 'Nobody would on an evening like this.'

'No,' she said. 'But I don't see that that gives me any hint of what I ought to do next.'

'We can keep together and go down towards Trafalgar Square. We might look along the Embankment. When we are tired we can get some dinner somewhere. You can get a sort of dinner almost anywhere I suppose. We shall want our dinner. . . . Perhaps it's not so hopeless a job as it seems at first. A big job but not a hopeless one. There are limitations to what he may do. Limitations in himself I mean. I don't think he'll go into uninteresting streets. His feeling is – spectacular. He's much more likely to keep to open spaces and near conspicuous buildings. That cuts out a lot of streets. And he won't go far east. In another hour the city will be shutting up and going home and putting out its lights. He'll turn back out of that – westward.'

'You can spare the time?'

'I've no engagements at all to-night. It was to have been an "off" night. And this business attracts me. It is interesting to see just how far we can infer and guess his proceedings. It's a curious mental exercise. . . . Do you know I think we shall find him!'

She stood quite still for some moments.

'It's awfully good of you to come with me,' she said.

'I come on one condition. . . . That you don't walk too fast. We've never walked much together, Christina Alberta, but I've seen enough of you to know that you walk abominably fast.'

§ 8

Every one knows the Café Neptune near Piccadilly Circus and the various crowd that assembles there. There you see artists and painters that are scarcely artists, poets and

155

mere writers, artists' models and drug-fiends, under-graduates in arts and medicine who are no better than they should be, publishers and gay lawyers, Bolsheviks and White Refugees, American visitors who come to scoff and remain a prey, stray students from the Far East and Jews and Jews and Jews – and Jewesses. And hither at about half-past nine that night came a stout, large, and wearily-distinguished-looking man accompanied by an attractive young lady in short skirts and bobbed hair who carried a large and shapely nose high and sternly, and they threaded their way among the tables through the smoky atmosphere, seeking a congenial place. Out of the garrulous confusing mirk arose a young man with a mop of red hair and pro-truded a rampant face and asked in a large whisper: '*Have you found him?*'

'Not a trace,' said Paul Lambone.

Fay Crumb's face looked up from the table through a haze of cigarette smoke.

'Nor we. *We*'ve been looking too.'

'As well here as anywhere,' said the stout man. 'Where have you looked?'

'Here,' said Harold, 'and hereabouts. It seemed a suit-able rendezvous.'

'We've ranged far and wide,' said Lambone. 'We've done miles – oh! endless miles. And Christina Alberta has refused all nourishment – for me as well as for herself. At last I said, either I sit down and eat or I drop down and die. May we take these chairs? You have that one, Chris-tina Alberta. Waiter! It is a case of extreme fatigue. No – neither Munchner nor Pilsener. I must have champagne. Bollinger 1914 will do and it must be iced – rather over-iced, and with it, sandwiches – a very considerable number of sandwiches of smoked salmon. Yes – a dozen. Ah!'

He dropped his wrists on the table. 'When I have had some drink I will talk,' he wheezed and became silent.

'When did you leave the Mews?' Christina Alberta asked Fay.

'Half-past eight. . . . Not a sign of him.'

'Have you been far?' Harold asked Lambone.

'*Far!*' said Lambone and for a time was incapable of more.

His voice seemed to recede in perspective. 'Asking policemen for a small, hatless man. Over great areas of London. On and on – from one policeman to another. . . . She's a most determined young woman. God help the man who wins her love! Not a soul had seen him. But I can't talk *yet*. . . .'

Harold clawed his chin softly with long artistic fingers. 'It is just possible,' he said slowly, 'that he went in somewhere and bought a hat.'

'Of course he must have got a hat,' said Fay.

'It never occurred to either of us that he would do anything so sane.'

'We never thought of asking in the hatters' shops,' said Christina Alberta.

'Happily,' said Lambone, and turned to welcome his refreshment. 'That would have been the last straw.'

'For a long time we were on the trail of another hatless man,' said Christina Alberta. 'We ran him down in the Essex Road after tracking him all up Pentonville. But he was just a vegetarian in sandals and a beard. And there was a report of a hatless man near the Britannia, but that came to nothing. He seemed just to have come out of his house somewhere to buy fried fish off a barrow in the Camden Town High Street.'

'Extraordinary how a crowd collects when you ask the simplest questions,' said Lambone with his mouth full of sandwich. 'And how urgently helpful it can be. They almost forced us up a staircase after that fried-fish man, who struck me as an extremely pugnacious, suspicious-looking fellow. The crowd would have it we wanted him, and he didn't seem to want in the very least to be wanted. If I hadn't had an inspiration something very disagreeable might have happened. I just said "No, it's not this gentleman, it's another of the same name." '

'But what did he say?'

' "You *better*," he said. But anyhow it satisfied the crowd, and afterwards we got away quite easily on an omnibus that took us down to Portland Road Station.'

The champagne arrived in its ice pail. 'Hardly cold, sir, yet,' said the waiter, feeling the bottle.

'It's not a time for fastidiousness,' said Lambone and took a third sandwich. 'You're not eating, Christina Alberta. And I insist upon your having at least one glass of this.'

Christina Alberta drank a little and ate mechanically.

'I wonder if we shall ever see him again,' said Harold. 'London is so vast. So *vast*! But I always feel that, when I see anyone go out anywhere. There is a tremendous courage in going out. London must be full of lost people. I used to be afraid of London until I discovered the Tubes and the Underground. I felt I might be sucked up side-streets to God knows where. And keep on going round corners into longer and longer streets for ever. I used to dream of the last street of all – *endless*. But whenever I get nervous I just ask for the nearest Tube station and there I am.'

'He *may* be back at the studio now,' said Fay.

Paul Lambone reached his fourth sandwich and his third glass of champagne with great rapidity. He became more leisurely in his refreshment.

'I am disappointed,' he said, 'that I didn't think of the possibility of his buying a hat. It has disorganized all my inductions. You see I was so concentrated on what was going on inside his head that I never troubled about what might be going on outside it. But a man of his neat and proper habits – acquired through a lifetime of orderly living – would get himself a hat almost mechanically. . . . We may have passed quite close to him in that.'

'I should have known him,' said Christina Alberta.

'But, until that Pentonville man drew a red herring across the trail, I am convinced we were close on his footsteps. You see Christina Alberta insisted upon my asking every policeman we saw – even men, overworked, irritable, snappy, *rude* men controlling the traffic – but at any rate I chose the route – I inferred the route. You see, my dear Watson' – he smiled faintly in weary self-approval at Crumb – 'the essential thing in a case like this is to put yourself in your man's place, to think his thoughts instead of your own. That is what I tried – so far as being out of breath would allow it – to impress on Christina Alberta. It's fairly straightforward. Here you have a man convinced, beautifully and enviably convinced, that he is the supreme lord of the world, unknown, unrecognized as yet, but on the eve of his proclamation. Will such a man go along any street just as easily as any other? Not at all? He will be elated, expansive, ascendant. Very well: he will go up hill and not down. He will choose wide highways and not narrow ones and tend towards the middle of the street – '

'He hasn't been run over!' cried Christina Alberta sharply.

'No. No. He would avoid traffic because that would hustle him and impair his dignity. Open spaces would attract him. High buildings, bright lights, the intimations of any assembly would draw him powerfully. So he certainly crossed Trafalgar Square from the Admiralty Arch in a diagonal direction, towards the conspicuous invitation of the Coliseum. . . . You see my method?'

He did not wait for Crumb to answer. 'But the more I think over our missing friend,' he went on, 'the more I admire and envy him. What crawling things we are! –

content to be subjects, units, items, pawns, drops of water and grains of sand, in the multitudinous, unmeaning muddle of human affairs. He soars above it. He soars above it now. He rejects his commonness and inferiority in one magnificent gesture. *His* world. The grandeur of it! Wherever he is to-night and whatever fate overtake him, he is a happy man. And we sit here, we sit here and drink – I am ordering another bottle of that wine, Harold, and I expect you and Mrs. Crumb to abandon that warm and sticky beer and join me – Waiter! Yes – another, please – we sit here in this crowded, smoky gathering (*look* at 'em!) while he plans the salvation of the world that we let slide, and lifts his kingly will to God. Glorious exaltation! Suppose that all of us could be touched – '

Christina Alberta interrupted. 'I think we ought to telephone to the hospitals. I didn't think before of the possibility of his being run over. Always he has been a little careless at crossings.'

Paul Lambone lifted a deprecating hand and searched in his mind for some excuse for rest.

'A little later,' he said after a slight pause, 'the hospital staffs will be more at leisure. It is their rush hour now – ten to eleven. Yes, the Rush Hour. . . .'

§ 9

Teddy Winterton appeared wading through obstructive seated people. His eye was fixed on Christina Alberta. 'Hullo!' said Lambone in not too cordial greeting, and glanced at Christina Alberta and back at the new-comer.

Teddy struggled for an unoccupied chair over which some lady had thrown a sealskin coat, and captured it with profuse apologies to the owner of the cloak and squeezed it in at the end of the table between Harold and Fay, who barred his way to Christina Alberta. 'Have pity on a lonely man,' he said genially and tried to catch the eye of Christina Alberta.

'You shall have one glass of champagne,' said Lambone with a slightly forced welcome in his tone.

'How do, Christina Alberta!' said Teddy, forcing her attention.

Christina Alberta turned to Fay. 'Will you come back with me now,' she said to her. 'Back to the flat? I must do that telephoning to the hospitals now or it won't be done.'

Fay looked at her curiously. 'It's serious,' said Christina Alberta's eyes, and Fay stood up and struggled with her coat. Teddy leaped to his feet to assist her. Christina Alberta had not removed her cloak, and was ready. 'I say, Christina Alberta,' said Teddy. 'I want a word with you.'

'Go on, Fay,' said Christina Alberta, giving her friend a little dig in the back and pretending not to hear him.

Teddy followed them out to the Piccadilly pavement. 'Just a word,' he said. Fay was for standing a little way off, but Christina Alberta would not let that happen.

'I don't want a word,' she said.

'But I might help you.'

'You might have done. But it's too late. I never want to see you again.'

'Give a fellow a chance.'

'You've had your chance. And tried to take it.'

'You might at least keep up appearances,' said Teddy.

'Damn appearances!' said Christina Alberta. 'Oh! *Come* on, Fay.'

She gripped her friend's arm.

Teddy was left hovering. He hesitated and then went back into the café to rejoin Crumb and Lambone.

The two young women went on in silence for a little while.

'Anything up?' Fay ventured.

'Everything's up,' said Christina Alberta. 'I wonder if there's a ghost of a chance of finding Daddy at the studio.'

They made their way to Chelsea without much further conversation. Fay had never before seen Christina Alberta looking tired.

When Fay opened the door Christina Alberta pushed in past her. 'Daddy!' she cried in the dark passage. 'Daddy!'

Fay clicked on the light. 'No,' said Christina Alberta. 'Of course he's not here. He's gone. Fay! What am I to *do*?'

Fay's pale blue eyes became rounder. Christina Alberta, the valiant, the modern, was in tears.

'There's the hospitals,' said Fay, doing her best to be brisk and cheerful.

Book the Second

THE WORLD REJECTS SARGON, KING
OF KINGS

CHAPTER THE FIRST

Incognito

§ 1

MR. PREEMBY had disappeared from Christina Alberta's world. For a time he must disappear almost as completely from this story. Mr. Preemby fades out. Taking over his outward likeness we have now to tell of another and greater person, Sargon the First, the Magnificent One, King of all Kings, the Inheritor of the Earth.

It is no doubt a very wonderful and glorious thing to discover that instead of being the rather obscure widower of a laundry proprietor with no particular purpose in the world one is Lord of the Whole World, but it is also, to a conscientious man anxious to do right, an extremely disturbing and oppressive discovery. And at first it is natural that there should be something a little confusing to the mind in this vast and glittering idea. It was an idea that carried with it an effect of release and enlargement. For purposes as yet obscure, he had been caught like a caged creature in that limited and uninteresting Preemby life. His imagination had rebelled against its finality; some deep instinct had warned him that his life was an illusion; in moments of reverie, and sometimes between sleeping and waking, there had been intimations of a light and purpose beyond the apparent reality. Now abruptly, as though a portal swung open, as though a curtain was drawn, that light poured upon him dazzlingly. His was no single life that begins and ends and is done with like an empty song. His existence was like a thread that shone and vanished and returned in the unending fabric of being; that was woven into a purpose. In the past he had been Porg in the city of Kleb, and he had been Sargon and Belshazzar. Many others had he been, but those memories still slumbered under the dark waters of forgetfulness. But the memory of Sargon shone bright. It was his Sargon self that had returned and no other of his selves. For some reason that was still obscure the Power that ruled his life needed him to be Sargon once again, in this great distressful world of to-day. Sargon had begun life humbly as an outcast babe and had risen to restore and rule and extend a mightier Empire than the old world had ever seen before. Certain qualities (h'rrmp) had been displayed by Sargon, and because of these qualities the Power had called upon him again.

A whole series of memories was unfolding in his mind. With an extraordinary convincingness he recalled his youth, memories of those distant days in Sumeria where the Power had set him on high. They were so bright and so pleasing that already they were thrusting his recollections of Sheringham and Woodford Wells into the background, making a fading phantom of his Preemby existence. He had never cherished these latter experiences, never turned them over in his mind with any pleasure. But his newly-restored memories were memories to dwell upon. There were pictures of his early life when he was a foundling, a mysterious foundling at the court of his predecessor. (That predecessor's name still escaped him.) Young Sargon was a fair and blue-eyed youth, a thing rare in brown Sumeria, and he had been found floating down the great river in a little cradle boat of rushes and bitumen, and he had been taken and adopted by the ruler of the land. And already as a lad he was pointed out as having an exceptional wisdom, as being able to do what other men could not do, he had the genius of the ruler. It was not that he had great cleverness nor great skill nor strength. Many of those about him excelled him in these minor things – in cleverness and

166

memory work in particular, Prewm, the son of the Grand Vizier, excelled him – but he had the true, the kingly wisdom beyond them all.

'The true, the kingly wisdom,' said Mr. Preemby-Sargon aloud and came into sharp collision with a tall, dark gentleman hurrying from St. James's Park towards St. James's Palace. 'Sorry!' cried Mr. Preemby-Sargon.

'My fault,' said the tall, dark gentleman. 'Late for an appointment.' And swept on.

Odd! Where had Mr. Preemby – or Sargon – seen that face before? Could it be – Something connected it vaguely with Sheringham and sunlit sand. And then Sumeria came uppermost and the tall, dark gentleman became the chieftain of a desert tribe, a desert tribe amidst the sands.

The ruffled surface became calm again, and that boyhood in Sumeria resumed possession of the mirror. Where were we? Even in those early days men had marked a gravity in the lad beyond his years. He had avoided puerile games. In all his lives he had avoided puerile games. No cricketer even at Sheringham. Modestly but firmly this youth had raised his voice in the council chamber and his words were seen to be wisdom. The old men had sat round marvelling. 'He sayeth Sooth,' they said in their antique Sumerian way. A soothsayer. He was also called the Young Pathfinder.

Before Sargon was fifteen the old childless ruler, beset by enemies, threatened with plots, had marked him. 'This boy might save the state.' Then, while yet only a few days over eighteen he was given charge of an expedition to pacify the mountain folk of the north and persuade them not to ally themselves with the Enemy of the North. He did more than he was told to do. He went through the mountain land into the plains beyond, and gave battle to the Enemy of the North and defeated him and smote him severely. After that all men perceived that he must be the new Lord and Master of Sumeria, the successor of his aged Patron. All applauded with sincerity except Prewm the Clever (already adorned with precocious sprouting whiskers) and he applauded with envy in his eyes. And then came the days of the Succession, and the Inauguration of the Harem, beautiful days. And after that the birth of the Princess Royal, his only child, and that great expedition into the deserts of the south. And more expeditions and great law-makings, wise laws and wiser, and crowds of applauding, grateful people and happy villages. Life became happy universally. Prewm plotted and rebelled and was dealt with after the simple custom of the time. That was a regrettable necessity, a thing not to be dwelt upon. The frontiers spread and the great peace spread; Russia, Turkey in Europe, Persia, India, Ancient Egypt, Somaliland, and so on and so forth, were conquered and made happy. America and Australia and the remains of Atlantis, still not completely submerged, were discovered. They were forgotten again afterwards, but they were really discovered then – and paid tribute. A League of Nations was established.

All the world told of the goodness of Sargon and lived golden days. For Sargon ruled by the light of justice in his heart. He mitigated the sacrifices in the Temples and introduced a kind of Protestantism into the creeds and services. The people made songs praising him. Passing men and women would run to kiss his hand. Nor did he deny himself to his people. That confidence was his end. Came alas! the assassin's knife, the black assassin, a madman, a stranger – !

It was wonderful. He could remember his people mourning after he was dead.

The white glove of a policeman against Mr. Preemby-

Sargon's chest just saved him from stepping in front of a motor-'bus. He recoiled dexterously. He was in Trafalgar Square, a great meeting-place, a confluence. Here in the warm light of the October afternoon was a crowd even greater than the Sumerian crowds. Here he would observe them. They were dark crowds, anxious-faced crowds. His coming back had to do with them. There had been a great war, much devastation; the world was wounded and unable to recover. The poor rulers and politicians of this age had no wisdom, had no instinct for the fundamentally right thing. Once more a leader and a saviour was required, one who had the wisdom that counts.

It was Sargon that walked under the noses of Nelson's lions and made his way past the statue of George the Fourth to the balustrading that commands the square. He took up his position there for a long survey. He looked down Whitehall to the great tower of the Houses of Parliament and Whitehall was full of a golden haze set with a glitter of traffic. The stream of omnibuses, cars, and motor-vans poured up to mingle with the streams that came out of Northumberland Avenue and the Strand, and the joint flow sundered again to the left of him and to the right away to Pall Mall, across the square there. No street lamps were lit as yet, but in the rounded bluffs of building to the left a few windows were warm with lights. Below, across the square, thin streams of pedestrians flowed like ants from one point to another and the squat little station of the Tube Railway perpetually swallowed up dots and clumps of individuals. Some sort of meeting was going on at the foot of the Nelson column, a mere knot of people without evident enthusiasm. Men with white and red placards about Unemployment were distributing white handbills and shaking collecting boxes. Immediately underneath a few poorly-dressed children ran about and played and squabbled. . . .

Just a little patch this was in one of his cities. For, you see, by the lapse of time and the development of his ancient empire, he was the rightful owner and ruler of this city and of every other city in the world.

And he had come back to heal the swarming world's disorders and reinstate the deep peace of old Sumeria once again.

§ 2

But how to set about this task?

That was the difficulty. There must be no Half Advent. He must take hold swiftly and decisively he realized, and from the balustrading in front of the National Gallery it looked a large, loose, scattering sort of world to take hold of. It might refuse to be taken hold of. If he began now, if he began to shout from this place, it was more than likely that no one would heed him. He must watch warily for his opportunity and *make no mistakes*. It did not become the Lord and Restorer of the Whole Earth to make mistakes.

Now, for example, that had nearly been a mistake at Buckingham Palace. It had blown over all right, but it might have had serious consequences. People did not know the Master yet, had no inkling. 'They might,' said Sargon, lapsing into a Preemby homeliness 'have run me in. And a Pretty Fool I should have looked then!'

There must be no more hasty action of that sort.

No. Indeed it became him rather to wait for guidance. The Power that had brought him back into the world and awakened him to a sense of his true identity and his mission, might be trusted presently to send him an enlightened supporter or so – who would recognize him. Because, of course, he must resemble the monarch he had

been – even as Hockleby had been recognizably like
Prewm. As he weighed this thought his hand sought
his moustache and he twisted it thoughtfully. It was in
effect a disguise. Meanwhile – ? Meanwhile he must see
what he could, determine the mood of the people and
learn their particular needs and distresses. He could go
among his people unsuspected – like Haroun al Raschid,
but for a wiser purpose. . . .

'Haroun al Raschid,' whispered Sargon and looked up to
Lord Nelson and nodded to him in a friendly way.
'Haroun al Raschid. Would that my pocket was full of
pieces of gold! But of that to-morrow. That man – what
was his name ? – Preemby had a bank somewhere.'

He felt for his breast pocket. The cheque-book was
still there. One signed the cheques '*A. E. Preemby*' –
queer, but one did. This A. E. Preemby had played the
part of a chrysalis. His hoard remained.

§ 3

In the Strand His Majesty caught a glimpse of his
reflection in a shop window. His hair was a little disordered, and he disliked to have his hair disordered. He
went into a hat shop that presented itself conveniently,
and bought himself a hat.

He took out his little note-case to pay – a reassuring
thing to do. For in it were no less than seven pound-
notes. He counted them with satisfaction. After paying
up at Tunbridge he had drawn again on his bank. He
hesitated whether he should give largesse to the shopman
– and did not do so.

It was not another grey felt hat with a black ribbon
he bought; it was an exceptional felt hat with a large brim
such as an artist or a literary personage might have

chosen. It was not the hat that Albert Edward Preemby, the restrained, the hesitating, would have bought; it was much more Sargon's sort of hat. Yet not pure Sargonesque; there was a touch of disguise about it still, a more manifest disguise. The brim came down over one's brow. One could see ever and again in shop windows and incidental mirrors that now a shadow of mystery lay upon those brooding blue eyes.

He made his way eastward towards Aldwych and so into Kingsway, looking now at the shops, now scanning the faces of the people.

To-day he was The Unknown. Scarce a soul that gave him a second glance. But soon would come discovery and then all this careless jostling crowd would be magnetized as he passed, would turn with one accord to him. They would salute and whisper and wonder. And he must be ready for them, ready to guide their destinies forthwith. It would not do to stand at a loss and say 'Er,' to stand collecting his thoughts and clear his throat, 'H'rrmp.'

Terrible the responsibility that lay upon him! But he would not shirk it. What should be his opening words to them when the moment of revelation came? 'First; – Let there be Peace!' Better words than that one could not imagine. He muttered to himself; 'Peace and not War among the Nations. Peace and not War among individuals. Peace in the street – in the workroom – in the shop. *Peace.*

'Love and Peace. I, Sargon the Magnificent, command it. I Sargon have come back after many ages to give Peace to the Whole World.'

A shop window drew him. It was a map shop and prominently displayed in the window was a map of *Europe after the Treaty of Versailles: – Two and Sixpence.* He stood looking at that. It would all have to be altered again. That was just part of his task. Then he surveyed the rest of the window. Behind the map of Europe there hung a wall-map of the world. He would need such a map of the world; you cannot rule the world without a map of it. Or you may forget large portions. Or would a globe be better? Maps are all to be seen at once, and besides they are more portable. Furthermore, the shop did not seem to sell globes and he did not know where globes were to be bought. He went in and bought the world map and emerged again on Kingsway after an interval, with a roll four feet long under his arm. He was also carrying an ingenious flat-paper planisphere which had caught his fancy as he stood at the counter. It might be useful, he felt, for astrological purposes.

He began to think vaguely of his possible destination. Whither was he going?

He was seeking quarters, he was seeking indeed some lonely hermitage. He had slipped away from the Princess Royal, who also had come back – rather needlessly he thought – into this modern world, because it was necessary for him to be absolutely alone for a time. He had to spend some days or weeks in spiritual struggle and meditation and mental purification before his revelation came. Even she might not minister to him during that period. She was devoted, but she hampered him. Indeed, she hampered him greatly. She did not fully understand. Her remarks and questions were generally disconcerting and sometimes downright annoying. It was quite probable that the metamorphosis might never occur with her about. And, besides, always in the history of great Visitants and marvellous returns there had been this opening phase of withdrawal and self-communion. Buddha, Muhammad; they had all done it. Perhaps he would fast. Perhaps fasting would be necessary. Perhaps there would be Celestial Visitants.

He wished he knew more of the technique of fasting.

173

Did one just stop having meals or were there ceremonies and precautions? But of that later. First he had to find that quiet room, his secret place of final preparation.

Presently he found himself in the grey squares of Bloomsbury and every house he passed displayed in its window a genteel card offering 'Apartments' or 'Bed and Breakfast.' Here also were 'Private Hotels' and even a plain 'Boarding House.' Well, here no doubt it had to be. A simple room amidst his unsuspecting people, a simple, simply furnished room.

§ 4

But though all Bloomsbury, to judge by the dark green and silver cards in its ground-floor windows, was offering shelter and sustenance to the homeless and the stranger, the new Lord of the World found it no easy matter to secure that simple room he needed for his own use. For more than an hour he was visiting one grey house after another, knocking, standing on doorsteps, entering passages laid with immemorial oilcloth, and demanding a sight of the accommodation offered, inspecting it, asking prices and – it became more and more evident – arousing suspicion. The people stared at his rolled-up map and his planisphere and seemed to dislike them instinctively. He had not expected such blunt demands for information; his vague mysteriousness was swept aside, he found himself difficult to explain. They wanted to know how he was occupied and when he would like to move in. None of them seemed prepared for him just to sit down in his room there and then. They expected him to go out and fetch his luggage. It undermined his confidence that behind him there was no luggage. All these people, he realized more and more distinctly, would expect him to produce luggage and might behave unreasonably if he did not do so. A mere readiness to pay in advance, he gathered, was not enough for them.

He had counted upon finding kind and simple people behind these lodging-house doors, people who would accept him and look up to him from the first and wonder about him and his planisphere, speculate about its significance and gradually realize the marvellous visitant that had come to them. But the people he saw were not simple people. Mostly they were dingy, sophisticated people. They came up out of basements in a mood of sceptical scrutiny, men in shirt sleeves, morose for the most part and generally ill-shaven; extremely knowing and anything but virginal young women, grimy looking older women, hungrily lean or unwholesomely fat. One had a goitre-like growth. And always there was something defensive in their manner.

And the rooms he saw were even less simple than the people. His consciousness was invaded by a sense of the vast moral changes that had happened to the world since he had ruled the white-robed honesty of his Sumerian irrigators. Then a room would have a table, a seat or two, a shelf with a few phials, an image or suchlike religious object, a clay tablet and a writing style, perhaps, if the occupant was educated. But these rooms were encumbered with contradictions. They had windows to let in the light and dark curtains to keep it out. Sargon's hidden second youth in the laundry had made him very sensitive to dirtiness, and the cotton-lace curtains of those places were generally very dirty indeed. Electric light was still rare in 'apartments'; mostly they were lit from gas brackets that descended from the centre of the ceiling and carried globes of frosted and cut glass. Always there was a considerable table in the centre and two uneasy arm-chairs. And there were lumpish sideboards of shiny, liver-coloured wood and comfortless sofas and incredible ornaments. Sometimes the rooms, and particularly the bedrooms, had a meretricious smartness and gaiety with mezzotints of ladies in the natural state trying to pass themselves off as allegorical figures or of the Baths in the congested harems of wealthy, rather than refined, Orientals. The overmantels were extraordinary affairs and much loaded with crockery ornaments, little jars, small gilt-winged angels, red devils, or encouraging looking ladies in bathing-dresses that were too tight for them. A common form of decoration was to fasten up plates on the wall much as one sees vermin nailed up on a barn.

A considerable number of these homes for hire were as shabby as roadside tramps. One stood out in his memory as faded and dusty and grey and threadbare beyond the possibility of reality. His self-absorption was penetrated by the wonder of who could live and who could have lived in such quarters. All his life had been amongst clean and bright surroundings; it was rare that he had any glimpses of that worn and weary stratum of English town life in which things are patched indeed, but in which it is rare for anything to be mended or cleaned and incredible that anything should be replaced. Even the air in these rooms seemed long out of date and the glass over the rusty engravings of the Monarch of the Glen and the Stag at Bay spotted by remote ancestral flies.

'Does anyone ever stay here?' asked Sargon of the shattered looking lady in charge.

He did not realize the cruelty of his question until he had asked it.

'My last gentleman stayed here fifteen years,' said the shattered lady. 'He was a copying clerk. He died in hospital this June. Dropsy. He always found this very

satisfactory – *very* satisfactory. I never knew him complain. He was a very good friend to me.'

A great desire for fresh air came upon Sargon. 'How
much are these rooms?' he asked. 'I must think it over.
Think it over and let you know.'

She asked her price, the usual price in that street, but
as she led the way down to the door she said; 'If it's too
much – If you made an offer, sir –'

Despair looked out of her grime-rimmed eyes.

'I must think about it,' said Sargon and was once more
at large.

Why did people get so dirty and dismal and broken
down? Surely in Sumeria there were never lives like that!
It would have to be altered; all this would have to be
altered when the Kingdom came.

§ 5

Then as the twilight deepened Sargon discovered just
the peaceful room he desired. It announced itself hope-
fully not by the usual printed card but by a hand-written
tablet saying 'A Room to Let,' in a window that had no
lace curtains but little purple ones enhancing rather
than concealing a bare-looking white room lit pleasantly
by the flickering of a fire. There were one or two pictures – real coloured pictures – hanging on the white wall.
Rather wearily Sargon lifted the knocker and supple-
mented its appeal by pressing the electric bell.

There was no immediate answer, and he knocked a second
time before the door opened. A slender young man
appeared holding a small girl perched on his shoulder.
She regarded Sargon gravely with very dark grey-blue
eyes.

'Everybody seems to have gone out,' said the slender

young man in a very pleasant voice. 'What can I do for you?'

'You have a room to let,' said Sargon.

'There *is* a room to let here, yes," said the slender young man and his appreciative dark eyes took in the details of the figure in front of him.

'Could I see it?'

'I suppose he might *see* it, Susan,' the young man hesitated.

'Of course the gem's got to see it,' said the small girl. 'If Mrs. Richman was here she'd show it him fast enough, old stoopid.' And she pulled the slender young man's hair – affectionately but very very hard.

'You see,' the young man explained. 'The landlady is out. *Don't*, Susan. And the landlady's lady assistant is out too. Every one is out – and we're sort of unofficially left in charge somehow. Properly, I ought not to have answered the door.'

'But I told you to – *silly*!' said the little girl.

The young man made no definite move. Instead, he asked a question. 'Is that a map, sir, you are carrying?' he asked.

'It is a map of the world,' said Sargon.

'Very helpful I should think, sir. And so you found your way here. Well – The room's upstairs if you'd come up. Hold tight, Susan, and try not to strangle me.' And he led the way up the staircase.

It was just the usual staircase and hall with oilcloth and wall-paper to imitate some exceptionally bilious coarse-grained wood. As they ascended the young lady ran great risks in her resolution never to take her eyes off Sargon and his map. She twisted round a complete circle and forced her bearer to stop on the first landing and readjust her. 'If you pull my hair once more,' said the slender young man, 'I shall put you down and never,

never, never, give you a ride again. It's on the next floor, sir, if you'd go first.'

The room appeared delightfully free from unnecessary furnishings. There was a little plain bed, a table under the window, and a gas-stove, and the walls were papered in brown paper, adorned with commonplace but refreshing Japanese colour prints. There was a recess one side of the fireplace with three empty shelves painted like the mantelpiece, a deep blue. The young man had clicked on an electric light, which was pleasantly shaded.

'It's rather plain,' said the young man.

'I like it,' said Sargon. 'I have no use for superfluities.'

'It used to be my room,' said the young man, 'but now I share the dining-room floor with the people downstairs and I've given this up. It's rather on my conscience –'

'People downstairs – what people downstairs? There aren't no People downstairs. It's Daddy and Mummy he means,' said the young lady.

'It's rather on my conscience,' said the young man, 'that I persuaded Mrs. Richman to alter the furniture. It isn't to everybody's taste.'

'May I ask,' said Sargon, 'how much the room might be?'

'Thirty shillings, I *believe*,' said the young man, 'with breakfasts.'

Sargon put down his map and planisphere upon the table. He felt that he must secure this room or be for ever defeated.

'I am willing,' he said, 'to take the room. I would pay for it in advance. And take up my quarters at once. But, I must warn you, my position in the world is peculiar. I give no reference, I bring no luggage.'

'Except of course these charts,' said the young man. 'Haven't you – for instance – a toothbrush?'

Sargon thought. 'No. I must get myself a toothbrush.'

'I think it would *look* better,' said the young man.

'If necessary,' said Sargon, 'I will pay for two weeks in advance. And I will get myself all necessary things.'

The young man regarded him with an affectionate expression. 'If it was my room I should let you have it like a shot,' he said. 'But Mrs. Richman is the landlady and in many respects she's different from me. Have you – travelled far, sir?'

'In space,' said Sargon, '*No*.'

'But in time, perhaps?'

'In time, yes. But I would rather not enter into explanations at present.'

The young man's interest and amusement deepened. He put Susan down on her feet. 'Might I look at your map?' he asked.

'Willingly,' said Sargon. He unrolled the map on the table and put his finger on London. 'We are here,' he said.

'Exactly,' said the young man helping to hold the map on the table from which it seemed likely to slip.

'It is still the most convenient centre in the world,' said Sargon.

'For almost any purpose,' said the young man.

'For mine, yes,' said Sargon.

'And that star thing – that must be a great help?'

'It is,' said Sargon.

'I suppose you would – *work* in the room? It would be just yourself? There would be no coming and going of people?'

'None. While I was here, no one would know me. Afterwards perhaps. But that does not concern us. Here I should remain incognito.'

'Incognito,' the young man repeated, as though he considered the word. 'Of course. Naturally. By the by, sir, might I ask your name. (If you hit me again, Susan, I shall do something cruel and dreadful to you.) We'd have to know your name.'

'For the time I think Mr. – Mr. Sargon.'

'Of course,' said the young man, 'for the time. Sargon – wasn't that an Assyrian king, or does my memory betray me?'

'It is not the Assyrian Sargon in this case, it is the Sumerian Sargon, his predecessor.'

'Not a word more, sir – I understand. You must be fatigued after your long journey and I should love – I should dearly love to let you the room. *Wow!* Susan, you go downstairs. Pinching I can't stand. Come along. You go down to your own proper room and let's have no nonsense about it. *Come!*'

Susan backed to the wall and prepared to resist tooth and nail. 'I didn't *mean* to pinch, Bobby,' she said. 'I didn't mean to pinch. Troof and really! I was just feelin' your trousis. Oh, don't take me down, Bobby! Don't take me down. I *will* be good! I'll be awful good. I'll just stay here and look at the funny geman. If you take me down, Bobby – '

'Now is this a real reformation, Susan – a conversion, a change of heart? Will you be a *jeune femme rangée* and all that, if I forgive you?'

'I'll be anyfing, Bobby dear, flet me stay.'

'Well! cease to exist then – for all practical purposes and I'll forgive you. What can the nice gentleman think of you, Susan? And you more than five! *Bah!* We were saying, Mr. Sargon – ? Yes, of course, I was saying that you ought to take the room. Payment in advance will be accepted. *But* – there is that toothbrush. And other small – what shall I say? – realistic touches. *I* shouldn't mind personally, but I'm only an agent, so to speak. Properly I am a sort of writer. Properly I ought to be writing a novel now, but, as you see, Mrs. Richman has left the house on my hands and my friends downstairs have left this charming young lady on my hands – Put that tongue back at once, Susan. Unladylike child! – and here we are! But as I'm saying, Mrs. Richman is the principal. She has her fancies about lodgers. It is useless to dispute about them. She will want a show of luggage. She will insist. But that is really not an insurmountable difficulty. This – you will remember the name? – is Nine Midgard Street. If you go out from here and turn to the left, take the third to the right and go straight on, you will come to a main thoroughfare full of 'buses and trams and traffic and light and noise, and at the corner you will find a shop where they sell second-hand trunks and bags. Now if you bought an old, battered, largish bag – and then went across the road to a chemist's shop and got those washing things you need – Oh! and a reserve collar or so at the outfitter's next door – You *must* get such things. . . . You see the idea?'

Sargon stood in front of the unlit gas-stove. 'This seems to be acting a falsehood.'

'But you must have clean collars sometimes,' protested the young man.

'I admit that,' said Sargon.

'And then you can settle down here and tell me about that business of yours. Otherwise, you know, you'll just wander about.'

'Your suggestion is really quite a helpful one,' said Sargon, getting the thing into focus. 'I shall adopt it.'

'You won't lose the way back?'

'Why should I?'

'Nine Midgard Street.'

'I shall remember.'

'Queer world it is,' said the young man; 'Isn't it? How did you leave the old folks in – Sumeria?'

'My people were happy,' said Sargon.

'Exactly. I've been there since. *Quite* recently. But the weather wasn't good and I got knocked about by a shell and had a nasty time as a wounded prisoner. Hot. Crowded. No shelter. Nothing cool to drink. But in your time it was different.'

'Very,' said Sargon.

'And now – by Jove! that kettle is boiling over all by this time, Susan. Come down to my room, such as it is, and have a cup of tea, Sir. And then you can go out and make those little arrangements of yours and dig yourself in so to speak before Mrs. Richman comes back. This, by the by, is your gas meter. You get gas by the shilling in the slot arrangement.'

'You are being very very helpful to me,' said Sargon. 'It shall not be forgotten when my time comes.'

'Nothing. It just happened you came into my hands so to speak. No, Susan, we don't. You *walk* downstairs. Pinching is forgiven but not forgotten. You can leave your map, Sir – and that star thing – as visible signs of your occupation. No, Susan – on foot.'

§ 6

The young man's room was bookish and rather untidy, and Susan had been killing toys on the carpet – a china-headed doll and something or other of yellow painted wood appeared to be the chief victims. The doll had bled saw-dust profusely. Dark curtains were drawn and a green-shaded electric light threw all the apartment into darkness except the floor. There was a gas-fire with a gas-ring on which a boiling kettle steamed like an excited volcano; there was a deal table on which was a big pile of letters addressed to '*Aunt Suzannah*' c/o Editor of *Wilkins*'

Weekly, and there was a large untidy desk on which was another litter of letters evidently receiving attention, and in the midst of the desk a writing-pad, on which reposed a squeezable tube of liquid glue and a half-mended toy. The glue oozed upon the face sheet of the writing-pad beneath these words, written in a beautifully neat handwriting:

UPS AND DOWNS

A Pedestrian Novel

BY ROBERT ROOTHING

CHAPTER THE FIRST

WHICH INTRODUCES OUR HERO

Beyond that the novel did not seem to have progressed. With the dexterity of long established usage Bobby made tea and produced plum-bread and butter. Meanwhile he kept a wary eye on Susan who had sat down by the waste-paper basket and was tearing up paper, and attended to the remarks and attitudes of his remarkable visitor.

Sargon already liked this young man enormously. It was extremely reassuring and encouraging to meet such kindly acceptance and understanding after the chill and doubt and ugliness of the previous hour's experiences. And it was nice and refreshing to have tea. A sort of grey insecurity, a threat of suppression that had come over his mind, vanished in this genial atmosphere. The shrivelled incognito expanded. The hidden mystery beneath it grew rich and full once more. This young man – he seemed ready to believe anything. Sargon walked up and down with his hands behind his back as if in the profoundest meditation. He would have muttered a few phrases in Sumerian, but for some reason he had quite forgotten that forgotten tongue.

'And so you write books?' he said regally.

'Not books,' Bobby answered over his shoulder; he was now toasting a circle of plum-bread. 'Not books *yet*. But – it *is* ridiculous, isn't it? – I am a bit of a poet and all that sort of thing, and a journalist of sorts. Just answers to correspondents – laborious, but a living.' He indicated the piles of letters on the deal table. 'As for books – I have as a matter of fact *started* a novel – it's on that desk – but that's only in the last few days. And it's so difficult to get a lot of time to oneself to really let oneself go with it.'

'Inspiration,' said Sargon understandingly.

'Well, one must let oneself go a bit, I suppose; particularly at first. But there's always something one must do cropping up to prevent it.'

'With me also.'

'No doubt.'

'That is why,' said Sargon, 'I am withdrawing into this solitude. To collect my forces. In Sumeria it was always the practice, before any great undertaking, to go out into the wilderness for a certain tale of days.'

'If I go out into the wilderness I get so lonely in the evenings,' said Bobby. '*Ssh!* That was the front door.'

He went out upon the staircase and stood listening.

'Mrs. Richman,' Sargon heard him call.

'S'me,' said a lady's voice.

'Here's a lodger for the second floor front.'

'I bin to the pictures,' said the voice outside. 'Mary and Doug – a fair treat.'

A corpulent lady in a black bonnet appeared breathing heavily. She panted a few obvious questions and Bobby hovered helpfully at Sargon's elbow to prevent him making any mistakes. 'He'll pay in advance,' said Bobby.

'That's awright,' said Mrs. Richman. 'When will he move in?'

'He's getting his luggage right away,' said Bobby.

'I s'pose it's all right,' said Mrs. Richman.

'I know his people. At least I know about them. I've been in his part of the country. You can be quite sure he's all right,' said Bobby.

'Well, if *you* say so,' said Mrs. Richman. ' 'Ope you'll be comfortable Mr. –'

'Mr. Sargon.'

'Mr. Sargon.'

And after a few rather vague comments on the weather Mrs. Richman withdrew. 'And now,' said Bobby, 'I'll just unload Susan on her and come with you for that bag. It's extraordinary how people lose their way in London at times.'

§ 7

'I've let the second-floor front to a lunatic,' said Bobby, breaking the news to his ground-floor friends, Mr. and Mrs. Malmesbury.

'Oh *Bobby*! and with Susan about!' cried Mrs. Malmesbury reproachfully.

'But he's a quite *harmless* lunatic, Tessy – and he had to be taken in somewhere.'

'But a lunatic!' said Mrs. Malmesbury.

'I only said that for effect,' said Bobby. 'He's really morbidly sane. I wouldn't have let him go for anything. Some day when I really get to work on that novel I'll put him in. I *must* have material, Tessy. And he's wonderful.'

He was preparing supper for the Malmesburys and himself. He was frying some sausages and potatoes over a gasring. Previously Bobby had done most of the putting of Susan to bed, and he had sat and told her stories according to custom until she was fast asleep. Tessy Malmesbury was out of sorts; she had a neuralgic headache, Billy Malmesbury had taken her for a walk in Regent's Park and she had come home exhausted; things would have gone to pieces badly if Bobby had not taken them in hand.

Tessy was never very well nowadays; she was a slight and fragile little thing and Susan had been a violent and aggressive child long before she was born. In the long lost days before the war when Bobby had seen Tessy first she had been the lightest, daintiest, most perfect thing imaginable; he had compared her to a white petal drifting down through sunlight, and almost written a poem about her; he had loved her tremendously. But it had seemed to him impossible to make love to so exquisite a being, and Billy Malmesbury, who was less scrupulous, had slipped in front of him and married her; she had not appreciated the delicacy of not making love to her. And then came the war and wounds and here they all were again, fagged and near the thirties, in a world where their small annuities brought them far less than they had promised to do. Billy was the junior partner of an architect and much encumbered with drawing-boards. He was a large-framed young man with a big, round, good-looking, slightly astonished face, pleasantly dappled with freckles. He had a great protective affection for Bobby. He sat now and designed a new sort of labour-saving pantry and, with a sense of infinite protection, let Bobby get the meal.

'And now I can tell you,' said Bobby, when at last all three of them were sitting at table.

'It's a little dear of a lunatic,' he said. 'If it's a lunatic at all.'

'I hope it isn't,' said Tessy.

'He's quite tidy in his person and he hangs together – mentally he hangs together – and his eyes aren't in the least wild. A leetle too bright and open perhaps. But he *does* think the world belongs to him.'

'Well, Susan does that,' said Billy.

'And so does Billy,' said Tessy.

'But not quite with the same air of magnificent responsibility. You see he thinks he's a certain Mesopotamian monarch called Sargon – I've heard of him because we had a little dust-up with the Turks round and about his stamping ground – he thinks he's this Sargon come again and come somehow – that bit's a little difficult – into the empire of the whole earth. It was Sargon, you know, who started all these British Lions and Imperial Eagles in the world. And so he proposes to take possession of the planet, which is in such a frightful mess –'

'Hear, hear!' said Billy.

'And put it in order.'

'What more simple?' cried Tessy.

'Exactly. Why haven't we *all* thought of that?' said Billy.

'But where does he come from?' asked Tessy.

'Not a sign. He might be a suburban nurseryman or a small draper or something of that sort. I can't place him. One or two phrases he used suggested a house-agent. But he may have picked them up from advertisements. And his first proceeding – perfectly rational – was to buy a map of the world. Naturally if you are going to rule the world, you ought to have a map of it handy.'

'Has he any money?'

'Enough to pay his way. He's got a small note-case. That seems to be all right. After we'd got a bag for him – he hadn't any luggage, and I thought he'd better buy a bag to satisfy Mrs. Richman – we sat down upstairs and had a simple straightforward talk about the world and what had to be done with it. Most instructive.'

Bobby helped himself to some more fried potatoes.

'And what *is* going to be done with it?'

'Let me see,' said Bobby; 'it's quite an attractive little programme. Rather I think on the lines of the Labour programme. Only simpler and more thorough. The Distinction of Rich and Poor is to be Abolished Altogether. Women are to be Freed from all Disadvantages. There is to be No More War. He gets at the roots of things every time.'

'If those are the roots,' said Billy.

'But isn't the real question how to do it?' asked Tessy. 'Aren't we all agreed about those things – in theory?'

'In theory, yes,' said Bobby. 'But not in reality. If every one really wanted to abolish the difference of rich and poor it would be as easy as pie to find a way. There's always a way to everything if you want to do it enough. But nobody really wants to do these things. Not as we want meals. All sorts of other things people want, but wanting to have no rich and poor any more isn't real wanting; it is just a matter of pious sentiment. And so it is about war. We don't want to be poor and we don't want to be hurt or worried by war, but that's not wanting to end those things. *He* wants to end them.'

'But how's he going to set about it?' said Billy.

'That is still a little vague. I think there is to be a sort of Proclamation. He's thinking that out upstairs now. He seems to think that he has to call up some sort of disciples. Then I think he will go down to Westminster and take the Speaker's place on the Woolsack or something of that sort. It *is* the Speaker sits on the Woolsack, isn't it? Or is it the Lord Chancellor? Anyhow, there are to be demonstrations – on a large and dignified scale. The people have forgotten the ancient simple laws, he says. He himself had forgotten them. But he has remembered them now; they have come back to him, and presently every one will remember them, all the great old things, justice, faith, obedience, mutual service. As it was in Ancient Sumeria. Dreamland Ancient Sumeria, you know. The dear old Golden Age. He has come to remind people of the true things in life – which every one has forgotten. And when he has reminded them every one will remember. And be good. And there you are, Tessy! I hope it will affect Susan – but I don't feel at all sure. I have a sort of feeling that Susan could stash up any golden age they started in about five minutes, but then perhaps I'm a bit prejudiced about her.'

'It's rather wonderful all the same,' said Billy.

'He *is* rather wonderful. He sits up there and looks at you with his little round innocent face and tells you all these things. And, assuming he's Lord of the World, they're perfectly right and proper. He sits with the map of the world unrolled on the table. I ventured to suggest that he would require a lot of subordinate rulers and directors. "They will come," he said. "No office, no duty shall be done henceforth except by the Proper People. That has been neglected too long. Let every man do that he is best fitted to do. Then everything will be well." '

'And when's all this to begin?' asked Billy.

'Any time. I don't think –' Bobby's expression became profoundly judicial. 'I don't think he'll do anything for a day or so. I pointed out to him that he ought to consider his demonstrations very carefully before he makes them, and he seemed inclined to agree. Some mistake, he says, has occurred already – I couldn't find out what. Apparently to-morrow he is just going to look at London, quietly but firmly, from the Monument and from the Dome of Saint Paul's. And also he wants to observe the manners of his subjects in the streets and railway stations, and wherever there is a concourse of people. The scales have fallen from his eyes, he explains, and now that he knows that he is Lord of the World he realizes how dis-

tressed and unsatisfactory everybody's life is – even when
they don't know it's unsatisfactory. His own life was
terribly unsatisfactory he says, unreal and frustrated,
until he awoke and realized the greatness of his destiny.'
'And what was that life of his?' asked Tessy.
'I tried to get that. And he caught the eager note in
my voice I suppose, and shut up like an oyster. The
draper's shop perhaps. Or a milk-round. I wonder.'
'But Bobby,' cried Billy in the expostulatory tone of one
who remonstrates with wild unreason; 'he must come from
somewhere!'
'Exactly,' said Bobby. 'And somewhere must be looking
for him. But you can't always hurry these things. And
meanwhile I take it it's our bounden duty to keep
an eye on him and see that he doesn't bump himself
too hard or fall into the wrong hands. . . . Until some
one comes along. . . . Don't you get up, Tessy, you're
tired.'
And Bobby jumped to his feet and proceeded to change
the plates and dishes while Billy fell into a profound
meditation upon the problem of the new neighbour
upstairs.
Presently he smiled and shook his head in kindly
disapproval.
'This will suit Bobby all right,' he said to Tessy. 'Whenever he ought to be upstairs in his own room getting
on with that novel of his he will be up on the second
floor talking to – what is it? – Sargon.'
'Accumulating material,' corrected Bobby from the
Welsh dresser, where he was turning a tin of peaches
out into a glass dish. 'Accumulating material. . . . Not
even a spider could spin a yarn out of an empty stomach.
Tessy, have you just simply *lost* the cream or have you
put it away in a new place very carefully for me to guess.
Oh right-o! I've got it.'

§ 8

Let us be frank about it; Sargon had his doubts.

Not always. There were times when his fantasy was bravely alive and carried him high above any shadow of uncertainty, and he was all that he could have ever wished to be. Then Mr. Preemby was almost forgotten. But there were moments, there were phases, when he became aware of a cold undertow of conviction that he was after all just Mr. Preemby, Mr. Preemby, formerly of the Limpid Stream Laundry, making believe, carrying it off and perhaps presently failing to carry it off. This chill flow of doubt could even oblige him to reason with himself, force him into a definite reassurance of himself. He would debate the whole question, candidly, fairly. Surely there was no deception, could have been no deception, about that séance. 'Told me things no one but I could have known,' he would repeat. 'I pin my faith to that.'

He knew that Christina Alberta had not really believed. It was just because of her revealing scepticism that he had fled from her. She had asked questions, tearing, rending questions, and she had said 'Um.' It is not proper to say 'Um' to world emperors. If presently he fasted or went into a trance, he felt sure that she would come and stand about beside him and say 'Um,' and spoil everything. Well, anyhow, he was away from that for a bit. But to be away from doubt was not enough. The great discovery threatened to evaporate. He wanted the comfort of the disciple. He wanted help and reassurance.

Bobby had comforted him greatly. While Sargon had been going from one suspicious lodging-house keeper to another, the faith of the new Saviour of mankind had weakened dreadfully. But Bobby from the first had had something deferential in his manner, had seemed to understand. His questions had grown more and more intelligent. Perhaps he was to be the first of the reawakened adherents. Perhaps presently he would be recognizable as some faithful servant in that still so largely forgotten past, a trusted general perhaps, or some intimate court official.

Yet even when Sargon doubted he believed. It is a very comprehensible paradox. He knew clearly that to be Sargon was to be real, was to signify and make all the world signify, was to go back into the past and reach right out into the future, was to escape altogether from the shrivelled insignificance of the Preemby life. To be Sargon was to achieve not only greatness but goodness. Sargon could give and Sargon could dare. Sargon could face lions and die for his people, but Preemby could go round three fields, had been known to go round three fields, to evade the hostility of a barking terrier. Preemby's world was dust and dirt, a mud speck in infinite space, and there was no life on it but abjection. Preemby was death; Sargon was rebirth into a world of spacious things. Not very clearly did Sargon achieve these realizations, but he felt them throughout his being. Something had happened to him of inestimable value and truth; he had to cling to this gift and hold it and keep it or be for ever fallen. Christina Alberta notwithstanding, the whole world notwithstanding.

So he walked up and down his little upper room in Midgard Street and elaborated his conception of his new rôle as lord and protector of the whole world. Twilight gave place to night but he did not turn on the light. He liked the friendly darkness. All visible things are limiting things, but the darkness goes out and beyond everything to God. 'I must look,' he said. 'I must watch and observe. But not for too long. There is action. Action gives life. That fellow Preemby, poor soul, he could look at things, but dared he lift a finger? No! Everywhere suffering, everywhere injustice and disorder, the desert and the wilderness breaking back in on us and he did nothing. If one does not call and call aloud, how can one expect an answer? In this world, vast, terrible – strikes – hoardings – adulteration – profiteers. . . . Nevertheless men who once lived bravely and did their duty. . . . Who may do it again. . . . Once they hear the call. Awake! Remember! The High Path. Simple Honour. Sargon calls you. . . . H'rrmp. . . .'

He came to a halt at his uncurtained window and looked out on the plain flat face of the opposite houses, pierced here and there by a lit window. Most had the blinds drawn, but just opposite a woman worked by lamp-light at a table, sewing something, her needle hand flew out perpetually and the book and one hand and the cuff of a reader came also into the picture, the rest of him hidden behind the curtain. At a bedroom window there was a looking-glass, and a girl tried on a hat and looked at it this way and that; then suddenly she vanished, and after a little interval the light went out.

'All their scattered lives,' said Sargon, holding out his arms with a benevolent gesture, 'knitted – drawn together by wisdom and love. A rudder put on the drifting world.'

Came a knock at the door. 'Come in,' said Sargon.

Bobby appeared. 'Getting on all right, sir?' he said in his engaging subaltern manner. He clicked on the electric light and came into the room. (Cadaverous and pleasant face he had; surely one would remember presently what he had been.) 'Wondered if you were eating anything to-night?' he asked.

'I quite forgot eating,' said Sargon. 'Quite. My mind – troubled by many grave matters. I have much to think of, much to plan. The hour grows late. The time is near. I wonder if the serving woman here –?'

'Only breakfasts,' said Bobby. 'Here we are on bed and breakfast terms strictly. The rest is with ourselves. For an emergency like this there is nothing so good as the Rubicon Restaurant. The Grill Room keeps open quite late. They will do you a chop or a cutlet. Or ham and eggs. Very good ham and eggs – crisp ham. You go out from here, turn to the left at the second corner, and go right down Hampshire Street until you come to it. You'll have no difficulty in finding it.'

The word 'crisp' had settled it.

'I will avail myself,' said Sargon.

'And it's equally easy to find your way back,' said Bobby with a faint flavour of anxiety in his voice.

'Have no fear, young man,' said Sargon in a tone of jolly reassurance. 'Have no fear. I've found my way in many climes and under many conditions – the wild mountains – the trackless desert. Time and space.'

'Of course,' said Bobby. 'I forgot that.'

'Still – London is different,' said Bobby.

§ 9

The next day at about half-past four in the afternoon a small but heavily moustached figure, with eyes full of blue determination, emerged from Saint Paul's Cathedral and stood at the top of the steps before the great doors, surveying the jostling traffic of Ludgate Hill and the Churchyard. There was a sort of valiant uncertainty in the figure's pose, as though it was equally resolved to be up to something, and uncertain about what it meant to do. London had been looked at from the top of the Monument and from the Cathedral dome on a crystal-clear October day, and it had betrayed an unusual loveliness and greatness under the golden sunshine. But it had shown itself too as a vast dreamy multitudinousness in which none but those who are resolute and powerful in action can hope to escape being swallowed up. It had stretched away to wide sun-lit stretches that seemed to be the horizon, and then up in the leaden-blue other stretches had been visible of houses, of shipping, of distant hills. The vans and carts in the shadowed streets below had looked like toys; the people were hats and hurrying legs and feet, curiously proportioned. And over all an immense dome of kindly cloud-flecked sky.

He had walked round the little gallery under the ball muttering: 'A wilderness. A city that has forgotten. . . .
'How fair it might be! How great it might be!
'How fair and great it *shall* be!'

And now he had come down again from these high places and the time had come for him to gather together his disciples and ministers and inaugurate the New World. He had to call them. Followers would not come to him unless he called them; they would wait for him to act, not know even of what awaited them until he called them, but when he called them they would surely come.

It was with an extraordinary sense of power over men's destinies that he stood now upon Saint Paul's steps and reflected that even now men and women might be passing by, among these busy men thronging the pavement, among the people in omnibuses, among the girls clattering away at their typewriters behind the upstairs windows, over whose busy, petty, undistinguished lives hung the challenge of his summons. Yonder perhaps was his Abu Bekr, his right-hand man, his Peter. Let them wait a little longer. He waved the traffic onward with a gesture of kindly encouragement. 'Soon now,' he said, 'very soon. Go on while ye may. Even now the sorting of the lots begins.'

Yet a moment more he stood still and silent, a statuette of destiny. 'And now,' he whispered; 'and now . . .

'And first –'

He was no longer troubled by his oblivion of the Sumerian tongue. In the night he had recovered the gift of tongues; he had muttered strange words in the darkness, and understood.

'H'rrmp,' he said, a word common to many tongues, clearing the way after five thousand years for the return of the forgotten sounds to a renewed use in the world of men.

'Dadendo Fizzoggo Grandioso Magnificendodidodo – yes,' he whispered. 'The Unveiling of the Countenance. The First Revelation. Then perhaps they will see.'

And slowly he descended the steps, his eyes searching the convergent frontages of the Churchyard for some intimations of a barber's shop.

CHAPTER THE SECOND

The Calling of the Disciples

§ 1

THERE are already wide differences of statement and opinion about the order and the details of the calling of the followers of Sargon. Happily we are in a position to give the circumstances with all the exactitude that may be necessary, and with an authority that will anticipate vexatious criticism. It was about half-past six that Sargon appeared in Cheapside, and the day's traffic was already ebbing in that busy city thoroughfare. His countenance was transformed and shone with that kind of luminosity that only the most thorough and exhaustive shaving can give. A youthful smoothness had been restored to it. The facial mane, the vast moustache, that had veiled it for so many years from mankind was abandoned, a mess of clippings and lather now in a barber's basin. Now the face was as bare as the young Alexander, a fresh-complexioned, sincere and innocent countenance speaking clearly with an unfiltered voice. It was flushed with a natural excitement as it went along Cheapside scrutinizing the faces of the foot passengers on a momentous and mystical search. The blue eyes beneath the brim of the distinguished looking hat were alight. Was it to be this man? Was it to be this?

§ 2

The first to be called was a young man of Leytonstone named Godley, a young man with a large and excessively grave grey face and a deliberation of utterance amounting to an impediment. He was carrying a microscope in a wooden box. He was a student of biology with a cyto-

logical bias; naturally very polite and temperamentally disposed to be precise and deliberate in all he said and did.
He was making his way from Liverpool Street station to
the Birkbeck Institute by a circuitous route because he had
nearly an hour in hand before his class began. He stood
poised on the pavement edge at a street-corner waiting for
two vans to pass, when his call came to him.

He found a very earnest barefaced little man beside him
whose blue eyes searched his countenance swiftly, and who
then gripped his arm.

'I think,' said Sargon, 'that it is you.'

Mr. Godley, who was not without a sense of humour,
attempted to reply that it certainly was him, but that
impediment of his, partly natural but greatly developed by
affectation, arrested him about the word 'certainly,' and he
was still sawing the air with his profile when Sargon spoke
again.

'I have need of your help,' said Sargon. 'The great task
is beginning.'

Mr. Godley went through the preliminary convulsions of
explaining that he had the better part of an hour to spare
and that he was willing to give help in any reasonable
matter provided it was first explained to him clearly just
exactly what the matter was. But he could only give help
for a limited time. His engagement with his class at the
Birkbeck was imperative. Sargon paid little heed to the
significance of the various sounds that Mr. Godley was
biting off and swallowing. He led his captive by the arm
and explained, with helpful gestures of his free hand, the
full significance of this call. 'You are I perceive, a young
man of scientific qualifications. They will be needed. I do
not know if you recognize me – your memory may still be
imperfect – but I recall your face, chief among the wise
men of our ancient court. Yes, indeed, chief among our
wise men.'

'N-no-no-not as-as-asure that I follow you aw-ow-ow-quite,' said the young man. 'My my – my aw-ow-ow-work issferr'll aw-ow-ow-known as yet.'

'*I* know it,' said Sargon boldly. '*I* know it. I have been seeking you. Do not be deceived by my plain incognito. Believe me I have tremendous powers behind me. In a little while all men will understand. The age of confusion draws near its end; a new age begins. We are the first two particles, the very first, in a great crystallization –'

'Where aaare we g-g-g-oing agg-aggs-aggs-exactly?' asked the young man.

'Trust me,' said Sargon bravely. 'Keep with me.'

The young man struggled with some complex question. But now three fresh individuals came under the magic attraction of the call and the young man's question fell in unheeded chunks. These new adherents were a little group of men standing at the kerb, about a small, almost inaudible hurdy-gurdy on which was a placard stating: 'We want Work not Charity; but there is no Work for Us in this So-called Civilized State.' They were clad in faded khaki, and were all youths of less than five-and-twenty.

'Now look at that!' said Sargon. 'Is it not time the new age began?'

He addressed himself to the man on the right of the organ-grinder.

'All this is to be altered here and now,' he said. 'I have work for you to do.'

'Oh!' said the ex-soldier in the accent of a fairly well educated man. 'What sort of work?'

'We're straight,' said the organ-grinder. 'We'll take it. If it's work we can do. We ain't fakers. Wot work is it?'

'Shillin' an hour?' said the third.

'More than that. Much more than that. And very great and responsible work. A harvest! A splendid harvest! You shall be leaders of men. Follow after me.'

'Far?' asked the man who had spoken first.

Sargon made a gesture that effectually concealed his own lack of a definite plan, and led the way.

'Lead on, Macbeth,' said the organ-grinder, and swung his hurdy-gurdy into its carrying position on his back. The two other ex-soldiers exchanged views that it was all right and that anyhow they'd see what was offered them. Mr. Godley, keeping abreast of his leader, began an immense and ultimately futile struggle with a fresh question.

The next disciple was not so much called as fell into the gathering body of Sargonites. He was a tall gentleman of a rich brown colour with frizzy black hair, and a vast disarming smile. He was dressed in an almost luminous grey frock-suit, a pink tie, buttoned shoes with bright yellow uppers, and a hat as distinguished as Sargon's own. He carried a grey alpaca umbrella. He held out a sheet of paper in a big mahogany hand and emitted in a rich abundant voice the word 'Escuse.' The paper had printed on it at the head the words, 'Lean and Mackay, 329 Leadenhall Street, E.C.,' and below written in ink, 'Mr. Kama Mobamba.'

Sargon regarded his interlocutor for a moment and then recognized him. 'The Elamite King!' he said.

'Non spik English,' said the black gentleman. 'Portugaish.'

'No,' said Sargon with a gesture that explained his intention. 'Providence. Follow after me.'

The coloured gentleman fell in trustfully.

'Look here!' protested one of the ex-soldiers. 'There ain't going to be coloured labour on this job?'

'Peace!' said Sargon. 'Very soon everything will be shown to you.'

'I don't think you have any ub-ub-business to mislead ap-ap-people,' said Mr. Godley, who was becoming more

and more interested in, and perplexed by, Sargon's proceedings.

Sargon quickened his pace.

'This – this gentleman s-s-s-simply wa-wa-wanted tu-tu-
tu-tu-to go to that address,' said Mr. Godley.

In his eagerness to get the idea home to Sargon he
became a little disregardful of his microscope box which
inflicted a sudden sharp blow on the knee of a passing
gentleman, a business man in a silk hat. The victim cursed
aloud with extraordinary vehemence and stood hopping on
the pavement with his hand to his knee. Then he suc-
cumbed to a passionate impulse to tell Mr. Godley exactly
what he thought of his conduct, his upbringing, and his
type of human being. He joined the followers of Sargon
at a brisk limp, occasionally saying 'Hi!' in a breathless
voice. A rather intoxicated man in deep mourning had
witnessed the incident. He came hurrying, with a certain
margin of error, to the side of the angry gentleman in the
silk hat.

''Sgraceful salt,' he said. ''Sgraceful! F'want a witness
I'm your man!'

His general intention was to go forward at the side of the
gentleman in the silk hat, but there were chemically
emancipated factors in his being that drove him sideways.
The resultant was a sinuous course that presently involved
him with a display of oranges in a barrow at the pavement
edge. It was not a serious nor a prolonged contact, but it
involved a certain scattering of oranges in the gutter and
added a new ingredient, a very angry costermonger's
assistant with a remonstrance and a claim for damages, to
the gathering body of Sargon's followers.

The moral of a proverb depends entirely upon the image
chosen, and though a rolling stone gathers no moss, a rolling snowball grows by what it rolls upon. A small hurrying group of people in a London street is a moving body

of the snowball type; its physical pull is considerable; it appeals to curiosity and the increasing gregariousness of mankind. Sargon, blue-eyed and exalted, with Mr. Godley intent and eloquent upon his left hand, and Mr. Kama Mobamba, tall, silent, smiling, with a shining confidence upon his ebony face that soon he would be led into the presence of Messrs. Lean and Mackay, formed the spearhead of the procession. Behind came the three out-of-work ex-soldiers, who were now involved in obscure protests and explanations with the gentleman in the silk hat, and a smart but rather incomprehensible young newspaper reporter, who had acquired his native tongue in Oldham, and had just come up to London to push his fortunes, and was anxious for something called a 'scoop.' He seemed to think that Sargon might be the 'scoop' he sought. Two ambiguous-looking individuals in caps and neck-wraps had also fallen in, possibly for nefarious purposes, a vague-faced young woman of the streets in a weather-worn magenta hat was asking what was '*up*' and the intoxicated man in mourning was explaining as wittily and obscurely as possible. There was also a fringe of skirmishing juveniles. And an Eton boy. He was very very young and fresh-faced, a scion of one of the oldest and best families in England and a convinced and fierce Communist. He had been on his way with a bosom friend to the celebrated model engine shop in Holborn when Sargon had swept past him and the inscription on the organ had caught his eye.

He was a boy of swift initiatives and with a highly developed dramatic sense.

'Sorry, old Fellow,' he said to his friend. 'But I feel the time has come. Unless I'm very much mistaken that little bunch is the beginning of the Social Revolution, and I must do my duty.'

'Oo I *say*, Rabbit!' said the friend. 'Come and buy that steam-launch first, anyhow.'

'*What's* a model steam-launch?' said Rabbit scornfully, and turned to follow Sargon.

He would have liked to have had a swift strong hand-clasp first, but you can't do that sort of thing with a chap who will always keep both hands in his trouser pockets. He darted off, and his friend followed discreetly in a state between amusement and dismay, and at such a distance as seemed to him to exonerate him from any personal complicity with the social revolution.

'Where are we going?' asked the young Etonian as he came up with the hindmost of the out-of-work ex-soldiers.

'*He* knows,' said the out-of-work ex-soldier, indicating Sargon.

§ 3

But that was exactly what our dear Sargon did not know. By this time he was no longer a convinced and complete Sargon. A scared and doubting and protesting Preemby was struggling back into his being.

Up to the beginning of the calling of the disciples Sargon had ruled in his own soul assured and unchallenged. But he had expected his disciples to respond to his call, to recognize and remember, to be immediately understanding and helpful. The calling was to have been like the lighting of a lamp in their minds and the world about them. He had expected not only his own clear and un-questioning conviction but accession and reinforcement for it. And so leaping from soul to soul the restoration of Humanity, the Empire of Sargon would have spread. For disciples who made conditions, for disciples who followed, gesticulating strangely and spluttering and bubbling and stammering injurious criticisms, for disciples who asked for a minimum wage, and for disciples who came limping after one calling 'Hi!' as though one was a cab, Sargon was totally unprepared.

Had he called these disciples rashly? Had he been premature again? Had he made another mistake?

These were unpleasantly urgent questions for a Master to solve while he was going briskly to nowhere in particular about four miles an hour along Holborn with his following gathering at his heels. Perhaps all leadership is a kind of flight. In every leader of men perhaps the fugitive has been latent. In Sargon now it was more than latent; it was awake and stirring, and its name was Preemby.

Since first mankind in its slow ascent from mere animalism became susceptible to Prophets and Great Teachers and Leaders there must always have been something of this internal conflict between the greatness of the mission and something discreetly less, and there must also have been always something of this clash of the disciples' quality and motive with the teacher's expectations. The very calling of disciples seems to admit a sense of weakness on the prophet's part. Their calling puts him in pledge. He puts himself in pledge to them. They will, he knows, hold him to it when he falters; deep gregarious instincts assure him he will not desert his declaration to them even when he might desert himself. They desert him – inevitably. In the whole record of the world there is only one unvarying, faithful disciple, Abu Bekr. All other disciples failed and crippled their Masters and misled them. They deserted or they drove the prophet whither he would not go. Great things and little things of the same kind follow the same laws. At the head of that small wedge of commotion driving along lamp-lit Holborn in the October twilight went Sargon the Lord and Protector of Mankind, the Restorer of Faith and Justice, the Magnificent One, and though he was already aware of an error made and dangers incurred, he was still resolved to pull a great occasion by some stupendous gesture out of the jaws of disaster. And closer than his shadow was Preemby, scared nearly out of his wits, ready for a desperate headlong bolt down any side turning, a bolt from explanation, a bolt from effort, a bolt back to Preembyism and infinite nothingness.

Suddenly there came to Sargon a reassuring voice, the voice of one who had at least seemed to believe and accept.

There had been a slight altercation with Billy before Bobby came hurrying across the road. 'There he goes!' said Bobby.

'That isn't him,' said Billy. 'Where's his moustache? He was pretty nearly all moustache.'

'Shaved,' said Bobby. 'I'd swear to him anywhere. A sort of prance in his walk. It's our prophet, Billy, and he's heading for trouble.'

'Looks more like a welsher,' said Billy. 'Where'd he get that ecstatic nigger? It's too rummy for me altogether, Bobby. You keep out of it. There's a policeman tacking on now.'

Bobby hesitated. 'Can't let him go like that,' he said, and dodged across the road just as four racing omnibuses blotted out the Sargonites from Billy's eyes.

'Forgive me, but where are you going?' said Bobby, stooping to Sargon's grateful ear in spite of a considerable push from Mr. Godley.

'I have declared myself,' said Sargon, and straightway reassurance came. This was the First of the Disciples, and he had found his way to his Master. Quite clearly now did Sargon see what he had to do. These first followers had to be instructed. The Teaching had to begin. To do that it was necessary to lead them apart out of the hurry and tumult of the street. A vision came to Sargon of a long brightly lit table, and of an array of disciples asking questions, and of memorable answers and great sayings. And straight ahead, glowing, bursting with light, already a friend, there towered up the inviting mass of the Rubicon Restaurant, pioneer in the great enterprise of supplying dinners de luxe at popular prices.

'Yonder,' said Sargon with a sweeping gesture of the hand, 'we will rest and sit at meat, and I will talk, and all things shall be explained.'

The bright vision of a discourse to a gathering of disciples at a table had so restored the gloriousness of Sargon that by the time he reached the entrance of the Rubicon Restaurant, which bulges invitingly at a corner, he had called two further disciples. One of these acquisitions was a matchbox-holding beggar of venerable appearance, and the other a highly intelligent looking man of perhaps fifty, lean and thinly bearded, carrying a book on the Doukhobors and wearing mittens and a tall black felt hat – a hat of an unusual shape rather like the steam-dome of a railway engine. This last acquisition was made at the very door of the Restaurant.

'Come in here,' said Sargon, seizing his arm, 'and take meat with me. I have things to tell you that will change your whole life.'

'This is very *suddan*,' said the intelligent-looking man, speaking in the high neighing protesting accent of an English scholar and gentleman, as he yielded himself to Sargon's grip.

§ 4

The actual invasion of the Rubicon Restaurant was a confused and swift affair. Sargon's mind was clear and simple now; he had to make that vision of a long white table with his disciples grouped about him a reality or incur a great defeat. His following was animated by a

mixture of unequal and incompatible motives, as all fol-
lowings are, and it was now swollen to something near
thirty – the exact number is uncertain because it passed
marginally into mere onlookers and passers-by – by the
action of the least worthy of the three out-of-work ex-
soldiers, who had been uttering these magic words, 'A
Free Feed!' ever since the Rubicon Restaurant had been
in sight.

The attention of that challenging individual, the outside
porter, had happened to be distracted by the arrival of
guests in a motor-car when the Sargonites came along.
They therefore swept through the outer entrance without
encountering any obstacle other than the rotating door,
which chopped the little crowd into ones and twos before
it reached the entrance hall. Perhaps twenty got into the
entrance hall, that space of marble and mahogany and
hovering cloakroom attendants, before the mechanical
incompetence of the man in deep mourning and his subsequent extraction by the politely indignant outer porter,
the costermonger's assistant intervening unhelpfully,
jammed the apparatus. The man with the bruised shin
seems to have fallen out before the Restaurant was reached,
and the vague-faced young woman in the magenta hat
drifted away at some unnoted moment.

In the spacious, glittering and observant outer hall a
tendency to dispersal manifested itself. The out-of-work
ex-soldier with the organ, seized by a sudden shyness,
made for the gentleman's cloakroom to deposit his instrument and became involved in an argument with his colleagues. The two ambiguous young men in caps and neck-
wraps seem to have hesitated about the correctness of their
costume. But Sargon held the newly caught gentleman
tight, and the venerable match-seller did not mean to be
separated from his patron in this bright, luxurious, dangerous place. Mr. Kama Mobamba, tall and smiling and

shining, handed hat and umbrella to an attendant and followed closely upon the Master, serene in his assurance that these were the lordly portals of the long sought firm of African traders, Lean and Mackay. And Mr. Godley, with his natural passion for explicitness, would not leave Sargon until he had made it perfectly clear to him why he did not feel bound to accompany him further. He came next after the others into the Large Restaurant, making noises like a cuckoo clock that has lost control of itself. The reporter from Oldham was also holding on, though in considerable doubt now what sort of story he would have to write. The Eton boy, more than half aware now of his error, and so disposed to be a little detached also, came into the Restaurant after depositing hat and umbrella without.

Bobby never came through. He was overtaken and held up in the entrance hall by Billy. 'This isn't your affair, Bobby,' said Billy. 'This really isn't your affair.'

'I can't make out what he's up to,' said Bobby. 'He's bound to get into trouble.'

'Never mind.'

'But I do mind.'

'The management's scared,' said Billy. 'They're sending for the police. There's a crowd gathered outside. Look at the faces looking in. See that chap peering through the hole in the glass? Nice thing for Tessy and Susan if we get into some police-court scrape.'

'But we can't leave him to get into a mess here.'

'But how can we help him?'

§ 5

Within the Restaurant Sargon made his supreme and final effort and encountered swift and overwhelming defeat. But at any rate he did not run away. He made a frontal attack on the world he had set out to subdue – as Sargon. As Sargon, invincibly Sargon, he met disaster.

Things had not begun to be very brisk yet in the Rubicon Restaurant. But indeed it is never so brisk in the Rubicon of an evening as it is at lunch time; it is too far from the west, pre-eminently a luncheon place. And the hour even for such briskness as is customary had not yet come. The neat lines of the little white tables, each with its lamp and flowers, were only broken here and there by occupants. A family group going to a circus; a little knot of people going to a meeting in the Kingsway Hall; three or four couples of theatre-goers in evening dress; three or four of those odd couples of a rather inexperienced looking middle-aged business man and an extremely inexperienced looking young woman in imperfectly conceived dinner dress who are to be seen everywhere in London, and a group of three business men from the north dressed in a canny grey and dining with a resolute completeness from cocktail to liqueur, was all the company yet assembled in the body of the restaurant. There were one or two occupants in the lower gallery, dimly seen; the upper gallery was unlit. The atmosphere was still timorous and chilly; even the three men from the north exacted their tale of London luxury in a subdued and even furtive manner.

The staff was still largely unemployed. The head-waiters, wine-waiters and table-waiters fidgeted serviettes and glasses, or stood about with that expression of self-astonishment and melancholy upon their faces habitual to waiters. A slight hubbub in the entrance hall and the sound of the smashing of the glass in the rotating door by the last effort of the man in mourning preceded the entry of Sargon.

Every one looked up. The guests forgot their food and their company manners; the waiters forgot their secret sorrows. Sargon appeared, an inconspicuous figure, a little white, almost luminous face, round bright eyes. With one hand he still gripped his last disciple. With the other he waved aside the gobbets of speech which Mr. Godley proffered him. A tall expectant negro face rose like a shield of ebony and ivory above him. Behind were the match-seller and other followers, less clearly apprehended.

A head-waiter faced him. Behind hovered a manager and a little further off an assistant manager fiddled with the fruit on the buffet.

Sargon released his latest catch and stood forward.

'Set a table here,' he said with a fine gesture. 'Set a table here for a great company. I have called a following and must needs discourse with them.'

'Table, sir,' said the head-waiter. 'For 'ow many, sir?'

'A great company.'

'Well, sir,' said the head-waiter with an appealing glance at the manager, 'we'd like to 'ave an idea 'ow many.'

The manager came up to take control and the assistant manager deserted his piles of fruit and came up behind helpfully. Sargon perceived he was against opposition and gathered all the forces within him. 'It is a great company,' he said. 'It must sit at meat with me here and I must discourse to it. These people yonder may join. Set all the tables one to another. The day of separate tables and separate lives is at an end. Let even the tables manifest the Brotherhood of Man. Under Our Rule. Set them together.'

At the words 'Brotherhood of Man' one of the three business men from the north was smitten with understanding. 'It's a blood-stained Bolshevik,' he said, or words to that effect. 'Shovin' in here! Of all places!'

'Oughtn't to be allowed,' said his friend. 'Aren't we to have *no* peace from them?'

The first business man expressed a general antipathy for incarmined Bolsheviks and went on eating bread in a hurried, fussed, irritated manner. 'When's that Fricassee of Chicken coming?' he said. 'They must have dropped it or something.'

But the manager's intelligence had been even quicker than the business man's. A swift signal had been given at the very beginning of Sargon's speech. The waiter sent to summon the police had already sped past Billy and Bobby and the rest of the uncertain crowd in the entrance hall, draughty now and uneasy because of the broken glass in the rotating door that the man in mourning had broken.

But Sargon heeded nothing of this byplay. He held on to the only course that he could see before him, which was to overwhelm the opposition that gathered against him.

'We don't have banquets in this room, sir,' said the manager, playing for time. 'Banquets you can have in the Syrian Hall or in the Elysian Chamber or in the Great Masonic or Little Masonic Hall – given due notice and after proper arrangements, but this is the general public restaurant. You can't *suddenly* give a banquet to an unknown company or society or something here. We don't cater for that. It isn't done.'

'It will be done to-night,' said Sargon, with a glance and intonation and gesture that would have bent all dream Sumeria to its knees.

But the managers of European restaurants are made of sterner stuff, it seems, than were the old Sumerians. 'I'm afraid *not*, sir,' he said, and stood blandly obstructive.

'Do you know,' cried Sargon, 'who it is with whom you have to deal?'

'Not one of our regular customers, sir,' said the manager, with the apologetic air of one who scores a point perforce.

'Listen,' said Sargon. 'This day is an Epoch. This is the End and the Beginning of an Age. Men will count this banquet I shall hold here the sunrise moment of a new world. I am Sargon, Sargon the Great, Sargon the

Restorer, come to proclaim myself. This multitude of
my followers must be fed and instructed here, fed bodily
and fed spiritually. See to it that your share is done.'

He made a gesture behind him when he spoke of his
followers, but indeed there was no following behind him
now save that one faithful but deluded African, and that
perplexed but persistent Oldham reporter. The Eton boy
had detached himself completely now. He was sitting at a
table afar off, where he had been joined by his friend, and
they conversed in undertones and watched. Even Mr.
Godley with his microscope, and the gentleman with the
book about the Doukhobors, had faded out of this story by
this time, and were going along Holborn exchanging and
interrupting each other's explanations and surmises about
this singular affair that had so unexpectedly deflected their
high and reasonable progress through life.

'I can only sus-sas-sas-suppose that-the-fellow-was-mad,'
said Mr. Godley.

While Sargon's retinue had melted the manager's had
gathered. Behind him now stood an array of waiters of
every description, three dozen perhaps of various and yet
uniform waiters, tall waiters and short ones, fat and thin,
hairy and bald, young and old, waiters in aprons and one
in shirt-sleeves.

'I'm afraid you're creating a disturbance here,' said the
manager. 'I'm afraid I must ask you to go, sir.'

Should he go? Never!

'Oh, generation of blind and deaf!' he cried, lifting his
voice in an attempt to reach the scattered diners beyond this
lowering crowd of waiting men, 'do you not recognize me?
Have you neither memories nor vision? Do you not see the
light that offers itself to you? Can you not hear the call that
thrills throughout the world? The hour for awakening has
come. It is to-day; it is now. You may cease to be things
of habit and servitude, and you may become masters of a

213

world reborn. Now! This moment. *Will* the change with me and the change is upon you! Sargon calls you, Sargon the Ancient and the Eternal, the Wise Ruler and the Bold One, calls you to light, to nobility, to freedom –'

''Fraid we can't let you make speeches here,' said the manager with hand extended.

'Let's chuck 'im out *now*,' said a short, thick-set waiter.

'Chuck him out!' said the anti-Bolshevik business man, standing up and speaking in a voice replete with indignation and gathering volume as he went on. 'And then bring us our Fricassee of Chicken. We have been waiting Ten Minutes for THAT FRICASSEE OF CHICKEN!'

And then a voice could be heard saying: 'Wot's it all *about*?' and suddenly a policeman stood beside Sargon and overshadowed him.

A wave of horror went through his soul, a wave of horror that was entirely Preemby. Throughout his whole virtuous life he had never once been in antagonism to the Police. 'Oh Lord! oh Lord!' cried this horror in his soul. 'What have I done now? I'm going to be run in!' The blue eyes grew rounder and he gasped for air, but no one there perceived how close he came to ignominious collapse. Preemby shivered and passed. Sargon choked and then spoke stoutly. 'What is this, Officer?' he said. 'Would you lay hands on the Master of the World?'

'My duty, sir, if he makes a disturbance,' said the policeman. 'Master or no Master.'

Very rapidly did Sargon adjust himself to this new phase in his affairs. He was defeated. He was to be led away. Yes, but he was still Sargon. The Power that ruled him had thrust him into defeat, but that could only be to try him. He had not expected this of the Power, but since the Power willed it, so it had to be.

'You understand, Officer, what it is you are doing?' he said, magnificently and gently.

'Quite, sir. I 'ope you don't intend to give us any trouble.'

A captive! Not thus had he foreseen the revelation of the Master. He gave one last look at the rich decorations of the great restaurant in which the opening banquet was to have taken place. Not here then but in some squalid police-court it was that the New Empire of Justice and Brotherhood had to be proclaimed.

He turned in silence and went out at the policeman's side quietly, deep in thought.

§ 6

So ended Sargon's first effort to enter into his Empire. Unless we count the visit to Buckingham Palace as his first attempt.

But before we go on to tell of the unexpected and dreadful experience that now came upon him, we must record one or two minor incidents of his capture.

One is the behaviour of Mr. Kama Mobamba. He watched the closing incidents in the Restaurant with a growing amazement upon his great bronze face. Had this little blue-eyed man been, after all, leading him wrong? When at last Sargon was led away, Mr. Mobamba moved at first as though still half inclined to follow him. Then he stood still, frowned reflectingly and fumbled at his ticket-pocket. With some effort he produced the sheet of paper that seemed to be his one intelligible link with London; it was now in a rather crumpled condition. Smoothing it out with his great hands, he advanced upon the manager with it extended.

'What's this?' said the manager.

The black gentleman bowed with infinite suavity, still tendering his paper. 'Non spik English,' said the black gentleman. 'Portugaish. Lean-a-Kay. Lemonallstree.'

He was difficult to direct.

Meanwhile in the entrance hall Bobby tacitly denied all knowledge of Sargon. He was still hovering there with Billy, held by a curious half-maternal solicitude. The ex-soldiers had 'mizzled,' to use the expressive word of the man with the organ, at the appearance of policemen; the man in mourning and his troubles had been cleared up; but there were still quite a number of people hanging about in a state of vague expectation, and the young reporter was trying to find some one who understood the rare and obscure language of Oldham in order to verify his facts. And there were several policemen; one evidently a superior officer, a very good-looking man in a peaked cap and a frogged coat.

'Here he comes!' said Billy, and Sargon was led out.

There was a silence as he passed through the hall to the rotating door. And upon Sargon, it seemed to Bobby, there rested a hitherto unnoted dignity. He looked neither to the right nor the left, and his eyes were exceedingly mournful.

'But what will they do with him?' asked Bobby.

'You don't happen to know him, sir?' asked the superior officer abruptly.

'Not a bit,' said Billy, taking the answer out of Bobby's mouth. 'Never seen him before. We just came in here to see what was up.'

And by his silence Bobby acquiesced.

'I've got no power to move you on here,' said the police officer, and smiled a suggestion of inopportuneness to Billy, and motioned to his satellites that the business there was at an end.

'We'd better go home,' said Billy, interpreting the smile.

§ 7

The three friends sat round a fire in the white room with the purple curtains, and Bobby poured out his regret that he had denied Sargon. 'They've taken him off, Tessy,' he said for the third time, 'and I do not know what they will do with him.'

'Discharge him with a caution,' said Billy with a drawing-board on his knee. 'He hadn't committed very much of an offence that I can see.'

'And then?' said Bobby, and meditated on the fire.

'I shall go round to the police-court and try to pick him up again afterwards if they let him go,' he said presently.

' Better leave it all alone,' said Billy.

But Tessy sat in her arm-chair between Billy and the fire and looked at Bobby's preoccupied profile rather sweetly out of the warm shadow. And nobody in the world saw her.

'They'll warn him and he'll come back here of his own accord, Bobby,' said Tessy comfortingly.

'Of course he'll come back,' said Billy.

'Very likely, Tessy,' said Bobby. 'But suppose they don't.'

He got up and stood by the fire. 'I suppose I ought to go upstairs and do some work.'

'I suppose you had,' said Billy.

'How is the novel getting on?' asked Tessy.

'Not much done yet,' said Bobby. 'The Prophet has disorganized the actual writing. But I've learnt a lot of things that will tell some day. And of course I have to do all my Aunt Suzannah stuff. Aunt Suzannah gets more and more popular. You can't imagine the things they ask me. It's all material in the long run. Still – it takes time. . . . I suppose they've locked him in a beastly little cell somewhere. And he's wondering why they don't see that he's

217

truly the great Sargon, come again to this world. . . .
Billy, the world's a dangerous place, a dangerous, unkind
place. Why couldn't they let him rip a bit? And his poor
little map of the Whole World upstairs – he always called
it the Whole World – and his little paper star-machine, and
his poor little empty room and his poor little empty bed.'

'I protest,' said Billy, putting his drawing-board aside.
'Bobby, you are a case of morbid overgrowth of the sympathies. You are a new disease. You are the type case of
Bobbyism. It's bad enough that you should sympathize
openly with that little devil Susan when I have spanked
her, and so undo all my teaching. It's bad enough that
you should do about a third of Mrs. Richman's work
because she needs light and air. I can even understand
something of your emotional relationships with various
stray cats and pigeons. But when it comes to your being
sorry for a poor little empty lodging-house bed, I draw the
line. Absolutely, Bobby; I draw the line. Poor little empty
bed! It's – it's *morbid*, Bobby.'

'But of course he was thinking of Sargon,' said Tessy.
'You'll go to the police-court to-morrow, Bobby?'

'I'll go – in spite of Billy. I don't care if it is a disease.
I'm worried about that little man. I'm afraid. He's too
round-eyed for this cruel world.'

And next morning Bobby went. He went to Lemon
Square Court and sat through a frowsty morning and
waited for Sargon who never appeared. He heard all the
morning 'drunks' and such-like come up for judgment, a
case about stolen soda-water syphons, two matrimonial
differences, and all about the wilful smashing of a plate-
glass window with intent to rob, but nothing about Sargon.
The magistrate vanished and the court began to disperse.
He asked questions of a policeman who had never heard of
Sargon and the little trouble at the Rubicon Restaurant.
Had he come to the right court? the policeman asked.

Bobby hurried headlong to Minton Street. Minton Street, too, it seemed, had never heard of Sargon. It did not occur to Bobby to ask in either police station. He retired baffled. He tried to find something about Sargon in the evening newspapers; there was not a line about the Rubicon or him. Perhaps he had not been charged! He hurried back and rushed upstairs full of a vain surmise; the room was desolate, the window open, the map of the world on the floor. Had Sargon been spirited out of existence?

Next day brought neither Sargon nor news of Sargon. Bobby lay awake of nights.

After three full days Billy, who had been watching his friend furtively, remarked in a casual manner: 'Why don't you go and see the Head Panjandrum at the Lemon Square Police Station about it? He'd be sure to know if anyone does.'

Shown in to Inspector Mullins, Bobby found himself confronted by the same good-looking officer he had seen in the entrance hall of the Rubicon Restaurant. 'You're the young man who didn't happen to know anything about him, three nights ago,' said Inspector Mullins, not answering Bobby's questions.

Bobby explained the situation candidly.

'Doesn't help much now,' said the Inspector. 'Still it's all in order. We took him, in the exercise of our discretion, to the Workhouse Infirmary – for observation as to his mental state. Three clear days they keep them there. Then they're either certified or let go. Or charged.'

'Certified?' asked Bobby.

'As a lunatic,' said Inspector Mullins.

'And what happened to him?'

'Usual thing, I suppose. He was a pretty clear case. By this time he's a certified lunatic, I suppose, and either at Cummerdown Hill or on his way there. Or if that's full – somewhere else.'

'Phew!' said Bobby. 'Pretty quick.'

He sat disconcerted. 'Can I go and see him at Cummerdown Hill?' he asked.

'Probably not,' said Inspector Mullins. 'Seeing you're not a relation.'

'I'm interested in him.'

'It isn't your business.'

'Exactly. But I like him. And I don't think he's exactly mad. . . . Seems odd of his people – Do you know anything about his people? I might go and talk to them about him.'

'That's possible,' said the Inspector. 'I don't know who they are. You might find out at the Workhouse Infirmary or they might tell you from Cummerdown. I don't know. Very likely *they* don't know who his relations are. There's all sorts of such stragglers in the world. Possibly he hasn't any relations – the sort of relations, I mean, who would want to bother about him. My impression is that once a man or woman is certified and put away it's rather hard for an outsider to get through. But, as you say, you can but try. Sorry I can't tell you any more. I never saw him myself at all – except as he went past me. Not my affair. . . . Yes, our usual procedure in such a case. . . . Oh! no trouble. Good morning.'

Left sitting squarely, an embodiment of implacable and indifferent law and rule.

CHAPTER THE THIRD

The Journey of Sargon Underneath the World

§ 1

IT has been said in an earlier chapter that Mr. Preemby, after his wife's death, was like some seed which germinates and thrusts out bold and unexpected things. A new phase in that belated germination began as he walked through the London streets beside his captor policeman. If the thing had happened to Mr. Preemby while he was still Mr. Preemby, it would have been merely a dreadful, shameful horror. It would have been an insupportable experience, a thing to regret, a thing to get through and conceal and if possible obliterate from record and memory. If, again, it had happened in the early days of Sargon's dreams it would have been an occasion for an immense dramatic improvisation. He would have thought of the effect upon the spectators and passers-by, he would have posed and gesticulated and said profound, memorable words. But some power of growth had taken possession of him now and he did none of these things. He posed now neither to the world without nor to himself within. For the first time in his life almost he was looking directly at himself and at what he had done and what had befallen him, and so full of wonder was he at this ultimate discovery of reality that he forgot all the vast fabric of make-believe, imaginative response, and deliberate self-delusion, up which he had clambered to this new phase of vision. He walked so quietly through the lit streets that only the most observant noted he was in charge and that the policeman was on duty; to the rest he might have been any casual companion of a home-going policeman.

One determination had been released in this renascent mind with an extraordinary strength and clearness, that he

was not, and never would again be, that Albert Edward
Preemby who had launched him into existence. He was a
being called, it mattered not what, in reality, but for his
present purposes, Sargon, Sargon the Magnificent King.
The first concrete visions of Sumeria and his ancient
glories had passed now into the background of his mind.
He had not lost his belief in them at all, but they were now
ancient history to him, and even the revelation at the
boarding house seemed very far away. His ideas had
travelled long distances and gathered much in the past
week. The expectation of an immediate sensational splendour had been rudely shattered. The Power that had
called him had surprised him exceedingly, but had not
overwhelmed him. He knew quite clearly that he had to
be Sargon who lived not for himself but for the Whole
World, and that to relinquish or deny that was to perish
utterly. It had not seemed to be necessary to him that his
own faith should be tried, but manifestly the Power had
determined that it should be tried. And manifestly he was
to be put through some austere process of preparation
before he entered into his Empire. He was to know what
prison was and to stand a trial. He would be asked to deny
himself.

What should he say to them? I am not He – I am not
Him – which was it? I am not Him you suppose I am.
He muttered it to himself.

'Whassay?' said the policeman.

'Nothing. Is it much further?' asked Sargon.

It was just round the corner. Sargon found himself in a
little austere room with half a dozen quite amiable but
slightly disrespectful men in uniform. He was asked his
name and address by one who sat at a table. 'Sargon,' he
said. 'Sargon the First.'

'No Christian name?'

'Pre-Christian,' said Sargon.

'No given name, I mean,' said the questioner.

'No.'

'And the address?'

'None at present.'

'Just anywhere?'

Sargon did not answer.

'Case for Gifford Street,' said a voice behind him.

'Memory case or something,' said the man at the table. 'Anyhow, it's Gifford Street.'

Sargon reflected. 'What's Gifford Street?' he asked.

''Ospital. Where they'll give you a bit of a rest and quiet.'

'But I want to meet a magistrate in open court. I have a message. I am in no need of rest or quiet.'

'They'll tell you all about that at Gifford Street. Buxton, will you take 'im round?'

'But I am perfectly well! Why should I go to hospital?'

'Routine I suppose,' said the seated policeman and gave his mind to other things.

§ 2

Queer! Why should it be a hospital? The way the Power was treating him was a strange way. He had to submit to the Power; he had to maintain himself Sargon. Still he could have wished for more explicitness.

He was so turned inward now that he went along beside Constable Buxton, not noting the streets nor the traffic nor the passers-by. Presently they were at a door in a high wall, within which there were buildings. Then they were in a little office and a large, grey-faced porter looked at him and exchanged muttered explanations with the constable. Then they were going across a wide yard and through large doors into a corridor where there was an unoccupied stretcher and two or three nurses in uniform. They came to a little glazed-in office and Sargon was asked to sit down on a bench against a wall while there was telephoning. Constable Buxton hovered down the corridor as though the task was nearly done.

A small bright-eyed man in a grey suit came and looked at Sargon. For some moments they regarded each other in silence. 'Well?' said the man in the grey suit.

'My name is Sargon. I do not know why I have been brought here. Is this a hospital? I understand it is. I am not ill.'

'You may be ill without knowing it.'

'No.'

'We just want to have you here for a bit to have a look at you.'

Sargon shrugged his shoulders.

A very big man with exaggerated shoulders and a large, clean-shaven, intensely self-satisfied looking face appeared. He had a wide, thin-lipped mouth, protruding grey eyes and highly oiled and entirely subjugated sandy hair with an army 'quif' on the forehead.

'Busy evening,' he said. 'This is number three.'

'Pretty full then,' said the small man in grey.

'Too full,' said Mr. Jordan. 'You don't know where you are. This *'im?'* he asked and indicated Sargon by creasing his thick neck and depressing the corner of his mouth towards him.

'This,' said the little man in grey to Sargon, 'is Mr. Jordan. He's going to show you just where you have to go and just what you have to do.'

Immediately, instinctively, Sargon disliked Mr. Jordan. But he stood up obediently because his idea of submission to the Power seemed in some way to overlap and include this new coercion. Mr. Jordan produced a voice of flat, oily, insincere amiability. 'You come along, Old Chap, with me,' he said. 'We'll make you comfortable all right 'fyou don't give no trouble.'

They went round a corner and up a cheerless stone stair-case that turned back on itself; they came to a landing and double doors with glass panes in them that opened upon a very long, dark passage lit by a single very remote light. And suddenly it appeared to Sargon that behind him and already distant lay that outer world of freedom, the streets and the lights, the coming and going of people and things, the endless chance encounters, the events and the spec-tacle of life to which the Power had sent him, and before him were dark and narrow and dreadful experiences. Why should he turn his back thus voluntarily on the great outer world he had come to save? Was this again only another mistake he was making? He took a step or so away from Jordan and faced him.

'No,' he said. 'I do not want to go further into this place. I do not wish it. Let me return. I have disciples to call and many things to do.'

The full moon of Jordan's face displayed incredulous astonishment that passed into fierceness. '*Wot?*' he said.

He left a tremendous pause after 'Wot' and then spoke very rapidly. 'None of your tricks *'ere*, you thundering old Bastard.' With a swift movement his huge, raw, red hand gripped Sargon by the upper arm. His thin lips were retracted to show his teeth; his eyes seemed popping out. He gripped not to hold but to pinch and compress and injure, and he dug fingers in between muscle and bone, so that Sargon stared at him with dilated eyes and uttered a sharp, involuntary cry of pain.

The grip relaxed from the acutely painful to the merely uncomfortable, and the big face came down close to Sar-gon's. It was manifest that Mr. Jordan had been regaling himself on cheese and cocoa. 'Don't you try it on, you Old Fool! Don't you blooming-well try it on. Whatever it is, don't you try it on 'ere. You're right enough to understand what I say. See? You do exactly wot you're told 'ere. You do exactly wot you're told. You do your best to avoid givin' trouble and I'll do my best ditto. But if you start doin' tricks – Gawd 'elp you! See?'

And he crushed the arm again.

'Understan'?'

The blue eyes seemed to assent.

'Down that passage, blast you!' said Mr. Jordan.

A distressed and wondering and yet not absolutely abject Sargon was taken to a wet and untidy bathroom in which a broken chair, pools of water, great splashings on the wall, and some crumpled towels in the corner suggested a recent struggle. There he was made to undress and take a tepid bath, dried with a towel that had already been in action, put into a grey nightgown that was doubtfully clean, a grey shoddy dressing-gown that certainly wasn't, and a pair of down-at-heel slippers two sizes too big, and so garbed, was led by Mr. Jordan, a little propitiated now by alert obedience, into the ward in which he was to pass the night.

A rufous man with very light eyelashes appeared.

''Ere 'e is, Mr. 'Iggs,' said Mr. Jordan.

'I've got his bed ready,' said Mr. Higgs. ''Ow many more of 'em?'

'Perfec' shower of 'em,' said Mr. Jordan.

'Three,' said Mr. Higgs.

'Well,' said Mr. Jordan. 'So long.'

'So long,' said Mr. Higgs.

Neither of them addressed the Lord of the Whole World directly. He might have been a parcel passed from hand to hand.

§ 3

When Sargon entered the Observation Ward of the Gifford Street Infirmary his sense of having left life, ordinary current life, far away behind him, beyond these grey passages and corridors and staircases and glass offices and high walls and little doors, was enormously reinforced. Never had he seen anything so emptily bleak and cheerless as this place. A heartless great dingy room it was, with green-grey distempered walls discoloured in patches, lit by a few bare lights that gave neither high-lights nor shadows. Black night and a greasily lit brick wall stared in through uncurtained windows. Half-way down the length of the place projecting pieces of wall suggested that two former rooms had been thrown into one. The floor was of polished bare boards. Far off was a table set against the wall with two or three torn and crumpled magazines thereon, and at the end an empty fireplace. In the near half, on either side, there were iron bedsteads in rows, twenty or thirty perhaps altogether. There was a foul smell in the air, faint and yet indescribably offensive, a fæcal smell mixed with a heavy soapy odour.

Even had it been unoccupied, this cold, large, evil-smelling room would have seemed a strange inhospitable place to Sargon. For it had always been the lot of Mr. Preemby, even in the days of his early poverty, to live snug, to have carpets, even if they were shabby carpets, under his feet, and an encumbrance of furniture and silly human pictures and brackets and things about him on the walls. Here in this harsh plainness it was as though the fussy, accumulative, home-making imagination of man had never been.

But the strange soulless atmosphere of the place was but

227

the first instant impression of Sargon. It was followed by a far more vivid and terrible realization, that this place was inhabited by beings who were only at the first glance men. Then as one looked again it became clear that they were not exactly men, they did not look up at his entry as men should, or they showed their awareness of him by queer unnatural movements. Several were in bed; others were dressed in shabby and untidy clothes and either sat on their beds or were seated in chairs about the lower part of the room. One individual only was in motion; a grave-faced young man who was walking with an appearance of concentrated method to and fro in a restricted circle in the far corner of the ward. Another sat and seemed to remove a perpetually recurrent cobweb from his face by a per-petually repeated gesture. Two men were jammed behind the table against the wall, and one, a fleshy lout with a shining pink skin and curling red hair on his bare chest, was making violent gestures, hammering the table with a freckled fist, talking in a voice that rose and sank and occa-sionally broke into curses, while the other, a sallow-com-plexioned, cadaverous individual, seemed to be sunken in profound despair. In one of the beds close at hand a young man with a shock of black hair and an expression of fatuous satisfaction, that changed with dramatic suddenness to triumphant fierceness or insinuating lucidity, sat up and gesticulated and composed and recited an interminable poem – something in the manner of Browning. It was running in this fashion:

> 'God shall smite them
> And blight them
> They may prevail but God will requite them
> Light 'em.
> Burn 'em to ashes and burn 'em to atoms
> Atoms!

Burning atoms – exactly like stars. See?
Stars in the void and all over the place.
Atoms galore and God can't show his face.
(Triumphant discovery.)
He *hasn't* a face.
That's it! That's it, my Boys!
Atheists wrong and theology wrong,
Plainly and simply here's every one wrong!
And I have to tell 'em!
There's a God, *item* one, but he hasn't a face
So he can't show his face.
That's the kink of it.
Naturally every one thinks he's *non est*
But he's there as I know to my cost;
For I'm lost
But I've shown how it is all the same.
No face – what a game!
I found God in the void
Unmasked and a little annoyed.
Quod erat demonstrandum X.L. . . .'

'There's your bed,' said Mr. Higgs at Sargon's elbow, shoving him slightly.

Sargon moved a little unwillingly, his puzzled eyes still on the talker.

'You'll hear enough of him before you're done, Old Chap,' said Mr. Higgs. 'Hop into bed now.'

Impelled partly by the arm of Mr. Higgs and partly by his natural disposition to please, Sargon got into bed. Mr. Higgs assisted him in a rough brotherly fashion. But before Sargon could pull up the clothes about him Mr. Higgs, glancing over his shoulder, became aware of something that was happening down the room – Sargon could not see what.

In an instant the genial authoritativeness of Mr. Higgs

gave way to rage. 'Yaaps, you dirty old devil!' said Mr. Higgs. 'You're at it again!'

He quitted Sargon and ran down the room very swiftly. Sargon sat up in bed to see what was happening. Three or four of the other patients did the same. A very dirty old man with a face of extreme misery, who was sitting in a chair, was seized upon and bumped up and down and hit several times with great vigour by Mr. Higgs. Then Mr. Higgs departed and returned, still uttering admonitions, with a pail and a rag.

For Mr. Higgs was not only an attendant on the mentally afflicted but also, on account of economy, the floor-scrubber and general cleaner of the ward. He had been trained in the navy to ideals of a speckless brightness and he scrubbed better than he attended.

'Lie down there!' cried Mr. Higgs returning up the ward with his pail. 'It ain't nothing to do with you.'

The Lord of the World lay down.

§ 4

It was an extremely uninteresting ceiling to look at except for a streak of yellowish stains, but it was better to look at the ceiling for a time than to look too much at these distressing people around him. They were distressing and distracting, and Sargon knew that it was urgently necessary not to be distracted, but to think over his position very carefully before anything further happened to him. All this rush of consequences had been so unexpected, preposterous and violent since – a few hours ago – he had surveyed London from the dome of Saint Paul's and decided that the moment had come to take hold of his Lordship of the World, that he perceived he might very conceivably be overwhelmed. How serene and distant now was that spectacle of London spread out under the amber sunshine between its far blue hills and its shining river, with its dense clusters of shipping and the black ant-currents of folk below. From that he had come swiftly, inevitably, to this echoing prison. For prison he saw it was. He knew quite well that these men around him were demented men and that he had been seized upon as a lunatic, but he thought that the Workhouse Observation Ward in which he was, was a lunatic asylum already. In his wildest imaginations he had never imagined the Power over all things could treat him thus. The possibility of a brief interlude in prison, of a severe but very public and triumphant trial, had entered his mind; but not that he might be hustled away out of the possibility of any such appeal. He had to think his position out anew, to discover what all this monstrous experience was intended to show and to teach him, and what he had to do to meet this strange occasion.

And it was very difficult to do this with a raucous voice down the room uttering foul threats about the ward attendant and a great fist beating the table in sudden storms and with that smooth, fluctuating, unending recitation nearer at hand, that cosmic poem, now almost inaudible – so that one strained to catch the words – and now in high-pitched delight. For long stretches it was just incoherent jumble and Sargon would hold it almost completely out of his attention while he pursued his own perplexities, and then it would rush together into something that challenged its way to mingle with his inmost thoughts.

'Filthy old Nature, she drives us amain;
One goad is lust and the other goad pain.
And so we get back to old nowhere again.
Nowhere to start from and nowhere again.

Want and be hurt, want and be hurt,
Out of the dirt you came, back to the dirt.
Hunger for dirt and dirty regretting
Dirty our feeding and dirty begetting.
Smear yourself, paint yourself, wear a fine shirt,
Put a brave face on it, Yah! – you are dirt.'

'Now is that true?' asked Sargon of himself. Is that true? Dirt? What is dirt? But no! he must not wander off after this mad raving! What was it he had been thinking about? He had been asking why had the Power thrust him into this dreadful place? Why had the Power brought him to this place? If only the man would stop that improvisation of his for a little while it might be possible to think that out. Why had he been given over to the commands of Jordan and Higgs to live among the madmen and – sudden fantastic side question! – why had *they*?

If only that poem would cease! If only that voice would fade to silence! It was now mere rubble and rubbish, as though thought had been broken up with a pickaxe and loaded in carts and shot down a slope. Don't listen to it, Sargon! Don't listen to it! Concentrate!

In his endeavour to concentrate, Sargon forgot even Higgs. He sat up in bed and drew his knees nearly to his chin and thought.

He was Sargon; that was the great issue. He had to remain Sargon. He was probably in this place of trouble and torment because of the conflict between his being Sargon and the possibility of his relapsing into Preemby. The Power had called him to be Sargon and to serve and suffer for and at last to rule the Whole World, but manifestly it was not a simple direct call. There was something working in opposition to this destiny, an Anti-Power, opposed to the Power, which was trying to put him back to Preemby and Preembyism, to being little and insignificant, to living obscurely and to no purpose and so at last to dying and becoming utterly and finally dead. That Anti-Power it was that had been permitted to bring him here, to frighten and torment him, to din mad rhymes into his ears, to urge upon him in a monotonous persistent voice that he was dirt and that God was without a face, and a multitude of suchlike blasphemies. But they were not true. The Anti-Power might talk and talk – would God there could be a respite from his talking! – but the truth was outside this place and greater than this place and altogether comprehended it. He was one, Sargon was one, from the beginning in Sumeria, in many lands and now here, the same spirit, the ruler who serves; he was one just as London was one when it was seen from on high up above there, endlessly multitudinous yet drawn together into a single personality. And so was the whole world one. To be Preemby was to be like a wretched little back street house down below there, swallowed up in the general effect. Never more could he be Preemby, even if he would. That was what he had to keep hold of. He could only be Sargon by denying Preemby – even though he had to face the pains of death.

Yet all the while the Anti-Power was insulting life and himself through that disordered poet and his recitation. The man had now fallen under the spell of a fascinating but detestable word, if one may call such a thing a word, 'Tra-la-la.'

> 'Tra-la-la. Tra-la-la.
> That is the note of it.
> Get the full gloat of it.
> Tra-la-la. Tra-la-la.
> All times and places
> Happy derision for Gods without faces.
> Tra-la-la sunshine or Tra-la-la rain.

Eat, drink, and kiss 'em and at it again.
Tra-la-la. Tra-la-la.
Kiss 'em and Kiss 'em and at it again.
At it again!
Tra-la-la.'

He varied his recitation with a loud explosive noise made by his lips on the back of his hand.

'Pray don't think me cynical,' he said to Sargon. 'It is just pure Joy de Vive.'

Sargon could not stand it any longer. This was damnable teaching to fling out before the very regenerator of mankind. He suddenly thrust out a pointing finger. 'You are wrong!' he said loudly and sharply.

The poet stared for a minute and with a gesture of salutation said: 'Tra-la-la-la.'

'I tell you life is real,' cried Sargon. 'Life is immense. Life is full of meaning and order. I have come to tell you and all men so.'

The poet interrupted smilingly and politely with:

'Tra-la-la,
Tra-la-la,
Life is a hiccup and life is a sneeze,
A smell from a dunghill borne on the breeze,
A thing of no moment – so do as you please!
Tra-la-la. Tra-la-la.'

He was going on, but Sargon would not hear him. He lifted his voice to drown his antagonist. 'I tell you, you poor soul! you are utterly wrong and blind,' he said. 'For the light has come to me and understanding is mine. You are not the lost thing you deem you are, or at least you need not be. No! I, too, was a lost thing such as you are, a little while ago. I, too, thought I was a grain, a fragment, a thing of no account. But the call has come to me, and I have been called to call others to take part with me in a new awakening. I have had a vision and I have seen the world like one who awakens from a long sleep. All things are joined together and work together and continue for ever.'

The poet wrinkled up his nose and waved his hand at Sargon as who should wave aside some object of offence. 'Tra-la-la,' he shouted.

'All things I tell you are joined together and work to-gether – '

'Tra-la-la,' louder.

'I tell you,' much louder.

'Shuddup there,' cried the loud and wrathful voice of Sanity embodied in Mr. Higgs.

'You'll have the whole ward jabbering in a minute,' said Mr. Higgs, approaching and addressing Sargon in tones of earnest expostulation. 'Shud Dup.'

And after a brief pause of reflection the Lord of the Whole World obeyed.

With a gesture of extreme dignity he indicated to Higgs that his crude demands were conceded.

'That's o'right,' said Higgs. '*You* can hold in if you want to. So you better. *He* can't.'

The poet went on in a soft insinuating undertone, reviling and mocking Sargon's faith to a refrain of: 'Tra-la-la. Tra-la-la.'

§ 5

Sargon sat up in bed, motionless now except that his head turned slowly to look at the people about him, and silent. His recent outbreak had in some way assuaged the exas-peration of that endless recitation. It continued, now crazily persuasive, now strident and vehement, now a mere babble of words, it flowed past him and over him; it was now manifestly directed at him, but he was able to disregard it. He sat up and looked at the people about him and contemplated the vast dreadful hours that plainly lay before him.

He did not look beyond the coming night. That alone he foresaw as an eternity.

He knew that this harsh, naked electric light which prized up his eyelids however tightly he closed them, would be glaring all night; he knew that because he had noted a glance that Higgs had directed at the violent man with red hair. Instantly he knew that Higgs was afraid of that red-haired man with the shining pink skin and would never dare to have the ward in darkness, never dare to have even shade in it, whatever the custom or the regulations might be. And also he understood why ever and again Higgs went out of the room at the upper end; he went out to assure himself of the presence of Jordan or some such other helper, within call. Yes, this light would certainly keep on all night and the poet seemed as likely to keep on, and there would be occasional outbreaks of table hammering and shouting from the red-haired man and from another man who uttered a sudden flat shout ever and again. And there would be misadventures of various sorts; noises and comings and goings. So he might just as well sit up and think as lie down and make hopeless attempts to slumber. One could always think. Of course if one was too tired one would cease thinking onward, one would just think round and round, but it would be impossible not to go on waking and thinking. There was no sleeping in this place. Eyes, ears, nose were all too much offended. Did anyone ever sleep here, mad or sane?

There was nothing for him to do, therefore, but to sit up and think, sit up and think, doze perhaps and think into a dream, until some unexpected jolt or jar brought him back to his thinking.

The longest night must end at last.

Then suddenly Sargon, between sleeping and waking, saw something horrible. At least it struck upon his nerves as horrible. Two beds away from him there lay an extremely emaciated young man and his head was lifted up. It was not supported by pillows; it was six inches above the pillow. It was held up in an attitude that it was painful to realize. The young man's face expressed a serenely proud satisfaction at this fantastic rigidity. It was incredible. Was there such a thing as an invisible pillow? Or was this a delusion of Sargon's eyes, a waking dream?

In the bed beyond another man was lying down with his wakeful face towards Sargon. His eyes met Sargon's. Neither man said a word nor made a gesture, but to each came infinite comfort. For the eyes each encountered were as sane as his own and each gave support to the other. It is so, they said. It is strange, but your eyes are not deceiving you. That is the form of that young man's affliction.

Sargon nodded. The other sane man nodded in reply and then turned over in his bed as a reassured child might do, to sleep. But could he sleep?

Sargon's gaze went round the ward with a new discovery. Yes, several of these others might be sane – sane as he was – and caught like himself. There was another man across the corridor with a little beard, a very, very mournful man, but he also had sane eyes.

To-morrow Sargon must go and talk to these others and tell them about himself and discuss this dreadful situation, but not now because Higgs would certainly interfere. Many things had already conspired to annoy Higgs. It was plain he could be easily irritated and it would be well not to annoy him further. For the present one must just sit and think.

What were the mad and what did madness mean?

Why had he been lifted up by the Supreme Power, out of the common acts and imaginations of his daily life, to a knowledge of his immortal being, why had he been shown his endless destinies and a vision of the whole world as his sphere, merely to be cast out of life and light and freedom forthwith into this grey underworld of the demented? It could not be that this was for nothing. It must signify.

And then the wind of a second question blew across his mind. The Power that had called him, and called him it would seem only to bring him into this place, had also brought all these others to this same dreadfulness. *Why?* For him it might be a trial but what was it for these others, whose souls had indeed dissolved and gone? What was the Power doing with them?

The whole scheme of things in Sargon's mind began to shudder and dissolve. If the Power had not done this, then it must be the Anti-Power had done it. There must be an Anti-Power as strong almost as the Power then, able to snatch men out of life into confusion, indignity, and death for ever. Or else – *there was Nothing*!

He sat quite still with his chin on his knuckles and eyes staring blankly at the last black possibility.

Was the whole of this call and this mission of his a deception and a delusion? Had he been cheated at Tunbridge Wells when the call first came to him to arise and awake? Were those memories of Sumeria no more than dreams? Was he indeed just Albert Edward Preemby – gone crazy? In a crazy, pointless universe of commonplace inanities? If so he was indeed the most foolish of living men. He had left his comfort and securities, sound though insignificant; he had run away from his dear Christina Alberta – to obey a Power that was nothing more than his own imagination and to follow a phantom end. For days he had been shutting Christina Alberta out of his thoughts; she was a sceptic, an ally of the Anti-Power. Now she came back, over-valiant and rash, but just a girl. He had left her to shift for herself, left her beyond reach of his reproofs and cautions. What was she doing? What evil and danger might not be overtaking her even now? It had not occurred to him before that his disappearance might distress and endanger her. Now he saw plainly that it must have done so.

The enemy came and argued frankly with him. 'You have been a fool, Albert Edward Preemby,' said the enemy. 'You have got yourself into a position of great danger and discomfort, you have deserted your own proper life for a horror of nothingness. Go back. Go back while there is still a chance of going back.'

But could he go back?

Yes. That could be done. So easily! He could say plainly that now he remembered his proper name. He could ask to see the doctor or the director or whoever it was presided over Jordan and Higgs and their colleagues; he could give his name and the address of the studio and his bankers' address and the address of the laundry and so forth, speaking very plainly and quietly, he could admit that he had behaved strangely but that the fit was over, and so he would pass out of these grim shadows back into the world. It would rejoice the heart of Christina Alberta. . . .

He thought of that alert, kind, slightly antagonistic figure. If only he could see it now! Coming down the long ward to him, to rescue, to release. . . .

Then he would be just Preemby again for the rest of his days, comfortably Preemby, Preemby the bystander, Preemby the onlooker, the ineffective, speechless man in the background of the noisy studio. But certain things would be at an end. He would never go to any museums

239

again or browse in the dark shadows of bookshops over dusty forgotten books about vanished cities and enigmatical symbols. He would think no more of the wonder and mystery of Atlantis and of the measurements of the Pyramids and of all the high riddles of the past and the future. There would be no more wonder in his life at all, for he had sought to enter into wonder and had found it delusion. Those things would be old tales and fancies of things that would never arrive. Past and future would be dead for him. The days would be dull and empty as they had never been before. The bladder of his life would be pricked. . . .

And the other way lay pain, indignity, rough treatment, vile food, filthy circumstances, trials that might break him – but with the Power still beckoning.

He thought of the things that belonged to Sargon; of the Power, of cities that were like great single persons, of the Whole World, of the mystical promise of the stars, of all these things he must renounce now and be Preemby, Preemby plain and sensible, to the end of his days, if he would go out of this place. He sat as it seemed to him for an immense time, still and brooding, though his answer was already definite in his mind. And at last he spoke. 'No,' he said in a hoarse voice that was almost a shout. 'I am Sargon, Sargon the servant of God – and the Whole World is mine!'

§ 6

Long after midnight Sargon was still sitting up in that bleak greasy glare amidst the noises and disorder about him. He had lost all count of time; his watch had been taken from him. Somewhen in the small hours he was praying. And at times he wept a little.

He prayed. Sometimes he made sentences and whispered them to himself and sometimes the sentences never got to words but passed through his mind like serpents that are seen through deep, dark water. 'Great is the task thou hast put upon me. I see now I am not worthy, O Master, to do the least thing that is required of me. I am not worthy. I am a petty man and a foolish man and all I have done so far is folly. But thou hast called me, knowing my folly. Forgive thou my folly and help thou my faith.' Silent and still he sat with tears upon his cheeks. 'Any punishment and any trial,' he whispered at last, 'only that thou shouldst not desert me and vanish out of my world.'

He prayed that the Power would yet make him the servant of the world and added falteringly and feebly, 'even as it was in the ancient days.'

For had there ever been those ancient days? Sumeria was now very far away from him, and the white towns and the blue river and the river galleys had faded and the wor-shipping crowds were just a faint smear upon his mind no stronger than the fading memory of a dream. He said nothing for a time, and then in a very loud whisper he said: 'Help thou my unbelief.'

Sometimes he prayed in a whisper and sometimes he prayed silently and sometimes he sat quite still. Higgs came and looked at him once or twice but did not interfere with him. The poem in the adjacent bed still went on, but it had now become a mere rhyming stream of blasphemous obscenities.

For a time after he had made an end to his praying, Sargon must have slept; he must have slept because he was awakened by the dawn. It did not come gradually; he awoke to it.

A cold, shadowless light filled the ward and the electric lamps that had seemed so bright were just luminous orange-yellow threads. And Higgs was standing in the doorway peering intently at the red-haired man, who was lying with his head on the table as though he were asleep – but perhaps only pretending to be asleep.

§ 7

It was on the afternoon of the following day that two strangers came to see Sargon. He was taken to them and they talked a little with him, and then chiefly with each other. Higgs was off duty but Jordan hovered in the background.

Neither of these gentlemen explained their business with Sargon to him. One of them was a short man in a black coat; he wore a gold watch-chain and a rich-looking tie with a jewelled pin; he had a gold pince-nez, a little pointed nose, a fat, clean-shaven white face, and a mouth like an oblique spade-thrust in a lump of dough. He spoke with something between a sniff and a lisp, and he was evidently rather in a hurry and annoyed at having been called in to see Sargon. The other was large and grey and worn-looking; he impressed Sargon in some indefinable way as being a medical man who had private troubles. He seemed to consider himself in charge of the conversation, and would occasionally refer upon some point of fact to the hovering Jordan.

'Understand,' said the pasty-faced man, 'you wanted to give some sort of dinner party to all sorts of people. Eh? – at the Rubicon. I suppose it came on you sort of sudden like. Eh?'

'I wished to confer with certain people,' said Sargon. 'It may have been a mistake on my part.'

'No doubt it was a mistake, Mr. – Mr. –'

'Won't 'ave a Mister to it,' said Jordan from the background. 'Calls 'isself Sargon.'

The doctor became very acute in his manner. 'Now isn't that some sort of historical name?' he asked with a sideways searching look.

'It is,' said Sargon.

'But it isn't *your* name, you know.'

'Possibly not. I mean – It is my only name.'

'That's a bit of an answer, that is,' said the pasty-faced man. 'My *word!*'

'What is your *real* name,' asked the doctor persuasively.

'Sargon.'

'Not Mr. A. E. Preemby.'

Sargon started and stared, possibly with a certain wildness in his eyes. 'With God's help, *No!*' he said.

'Was it ever Mr. Preemby?' asked the doctor.

'That does not matter now. That is of no importance now.'

'It may be of *some* importance,' said the pasty-faced man.

'And now you're a King or a Lord or something and you own the world?' said the doctor.

Sargon made no answer. He felt he was in a net.

The doctor turned to Jordan and beckoned him in a whisper. Only one sentence came to Sargon's ears. ''Iggs 'eard it,' said Mr. Jordan.

'Aren't you called Sargon the Magnificent?' asked the doctor.

Sargon bent his head in sorrow. 'Better were it to call me Sargon the Unworthy. For in many things I have failed.'

The pasty-faced man looked at the doctor. 'Haven't we had about enough of this?'

'My conclusions are clear,' said the doctor. 'In fact, I have the certificate ready.'

'If you're satisfied, Dr. Manningtree, I am. If I'm to see those other fellers.'

'I've got all the papers in my room,' said the doctor. 'Right-o,' said the pasty-faced man.

'It's very good of you to come to-day. I wouldn't have bothered you until to-morrow but we are really getting overcrowded here. One chap's decidedly dangerous. The attendants here don't like the look of him. You need only just see him for a moment. Or any of them. All clear cases for summary reception orders.'

They spoke now as if Sargon were not present or as if he were an inanimate object. And indeed for them he had become so; he had passed for them already out of the comity of mankind.

'Why have you been talking to me?' asked Sargon suddenly with a vague fear of what had been said and done developing in his mind.

The doctor's manner altered. He spoke to Sargon as one might speak to a small child. 'You'll be going back to bed now,' he said. 'Jordan!'

'But I want to know.'

'Go with Mr. Jordan.'

'What are these papers you speak about?'

The doctor turned his back on Sargon without an answer and the man with the pasty face opened the door to depart. Sargon made a step towards them, but Jordan laid hold of his arm.

And while Sargon was being steered back to bed, firmly rather than gently, in the grip of Jordan, the justice and the doctor filled in and signed the forms that were necessary to deprive him of nearly every right he possessed as a human being. For there is no trial by jury and no writ of habeas-corpus in Britain for the unfortunate charged with insanity. He may not plead in public and there is no one to whom he may appeal. He may write complaints but they will be neglected; his most urgent expostulations will be disregarded in favour of any dull attendant's asseverations. He is handed over to the nearly autocratic control of under-educated, ill-paid, ill-fed, and overworked attendants. Every night and every day seems endless to him at first, and then the nights and days fall into a sort of routine and become unimportant and pass away more and more rapidly. He is almost always kept in a state of bodily discomfort, always rather ill from the ill-prepared and sometimes tainted food, and much incommoded by clumsy drugging and particularly by the administration of violent purgatives. In croton oil alone are our asylums truly generous. He has excellent reason for fearing many of his fellow inmates and for a servile obedience to the attendants in charge of him. A medical superintendent hovers in the background: a medical staff with no special training in mental science. They pass through the wards at the appointed times, avoiding trouble, seeing as little as possible.

And, after all, what can they do? They cannot raise the expenditure upon food or increase the number or salaries of the attendants. They are appointed to save and not to spend the ratepayers' money. The attendants work together and protect each other; they must hang together; many of them go in fear of the violent cases. Occasionally, after due notice, a visiting magistrate will pay a formal visit to the asylum. Everything is put in order for the occasion. The inmate with a grievance dares not accost him or does not know how to accost him nor how to frame his complaint. The attendants are at hand to interrupt, embarrass, and explain. So, with no possibility of redress, the poor half-lunatic will be roughly handled, badly fed, and coarsely clothed, and night and day he will have no other familiar company than the insane. It is bad enough for the sane to be afflicted by the vagaries, the violence, the exasperating mechanisms, the incoherences of the truly demented, but what must it be for those upon whom the penumbra of that same shadow has fallen? They have no privacy; no escape from those others; no peace. Our world herds these discards together out of sight, walls them up, spends so little upon them that they are neither properly fed nor properly looked after, and does its brave hopeful best to forget all about them.

And our Sargon, who even in the outer world of usage and freedom was sometimes a little at a loss, must now go on into this dark underworld. For two days more he will be kept in the Gifford Street Observation Ward awaiting the convenience of the authorities; then in the company of four other prisoners he will be sent to a still bleaker and more desolate and hopeless confinement within the clustering buildings and walls and railings of Cummerdown Hill.

So he passes now for a time out of sight of everyday mankind, and so also for a time he shall pass out of this story. It would be insufferable to tell with any fulness his daily tale of discomfort and indignity.

Book the Third

THE RESURRECTION OF SARGON,
KING OF KINGS

CHAPTER THE FIRST

Christina Alberta in Search of a Father

§ 1

HITHERTO Christina Alberta had faced life with a bold, disdainful, and successful gesture. The discretions and scruples of others were not for her. She had seen no reason for their prudent hesitations, their conventions and restraints. Now for the first time she knew dismay. Her Daddy had vanished into a world that she suddenly realized could be immensely cruel. Teddy was rotten, so plainly rotten that only a fool wrapped up in her own sensations would have touched him. She lay awake for most of the night after her Daddy vanished, biting her hands and damning Teddy. Lambone the great friend was lazy, incompetent, and futile. Harold and Fay seemed already a little tired of her misfortune and vaguely disposed to blame her for bringing her Daddy to London. She had no one else to whom she could turn. No one remained to her—except Christina Alberta herself, feeling a little soiled now and more than a little afraid. 'But what am I to *do*?' she asked the night, again and again, in her stuffy but artistic little bedroom.

Among the other disadvantages of her position she had less than a pound of ready money.

It has to be recorded that for two whole days Christina Alberta did not even take the obvious step of going to the police. She had a queer instinctive knowledge of the danger of bringing the police and the social system generally to bear upon her odd little Daddy. She had an innate distrust of official human beings. It was Paul Lambone who induced her to go to the police. He had the grace to be ashamed of his unhelpfulness, and after an interval of two clear days he came round to the Lonsdale Mews to offer his generous but sluggish help once more. He caught her having tea with Fay.

'Christina Alberta,' he said, looking a very large comfortable figure of sorrow, 'I've been worrying and worrying about you all the time. I didn't help enough. I thought he'd come back of his own accord and that all the fuss was a little premature. Have you heard anything?'

Christina Alberta was torn between the desire to snap his head off and a realization that he was, after his fashion, quite sincerely friendly to her and could be very useful.

'*Say* it!' said Lambone. 'You'll be better, my dear, after you've said it and then we can talk matters over.'

He got the reassurance of a smile. He brightened visibly. He was the sort of man who would hate to feel hated even by a cockroach. 'I won't sit in that chair, thanks,' he said to Fay. 'It's too comfortable. And at any moment we may think of something and I may have to leap up and act.' 'Spartan,' he said, sitting down.

'Eh?' said Fay.

'Spartan. My doctor tells me to say it before every meal and especially before tea. I don't know why. Magic or Coué or something. Are these things cocoanut cakes? I thought so. . . . Good they are. And what are we going to do about it, Christina Alberta?'

He became sane and helpful and more and more like the man who wrote *What to Do on a Hundred and One Occasions*. He made Christina Alberta admit to bankruptcy, and made it clear to her that it was her duty to accept a loan of twenty-five pounds from him. He then dealt with the point about reporting the disappearance to the police, and convinced Christina Alberta upon that. If Mr. Preemby had fallen into bad hands the sooner the police looked for him the better. But he did not think that likely; he was much more inclined to the idea that Preemby had made a disturbance and been taken up. He guessed he would be dealt with as a mental case. He had consulted those useful books *The Justice of the Peace* and the *Encyclopædia Britannica*, and displayed the excellence of his mental digestion. Christina Alberta perceived that he had in him the makings of a competent barrister.

He carried off Christina Alberta in a taxi to Scotland Yard. 'Either they'll tell us there or tell us where we shall be told,' he said.

Fay was impressed by the originality of that. 'Now if it was a lost umbrella,' she said, 'I could understand it. But I'd never have thought of going to Scotland Yard for a lost father.'

By six Mr. Preemby had been traced to Gifford Street. But there was no seeing him at Gifford Street. He had been certified as a lunatic and he was bound, the attendant thought but wasn't quite sure, for Cummerdown Hill. Paul Lambone tried to be dignified and important and to prevail over the attendant and extract further information, but not very successfully. In the end he and Christina Alberta departed with little more than one immense discouraging fact. They would not be able to see Mr. Preemby nor to learn anything very material about his condition until the next visiting day, whenever that might be, at Cummerdown Hill. Then if he was 'fit to be visited,' they might go and see him. The attendant was rigid in his statements and had the air of disliking both Lambone and Christina Alberta extremely.

As they came away from Gifford Street Christina Alberta observed that Lambone was angry. She had never seen him angry before. It was a very transitory phase. There was an unusual depth of pink in his cheeks.

'Dog in office,' he said. 'Just there to annoy people – anxious people. One would think . . . man in my position . . . certain standing. . . . Some attention. . . . Any other country but this, Man of letters has respect.'

Christina Alberta agreed mutely.

'Manners in a public official – primary.'

'He was detestable,' said Christina Alberta.

'Not at the end of my resources,' said Lambone.

Christina Alberta waited.

'Ought to have gone to Devizes in the first place. Knows more about mental cases and lunacy law than any other man in London. Wonderful fellow. I'll go back to my flat and I'll ring him up and make an appointment. Then he'll put us wise about the whole business. And I want you to meet him anyhow. You'll appreciate Devizes. Come to think of it, you're remarkably like him.'

'How?'

'Got the Life Force and all that. And physically like him. Very. The same nose – much the same profile.'

'It's a nose more suitable for a man,' said Christina Alberta. 'I suppose *he* carries it off all right!'

'It's a damned good nose, Christina Alberta,' said Lambone. 'It's a valiant nose. Don't you break down to any modesty about it. It was your nose attracted me first to you. You'll spike a husband with it yet, and he'll adore it and follow it even as you do. Nowadays women have to be free and individualized; they have got to have features and distinction. The days of the wanton curl and the swan neck and complexion have gone. Not that you haven't the clearest skin I've ever set eyes upon, Christina Alberta.'

'Tell me some more about Dr. Devizes,' said Christina Alberta.

§ 2

But it wasn't the next day that Christina Alberta met Devizes. She put that off for a day and fled down to Woodford Wells in response to a remarkable communication from Mr. Sam Widgery.

The Widgerys had never been correspondents of the

Preembys except in so far as the payment of the dividends upon Mr. Preemby's interest in the Limpid Stream Laundry necessitated letters. There had been a certain amount of friction in the flotation of the company, and Mr. Widgery had remained resentful and sought to show as much by a studied curtness in his communications. But now came this letter addressed to 'Miss Chrissie Preemby.'

'*My dear Chrissie,*' the letter began.

'*This is a shocking business about your poor father I can't tell you how shocked I am I went up post haste to the work-house where you had put him as soon as they wrote to me and got his watch and cheque book. It is fortunate they found my address in his pocket or I suppose I should have been kept in the dark as per usual about all this he did not know me and denied his own name but afterwards he said he knew me for a filching commercial wrogue and would have my ears cut off and threatened me. I was to be unpailed whatever that may be. I have been thinking over all this business and since you are not yet of age I suppose I am a sort of guardian to you and have to look into your interests at the laundry which is not paying nearly so well as your father led me to believe. I think he was already queer at the time and didn't fully under-stand what he was doing and I doubt if all that of his about preference shares which I never held with really but did to humour him ought to stand. Luckily there is no hurry about this has you won't have to pay anything for him where he is Mr. Punter says so long as you leave well alone and we can see about these other things when you have got over the first shock of your father's breakdown. My wife sends her love and kind sympathy. You must keep calm and not let these things disturb you too much because very often it is here-riterary and one cannot be too careful so leave everything to me and believe me to remain*

'*Your affectionate cousin*

'*Sam Widgery.*'

'Rather!' said Christina Alberta and telephoned forthwith to put off Paul Lambone and Wilfred Devizes and hurried off with a combatant light in her eye to the Underground and Liverpool Street Station.

§ 3

When Christina Alberta got down to Woodford Wells it seemed to her that the laundry was just a little smaller than it used to be and that a slight tarnish had fallen upon the bright blue delivery vans. The swastika upon them had been covered over by paper bills in red lettering saying: 'Under Entirely New Management. Address all Communications to the Managing Director Samuel Widgery Esq. By Order.'

She went up the garden path to the door that had been home to her for nearly all her life, and it was opened to her by Sam Widgery himself, who had seen her coming. 'So you came down,' he said, and seemed to hesitate about admitting her. He was a tallish, stooping man with a large bare pock-marked face, a dropping nether lip, a large nose that snored occasionally when he breathed, and furtive very small brown eyes. He was clad in dark grey ill-fitting garments, with a frayed collar and a very worn made-up black satin tie. His waistcoat was mainly unbuttoned and he fidgeted with his hands. He looked at Christina Alberta as though he found her more formidable than he had thought her.

'Did you see Daddy?' said Christina Alberta, coming straight to the point.

He compressed his mouth and shook his head from side to side as though he recalled painful things.

'Was he bad? Was he queer or—*dreadful?*'

'Not too loud, my dear,' he said in his husky whispering

254

voice. 'We don't want *every one* to hear about your trouble. Come in here where we can talk properly.'

He led the way into the little living-room in which her father had so recently planned the conditions for the conversion of the laundry into a limited company. The familiar furniture had been rearranged rather amazingly, and a large, dark bureau had been placed under the window. With discreet gestures, Sam Widgery closed the door and came towards her. 'Sit down, Chrissie,' he said, 'and don't get excited. I was afraid you might come rushing down here. But of course I was bound to write to you.'

'Did you see him?' she repeated.

'Mad as a hatter,' he said. 'They say he made a riot at the Rubicon Restaurant. Wanted to give a great banquet there to all the beggars in London.'

'Did you see him? Was he well? Was he unhappy? What have they done with him?'

'You mustn't *pelt* me with questions, Chrissie. You mustn't let your mind go on at such a pace. I told you in my letter I went up and saw him. They called him out and he came to me in a little room.'

'Where was it? Where was this workhouse?'

'There you go again. Just sit down and take things quietly, my girl. I can't answer all these questions at once.'

'Where was it you saw him? Was it at Gifford Street?'

'Yes. Where else could it be? They was waiting to remove him.'

'Where?'

'Some asylum I suppose?'

'Cummerdown Hill?'

'Come to think of it, it *was* Cummerdown Hill. Yes – they said Cummerdown Hill. He came out. He looked much as usual, bit more vacant perhaps, until he set eyes

255

on me and then he gave a sort of start and said, "Don't
know you," he said. Like that.'

'Well, that wasn't mad. Did he *look* mad? I suppose he
didn't want to talk to you – after all the disagreeable
things that have been said.'

'Very likely. Any'ow I said to him, "What! don't know
me?" I said; "not know old Sam Widgery what you planted
your laundry on?" Just like that – joking at him like.
Quite kindly but – humorous. "I don't know you," he
says and tried to go. "Hold hard!" I said and took him by
the arm. "You're a base, complaining scoundrel," he says
to me and sort of tried to push me away. "You'd rewin
any laundry!" he says – him to me, what was in the laundry
business a dozen years before he married your poor
mother. "Any'ow I 'aven't your complaint," I says, "Mr.
Albert Edward Preemby." He sort of stiffened. "Sargum," he says, "if you please. . . ." '

'Sargon,' Christina Alberta corrected.

'Maybe. It sounded like "Sargum." And "Sargum" he
would have it. Mad as a hatter on that. I tried to talk but
what was the good of talking? I couldn't get anything
plain or straight out of him at all. Started threatening me
with the bastinado – whatever that may be. I asked him
to be decent with his language. "I've 'ad enough," I says
to the attendant at last and the attendant took him away.
And so we're quit of him, Chrissie.'

'Quit of him!'

'Quit of him. What can anyone do?'

'Everything. Did he look very unhappy? Did he look
frightened or ill-treated?'

'Why should he? They're taking proper care of him and
he's out of harm's way.'

'You're sure he looked – serene?'

'Bit jaded perhaps. That's his own internal workings I
expect. But he's where he ought to be, Chrissie. I feel

that. What we've got to do, from what Mr. Punter says, is to let well alone. There he is with everything he wants, living on the ratepayers' money. We've got ourselves to consider. We've got to think of that crazy preference-share idea he's saddled the laundry with. *That's* urgent. It's a charge of nearly five hundred a year as things are, nearly ten pound a week. There isn't a laundry in London could stand it.'

'I shall have to see my Daddy,' said Christina Alberta. 'I don't believe he *is* so comfortable. I've heard horrid stories of asylums. Anyhow, I ought to go right away and see him.'

'Can't do that, Chrissie,' said Mr. Widgery, shaking his large grey face slowly from side to side and watching her as he spoke. 'They don't have visitors running in and out of these mad-houses just whenever they want to. Wouldn't *do*, you know. The poor creatures have to be kept quiet and not excited. I daresay I could give you a letter for next visiting day –'

'*You!* Give *me* a letter!'

Mr. Widgery shrugged his shoulders. 'It would help you to get in. But you won't make anything of him, Chrissie, even if you see him. And you'll have to wait for a visiting day. You must do that.'

'I want to see him.'

'Very likely. But regulations are regulations. Meanwhile there's all this business muddle we got to put straight. While he's in that asylum I think what I ought to do is to give you 'n allowance, five pounds a week say, and keep back the rest until we're able to get something settled up. Or four. Or perhaps as you want it – not a definite sum. I don't know. I haven't thought it out yet. You can't possibly want to do with all that ten pounds a week with him off your hands. Then we'll be able to see where **we** stand and everything will be all right again.'

He paused and scratched his cheek and watched her with his little sidelong eyes. 'See?' he said as if to stimulate her to speech.

Christina Alberta looked at him in a silence that became painful. Then she stood up and regarded him – her arms akimbo and her face alight.

'I see now,' she said. 'You damned old Rascal!'

Mr. Widgery had nice old-fashioned ideas about young ladies and ladylike language. He was taken aback. 'Now!' he said. '*Now!*'

'Always I should think,' said Christina Alberta.

'You mustn't say things like that, Chrissie. You mustn't use words like that. You mustn't get wrong ideas about all this. What d'you mean? Old rascal! Something old rascal! Why? I'm only doing what I got to do. You aren't really of age yet, you're just a mere child legally speaking, and it falls to *me* naturally, *me*, his nearest relative so to speak, to make such arrangements as have to be made about his affairs. That's all. You mustn't get wrong ideas about it all and you mustn't get excited. See?'

'I called you,' said Christina Alberta, 'a damned old Rascal.'

He did not meet her eye. He spoke as if he appealed to the bureau.

'And does it do you any good to use such horrible expressions? And does it do me any harm? And does it alter the fact that whether I like it or not, I've got to look after his property now and see about it and see you don't get into any trouble or mischief? All me and your aunt have been thinking about is just what's right and proper to be done for you. And then you turn on me like a serpent and use language – !'

Words failed Mr. Widgery, and still seeking sympathy from the bureau, he shrugged his shoulders and threw out his hands.

258

'You're no relation of his,' said Christina Alberta. 'I guessed when I read your letter that this was the sort of thing you'd be up to. You're glad to have him out of the way because he was such a one for punctual payments. You think I'm all alone; you think I'm just a girl and that you can do what you like now with me. You've made a mistake. I'll make you pay up every penny that's due on the laundry and I'll see you do it more punctually than ever. And why didn't you do something to get him out as soon as you heard they'd taken him?'

'Now don't you go getting excited, Chrissie,' said Mr. Widgery. 'Even if I ain't a blood relation of his, I am of yours. I'm your next-of-kin and your best friend and I got to think what's got to be done about *you*. I got to act for *you*. In spite of bad language and everything. I tell you he's right and safe where he is and I'm not going to have anything done to disturve him. Nothing at all. There he is and there he's going to stay, and I'm going to act as Mr. Punter advised me to act. I'm going to keep back his dividends as they fall due, and pay you what I think proper to pay you for your keep and so on and charge it to him, and I'm going to see you live an orderly sort of life in future now too, same as my poor cousin Christina would have wanted you to do. You've been knocking about the world in a perfectly scandalous way and learning to curse and swear. It can't go on. That's how things are, Chrissie, and the sooner you see them the right way round the better.'

The young woman stood speechless while Mr. Widgery unfolded his intentions.

'Where's Mrs. Widgery?' she said at last with an effort of stupendous self-control.

'Up in the laundry seeing to things. No need to bother her. We been talking about all this, over and over, and we're quite of one mind in the matter. It's *our* right to look after you and it's *our* responsibility to look after you, and we mean to do our duty by you, Chrissie, whether you like it or not.'

Unpleasant doubts assailed Christina Alberta. She was still two months short of one and twenty, and it was quite conceivable that the law gave this ugly, oily creature all sorts of preposterous powers of interference with her. Still it was her style to carry off things with a brave face.

'All this is just nonsense,' she said. 'I'm not going to have my Daddy put away like this without a word from me, and I'm not going to let you muddle about with his property. Everybody in the family knows you're a crooked muddler. Mother used to say so. I'm going to see about him myself, and I'm going to have him sent off to some special sort of mental nursing place where he can have proper attention. And that's what I came to tell you.'

Mr. Widgery's little eyes seemed to weigh and judge her. 'You're giving yourself high and mighty airs, Chrissie,' he said, after a little pause. 'You'll do this and you'll do that. You've got a sort of wrong idea of what you can do in the world. You haven't got any money and you haven't got any authority, and the sooner you get that into your head the better.'

That scared feeling was gaining upon Christina Alberta. In order to counteract it she deliberately lost her temper. 'I'll jolly soon show you what I can do and what you can't,' she said with a flaming face.

'Now don't *yew* go getting excited,' said Mr. Widgery. 'You of all people shouldn't get excited.'

'*Excited!*' said Christina Alberta, rallying for a repartee, and then struck by an ugly thought she stopped short and stared at the little bright brown eyes in the pock-marked face. Mutely they answered her mute amazed question. This was the third or fourth time he had used the word 'excited' and now she knew what he was aiming at. Suddenly she realized the train of ideas that her Daddy's extinction had set going in his head. He also had been studying the lunacy laws – and dreaming dreams.

'Exactly,' said Mr. Widgery. 'You've always been a queerish sort of girl, Chrissie, and the rackety life you lead and now this affair has been a strain on you. Must have been. You've got no quiet friends but your aunt and me and no quiet place to come to but here. Don't you go flaring out at me, Chrissie; I mean well by you. I'm not going to go paying you money to keep you up there in London. Why! – you might go getting drugs or anything. Call me a something rascal if you like. Swear at me as though you were out of your senses; it won't alter what I mean to do. I want you to come down here and rest your mind and nerves for a time, and let me get in someone to see you – see what ought to be done about you. . . . You'll thank me for it some day.'

His big grey face seemed to expand and swim about before her eyes and the room grew small and dark.

'It's my duty to see after you,' he said. 'It can't hurt you or anyone for us to have advice.'

In the train from Liverpool Street she had told herself she had intended to wipe the floor with Mr. Sam Widgery, but things hardly seemed to be happening like that.

'Bah!' she cried. 'D'you think I'd come back here?'

'Better than being lost in London, Chrissie,' he said. 'Better than being lost in London. We can't have you wandering off in London, same as your father did.'

She felt that the time had come for her to go, but for a second or so she could not move to do so. She could not move because she feared he might do something to detain her, and if he did she did not know what she would do. Then she pulled herself up by the feet.

'Well,' she said with a step past him doorward that turned him on his heel; 'I've told you what I think of you. I'd better be getting back to London.'

In his eyes she saw the thought of obstructing her flash into being and die. 'Won't you stay and have something,' he said, 'before you go back?'

'Eat *here*!' she cried and got to the door.

Her hand trembled so that it was difficult to turn the handle. He stood motionless staring at her with his lower lip dropping and an expression of doubt upon his face. It was as if he was not quite sure of himself nor of the course he meant to pursue. The course he wanted to pursue was appallingly plain.

§ 4

She walked with dignity out of the open front door and down the garden path. She did not look back, but she knew his face came up close to the window and watched her. Never in her whole life had panic come so near to her. She would have liked to run.

After the train had started she felt a little safer. 'How the devil can he get at me?' she said aloud to the empty compartment.

But she wasn't at all sure that she couldn't be got at, and she found herself trying to estimate just how much support and friendship she might find in her London friends. Could she, for instance, count upon Mr. Paul Lambone? If supplies were cut off could she get some sort of job and keep herself for a time until she could extract her silly Daddy from the net into which he had fallen? How would Harold and Fay, perennially hard-up, behave if supplies ran out? And meanwhile there was Daddy, wondering why no help came to him – puzzled by what had happened to him and no doubt getting sillier and sillier.

Christina Alberta was growing up fast now. Beneath all her radicalism and rebellion there had always hitherto

been a belief, tacit, subconscious, in the rightness and
security and sustaining energy of the social framework.
There is under most youthful rebellion. She had assumed
without thinking very much about it that hospitals were
places of comfort and luxury, doctors in full possession
and use of all existing science, prisons clean and exemplary
places, that though laws might still be unjust that the
administration of the law was untouched by knavery or
weakness. She had had the same confidence in the ultimate integrity of social life that a little child has in the
invincible safeness of nursery and home. But now she was
awakening to the fact that the whole world was insecure. It
was not that it was a wicked or malignant world, but that
it was an inattentive and casual world. It dreaded bothers.
It would do the meanest, most dangerous, and cruellest
things to escape the pressure of bothers, and it would
refuse to be bothered by any sufferings or evil it could
possibly contrive to ignore. It was a dangerous world, a
world of bothered people in which one might be lost and
forgotten while one was still alive and suffering. It was a
world in which it is not good to be alone, and she was beginning to feel herself very dangerously alone.

She had never, she reflected, thought very much of her
family, but now she perceived a family may dissolve away
too soon. She wanted a wall to put her back against if
after all Sam Widgery screwed up his courage to be
aggressive; she wanted some one who would be her very
own, a safe ally, some one she could count upon, some one
closer than law or custom, some one who would go about
and find out exactly what had happened to her if she fell
into disaster, who would refuse to accept her downfall,
some one who would care for her more than he cared for
himself and not be lightly turned away.

Himself? Not *herself*. In fact, a lover.

'Damn Teddy!' cried Christina Alberta, and knocked a

puff of dust out of the railway cushion with her fist. 'He messes it up.

'And I knew what he was. I knew all the time exactly what he was!

'I've got to stick it alone,' said Christina Alberta.

'And besides who'd have cared for me, anyhow, with a nose like mine?

'Even if there were such things in the world as lovers who loved like that! But it's a world of people who don't care. It's a world of people who haven't the guts to care. It's a dust-heap of a world,' said Christina Alberta.

§ 5

Her thoughts began to flow into a new region. After all, wasn't there something too disagreeably justifiable in the suggestion that she was – how to put it – *queer*. Hitherto Christina Alberta had always regarded herself as a model of sanity and mental directness – with no fault indeed except possibly her nose. Now the word 'queer' stuck in her mind like a thorn that has gone right home. She could not get it out again.

She had always, she knew, been different. She had always had a style of her own.

Most of the people she had met in the world had impressed her as being colourless, weak in speech and action, evasive – that was the word, 'evasive.' They evaded the use of all sorts of blunt words, they didn't know why. Christina Alberta was all for saying 'Damn' and 'guts' and so forth until some one convinced her of some better reason for avoiding them than merely that they weren't used by 'nice' people. These others were always not saying things because they weren't said and not doing things because they weren't done. And for what was said and what was done, however manifestly preposterous it was, they had a sort of terrified imitativeness. They just ran about being as far as possible somebody else until they died. Why exist at all then? Why not get out of it and leave some one else in possession? But, anyhow, they got through life. They didn't get into trouble. They supported one another. And, on the other hand, if you didn't evade? You puzzled other people. You left the track. You were like a train leaving the rails and trying to take a cross-country short-cut. You hit against – everything.

Was this evasive life she had always despised really the sane life? Was ceasing to evade ceasing to be sane? Sheep, she had read, had a disease called gid; then they wandered alone and died. Was all this originality and thinking for oneself and not going with the crowd and so forth, that had been her pride and glory, just the way out from the sane life? Originality, eccentricity, queerness, craziness, madness; was that merely a quantitative scale?

Was not her Daddy's queerness this, that after years of the extremest evasion he had at last tried to break away to something real and strange? And had she, after her fashion, been attempting anything else? Was she, too, lopsided? Lop-sided in a different direction perhaps, but lop-sided none the less. An inherited lop-sidedness?

Her mind went off at a tangent on the question whether she had really inherited anything whatever from her Daddy. Was his queerness her sort of queerness at all? It ought to be, seeing that they were father and daughter.

How different they were! For a father and daughter how amazingly different they were! . . .

But were they father and daughter? A much repressed fantasy came back to her – a fantasy based on the flimsiest foundations, on chance phrases her mother had used, on moments of intuition. Once or twice a reverie had arisen out of these lurking particles of memory and had taken her by surprise only to be thrust aside again with contempt.

Blup. Blup. Blup. There came a familiar variation to the familiar sounds of the train. Christina Alberta was running into Liverpool Street Station and her perplexities were all unsolved.

The old fantasy lost heart and faded away. What was the good of such dreams? There she was.

§ 6

Christina Alberta's meeting next day with Wilfred Devizes turned out to be a much more exciting affair than she or he had expected it to be.

Acting on the advice of Paul Lambone, she had brought photographs and a letter or so in her Daddy's handwriting with her, and she had thought out what she judged would be significant things to tell about him. She went in a taxi with Paul Lambone to Devizes' house just off Cavendish Square, and they were shown up at once past a waiting-room and a consulting-room to a dignified little sitting-room with an open fire and a table with tea things and a great array of bookcases. Devizes came in to them forthwith.

She was a little shocked to think that this lank, dark, shock-headed man could be recognizably like her. He was younger than she had expected him to be, younger she thought, than her Daddy or Mr. Lambone, and he wore a long unbuttoned morning coat. He carried the nose all right; he was indeed very good-looking.

'Hullo, Paul,' he said cheerfully. 'Is this the young lady whose father's been stolen? We'll have some tea. It's Miss –?'

'Miss Preemby,' said Paul Lambone, 'but every one calls her Christina Alberta.'

266

Devizes turned an eye that was by habit and disposition a scrutinizing eye upon her. He betrayed a faint momentary surprise and came and shook hands. 'Tell me all about it,' he said. 'You don't think he's really mad, but only rather exceptional and odd. That's it, isn't it? Lambone tells me he is sane. It's quite possible. I'd better go over the state of his mind first, and then we can discuss the question of the asylum afterwards. I gather you want to get him under your own care – outside. That isn't by any means simple. We'll have to study the obstacles. Meanwhile tea. . . . I've been disentangling the delusions of a perfectly terrible old lady, and I'm rather deflated. Just tell me all about it in your own way.'

'Tell him,' said Paul, settling his shoulders into his armchair, and preparing to interrupt.

Christina Alberta began to unfold her premeditated discourse. Every now and then Devizes would interrupt her with a question. He kept his eyes on her, and it seemed to her even from the beginning that they betrayed something more than attention to what she was saying. He looked at her as though he had seen her before and couldn't quite remember where. She described her Daddy's talks to her when she was a girl, about the Pyramids and the Lost Atlantis and so forth, and the odd spirit of release and renewed growth that had followed the death of her mother. She told of the spiritualistic séance and the coming of Sargon. Devizes was very keen on various aspects of the Sargon story. 'It was odd that the suggestion fell in so aptly with Preemby's mental disposition. What was that young man up to? I don't quite understand him.'

'I don't know. I think he just hit by chance on the stuff he talked. It was just bad luck that it fitted.'

'Undergraduate idea of fun?'

'Undergraduate fun. It might have been Tut-an-ka-man.'

'But it happened to be Sargon.'

'He may have been reading some ancient history.'

'He didn't, I suppose, know anything about your father?'

'Couldn't have done. I suppose he thought my – my Daddy looked a little small and absurd, and I suppose it appealed to his sense of humour to single him out from the others and make him a great king. I'd like to have a few minutes' straight talk with that young man.'

'This you see isn't a delusion, Devizes. It's a deception,' said Paul Lambone.

'Is he generally coherent?' asked Devizes.

'Granted his thesis, he's amazingly coherent,' she said.

'He doesn't sometimes become some one else, God or a millionaire, or anything of that sort?'

'No. He believes in reincarnation and hints at having lived other lives, but that's all.'

'Thousands of people do that,' said Lambone.

'And nobody is persecuting him? Nobody makes noises to trouble him or gets at him with X-rays or anything of that sort?'

'Not a shadow of that sort of thing.'

'The man's sane. Unless he went mad when he walked out of your friends' studio.'

'I'm for his sanity right out,' said Lambone. 'I wish I'd had a chance to talk to him. There's something – everybody's chattering now about an Inferiority Complex. Well, isn't it common for people who have been rather put upon and deceived and so forth, and who don't want to face the facts of life, to take refuge in an assumed personality? And putting the reveries, the spiritualist séance and so forth all together, doesn't it work out on those lines?'

'He knows he is really, *au fond*, Preemby?' Devizes asked.

'It annoyed him to tell him so,' said Christina Alberta. 'I think one reason why he went away was because I and my friend, Mrs. Crumb that is, at the studio where we live, would try to make him be sensible about that. It drove him away. He knows he is really Preemby and he hates it. He knows this is all a make-believe.'

Paul Lambone took up the discourse. 'I do so sympathize with that. So far from that being insane it's perfectly rational. Becoming somebody else greater than oneself is part of half the religions of the world. All the Mithraists used to become Mithra. The Serapists, if I remember rightly, used to become Osiris. We all want to be born again really. Every one with any sense and humility does. Into something greater. "Who will deliver me from the body of this death?" That's why Christina Alberta's Daddy is so tremendously interesting. He's got imagination; he's got originality. He may be a feeble little chap, but he has that.'

'Having an exceptional mind isn't insanity,' said Devizes, 'or else we should put all our poets and artists in asylums.'

'Few would come up to that standard,' said Lambone. 'I wish they did.'

Devizes reflected. 'I think I've got things clear. He's coherent. He's neat in his dress. He isn't persecuted. He's unselfish in his thoughts, almost romantically so. And he's not fattish and lumpish, and he's never had any sort of fit. There's no insane type a properly qualified doctor could class him under, but then most doctors are altogether unqualified for mental practice. A stupid doctor might mistake his imaginations for the splendour of paranoia or take his abstraction in reverie for *dementia præcox* or think he was a masked epileptic. But all these are cases of mental disease, and your father is probably not diseased at all. He's mentally disturbed, but that's all. The difference between him and a real lunatic is the difference between a basketful of fruit that's been overturned, and a basketful that's gone rotten. Overturned fruit gets bruised and rots very easily – but being overturned isn't being rotten. What sort of man is he to look at?'

269

'She's got photographs,' said Lambone.

'I'd like to see them,' he said, and was given a recent one of Mr. Preemby as laundryman. 'Too much moustache by a long way,' he said. 'Is there anything – with some at least of his face uncovered? There's nothing here but his eyes.'

'I thought you'd feel that,' said Lambone. 'There's one of Mr. Preemby as a young man, taken soon after his wedding with Mrs. Preemby. Have you got it, Christina Alberta? . . . Here we are. . . . That's Mrs. Preemby in the chair. The moustache – in bulk – has yet to come.'

'He married young?' Devizes asked Christina Alberta.

'He must have done,' she said. 'I don't know his exact age. My mother never told me.'

Devizes scrutinized the photograph. 'Queer,' he said, and seemed to be searching his memory. 'Something familiar. I've met people like this.'

'They were both London people, I suppose,' he said, looking hard at Christina Alberta.

'Woodford Wells,' said Christina Alberta.

'My father was born at Sheringham,' she added as an afterthought.

'Sheringham. That's queer.' With a manifestly deepened interest he looked at the couple posed against one of those rustic backgrounds dear to Victorian photographers. 'Chrissy,' he repeated to himself. 'Chrissy. Christina Alberta. It *can't* be.'

For some moments Dr. Devizes ceased to attend to his consultants and they remained intently observing him. He tried to fix his attention on the young man's face in the picture, but it was the young woman who sat on the rustic stile that absorbed his interest. Amazing how completely he had forgotten her face, and how she came back now incredibly unlike and yet like his memory of her. He remembered the glasses and the neck and shoulders. And a sort of stiff defiance. 'When were your mother and father married?' he asked. 'How long ago?'

'Eighteen ninety-nine,' she answered.

'And then you were born straight away?' He asked the question with an affectation of ease.

'There was a decent interval,' said Christina Alberta with a clumsy levity. 'I was born in nineteen hundred.'

'A little, fair, blue-eyed chap with rather an absent-minded manner. I seem to see him,' Devizes said, and resumed his examination of the photograph. Nobody spoke for the better part of a minute. 'Good Lord!' whispered Lambone to himself. Devizes drank a cup of tea absent-mindedly. 'Extraordinary,' he ejaculated. 'I never dreamt of it.'

'What is?'

His answer went off at a tangent. 'Christina Alberta's resemblance to my mother. It's amazing. It's been worrying me ever since I came into the room. It's been distracting my attention. I've got a little picture. . . .'

He jumped up and went out of the room. Christina Alberta, puzzled, excited, turned instantly on Lambone. 'He knew my father and mother,' she said.

'Apparently,' said Lambone with something defensive in his voice.

'*Apparently!*' she echoed. 'But – he *knew* them! He *knew* them well. And –. *What's he thinking of?*'

Devizes reappeared holding out a small gold-framed picture. 'Look at that!' he said and handed it to Paul Lambone. 'It might be Christina Alberta. Don't you see how like it is? Allowing for that preposterous hair piled upon her head and the way her dress goes up round her neck.'

He handed the picture to Christina Alberta and looked at Lambone in amazed interrogation.

'It might be me in fancy dress,' Christina Alberta agreed, with the picture in her hands. There came a long pause.

She looked up and saw the expression of his face. Her mind gave a fantastic leap, so fantastic that it instantly leapt back to the point of departure. It was like a flash of lightning in a night as dark as pitch. She made a great effort to pull the conversation together, to behave as though her mind had never leapt at all. 'But what has all this to do with my Daddy's case?' she asked.

'Nothing directly. Your resemblance to my mother is a pure coincidence. Pure. But it's a curious coincidence! Just for the moment it pulled my attention aside. Forgive me. I've a belief that where there's a resemblance of this sort there's a blood relationship. I suppose your mother's people – what did you say they were called – Hoskin?'

'Did I say? I don't remember. I *didn't* say. I didn't. Her name was Hossett.'

'Ah, yes! – Hossett. I suppose that two or three generations back the Hossetts and Devizes intermarried. And there we are! Cousins – at we don't know what remove. But types go under in a family and then bob up again. It sort of links us, Christina Alberta, doesn't it? It gives me a special interest. I don't feel now that you're just any old patient. Or, rather, just Paul's friend. I feel linked. Well – That's that. Let's come back to your father. Who married your mother just when they were starting the old South African war. He's always been a dreamy, unobservant type. As we were saying. Even from the beginning. . . .'

He stopped short.

'Always,' said Christina Alberta, after a long pause.

'We've been into all that,' said Devizes and paused, and was for a minute entirely at a loss for words. 'Yes,' he said at last.

Her heart was beating fast and there was a flush of excitement on her cheeks. Her quick wits had filled in all the gaps. She understood now – and then again it vanished.

She would have liked to have gone away and thought it all over at once. But that wouldn't do. She must disregard the questions that surged up within her. Her mind went forward like an obstinate traveller caught in a whirlwind. Her mother for example. She was trying to recall something about her mother that had long been stifled in her mind. 'Went away and left me to it,' was it? 'Went off and left me to it?' Her mother lying in bed and wandering. Who had left her to what? That standing perplexity. That suspicion. That dream. But attend to him now, Christina Alberta; attend to him! She was observing him with all her being, and yet she seemed deaf to what he said.

He was saying that now that he agreed with them that Preemby was sane, he could see his way to the real business before them. It was the old, old story of making lunatics out of sane people which they encountered in Preemby's case. It was the old, old story of making lunatics out of sane people which they encountered in Preemby's case. (He repeated his sentence word for word without apparently realizing he had said it twice.) All exceptional people were in danger of being misunderstood, but such a type as Preemby, original and yet incapable of abstract expression or philosophical method, which sought fantastic expression for its feelings and impulses, was particularly liable to give offence, awaken suspicion and dread and hostility. It was just these borderland cases he was always trying to save from asylums, and just such cases that were always going there. And they were the last people to bring into contact with real insanity. 'To go back to my metaphor, the basketful of fruit isn't rotten, is scarcely speckled with decay, but it is disordered and overturned. A mind is a delicate thing to knock about. It will rot very easily, and a mind like your father's particularly will rot very easily under asylum conditions. After all this rigmarole I come to just the conclusion you've already reached, that we have to get Preemby out of Cummerdown Hill and away under restful conditions as soon as possible. When we'll comb out his particular complex and get him into working relations with the world again. I'm quite sure we can do that somehow, make his incognito permanent, make him an Emperor in exile, restore his proper name, organize a common daily round for him and get him back more and more to be a chastened and released Preemby.'

He paused.

'That's it,' said Lambone, roused from a profound contemplation of the two interesting faces before him.

'It isn't easy. Even to get at him isn't easy. There will be delays. A careless magistrate and a silly doctor can make a lunatic in five minutes. It takes no end of time to unmake one.'

'That's what I want to set about doing,' said Christina Alberta.

'Naturally,' said Devizes, 'and I'm with you.'

He explained one or two points in lunacy law, began sketching a scheme of operations, considered the people to whom she ought to write and the people to whom he ought to write, and how soon it would be possible to see Preemby, and give him a word of encouragement. Already Devizes had had several brushes with lunacy organization; he was considered a troublesome but dangerous man for a medical superintendent to be up against. That might arouse either hostile obstruction or the propitiatory spirit. They must go carefully.

Lambone scarcely interrupted now at all. He had ceased to be acutely interested in Preemby, immured away there in Cummerdown. He was lost in admiration of the self-control his astonishing friends displayed. He tried to imagine what an undertow of strange excitement, of queer thoughts and confused emotions, there must be beneath their highly intelligent discussion of the case of Mr.

274

Preemby. They wasted very little attention upon the on-looker. Christina Alberta's face was faintly flushed, and her eyes glowed; Devizes was rather less of a conversationalist than usual and rather more like a university tutor with an exceptionally interesting student.

The subject was exhausted at last and the time came to depart. Devizes came to the door with them.

'Don't forget that I'm always round the corner, so-to-speak,' he said. 'I'm in the telephone directory. And don't forget, Christina Alberta, don't forget I'm your long-lost cousin, very much at your service.'

'I won't forget that,' said Christina Alberta, meeting his eye.

A little pause, and then rather stiffly they shook hands.

§ 7

'Am I mad?' said Christina Alberta as soon as she and Paul Lambone were in the street together. 'Am I dreaming?'

Lambone was clumsy. 'Mad? Dreaming? How?'

'Oh! don't pretend not to understand. That he's my real father? Don't pretend! oh please don't pretend! Is he or is he not?'

Lambone did not reply for a moment. 'You flash at things – like a lizard. How could it have happened?'

'Then you *did* think?'

'My dear Christina Alberta, he didn't know you existed until he set eyes on you. I'm sure of that.'

'But then. Wasn't it plain? He *knew them both!*'

'Devizes,' said Lambone, 'is ten years younger than I am. He's barely forty. He must have been – not more than eighteen. Nineteen at most. It's a little difficult.'

'That makes it easier. You never knew mother. If they were both young –'

'It's just possible,' said Lambone, 'there is some other **explanation.**'

275

'But what?'

'Can't imagine. I suppose he was at Sheringham – perhaps for a holiday – and met her. But –'

'It must have been something casual, a kind of accident. Mother used to have flashes. . . . I never quite understood her. She used to suppress me, and perhaps she was suppressing herself. . . . And at the end – she said something. Someone had left her to it. . . . Do you know – at times – I've had fancies – suspicions! It seemed as though she guessed that I was guessing. Now I know – I *was*. It's incredible. And yet it explains a hundred things.'

'He certainly never knew of you. He's – amazed.'

'And what's going to happen next?'

'Legally you're Preemby's daughter. Nothing can alter that. All the resemblances and coincidences in the world won't alter that.'

'And all the law in the world won't alter the facts. And –'

She turned on Lambone with a flushed face. 'Do you realize what it means to think you are the daughter of a certified lunatic? And then find you are not? All last night I was awake with that unendurable thought.'

'All night – at your age!'

'It seemed all night. Last night – I *tried* to imagine that something of this sort had happened. Tried – and couldn't. Tried to bring back all those old fancies. And here it is! I might have known. I did know and wouldn't know.'

'Tell me about this real father of mine. I don't know a thing about him. Is he a good man? Is he a bad man? Has he a wife?'

'He adored his wife. And so did I. She was one of the loveliest and cleverest young women I've ever known. She was strong and jolly – and the beastly influenza and pneumonia got her. In a week. It cut him to ribbons. They'd had no children. They'd had only four years together.

He's attractive to women, but I don't think there'll be a second Mrs. Devizes for a long time. I can't imagine it. Any other woman! Why! All that house – it's full of her presence.'

'Yes,' said Christina Alberta, and thought for a time.

They were detached for a time in crossing Bond Street, and the pavement was too crowded and Piccadilly was too congested for them to talk again until they were in St. James' Street.

'Daddy,' said Christina Alberta, 'seems ten thousand miles away. But when I'm over the amazement of this I expect I'll get back to him all right. But just for a time – he must wait.'

'You'll come in for a bit?' said Lambone at the corner of Half Moon Street. 'I could give you some dinner.'

'No, thanks. I'll walk all the way to Chelsea,' said Christina Alberta. 'I want to think this out by myself. I want to get alone with this spinning head of mine and try to slow it down. My life's gone topsy-turvy. Or it's been topsy-turvy and it's suddenly come right side up. I don't know which. Oh! – I don't know anything. I've got to begin all over again.'

She shook hands and paused. Lambone waited, for manifestly she had something to say. She got it out at last.

'Do you think – he liked me?'

'He liked you all right, Christina Alberta. Don't you worry about that.'

§ 8

It was a little more than two days before Christina Alberta, to use her own expression, 'got back' to her lost Daddy.

Those two days were full of an immense excitement. Devizes was the most wonderful fact in the world. She exploded into love for him. She had the most vivid impression of him, dark and tall, rather grave, watchful and amazingly understandable. Yet vivid as her impression was she doubted every detail of it, and wanted to go back to him and verify it all over again. It was their quality of mutual understanding that was at once the most delightful and the most incredible aspect of the whole affair. Their brains no doubt were unlike, as every two individual brains must be, yet their unlikeness was not a mere accumulation of accidental differences, but the unlikeness of two variations of one theme. She could feel his intentions beneath his words. Her mind had jumped with his realizations and there must be kinks and turns in her brain, kinks and turns that just made her difficult and queer for most people, which would find the completest parallels in his. She didn't believe there was a thing in her thoughts and acts that she would be surprised at his knowing and comprehending.

She had never before thought of parentage with any enthusiasm. She had viewed it rather in the spirit of Samuel Butler and Bernard Shaw, and conceived of parents generally in relation to their children as embarrassed hypocrites with an instinctive disposition towards restraint and suppression. She had made an exception of her own particular pair; Daddy had been a great friend anyhow, though mother for the most part had been a concentrated incarnate 'Don't.' But she had never realized there might be something rather intimately interesting in consanguinity. And then suddenly a door had opened, a man had come in and sat down and talked to her and discovered himself the nearest thing in life to her. And she to him. She wanted to go to him again; she wanted to see more of him, be with him. But he made no sign and she could think of no decent excuse for a call upon him. The very intensity of her desire made her unable to go to him easily.

She wrote the various letters they had agreed she should write, and then decided to master mental science and lunacy generally. That and the case of her 'Daddy' she perceived to be her formal link with Devizes.

She set out for the Reading Room of the British Museum, for which she had a students' ticket, and she tried to concentrate her mind upon the book she had requisitioned, instead of letting it wander off into the strangest reveries about this miraculously discovered blood relation. In the afternoon she rang up Lambone to be given tea, with the intention of learning everything that the wise man could tell her about Devizes and generally turning him over conversationally. But Lambone was out. The next day the craving for Devizes was overpowering. She rang him up.

'May I have some tea?' she asked. 'I've got nothing much to say, but I want to see you.'

'Delighted,' said Devizes.

When she got to him she found herself shy, and him as shy as herself. For a little while they made polite conversation; it might almost have been the conversation of two people at a formal call in a country town. He called her 'Christina Alberta,' but she called him 'Doctor Devizes,' and he asked her if she played or danced, and whether she had ever been abroad. She sat in an arm-chair and he stood over her on the hearthrug. It was clear that the only way to intimacy lay in a frank treatment of her Daddy. She felt that if this sort of talk went on for another minute she would have to scream or throw her tea-cup in the fire. So she plunged.

'When did you first know my mother?'

Devizes' attitude stiffened, and he smiled faintly at her boldness. 'I was a Cambridge undergraduate reading for the Natural Science Tripos, and I went down to Sheringham to read. We – we picked each other up on the beach. We made love – in a scared, furtive, desperate, ignorant sort of a way. People were primitive in those days – compared with what they are now.'

'Daddy wasn't there.'

'He came in afterwards.'

Devizes considered for a moment. He decided that it wasn't fair to oblige her to go on questioning him. 'My father,' he said, 'was a pretty considerable old bully. He was Sir George Devizes, the man who invented the Devizes biscuit and cured old Alphonso, and he was celebrated for being rude to his patients. He would smack their stomachs and tell them they ought to be scooped out. He helped make Unter Magenbad. He suspected me of being a bit of a soft, though as a matter of fact I wasn't, and he generally had the effect of laying up for a quarrel with me. He kept me pretty short. He wasn't particularly nice to my mother. He used to get at my mother through me. I didn't dare to have a scrape of any sort. I was really afraid of him. If I saw a scrape blowing up my habit and disposition was to run away.'

'I see.'

Devizes considered the implications of that 'I see.' 'Not that I ran away from any definite scrape that I knew of at Sheringham,' he said very carefully.

'What was my mother like in those days?'

'A sort of subdued fierceness. A flushed warm face. She was pretty, you know, and very upright in her carriage. And she had a swift decision beneath her stiffness. Her wishes would suddenly crystallize out, and after that there was no bending her.'

'I know.'

'I suppose you do.'

'She wore glasses then?'

'Oh yes.'

'Was she fresh then? Was she happy?'

'A little too fierce to be happy.'

'Did you – ever – love her?'

'It is a long time ago, Christina Alberta. There was – seaside love-making. Why do you cross-examine me like this?'

'I want to know. Why' – Christina Alberta had a momentary terror at her own boldness – 'Why didn't you marry her?'

Devizes made no pretence of surprise at the question. 'There was no reason manifest why I should have married her. None at all. I can't conceive what my father would have done if I had come back from Sheringham engaged to a chance acquaintance. And anyhow, why should I have done anything of the sort?'

His eyes defied hers. 'I left her my address,' he added. 'She could have written to me. She never did.'

'Did a letter go astray?' said Christina Alberta, and added hastily, 'my imagination is running away with me.'

She hesitated and trembled at the next words she had resolved to say, but she said them, with a forced offhandedness. 'You see – I might have fancied you as a father?'

It produced no catastrophe. He looked her in the face and then smiled. After that smile she felt that they understood each other completely, and it was very pleasant to think that. 'Instead of which, you have to adopt me as a cousin,' he said deliberately. 'Cousins it is, Christina Alberta. It's the best we can do. We have to put our heads together and think of your Daddy. He's our common concern. I'm interested in that little man. He's defended himself against many things by those dreams of his. Very wilful dreams they may have been. Who knows? Necessary protective dreams.'

Christina Alberta did not speak for a little time. She nodded. She was glad at their manifest understanding and yet she was disappointed, though she could not have told herself what else she had expected. This man a yard away was the nearest thing in the world to her, and always there

281

might be this invincible barrier between them. They were linked by an invisible tie and they were separated by an unfathomable necessity. Never before in her life had she known what love could be; she wanted to be free to love him; she wanted him to love her.

She realized that she was standing quite still, and that Devizes was standing just as still upon his hearthrug, watching her face. His mouth and eyes were quiet and serene, but she imagined he must be gripping his hands together behind him. She had to obey him. There was nothing for her to do but follow his lead.

'Daddy's our common concern,' she said. 'I suppose I shall begin to hear from some of those people to-morrow.'

§ 9

Christina Alberta got back to her Daddy in a dream.

It was a queer dream. She was going about the world with Devizes and they were locked together in such a way that she and he could never look at each other, but were always side by side. But also with the sublime incoherence of dreams they were at the same time great ebony images, and they sat stiffly side by side like a Pharaoh and his consort, and they looked over a great space; they were very big effigies indeed and their profiles were alike. All through the dream she thought of Devizes and herself as black. The space before them was sometimes a sandy desert and sometimes a grey cloudy expanse. Then suddenly something round and white came bounding into the midst of this arena and became a little man, a familiar little blue-eyed man, tied up into a ball with ropes and sorely maimed, who rolled about and panted and struggled to be free. Oh! but he struggled pitifully. Christina Alberta's heart went out to him, and yet impelled by some tremendous force within her she rose and Devizes rose beside her and they marched stiffly forward. She could not help herself, she could not control the rigid movements of her hands and feet. They stepped high and forcibly. She was voiceless, she tried to cry out, 'We shall trample upon him! We shall trample upon him!' but there was no more than a hoarse inarticulate sound of horror in her throat. . . .

They were upon him. She felt the body of her Daddy writhe under her. He was like a bladder. His soft, ineffectual body, with her feet upon him, bent and bulged about. She forgot there was anything else but her Daddy and herself. Why had she treated him like this? Devizes disappeared. Her Daddy was clinging to her knees and now a crowd of vile figures had appeared and sought to drag him away. 'Save me, Christina Alberta,' he was pleading, though she heard no sounds. 'Save me. Save me! Every day they torture me.' But they dragged him away and she could not put out her arms to him. Because she was made of ebony and all of one piece with Devizes.

Then some one, a bird or a Sphinx with the face and voice of Lambone came into the dream. 'Listen to your Daddy,' he said. 'Do not despise him or simply pity him. He has much to teach you. The world will never learn anything until it will learn from ridiculous people. All people are ridiculous. I am. I am ridiculous. We learn in suffering what we teach in song.' She saw that her Daddy was now sheltering between the paws of the Sphinx, and that the evil men had vanished.

She became intensely aware of a revealing absurdity in her dream. No previous incompatibility had shocked her at all, and she had never thought that she was dreaming up to this point. But now she became intensely oppressed by the idea that the Sphinx was an ancient Egyptian and classical figure, and that Sargon was a still more ancient

Sumerian. The dream was going wrong. The periods, the cultures, were mixed. She conveyed this to Sphinx-Lambone, and he turned his head to answer her, and immediately the evil figures were back, and taking advantage of Lambone's inattention, were dragging her Daddy away. She tried to call Lambone's attention to that, but he said there would be plenty of time to recover her Daddy when the point about the Sphinx was settled. He wasn't a Sphinx, he explained, but a Winged Bull. He never had been a Sphinx. Or why should he be wearing a long curly stone beard? She wanted to argue that it was a false beard and that he had only just put it on. And anyhow it was just like him to start an inopportune discussion. Meanwhile her Daddy was receding into wretchedness. She became aware of this rapidly and painfully. It was her Daddy still, but his body was different; it was not a human body any more, but a basket of fruit overturned. Unless she did something at once it would go rotten and be bad for ever.

She tried to cry out words of comfort and reassurance to the poor tragic little figure before the dream came to an end – for now she knew surely that it was a dream. Of course he was suffering intolerably. Why had she not written to him or telegraphed to him? Surely they would give him a letter or a telegram! A profound self-detestation for her incompetence and negligence, and a great horror of pain and cruelty came upon her, and she awoke completely to black night and infinite dismay in her little hard bed in her stuffy little bedroom in Lonsdale Mews.

§ 10

But the impression of her Daddy, desolate and broken-hearted and in danger, remained with her, terribly vivid.

It clung to her. She got up in the morning anxious and depressed by it.

'I am not doing enough for him,' she said. 'I am letting days slip by – and for him they must be days of despair.'

'Sure th' 'Sylums 'nt so ba-s-at,' said Fay. 'Sure yr over-rating it.'

'But to live among lunatics and be classed as a lunatic!'

'They've *bans* play-them. Foxhill 'Sylum there's *buful* ban. 'Ntainments nors-sorts treats,' said Fay.

Christina Alberta refrained from bad language.

'You getting ill ove' all this,' said Fay. 'You doing no good 'n Lun. Youffar be'r come dow' Shore'm. The's th'ouse spoilin'. In this las bit of fine w'r.'

For the October weather was holding out that year quite wonderfully, a succession of calm golden days, and the Crumbs had been offered the loan of a bungalow on the beach at Shoreham by a friend who had used it throughout the summer. They wanted to go down to it before the weather broke, but going down to it meant leaving Christina Alberta all alone in the studio, and they did not want to do that. But they meant to go to Shoreham. Christina Alberta, now that she had discovered Devizes, could not endure the thought of getting out of telephone range of him. London, she argued, was manifestly her proper centre. She could get down to Cummerdown Hill in an hour; she could keep in touch with everything. The Crumbs might go but she *must* stay.

Fay would not understand. She pestered.

About eleven o'clock Christina Alberta went to the Post Office telephone booth and rang up Devizes.

'Can't something be done to hurry things up?' she asked. 'I've got Daddy on my nerves. I can't bear to think of him there day after day. I've been dreaming of him.'

'Worrying is no good. We – I've got some bad news for you. So put all your controls on.'

He paused. Christina Alberta, for all her love of Devizes, had to restrain her violent desire to snap, 'Oh! what is it?'

'Visiting day was yesterday. He had one visitor. I suppose that's the agreeable relation you described – what was his name? Wiggles? Mr. Widgery. But your Daddy can't be seen again by the outer world for a week. Not until next Tuesday.'

'Oh damn!' said Christina Alberta.

'Exactly. I'll do what I can to arrange some sort of special access. I got on to the Medical Superintendent himself. But he's queer. He's evidently quite friendly and well disposed, but he fences about. He can't say either Yes or No. Odd! I'm free to-day in the afternoon, but I'm tied up to-morrow. I was for going down to see *him* – the superintendent I mean, for a talk after lunch. "Better in a day or so," he says. Hope there's nothing wrong that he's keeping back. Afterwards he promised me to ring me up later, and then abruptly he switched off. So hold yourself ready, there. What's your telephone number?'

'Haven't got one. You must telegraph.'

'Or I'll chase round in a taxi and pick you up. Sorry to hold you up like this, Christina Alberta.'

'I don't mind anything so long as it's getting towards Daddy.'

'Right-o,' and the voice was cut off.

The telegram came after an interval of two hours, two hours which had been devoted to a rambling dispute with Fay about the Shoreham difficulty. The message ran as follows: '*Has your father turned up he escaped at dawn this morning in slippers and dressing-gown and nothing seen of him since if not appeared meet me Victoria two-seven for Cummerdown telephone Gerrard 0247 if there.*'

286

§ 11

But Mr. Preemby did not turn up anywhere. He just vanished.

Christina Alberta, in a state of incredulous astonishment at this fresh disappearance, went down with Devizes to Cummerdown. They found a Medical Superintendent by no means so amazed as they were. Sargon had been missing at breakfast time; everything seemed to point to his just walking out of the Asylum. That sort of thing had happened before. It showed a certain sleepy negligence on the part of one or two attendants, and they would be reprimanded. But as for wonder, the Medical Superintendent refused to wonder. Lunatics often stray or escape, and unless they are dangerous the authorities make no great commotion about it. They kept it out of the newspapers as far as it was possible to do so.

'This place isn't Portland,' said the Medical Superintendent. 'They get back all right. I give him a day. He's probably coming back now. He may be hiding up a mile away. I'm chiefly anxious about his catching cold. Pneumonia is the standard death of a lunatic. But it's wonderfully warm for the time of year. I've never known such an October.'

He was much more desirous to talk to Devizes about lunacy reform, and convince him that he was a highly progressive and able Medical Superintendent, than to discuss the special case of Mr. Preemby. 'We do what we can,' he said, 'but we're fixed by the extreme economy we have to practise. Low-grade attendants and not enough even of them. The public indifference to lunatics is monstrous. Everybody – even the people with insane relations – wants to forget all about them.'

'But how could Preemby have got out of the grounds?' asked Devizes. 'Aren't there walls all round?'

'Like everything else about lunacy law, the back is not as good as the front,' said the superintendent. 'But here we have got at least a complete wall of sorts all round. The original building used to be a private mansion with a walled park. For a time – in the eighteenth century – it was a boys' school.'

He showed them from his window over the roofs of a clump of outbuildings the limits of the garden and farm at the back, dropping towards a streamlet and defined by a roadside wall and old thorn and oak trees. 'For my own part,' said the Medical Superintendent, 'I admit the urgency of very drastic reforms.'

'I wonder if Cousin Widgery can throw any light on this,' said Devizes.

'Widgery?'

'That was his visitor yesterday.'

'*Was* it?' said the Medical Superintendent, and reflected and went to his desk as if to look for a paper. 'I thought it was a different sort of name – rather more like Goodchild. Perhaps I've mixed up the names.'

'Mr. Sam Widgery,' said Christina Alberta, 'would be the last person who'd want Daddy to get out. He probably came to make sure that he wouldn't. He may have come just for the pleasure of gloating over him. Uncle Sam's not a pretty soul. He may have wanted to make sure the wall went all the way round.'

The Medical Superintendent forgot his doubt about the name and the paper and turned with a fresh idea to them. 'You don't think there was any animus? You don't think he may have made for Mr. Widgery? Where does this Mr. Widgery live?'

But neither Devizes nor Christina Alberta thought there

was any great possibility of Mr. Preemby beating back to Woodford Wells.

'He's much more likely to go to Canterbury or Windsor, or start straight off for Rome,' said Christina Alberta.

'Or Mesopotamia – or the British Museum,' said Devizes.

'Or *anywhere*!' said Christina Alberta with a note of despair.

They returned to London completely baffled. Christina Alberta was for a visit to the Cummerdown Police Station and for a search in the villages round about, but Devizes explained that this might do more harm than good. Until now Christina Alberta had never heard of that one kindly weakness in the British lunacy laws, the release of the fourteen days freedom. If the lunatic can get away from the Asylum and remain at large for that period, he or she becomes legally sane again, and cannot be touched without a fresh examination and a new certificate. To set the whole countryside hunting for Preemby might merely lead to his recapture by the Asylum authorities. And whatever happened the mystery must not get into the papers.

'But while we do nothing, he may be lying dead in some out-of-the-way ditch,' said Christina Alberta.

'If he is dead he won't mind a little delay in finding him,' said Devizes.

No, the only thing was to wait at Lonsdale Mews against the chance of his returning thither. The Crumbs went off to Shoreham and Christina Alberta was left alone in the studio, but after one endless day of it Paul Lambone thought of a convenient agency called 'Universal Aunts,' and a suitable lady was sent to relieve her from a continuous vigil.

One, two, three days passed. There came no sign from Sargon, no news of any fresh calling of disciples or visits to the King. He had evaporated. A vision of a little crumpled-up body in a ditch replaced the tormented figure in the cell in the distressed imagination of Christina Alberta. But the mind refuses to go on with a painful fancy that leads to nothing, and Christina Alberta's imagination presently ceased further dealings with her Daddy until fresh material came to hand. 'He will turn up somewhere,' she repeated feebly, and became a great consumer of evening papers. 'He will turn up somehow.' Her chief anxiety was that he should not turn up with too tremendous head-lines. She began to adjust herself like an early Christian for the Second Coming. The riddle of her Daddy's disappearance became a habit of mind, became, as it were, a frame, a proscenium arch to her current activities. Beneath it she returned to the urgent and extraordinary problem of herself and her relationship to Devizes.

§ 12

It was manifest that he was almost as excited as she was at their mutual discovery. The possible proceedings of Sargon, fantastic as they might prove to be when they came to light, remained for him as for her a matter of urgent importance, but the thought of this strange relationship completely overshadowed it. Each had a reciprocal desire to get at the other, to discover what magic of sympathy and understanding might not be latent in their consanguinity.

The evening after the Universal Aunt was installed he took Christina Alberta out to dine with him at a pleasant little Italian restaurant in the corner of Sloane Square, and afterwards he came back to the studio with her and talked until nearly one in the morning. He showed himself shyly anxious to find out her aims and purposes in life, and what she was doing and what might be done to let out her possibilities. He was evidently disposed to shoulder just as much parental responsibility as he could, subject to the preservation of appearances and a proper care for the self-respect of the vanished Sargon. She attracted him and he liked her. Her feelings for him were more tumultuous and abundant and indefinite. She didn't particularly want help or support from him. The idea of being dependent upon him for anything repelled rather than attracted her, but she wanted to get hold of him, to please and satisfy him, to be better than he had expected and interesting in fresh ways. She wanted him to like her – to care for her more than mere liking. She wanted that anxiously and tremendously.

She liked a sort of ease and confidence he had with waiters and cabmen and the common services of life. He seemed to know just what people would do and they seemed to know just what he would do; there was no tension in these matters, no nervous 'h'rrmping.' These common attributes of habitual prosperity were so little in her experience that they seemed a distinction of his; and they threw a flavour of knowing what he was about, and being serenely in control over most of the conversation, when indeed he was as curious and experimental and emotionally stirred almost as she was. The eyes that met hers when she talked were steady, friendly, interested, intimate eyes, and her heart went out to them.

Over the dinner he talked at first about music. He had had no music in his education, and now he was discovering it. A friend of his had been taking him to concerts, and he had got a pianola, 'so as to spell it out at home first.' But Christina Alberta's education had missed out music too, and she hadn't as yet discovered it. So that topic died out presently. He tried her about pictures, but there again she wasn't particularly interested. They had a little silence.

He looked across at her and smiled.

'I'd like to ask you all sorts of questions, Christina Alberta, if I dared,' he said.

She blushed – absurdly. 'Any questions you like,' she said.

'Immense questions,' he said. 'For example – generally – what do you think you are up to?'

She understood what he meant at once. But she was so unprepared with an answer that she became evasive.

'Up to!' she said, playing for time. 'I suppose I'm looking for my lost Daddy.'

'But what are you up to generally? What are you doing with your life? Where are you going?'

'I'm at sea,' she said at last. 'Lots of my generation are, I think. The girls especially. You are older than I am; I'm only beginning. I don't want to seem cheeky, but aren't you better able to say what *you* are up to? Suppose' – her slightly scared gravity broke into an impudent smile that Devizes found very congenial – 'suppose you play first?'

He considered that. 'Perfectly fair,' he said. 'I will. Have another olive. I'm glad you like olives. I do too. Nobody's called me to account for a long time. What *is* my game? It's a fair question.'

But not an easy one evidently.

'I suppose one ought to begin right back at one's philosophy,' he said. 'A long story. But I started the idea.'

Christina Alberta was greatly elated at her successful repulse of his projected cross-examination. Instead of making a display herself she could watch him. She watched him over the flowers on the table and had to be nudged by the waiter when he brought the pheasant to her elbow.

'How *should* one begin?' he plunged. She had heard of Pragmatism? Yes. She was probably better read in that sort of thing than he was. He was, he considered, a sort of Pragmatist. Most modern-minded, intelligent people he held were Pragmatists as he understood it. Pragmatist? As he understood it? He met her eye and explained. In this sense he meant it; we, none of us, had a clear vision of reality; nobody perhaps would ever do more than approach reality. What we perceived was just that much of reality that got through to us, through our very defective powers of interpretation. 'They've done this pheasant *en casserole* very well,' he broke off. 'Three minutes' truce we ought to give it. Do you find I'm talking comprehensibly? I doubt it.'

'I'm hanging on,' said Christina Alberta. . . .

'Perhaps I'm beginning rather too far off.'

Pheasant. . . .

'To come back to my confession of faith,' he said presently. . . . 'Mind you, Christina Alberta, you've got to say your bit afterwards.'

'It won't be as definite as yours,' she said. 'Some of yours I shall steal. But go on – telling me.'

'Well, keep hold, Christina Alberta. I feel I'm going to be at once hesitating and condensed. And I'm not sure of what you know or don't know. If I say I'm an Agnostic about the nature of the universe, and how it began and where it ends, does that convey anything to you?'

'Just what I think,' said Christina Alberta.

'Well.' He started afresh and got into parenthetical difficulties. The Pêche Melba came to interrupt and permit a fresh start. He unfolded a psychologist's vision of the world for her inspection, a curious and yet attractive vision to her. He expressed himself in terms of mind and understanding. She was used to hearing everything expressed in terms of labour and material necessity. Life, he said, was one continuous thing, all life was connected. He tried to illustrate that. The conscious life of most lower animals was intensely individual, a lizard, for example, was just itself, just its instincts and appetites; it received no teaching and no tradition, it handed on nothing to its kind. But the higher animals were taught when they were young, learnt and taught others and communicated with each other. Men far more than any animal. He had developed picture-writing, speech, oral tradition, scientific record. There was now a common mind of the race, a great growing body of knowledge and interpretations.

'People like ourselves are just cross-sections of that flow. Individually we receive it, react to it, change it a little, and pass away. We are just passing phases of that increasing mind – which may be, for all we can certainly say, an immortal mind. Does this sound like Greek – or nonsense to you?'

'No,' she said, 'I think I get the drift of it.' She looked at his intent face. He wasn't in the least talking down to her; he was simply trying to express himself as well as he possibly could to her. He was treating her like an equal. Like an equal!

That was his general philosophy. He was coming to the question of himself now, he said. He became very earnest over the coffee cups and ash tray on the swept tablecloth. He spread elucidatory hands before her. He was conscientiously explicit. He saw in himself two phases, or rather two levels of existence. Roughly speaking, two. They had links and intermediate stages of course, but they could be ignored when one just wanted to express the idea. First of all, he was the old instinctive individual, fearful, greedy, lustful, jealous, self-assertive. That was the primary self. He had to attend to that primary self because it carried all the rest of him, as a rider must see that his horse gets oats. Deeper lay social instincts and dispositions arising out of family life. That was the second self, the social self. Man, he threw out, is a creature that has become more and more consciously social in the last two or three hundred thousand years. He has been lengthening his life, keeping his children with him longer and longer, enlarging his community from family herds into clans and tribes and nations. The deep-lying continuity of life was becoming more apparent and finding more and more definite expression with this socialization of man. To educate anyone in the proper sense of the word was to make him more and more aware of this continuity. The importance of the passionate feverish self was then reduced. True education was self-subordination to a greater life, to the social self. The natural instincts and limitations of the primary self were in conflict with this wider underflow; education, *good* education, tended to correct them.

'Here am I,' said Devizes, 'as we all are, a creature in a state of internal conflict, quicker, fiercer mortal instincts at issue with a deeper, calmer, less brightly lit, but finally stronger drive towards immortal purposes. And I am – how shall I put it? – I personally am, to the best of my ability, on the side of the deeper things. My aptitudes and temperament and opportunities have brought me to psychology – as a profession. I work to add to the accumulation of human knowledge and understanding about the mind. I work for illumination. My particular work is to study and cure troubled and tangled minds. I try to straighten them out and simplify them and illuminate them. And above all I try to learn from them. I seek the mental or physical cause of their distresses. I try to set down as clearly and accessibly as possible, all I observe and learn. That's my job. That's my aim. It gives me a general direction for my life. All the stuff of my mere individual existence I try to subordinate to that end. Not always. My monkey individual gets loose at times and gibbers on the roof. And at other times it's rather good company as a relief from overwork. Vanity and self-indulgence have their uses. But never mind the monkey now. I do not want to be a brilliant person; I want to be a vital

part. That's my essential creed. I want to be the sort of
wheel in the machinery they call a mental expert. As good
a wheel as I can be. That's what I'm up to in general
terms, Christina Alberta. That's what I think I am.'

'Yes,' said Christina Alberta, reflecting profoundly. 'Of
course I can't produce a statement like that. You've got
your system – complete.'

'And finished,' said Devizes. 'You've got to tell your story
in your own way. At your age – you ought to be with loose
ends to all your convictions.'

'I wonder if I can tell you any story.'

'You've got to try your best now. It's only fair play.'

'Yes.'

There was a little silence.

'It's wonderful to talk to you like this,' said Christina
Alberta. 'It's wonderful to talk to anyone like this.'

'I feel that you and I – have to understand each other.'

She met his grave eyes for a moment. There was a wave
of emotion within her. She could not speak. She reached
out her hand to touch his, and for a moment their hands
were together.

§ 13

Christina Alberta only got to her confession of faith in
the studio after they had returned thither and relieved
the Universal Aunt. Even then they didn't settle down
to the business all at once. Devizes walked about and
looked for drawings by Harold; he deduced Harold
from his drawings to a quite remarkable extent, Christina
Alberta thought. He was curious about Fay. 'What's
Mrs. Crumb like?' he asked. 'Show me something of
hers, something that seems to give her.'

It pleased Christina Alberta very much to think that
he was shy with her. She felt that this was a recognition

of her equality. He was respecting her and she was very eager that she should be respected by him.

He got to an anchorage at last in the gaily painted seat by the gas-fire: and Christina Alberta, after flitting about the room for a time, came and stood before it, shapely legs wide apart and hands behind her back in an attitude that would have shocked all her feminine ancestors for many generations. But it did not shock Devizes; he found her more and more interesting to watch, and he sat at his ease and regarded her with a lively admiration. Most of us get used to our daughters so gradually; they grow up and we carry the wonder of them as Milo carried his ox; it isn't common for a man to get an unexpected daughter abruptly at the age of twenty-one.

She said she hadn't much in the way of metaphysics; she was a Materialist.

'No prayers at mother's knee? Religion of Mother and Daddy? School prayers and teaching? Church or chapel?'

'It all washed out and faded out I think, as they laid it on.'

'No fear of hell? Most of my generation went through the fear of hell.'

'Not a trace of it,' said the New Age.

'But – a desire for God in the night?'

Christina Alberta paused for a little while. 'I have that,' she said. 'It comes – sometimes. I don't know whether it's very important or not important at all.'

'It's part,' said Devizes slowly, 'of something that has to do with wanting to be more than a miserable worm – and disliking meanness – and so forth.'

'Yes. Do you know more about it?'

Rather oddly he didn't answer that. 'And how do you see yourself in relation to mankind – and the animals – and the stars? What sense of obligation have you? What do you think the road is along which you have to go?'

'H'm,' said Christina Alberta. She considered she was a Communist, she said, though she didn't belong to the Party. But she knew some other young people who did. She produced some of the phrases of the movement, 'the materialist conception of history' and so forth. He said he failed to understand and asked rather irritating questions; she thought controversially. She didn't realize at first how widely apart was their phraseology. As they talked this became apparent. He seemed to have nothing too good to say for the Communist idea, for wasn't it just his own idea of being a part of a greater being of life? but he seemed to have nothing too bad for practical Communism. Marxist Communism he said wasn't a constructive movement at all; it was merely a solvent. It had no idea, no plan. Christina Alberta was put on the defensive. 'Enthusiasm for an ideal Communist state isn't nearly so important as the question of immediate Communist tactics in a decaying society,' she recited, in an almost official tone. That was how her young friends in the Party talked. But when she talked like this to him it didn't seem so effective. He wouldn't leave her phrases alone. He wanted to know what she meant by decay in a society, whether there had ever been a society not actively in decay, and not also actively in growth, what good tactics were except in relation to general strategy and whether there could be any strategy without a clear war-end. She countered more vigorously than effectively and their manner became controversial.

He pressed the difference in their opinions. Communism for him meant a new spirit, a spirit of science reorganizing the world upon scientific collective lines, but the whole temper of party communism was contemporary. It was saturated with the feelings and ideas of existing social classes, with the natural resentment of the dispossessed. It had the angry dogmatism of desperate people not sure of their grip. It needed more of the passion of creative self-forgetfulness. Many Communists, he said, were simply reversed capitalists, egotists without capital; they wanted revenge and expropriation, and when they were through with that they would be left with nothing but social ruins and everything to begin all over again. And they were suspicious and intolerant because of their want of internal assurance. They distrusted their best friends, their proper leaders, scientific men like Keynes and Soddy.

'Keynes a Communist!' cried Christina Alberta in derision. 'He doesn't accept the first scientific fact of the class war.'

'It isn't much of a fact – certainly not a First Scientific Fact,' he replied. 'Keynes builds up slowly a conception of a scientifically organized exchange system. Most of your friends in Russia don't seem capable even of realizing that such a thing is necessary.'

'But they do!'

'Have they shown it?'

'What do *you* know of the Russian Bolsheviks?'

'What do *you*? You just look at the labels on people. Nothing genuine without the red label – and everything genuine with.'

She said he saw things from his 'bourgeois' standpoint, and he laughed cheerfully at her social classifications; there was no bourgeoisie in England, he said; she attempted some of the stock cynicisms and sarcasms of the movement but with an unusual lack of conviction. It was easy for him to criticize, she said, living as he did on invested capital.

'It would make it easier,' he smiled. 'But really I live on my fees.'

'You have invested capital.'

'Some. I don't live on it.'

They had exhausted the dispute for a time. After all, she reflected, she hadn't put up such a bad fight, considering her age and standing. The momentary glow of controversial exasperation faded again. They drifted to the more immediate question in which they were interested, the question of what she was to do with her life.

§ 14

'We progress, Christina Alberta,' said Devizes, 'but it's still generally the rule that a woman's life is determined very largely by the character and occupations of – the leading man in the play. Have you by any chance been in love yet?'

She wanted to tell him all the truth about herself, but some things are untellable. She hesitated and blushed hotly. 'Nowadays,' she said, and stopped. 'I've some imagination. I've run about London. I've perhaps imagined things –'

His eyes were very searching for a moment but none the less kindly.

'I've been in love – in a kind of way,' she admitted.

He nodded with a dreadful effect of complete comprehension.

'I don't want to run my life in relation to any man,' she extended.

'Clever girls never do. Any more than clever young men want to spend their lives adoring a goddess.'

'In any case I don't see myself becoming a child-producing housekeeper,' she said.

'Even if you married. No. I doubt whether you are that type. But if you are going to reject that easy way – and it *is* an easy way, in spite of what people say – if you are going to be a citizen on your own as a man is, then

300

you've got to do a man's work, Christina Alberta. There's to be none of the Pretty Fanny business, you know.'

'Well, *am* I?' asked Christina Alberta.

'No, I don't think you are. And in that case, I guess you want some more education. You're clever, but you're a bit patchy.'

'I'm good enough to get a job. And then learn.'

'Learn,' he said. 'That's enough to take you all your time. I'd rather we agreed it's got to be a student for two or three years more. You need have no anxiety about ways and means. You and I are of the same Clan – a clan of two practically – and I am the head. I'll see you through just as though you were a son. And now, what sort of work is it to be? Law? Medicine? a general education for journalism or affairs? Doors open to women now – fresh doors every day.'

To that Christina Alberta could speak a little more fully. She had been thinking out some of these things. She wanted to know about life and the world as a whole. Could she have a good year at physical science, biology and geology chiefly and anthropology? Would that be possible? And then if she was any good at medical work, another year at mental science or politics and public health? 'It sounds ambitious, I know,' she said.

'Ambitious! It's an encyclopædia in a year.'

'But I want to know about all these things.'

'Naturally.'

'Could I have longer than that?'

'You'd have to have longer than that.'

'It seems to be asking for so much.'

'It wouldn't be if you were in trousers. We've agreed to unsex you to that extent. Why shouldn't you be ambitious?'

'You think I might do work – scientific work – at last – as you do?'

'Why not?'

301

'A girl?'

'You're the sort of stuff I am, Christina Alberta.'

'Do you think – some day – I might even come to work – to work with you?'

'Kindred minds may follow kindred courses,' he said, with the completest recognition of their relationship. 'Why not?'

She stood and looked at him with a dark excitement in her eyes and he had a momentary intimation of all that he might be to her. Gallant she was and fine and ambitious; a wonderful life to come out of nothingness into his own. And she meant this relationship to grow, as well it might grow, into something very great and deep for both of them.

He went off at a tangent to talk of the contrast of men and women students and of men and women as workers. 'You'll never run parallel with men, you free women, so don't expect it. You've got to work out a way that is similar perhaps but different. Different down to the roots.' He argued that probably the whole fabric of a man had its qualities that a woman's did not possess, and vice versa, down even to a muscular fibre or a nerve tendril. A time might come when we should be able to put a drop of blood or a scrap of skin under the microscope or apply some subtle reagent to it and tell its sex. 'A man resists,' he said. 'A man is intractable. He has greater inertia, physical and mental. That keeps him to his course. Men compared with women are steadier and stupider. Women compared with men are quicker and sillier. Bludgeons and bodkins.'

He talked of his student days when women medical students were still rather novel intrusions, and from that he passed to his father's prejudices, to his father's treatment of his mother and his boyish days. Presently they were exchanging experiences of childish delusions and fancies. She forgot how much older and more experienced he was in the ease of his talk. He told her about himself because he recognized her right to know about him; he listened with a friendly eagerness to all she chose to tell him of her Daddy and herself and about her impressions and her few adventures in encounter as a suburban student in London. They shared their delight in Paul Lambone's kindly absurdity. Presently it occurred to her to offer him drink. The Crumbs had left a bottle of beer and a syphon. But Devizes asked her to make tea and helped her with the kettle. Meanwhile the mutual exploration went on. Their friendliness grew richer and deeper as they talked. She had never before met so intimate and delightful a curiosity as his. She had had friends before but no such friendliness; she had had a lover but never such intimacy.

It was one o'clock before he went away.

The talk had ebbed. He sat thoughtful for a moment. 'I must go,' he said, and stood up. They faced each other, a little at a loss for parting words.

'It's been wonderful to talk to you,' she said.

'It's a great thing to have discovered you.'

Another pause. 'It's a great thing for me,' she said lamely.

'We'll talk – many times,' he said.

He wanted to call her 'my dear,' and an absurd shyness prevented him. And she was aware of that suppression.

She stood up straight before him in the passage with a flush on her cheeks and her eyes alight, and he wondered he had not thought her beautiful from the beginning. 'Good-bye for the time,' he said, and smiled at her gravely and took and held her hand for a moment.

'Good night,' she said, and hesitated and then opened the green door for him and stood and watched him go up the Mews.

At the top he turned and waved his hand to her before he disappeared. 'Good night,' she whispered and started, and looked about her as if she feared that her unspoken thoughts had been audible.

Father. Her father!

So real fathers leave one aglow like this!

He had left her tense as a violin string on which the bow rests motionless. Now Daddy, who wasn't her father, she would just have hugged and kissed.

How Bobby Stole a Lunatic

§ 1

A MAN may be a mental expert and yet fail to take the most obvious hints in a detective investigation. The medical superintendent at Cummerdown Hill had doubted for a moment whether Widgery was the name of Sargon's visitor. He had thought it was more like Goodchild. But since there was no known Goodchild in the world of Christina Alberta, neither she nor Devizes had troubled to scrutinize this momentary uncertainty. Nor had she and Devizes asked themselves why Widgery should have made a second visit to his cousin. Indeed, he had not done so. It was a much younger man who had visited Sargon that Tuesday; he had falsely represented himself as Sargon's nephew and given the name of 'Robin Goodchild.' His real name was Robert Roothing, and he had come for the sole purpose of getting Sargon out of the asylum as soon as possible, because he could not endure the thought of his staying there.

Circumstances had conspired with a natural predisposition to give Bobby a great horror of all restraint. His mother, a gentle dark creature, the wife of a large blond negligent landowner, had died when Bobby was twelve; and he had been entrusted to the care of a harsh, old-fashioned aunt – to whom the cupboard seemed a proper place for discipline. When she discovered that he was really distressed by it, she sought to break his 'cowardice' by giving him quite liberal doses of it – even when he had committed no offence. He went to a school where discipline was maintained by 'keeping-in.' The war eliminated his father, who died suddenly of over-excitement while in command of an anti-aircraft gun

305

during an air-raid, and it led Bobby through some tiresome campaigning in Mesopotamia and the beleaguerment of Kut to an extremely unsympathetic Turkish prison. In any case he would probably have been a free-going easy creature, but now he had so passionate a hatred of cages that he wanted to release even canaries. He disliked the iron fences round the public parks and squares with a propagandist passion, he wrote articles about them in *Wilkins' Weekly* and elsewhere clamouring for their 'liberation,' and he never went by train if he could help it because of the claustrophobia that assailed him in the compartment. He would ride a push-bike except for long distances, and then he would borrow Billy's motor-bicycle. He did his best to prevent his craving for the large and open from becoming too conspicuous or a nuisance to other people, but Tessy and Billy understood about it and did their best to make things easy for him.

It was not only claustrophobia that Bobby had to fight against. He carried on a secret internal conflict with a disinclination to act upon most occasions, that he believed had developed in him as a result of war experiences. Sometimes it seemed to him to be just indolence, sometimes fastidiousness, sometimes sheer funk and cowardice. He could not tell. He had a rankling memory of a case of cruelty he had witnessed in the prisoners' camp when he had stood by and done nothing. He would wake up sometimes at three o'clock in the morning and say to himself aloud, 'I stood by and I did nothing. Oh God! Oh *God!* Oh GOD!' And at times he would walk up and down his study repeating: '*Act!* You vegetable! you hiding cur! Out and act!' Meanwhile he obeyed routines and did whatever came to his hand. As 'Aunt Suzannah' he was excellent, indefatigably considerate, lucid, really helpful. *Wilkins' Weekly* was proud of him. He was the backbone of the paper.

And now this affair of Sargon's had twisted him up very badly between his desire to free the little man, who had taken an extraordinary hold upon his imagination and sympathy, and his sense of the immense forces against which he would have to pit himself if he tried to give him any help. It was only after a considerable struggle with himself that he had called at the police station and the Gifford Street Workhouse. He was afraid of awkward questions, afraid above all of being 'detained.' The workhouse was a detestable place with high walls and a paved court and a general effect of sinister seclusion from the grubby street outside. For the best part of a day after his Gifford Street visit he hesitated whether he should do anything more.

'Bobby's got a grouch,' Susan told Tessy. 'He's stoopid. Just sits and says 'E 'as to fink sumpfink over. What's he fink fings over for? Said I was to come downstairs again, there was a good girl. . . . Meant it. . . . Said so. . . . Puss'd me 'way. . . . I do-o-nt fink I lo-o-o-ove Bobby 'nymore.'

Great distress. A storm of tears. Tessy was deeply sympathetic.

But after tea Bobby was brighter and drew Susan her 'Good night picture' and came down and sat on her bed and talked her to sleep the same as usual, and Tessy perceived that the worst of Bobby's trouble was over.

At supper Bobby unfolded his plans.

'I mean to go to Cummerdown Hill to-morrow,' he said compactly.

'To see Sargon?' said Tessy understandingly.

'If I can. But it won't be visiting day. That's Tuesday. I want to look round.'

Billy raised his eyebrows and helped himself to butter.

'But –' said Tessy, and stopped short.

'Yes?' said Bobby.

'You won't be able to see him. You don't know the name he's under.'

'They'll call him Mr. Sargon,' said Billy.

'His name's Preemby. He's a laundryman. They told me at the workhouse. His people *want him to be there!*'

'I can't stand the thought of it,' said Bobby after a brief silence.

'Don't follow,' said Billy.

'That nice little thing being made into a lunatic. Like a little blue-eyed bird he was. High walls. Great louting warders. Sargon, King of Kings. . . . I've got to do something about it or I shall burst.'

He looked at once weak and desperate. Tessy reflected. 'You'd better go,' she said.

'But what good will that do?' said Billy, and was quelled by a glance from Tessy.

'If you can lend me the old motor-bike and the side-car. You're not using it this week-end.'

'You can take off the side-car,' said Billy.

'I may want it,' said Bobby.

'You don't mean –!' said Billy.

Bobby came as near to an explosion as he ever did.

'Oh never mind *what* I mean. I tell you I'm going down to Cummerdown to have a look at the place. No doubt I'm a futile ass, Billy, but I just can't help myself going. The poor little beggar's got no friends. His own family's helped to put him away. Families do. It's an infernal world. I've got to do something. If it's only to shake 'em up. If I stay here another day I shall start smacking Susan.'

'Somebody ought to,' said Billy.

'If he can only keep away for fourteen days clear –'

'He's free?' said Tessy.

'He has to be certified all over again – anyhow,' said Bobby.

§ 2

Bobby discovered that the village of Cummerdown lies nearly two miles away from the Asylum, and does its best very successfully to have as little to do with it as possible. It nestles among trees just off the high road to Ashford and Hastings, and has one cramped little inn that gave him a bleak bedroom and accommodated his machine and side-car in an open outhouse crowded with two carts and a Ford and populous with hens. The day was still young, and after he had deposited the elderly rucksac in which he had brought his 'things' upstairs, he set out with a walking-stick and an air of detached interest to recon-noitre the asylum and develop his plans for the rescue of Sargon. That golden autumn was still holding out; the pleasant lane he followed to the high road was patterned with green and yellow chestnut leaves and the trees overhead were full of sunshine. It was a reassuring day. It encouraged him. It took him with a kindly seriousness and made him feel that rescuing people from lunatic asylums was the sort of work the sun could shine upon and nature welcome.

It had needed a great effort to get down from London. He had felt then like a midget setting out to attack an embattled universe. Amidst the Croydon traffic he had been half minded to go back, but he had felt that he could not face Tessy until he had been at least definitely defeated. It was delightful to note an increased assurance within himself as he drew nearer to his enterprise. He felt much more on the scale of the powers he attacked. After all, what were laws and regulations but just things patched up by men like himself? What were prison walls but the slow work of shirking bricklayers and evasive contractors? The attendants and custodians, the superintendents and so forth he was setting out to circumvent, were all as fallible as himself. And the thing was urgent and outrageous, this seizure of a harmless little fantastic, this frightful imprisonment. It had to be fought. The world would be intolerable unless such things were fought.

Queer world it was! Such beauty on these tree-stems, such a glow, and the delightfulness of rustling one's feet through these leaves! But all that was by the way; the real business of life was to fight evil things.

He came out from between the trees and saw the wide downs opening out before him and the blocked masses of the asylum with its broad bare grounds and walls, an eyesore. This was his objective. In that place some-where was Sargon, and he had to be released.

He seated himself on a convenient stile and inspected that heavy architecture and tried to frame a plan. That white building in the centre looked like a gaunt Georgian private house. That was probably the nucleus of the whole place. Two men were visible in front of it mowing the grass – patients perhaps. The wall and railings along the road looked implacable. Two stern-looking lodges there were, no doubt with a testy janitor lurking within, and there were iron gates – one open. A van was coming out, a furniture dealer's van. For a time Bobby's mind ran on the possibility of becoming a tradesman with parcels or a crate to deliver. . . . Many difficulties that way. . . .

'But why a frontal attack?' said Bobby with an effect of discovery. The place fell away behind, downhill. He would inspect the rear. If he worked round by the open down to the right, he would probably get on to slopes commanding a view of the asylum grounds.

An hour later Bobby was sitting on a heap of flints by the side of a minor road which ran over the rising ground behind the asylum. He found the rear of the place much more hopeful and much more interesting than the front. There were fields with a number of men working in them, and at one place near the buildings a row of men seemed to be digging a trench under the supervision of an attendant. There was quite a lot of movement closer to the buildings, under a sort of open shed half a dozen men seemed to be taking exercise by walking up and down. It vexed Bobby to think that any one of these figures might be his Sargon. If only he had the elementary common sense to bring a field-glass, he reproached himself, he might have been able to make out his little friend's features. 'No clearness of thought,' he whispered. 'No decision.' A lot of these people seemed to be going about very freely, carrying gardening implements and so forth. One he noted, walking about and gesticulating as if he talked to himself; he was manifestly a patient and quite unattended.

The wall bounding the asylum on this side had none of the austerity of the front wall. It seemed to be an old estate wall; in several places it was covered with ivy and here and there it was overhung with trees. The ground dropped away to his right, there was a little stream which ran out of the asylum grounds at the lowest corner; the corner was shaded by trees and seemed to be left to the trees and undergrowth; the stream ran under a low arch in the wall and went on down a widening valley towards London. The seclusion and shade of this corner appealed to Bobby very strongly. It seemed to him exactly the point at which Sargon ought to be got out of the place. He decided that presently he would stroll down and examine its possibilities as precisely as possible. If one could get Sargon to come down there –

He found the details difficult. He meant to have a plan

worked out in every detail and to communicate it to Sargon on the next visiting-day, but it was very hard to fit this plan together. He did not know when it would be most convenient for Sargon to attempt to slip away, whether this was to be a daylight or a night affair. He saw before him a great vista of inquiries to be made and suspicious people to be faced. 'Damn!' said Bobby, and for a time he was again for abandoning the attempt.

Why couldn't one go in at these gates, boldly and overwhelmingly, and say, 'There is a sane man here and I have come to set him free?' A superman might do that, or an archangel. How splendid it would be to be a sort of Archangel-Knight-Errant, a great flaming presence of light and winged power, righting wrongs, reproving oppressors, liberating every kind of captive creature. Then one might do things. Bobby lapsed into a childish day-dream.

Presently he roused himself, stood up and went down towards the exit of the stream. The wall struck him as quite climbable – even by a little old gentleman. The stream came out meandering among pebbles through a short tunnel. One could have got into the asylum grounds or out of them quite easily over the wall by the ivy or through the culvert. He resolved to come again at twilight and – just to satisfy himself about his own pluck among other things – get into the asylum premises and walk about a little.

Yes. He would do that.

He tried to imagine himself assisting Sargon over the wall. One could get on the top of the wall and reach down to his hands. A cripple could do it. The motor-bicycle would have to be waiting up there in the lane. And then? *Where would he take him?*

This was a new consideration. For a time Bobby's mind was appalled and paralysed by the complexities of his enterprise. He had not thought of taking him anywhere in particular.

The days that intervened before visiting-day seemed at once interminable and frightfully swift. He had been to Dymchurch in the summer with the Malmesburys, and liked the landlady of his lodgings very much; he wired to her 'Can I come with a relation not ill but overworked for week or so you will remember me last summer Roothing the Feathers Cummerdown ' and had got a reply, 'Glad to see you any time.' So that was all right. But the rest of the plan failed very largely to materialize. He made his nocturnal visit to the asylum grounds without misadventure.

The morning of visiting-day found him with half a dozen plans, and they all had gaps and none seemed much better or worse than the others. And he had walked round the asylum grounds at various discreet distances, by night and day just twenty-three times, not counting loops, returns and visits to particular points of interest. Fortunately asylums are much preoccupied with their internal affairs, and do not keep look-out men upon the battlements. They do not reckon with rescuers from outside.

Bobby made his final decision among these conflicting projects over his breakfast bacon. With a resolute sangfroid and his nerves all a-tingle, he set out for the asylum to see Sargon and begin the work of rescue as he had thought it out. First he had to find out what freedom of movement was permitted Sargon, when it might be possible for him to get away to the corner by the culvert, and he had to arrange a time for that meeting. Then he would have to provide also for alternative times if Sargon failed to keep his first appointment. Bobby would be waiting under the wall and the motor-bicycle and side-car would be hidden among the bushes up by

the road. In a trice Sargon would be over the wall. After
that they could laugh at pursuit. Off they would go to
Dymchurch, and there, safe and untrackable, Sargon
would keep indoors until the fifteen days needed to
make him legally a sane man again had passed. And then
Bobby could find out those relations of his and talk the
matter over with them, and get things on a proper footing.
So Bobby planned it out.

Just at the lodge gates he decided upon an assumed
name. He wasn't quite clear why he didn't give his own
name, but an assumed name seemed to him to be more
in the spirit of the adventure.

§ 3

When Sargon was informed that he was to be visited by
Mr. Robin Goodchild he was in a depressed mood. He
betrayed no surprise at the name. It seemed to him to be
as good as any other name. It might be the name of some
intelligent inquirer or possibly even some precursor of the
release he still hoped for. His spirits rose. He submitted
cheerfully to a searching examination of his personal
tidiness, and he nodded acquiescently to a warning not
to talk about '*every* blessed thing' he'd seen.

His spirits rose still more when he saw the dark kindliness of Bobby's face. It was the one disciple who had ever
seemed to believe. He held out both his hands in a little
storm of emotion. Whatever sort of muddler Bobby
might be to himself, to Sargon in that moment at least
he was strength and hope.

The meeting occurred in the reception-room downstairs, for no one from the outside world may ever
penetrate to the wards and the bleak realities of everyday asylum life. The reception-room had a baize-covered

314

table in the middle, a black horsehair sofa and numerous
chairs; it was totally devoid of small movables; there was
an A B C time-table and one or two illustrated weeklies
on the table, and the walls bore brown-spotted steel
engravings of Prince Albert and Queen Victoria in the
Highlands and of Windsor Castle from the Thames.
There were three or four groups, each of two or three
people, with their heads together conversing in tactful
undertones; there were several women and one little girl;
a tearful lady in profound mourning sat apart by the
empty fire-place and no doubt awaited a patient; two
attendants tried hard not to look as though they were
listening as intently as possible to the conversations going
on about them. The patients present were all in the sanest
phase, 'fit to be visited.' There was no madness visible;
at most only a little nervous oddity. Bobby had been
watching these other groups while he waited, and he had
been impressed by a certain quality of furtiveness in their
behaviour. The furtiveness he connected with the alert-
ness of the attendants. One affected to look out of the
window, the other half sat at a table holding an old
Graphic, and ever and again there would be a quick glance
at this patient or that. It had not occurred to Bobby that
his talk to Sargon would be semi-public; it was a disconcerting interference that would greatly hamper him in
giving his instructions.

Bobby saw at once that Sargon was very much thinner
than when he had taken his room in Midgard Street.
He looked ill and worn, an effect that was emphasized
by the fact that he was badly shaven and wearing ill-
fitting clothes. His eyes seemed larger and sunken under
his brows and his forehead more definitely lined. Yet if
he looked unhappier he also looked more intelligent.
He seemed more aware of the things about him – less a
man in a dream.

'I have come to see if I can be of service to you,' said Bobby, holding out his hands. 'Your friends and disciples are anxious for your welfare.'

'You have come to see me,' he said, and glanced sideways at the listening attendant and dropped his voice; 'me – *Sargon?*'

Bobby understood that note of doubt and it grieved him. 'You, Sargon, the King out of the Past.'

'They would have me deny it,' whispered Sargon.

Bobby raised his eyebrows and nodded his head as who should say, 'They'd do *anything*.'

The little man's manner changed. 'How is one to know?' he said. 'How is one to know?'

He sighed. 'Nothing seems certain any more.'

'Can we sit down and talk together,' said Bobby. 'There is much to be said between us.'

Sargon glanced round. There were two chairs in a corner, and in that corner they might be a little beyond the eavesdropper's range. 'I cannot understand this madness,' said Sargon as they sat down. 'I cannot understand this Riddle that has been set me. Why does the Power, why does God, permit men to be mad? When they are mad they are beyond good and evil. What are they? Men still? What becomes of justice, what becomes of righteousness – when men go mad?' His voice sank. His eyes became furtive. 'Dreadful things happen here,' he whispered. 'Dreadful things. Quite dreadful things.'

He ceased. For a little while neither he nor Bobby said a word.

'I want to get you out of this,' said Bobby.

'Are my friends doing anything?' asked Sargon. 'What is Christina Alberta doing? Is she well?'

'She is splendid,' he said haphazard. No doubt she was one of this beastly family of Sargon's that was content to leave him here. 'I want you to listen to me,' he said.

316

But Sargon had things to tell. 'Everyone in this place is always thinking about what their friends outside are doing for them. The poor souls come and talk to me. They know I am different from what they are. They write letters, petitions. I tell them that when God releases me I will bear them all in mind. Some mock at me. They have delusions. They think they are kings or emperors or rich men or great discoverers, and that the world has plotted against them. . . . Some are suspicious and cruel. . . . Darkened souls. . . . Some have dreadful habits. You cannot help but see. . . . Some are badly sunken – degraded – indescribably. . . . It is very painful, very painful.'

The blue eyes stared blankly at unpleasant memories. 'There can be no doubt that I am Sargon,' he said abruptly, and looked sharply at Bobby.

'I call you by no other name,' said Bobby.

The momentary acuteness faded again. 'That man Preemby was unawakened. He was asleep – scarcely dreaming of life. *But I have seen!* I have looked at the world from high places. And from dark places too. . . . Sargon. Sargon is a different person. . . . But it is difficult.'

He became silent.

Bobby felt that they were getting nowhere. In his anticipations of this conversation he had talked and Sargon had listened. And there had been no one to overhear. But this was all unexpected. Anyhow, the plan had to be told; Sargon had to be instructed in his part. He glanced warily at the people nearest to them. 'There are those among us,' he said quietly and quickly, 'who would set you free. I want to tell you –' On the spur of the moment he attempted a code. 'When I speak of a city in Central Asia it will mean this place, the Asylum. Do you understand?'

'This place – Central Asia. If I am Sargon. . . . Everything is possibly something else. But we are still in England nevertheless.'

'In reality. But I want to explain to you.'

'Yes, yes. Explain.'

'I shall speak of great discoveries in Central Asia. That will mean this.'

Did he understand?

'*Rescue!*' whispered Bobby in Sargon's ear, and glanced at the attendant and met his eye and was discomposed.

'Tell me about the discoveries,' said Sargon after a little pause as though he had not heard that whispered word.

'It is a symbol for this place,' said Bobby.

Sargon looked puzzled. The attendant was watching their faces now. Perhaps he suspected already. Bobby flushed hotly and plunged abruptly into an account of the discoveries of an amazing Russian he called Bobinsky. Bobinsky had found a walled city with no way out. 'Yes,' said Sargon interested. The attendant was now looking away. 'Like this place,' said Bobby, and more explicitly; 'I *mean* this place.' There was a river ran through the city, the city of confinement, and went out by the lower part. There it was the helper waited. The rescuers. That was the place for them to wait. Did he understand? At that point where the trees grew and the river went out through the wall. There they waited. There they would wait until the captive king came to them.

'It is a curious story,' said Sargon. 'What captive king do you mean?'

'It is meant for you.'

'The river you speak of may be the Euphrates,' said Sargon. 'I dream of the Euphrates.'

He had missed it all! He was out upon some woolgathering of his own. Euphrates! What had the Euphrates to do with Central Asia? Or the Asylum?

'Bother!' said Bobby. 'I say – It is a smaller river I mean, a streamlet – in the grounds here. Don't you understand?'

A tall sharp-faced woman in a hat of hard black straw came near them and sat down. Bobby, as he talked, observed her out of the corner of his eye. Was she the friend of a patient or what was she doing here? 'I speak in symbols,' said Bobby, still watching and thinking about this woman. 'This city is your prison.' He caught the woman exchanging a glance of intelligence with the male attendant who had moved a couple of yards up the room. They knew each other. Then she must be another observer. 'I want no other prison than this,' said Sargon, evidently quite at cross-purposes. 'One prison is enough.'

'I don't mean that,' said Bobby. 'Can you walk about here pretty freely?'

'Not freely,' said Sargon. 'No.'

'If you could come out into the grounds. To-morrow.'

The woman turned her long sharp foxy nose towards him and stared at him with rather stupid green-blue eyes.

Bobby's nerve was going to pieces altogether. He was always more afraid of women than men. This prim sharp-nosed figure so manifestly listening, and listening with a faint hostility to all he said, completed his discomfiture. He tried to improvise a story of lost and recovered cities that would be crystal clear to Sargon and yet incomprehensible to the listener. But his invention faltered at the difficult task. Where the river ran out of the city, he repeated; he harped upon that idea; where there were trees and ivy, there the faithful waited. When was the propitious hour for the Master to steal away to them? Everything was prepared. When could it be? When might it be? Fragmentally and mixed with many

319

irrelevancies Bobby tried to get the import of these suggestions over to his hearer. Now he would be explicit; now as the fear of the listener returned, vague and misleading. He did convey a sense of mystery and intention to Sargon, that was plain; but he felt he conveyed nothing more. The time was slipping by. Bobby could have throttled that infernal woman. More and more did she become audience to his floundering efforts. He maundered back to his starting point about Bobinsky. 'There is no such person as Bobinsky,' he threw in.

'Then how could he explore cities?' asked Sargon, manifestly more and more perplexed at Bobby's rigmarole.

'He is dead,' said Bobby. 'He was just a mask.'

'Some men are.'

'Don't mind about Bobinsky. Could you slip away to that corner? No, no. She's looking. Don't answer.

'*Now* answer.'

'I don't understand,' said Sargon.

Bobby felt that he was only puzzling Sargon. But what else was to be done? He could have kicked himself for not having brought a brief statement of his plan written plainly on a little piece of paper that he could have slipped into Sargon's hand – or pocket. It would have been so simple. He could have made a map and a drawing. Too late to do that now.

Despair came upon Bobby. Everything had gone wrong. He got up to go and then sat down again to make another attempt. He felt murderous towards that woman, towards himself, even towards slow-witted little Sargon.

'It was very good of you to come and see me,' said Sargon. '*Why* did you come? . . .

'Do you think anything will be done about me? . . .

'You will see Christina Alberta? When I saw you first I thought you had things to tell me – important things. One lives on such hopes here. Here – when there are no

320

visitors – nothing happens, nothing pleasant. And one is
distressed. . . .

'I am interested to hear of those cities in Central Asia
of course, but it is a little puzzling. Did you come
specially about them? Or just to see me?

'You will come again. Even to come down here to this
sitting-room is an event. . . .'

Then in a swift whisper. 'The food is frightful. So
badly cooked. It disagrees with me. . . .'

'That woman,' said Bobby as he went, 'She has spoilt
everything. I can't stand her.'

'That woman?' said Sargon, and followed the direction of
Bobby's eyes. 'Poor soul,' he said. 'She's a deaf mute.
She comes to see her brother. The whole family is defec-
tive or insane.'

A maddened Bobby returned towards his little inn.
Should he chuck the whole thing? Intolerable thought!
He must make fresh plans – fresh plans altogether. He
must begin all over again. The little man was evidently
wretched. But it was going to be harder to get hold of
him than Bobby had thought.

Bobby had no sleep that night.

§ 4

In the night just before daybreak suddenly Sargon woke
up and understood. He understood quite clearly what
the young man had been saying to him. He had said
'Rescue!' Of course he had meant to say 'Escape'! That
city in Central Asia was only a parable; he had said as
much. He had been describing a corner of the asylum
grounds, that corner where the stream ran out beyond
the workfields and the shrubbery where the patients were
supposed not to go. He had been telling of friends who

would wait outside. He had been trying to arrange an hour when these friends would come there. And Sargon had failed to understand. He sat up in bed very still.

It was perfectly clear, but through a sort of dulness that came upon him at times he had not grasped the drift of it at the time. The young man had shown irritation, naturally enough. What would he do now? Would he try again? Were the friends still waiting?

Who was this young man? His name was unknown or forgotten. But he believed. He had said, 'I call you by no other name.' Sargon! And there were these friends he spoke of, who waited outside for the king. They must know. How could they know, if there was nothing to be known? After all, perhaps it was no dream. Perhaps the world was awakening. . . But he had failed them. He had not understood. . . . They waited without. . . .

How still everything was! A strange unusual stillness. It was rare for this place to be so bereft of noise. It was dark and yet not altogether dark. The ward was dimly lit by a blue-shaded light. The three nearer beds were unoccupied, and beyond the man who tossed and muttered almost incessantly lay for a little while at peace. The man who raved had died three days ago; the man who gave sudden loud shouts had been taken away to another ward. Through the open door one could see across the landing into the little yellow-lit room where Brand the ward attendant sat with his arms crossed and chin on his chest and slept, his Patience cards spread out before him. He seemed to be alone and yet he could sleep like that! Where could the other man be – the new attendant whose name Sargon did not know? And yet he felt – someone had just gone out!

The uncurtained windows showed the night outside, a darkness that became translucent, a streak of very black cloud and five pale stars. Across the lower edge of that oblong picture one could see indistinctly a tracery of tree branches and the lumpish head of a young oak still bearing its leaves, the trees along the first hedge. These outlines grew distincter as he watched. It was like the slow development of a photographic plate in the dark-room. The stars dissolved. Had there been five? There were three; the other two had dissolved into the pale invading light.

Dared one venture on to the landing? If Brand awoke he could make some natural excuse. He stood well with Brand. But the other fellow –?

There was not a trace of him. Where had he gone? . . . *Do it now*! – wisest of maxims.

Very swiftly Sargon slipped out of bed and put on his dressing-gown and slippers. Hush! *What was that?* . . . Only some one snoring. Nothing more. He went out and stood on the landing. Brand slept on like a log.

The stone staircase was lit and empty and from the open door to the left downstairs came the harsh breathing of a sleeper. All the world seemed asleep for once, except Sargon and those friendly watchers outside the walls. Far away there were sounds of bawling and raving, but these were stifled by distance and an intervening door. They merely made the nearer silence more perceptible.

Something stirred, a little clicking sound that sent Sargon's heart racing. Then a resonant blow. A second blow. It was nothing; it was the clock downstairs striking six.

Very quietly but very resolutely he walked downstairs. An intuition, an instinct impelled him. He felt and peered at the door and behold! it was ajar! Unbolted! Unlocked! Brand's colleague was abroad upon some errand of his own. The cold air of freedom blew upon Sargon's face.

The door opened and closed softly and Sargon stood upon the doorstep of the left wing of the asylum, facing the dim world of a November dawn.

It was dark but it was clear, a world of ebony outlines and colourless forms. Everything looked as if it had just been wiped over with a wet rag. It was cold, but it was cold without any of the hate and bitterness of wind.

He crossed the gravel drive and came to a stop and stood looking about him. The heavy building of the left wing rose above him, a vast bulk that went up into the paler darkness of the sky. It receded in perspective and the central block beyond looked like the ghost of a house. Here and there there were orange-lit windows and others fainter lit by some remote reflected light. In the lodge to the left of the gates there was also a light. For where there is madness there is never perfect sleep.

But the asylum was as near complete silence that morning as an asylum can ever be.

He looked and listened. Not a footfall. It would not do to be found here by that other attendant. . . .

But the man was snugly away somewhere. No one would loiter here in this chill air.

What was it Sargon had to remember?

The friends and believers were waiting for him. They were waiting now. Where the river ran out of the city wall; that was to say where the little streamlet ran out of the grounds. That would be this way – to the left, where the fields dropped down-hill. He stepped on to the grass, for his feet made loud sounds on the gravel. The grass hissed crisply. It was heavy with white frost and his footmarks made black blots in the wet silvery grey.

He walked past and away from the ponderous dark mass of the asylum into the open, colder air of freedom. He unlatched and went through the small iron gate in the iron fencing that separated the trim grass plots of the front from the cabbage field. It complained a little on its hinge and he opened and closed it very carefully. He struck across the field. The path ran before him into a mist. It came out of the mist to his feet and vanished behind him. It was as if it went past him while he marked time. He could not remember whither the path ran, nor how it lay with regard to the corner he sought. But every moment things grew clearer.

Every moment things grew clearer. There had been something dark and brooding in the sky that hung over him and seemed to watch him. He had done his best to ignore the vague presence, because he was afraid of his own imagination. But suddenly he saw plainly that it was just the tops of trees showing above the mist. That must be the line of trees along the hedge parallel to the asylum front. He must go through these if he wanted to go down-hill. He left the path and made his way slowly along a frozen ridge of dug earth. He skirted long rows of stalky cabbages, black and shrivelled and unkempt, they looked like Cossack sentinels afoot. They all leant towards him as though they listened to the sound of him.

As he drew near the hedge and the trees he heard a sound like the feet of an army of midgets. It was the drip, drip of moisture from the trees.

Far away behind him and quite invisible to him a motor-car scurried along the high-road.

He had some difficulty in finding a way through the hedge and a bramble scratched his ankle. He told himself there was no hurry; the friends waited. Beyond the hedge the ground went down-hill and the mist grew whiter and thicker. The daylight was strong enough now to show the mist dead-white. It veiled the stream altogether.

He walked slowly. He had no sense of being pursued. Brand would not go into the ward for an hour yet; he might not miss him for a long time. . . .

What a wonderful thing, thought Sargon, is daybreak, and how little one sees of it! Every day begins with this miraculous drama and we sleep through it as though it did not concern us and rouse ourselves only for the trite day. A little while ago the world had been an inky monochrome and now it was touched with colour. The sky was blue. All the stars had gone – but no! not all. One still shone, a large pale star, the star of Sargon. And the sky about it was flushed with a faint increasing pinkiness. That must be the east and that star must be the morning star, hanging above the outhouse chimneys. Those chimneys were very distinct. The butt end of the asylum which had been a black and shapeless monster a little while ago, had now become a dark purple shape outlined with an exquisite clearness, eaves and ridges and chimneys and creasings and window-frames. Four windows shone a fading orange and two of them suddenly blinked and vanished.

Would anyone look out of a window there and see him?

It did not matter. He would go on down towards the stream. This friendly mist would hide him.

It was wonderful to be in this white mist and yet not in it. It was always a little way from him. And nevertheless it wetted him. How crisp the frosted ground was, but if one kicked through the surface, it was soft.

Overhead the blueness increased and there was now a rippled patch of pink cloud.

He went deeper and deeper into the soft mist. Presently he was walking on long wet shrivelled grass. When he turned presently to look back at the asylum it had altogether disappeared.

What was that? Was it something talking or was it the beating heart of some busy elfin machine? Listen! Peer! Think!

It was the stream.

Now everything was plain and easy.

He walked beside the stream. Near at hand trees became visible, attendant trees with mist about their waists, white-clad sentinel trees. The dry grass was ranker here. And

326

what was this, like a denser lower mist within the mist? This was the wall. Beyond that wall, almost within shouting distance now, the friends and believers would be waiting. How discreet they were! Not a murmur, not a footfall.

For a long time Sargon stood motionless beside the culvert beneath the wall. At last he roused himself and by a great effort and with the help of the ivy he scrambled to the top of the wall.

No one waited. Some dim four-footed thing bolted from the frost-bitten weeds below, and then there was silence. There was no sign of watchers nor helpers.

No matter. If it was God's will they would come.

He sat very still. He did not feel deserted nor alone. He was not in the least dismayed. He felt that the Power who had called him into being was all about him.

Slowly, steadily the light grew brighter. A little cloud like a floating feather caught fire very suddenly and then another. A great beam of light, like the beam of a searchlight, only very much broader, appeared slanting to the north. Then above a whaleback of distant downland came a knife-edge of dazzling light, an effulgence, like a curved knife, like a cap, like a dome, a quivering blazing firebirth. And then torn clear of the hill and round and red the November sun had risen.

§ 5

It was full daylight and the mist had dissolved away. The roofs of the asylum buildings were now visible over the crest, divested of all magic, bleak and commonplace. From some point in that direction a dog was barking.

It was strange that there should be no one here. That young man whose name he had never known, had made it very plain that there were friends in waiting here. Perhaps they had gone away and would come back presently.

Still it did not matter now very much. At any rate he had seen a sunrise of almost incredible beauty. How good a thing the sun was! The thing of all visible things that was most like God.

Perhaps there were no helpers here at all. Perhaps he had misunderstood. He was stupid he knew. He misunderstood more and more. Perhaps presently keepers would come in search of him and take him back to the asylum. It might be so that things were decreed. He would not let it distress him. Life was full of trials and disappointments. He was feeling now very cold throughout his substance and tired so that all his energy was gone. With a start he became aware that there was a man standing up the slope that overlooked the asylum grounds. He felt a thrill of renewed vitality. This man was standing quite still looking down at the asylum. It might be one of the staff looking for him. Or one of the promised helpers. One of the promised helpers?

Sargon was not so calm and apathetic as he had supposed. He was atremble from head to foot. He was not shivering with cold but trembling with excitement. He felt he must end this doubt one way or the other. Could he catch this man's eye? He waved a hand. Then he drew a dirty little pocket-handkerchief from his dressing-gown pocket and began to wave it. Now! Now it seemed the man was looking straight down at Sargon.

He was moving towards Sargon slowly, as if incredulous. Then he was signalling and running.

Sargon sat quite still. He knew all along they would come for him.

It was Bobby, close at hand now and crying out, 'Sargon! It is you! Sargon!' Sargon did not wait for him. He turned about and scrambled and dropped off the wall. They clasped hands. 'You have come to fetch me?'

'I was in despair. I didn't dream you understood me. I'm all amazed. . . . Let me think; what are we to do? This is splendid. My motor-bicycle is in the inn. Nuisance that. Yes, come along. I must hide you somewhere and fetch it. Then we will get away. I didn't think you'd have no clothes. Clothes? Won't show much. Cold? May be cold. I'll get a rug. There's a rug in the sidecar.'

He led the way back up the slope, glancing ever and again at the asylum fields. Sargon trotted beside him, calmly confident in God and Bobby, with the limitless docility of one who trusts his servant.

§ 6

Bobby's mind was fresh and bright that morning. He had wandered out to the asylum simply because he could lie in bed in a fever of regrets no longer. His extreme luck in encountering Sargon has restored all his confidence in himself and in the propitiousness of things. He made his plans quickly and with decision. It would be impossible to take Sargon back to the inn and give him coffee. So soon as he was missed they would surely go to the village. And every one would note this queer little figure with its dressing-gown and slippers and scarred ankles. He must get the little man into hiding somewhere close at hand. In that small beech wood just over the next crest. (Pity he was so scantily clad!) Then the motor bicycle must be fetched as quickly as possible.

Sargon was absolutely trustful and obedient. 'It is cold I know,' said Bobby, 'but unavoidable. I wish there were not so many wet dead leaves.'

'Only be quick and fetch help,' said Sargon.

'Don't stir from here,' said Bobby.

It was not the most perfect hiding-place in the world, a ditch, a clump of holly on the edge of a bare beech-wood, but it was all that downland was likely to provide. 'So long,' said Bobby and set off at a smart trot for the inn and the motor-bicycle. He arrived flushed, dishevelled, and out of breath and found the inn suspicious and reluctant when he announced that he wanted his bill instantly, refused any breakfast but a cup of tea and a chunk of bread and butter, and set about packing his little roll. There seemed endless things to do, taking an interminable time. To cap a score of irritating delays the inn was short of change and had to send out to the village shop. Billy's motor-bicycle, always a temperamental creature, gave great trouble with its kick starter. And meanwhile Sargon was shivering amidst the mud and dead leaves under the dripping trees or worse, being recaptured and led back into captivity.

It was nearly eight before Bobby came back along the cart-track into sight of the little beech-wood, and his heart jumped when he saw two heavy-looking men advancing towards him. He knew them for asylum men at once; they had the unmistakable flavour of subaltern authority that distinguishes prison warders, ex-policemen, time-keepers, and the keepers of the insane. As he throbbed near them they came into the middle of the road and made signs for him to stop. 'Hell!' said Bobby, and pulled up.

They came alongside and without evident hostility.

'Excuse me, sir,' said one – and Bobby felt better.

'That large place you see there, sir, is Cummerdown Asylum. Perhaps you know it, sir?'

'No. *Which* is the asylum? All of it?' Bobby felt he was being really clever and his spirits rose.

'Yesir.'

'Damn great place!' said Bobby.

'We've got one of our inmates astray this morning. Harmless little man, he is, and we ventured to stop you and ask you if you've seen him.'

Bobby had an inspiration. 'I believe I have. Was he in a sort of brown robe and slippers with nothing on his head?'

'That's 'im, sir. Where did you see him?'

Bobby turned round and pointed in the direction from which he had come. 'He was making off along the edge of a field,' he said. 'I saw him not – oh, not five minutes ago. Mile, or a bit more, away from here. Running he was. Along a hedge to the right – left I mean – near a chestnut plantation.'

'That's 'im all right, Jim. *Where* did you say, sir?'

Bobby's brilliance increased. 'If one of you will sit behind me and the other get into this contraption – bit of a load, but we can manage it – I'll run you back to the very place. Right away.' And without more ado he set about turning round. 'That's a real help, sir,' said Jim. 'Don't mention it,' said Bobby.

Bobby was now at the top of his form. He loaded them in with helpful words – even the smaller of the two was a tight fit for the side-car and the other sat like a sack on the luggage carrier – he took them back a mile and a half until he found the suitable hedge by the chestnut tree. He unloaded them carefully, received their hearty but hasty thanks with a generous gesture and sent them off at a smart trot across the fields. 'He can't have a mile's start,' he said. 'And he wasn't going particularly fast. Sort of limping.'

'That's 'im,' said Jim.

Bobby kissed his hand to their retreating backs. 'That's *you*,' said Bobby. 'God help you both and cleanse your hearts. And now for Sargon.'

He buzzed back to the place where he had left Sargon, turned his machine round again and then looked towards the corner of the wood by the holly clump where the little man ought to have been waiting. But there was no sign of a peeping head. 'Queer!' said Bobby, and ran up to the place where he had left Sargon crouching in the ditch. Not a sign was there of him. Bobby looked about him, baffled and frightened. After all, after everything, could things go wrong now?

'Sargon,' he called, and then louder, 'Sargon!'

Not a sound, not a rustle came in reply.

'He's hidden! Can he have crawled away and fainted? Exhausted perhaps!'

Fear touched Bobby with a chilly finger. Had he mistaken the place perhaps? Had Sargon strayed away in spite of his promise, or crept back numbed and wretched to the warmth and shelter of the asylum? Bobby followed the ditch down to the corner of the wood and beyond the corner in the ditch to the right, he suddenly beheld a little old woman, a little old woman sitting bunched in a heap on a litter of dry straw and fast asleep. She was wearing a battered black straw hat adorned with a broken black feather, a small black jacket bodice; a sack was drawn over her feet and a second sack thrown shawlwise over her shoulders. She was so crumpled up her face was hidden, all except one bright red ear, and behind her on the bank lay two large stakes tied in the form of a cross. To Bobby she was the most astonishing of apparitions. It was disconcerting enough to discover Sargon gone. It was still more amazing to find him so oddly replaced.

Bobby stood hesitating for the better part of a minute. Should he wake the old thing up and ask her about Sargon, or should he steal away. Nothing, he decided, would be lost by asking.

He went close up to her and coughed, 'Excuse me, Madam,' he said.

The sleeper did not awake.

Bobby rustled among the leaves, coughed louder, and asked to be excused again. The sleeper muttered a choking snore, woke with a start, looked up, and revealed the face of Sargon. He stared at Bobby without recognition for a moment and then gave way to an enormous yawn. While he yawned, his blue eyes gathered intelligence and understanding. 'I was so cold,' he said. 'I took these things from the scarecrow. And the straw was nice and dry to sit on. Shall we put it all back?'

'Oh, glorious idea!' cried Bobby, with all his spirits restored. 'It makes an honest woman of you. Can you walk in that sack? No, we haven't time to put it back. Shake it down off your legs and bring it with you. The side-car isn't two hundred yards away. You'll be able to put it on again then. This is magnificent! This is wonderful! Certainly we won't put it back. Off we'll go, and when we've a good ten miles between us and the asylum we'll stop and get some hot coffee and something to eat.'

'Hot coffee!' said Sargon, brightening visibly. 'And bacon and eggs?'

'Hot coffee and bacon and eggs,' said Bobby.

'The coffee there is – *beastly*,' said Sargon.

Bobby helped Sargon into the side-car and raised the hood over him, erected the wind-screen, and so packed him away. He became a quite passable aunt, dimly seen. And in another minute Bobby had kicked the engine into an impatient fuss and was in the saddle.

He felt himself now the cleverest fellow that ever stole a lunatic. Not that it wasn't the easiest thing in the world to get a lunatic away. If you knew how. . . . They quivered and jolted along the little minor road and so on to the smooth main highway to Ashford and Folkestone. The accelerator was urged to do its best. 'Good-bye, Cummerdown,' sang Bobby. 'Cummerdown Hill, good-bye!'

The little old motor-bike was going beautifully.

§ 7

They got their breakfast at an inn near a Post Office a mile or so beyond Offham. Bobby left Sargon dozing in the side-car and went to send a telegram to Dymchurch announcing his coming. There was some delay in the Post Office, as the post-mistress had mislaid her spectacles. Bobby returned to find the breakfast nearly ready and to assist Sargon out of his sack and into the little room of the inn. The landlord was a short, stout man, with a grave observant face. He watched this emergence of Sargon and his progress to a chair behind the little white tablecloth, with silent wonder. Then for a time he hid. Then he came back into the little room where the table was set. For some moments he stood regarding Sargon. 'Umph!' he said at last and turned about and went slowly into his kitchen where some sort of wife seemed to be cooking things. ''E's a rummun;' Bobby heard him remark, and so was prepared for discussion.

The ham and eggs and coffee were served and received with eagerness. The landlord stood over them scrutinizing their reception of his provisions. 'Hain't 'ad no breakfast, then?' he said.

'Having it now,' said Bobby, helping himself to mustard.

'Come far?' said the landlord after a thoughtful pause.

'Fairly,' said Bobby with judgment.

'Going far?' the landlord tried.

'So-so,' said Bobby.

The landlord rallied his forces for a great effort. 'We get some rummy customers here at times,' he said.

'You must attract them,' said Bobby.

The landlord could make nothing of that. He turned about and said 'Umph' – meaningly.

'Umph,' said Bobby, just saturating it with meaning.

The landlord made a cunning attempt as they were departing. 'Hope you enjoyed your breakfast,' he said. 'I don't know rightly whether it's a lady or a gentleman you got with you – still –'

Bobby's mercurial temperament was far too high just then. 'It's hermaphrodite,' he said in a confidential whisper and left the landlord with that.

But when they had gone a few miles further he told Sargon he had decided to buy him some socks and a jacket and trousers at the next shop they saw. 'As it is,' he said, 'you are ambiguous. And then we'll put that hat and jacket and the sacking by the wayside for anyone who wants to use them. And I'll have to send another telegram. I made a mistake.'

Bobby's mental state became more febrile as the day wore on. He developed a wonderfully circumstantial lie about a cottage and a fire and how his friend had only escaped with just a few articles of clothing hastily put on. 'Everything else,' said Bobby, 'practically incinerated.' They were going down to take refuge with a variable relation, a brother, an uncle, a maiden aunt. As the day progressed the circumstances of the fire became richer and more remarkable and the particulars of the escape more definitely thrilling. Bobby told such lies with great sincerity and gravity; they were a form of freedom – from reality.

Sargon himself said very little. For him this adventure was a severer endurance test than Bobby realized at the time. For the most part he was either cramped up and boxed in under the hood and wind-screen and being jolted and jumped along the hard high-road, or he was hastily changing some garment by the roadside, or he was sitting still in the side-car taking refreshment and being lucidly but perplexingly, and usually quite unnecessarily, explained.

§ 8

Mrs. Plumer, of Maresett Cottage, Dymchurch, was an anxious widow woman. She had a kind, serviceable heart, but it was troubled about many things. She saved and eked out almost too much. She let most of her rooms in the summer and some even in the winter, but she hated to think of the things careless lodgers might do to her furniture. She liked everything to be in order and lodgers better looking and better behaved than Mrs. Pringle's lodgers or Mrs. Mackinder's lodgers. She had taken a fancy to Bobby because he had fitted in nicely when she had had only one room to spare, and because he had shaved in cold water instead of calling down as every other man lodger did – there was no bell in that room – for hot. Also he talked agreeably when he came in and out and didn't want more at meals.

She was very pleased when he wrote to take her downstairs living-room and two bedrooms for himself and a friend for a fortnight. There were few people in Dymchurch who got 'lets' in November. They might come 'any time' after Tuesday.

She told Mrs. Pringle and Mrs. Mackinder that she was expecting two young gentlemen, and left them to suppose that her guests might stay on indefinitely.

On Wednesday she was excited and rather perplexed by a series of telegrams from Bobby. The first said plainly and distinctly: '*arriving with aunt about four Roothing.*' That disappointed her. She would have infinitely preferred two gentlemen.

But within an hour came another wire and this said: '*Error in telegram not aunt uncle sorry Roothing.*'

Now what was one to make of *that*?

Presently the child from the Post Office was back again. *'Uncle catching cold fire hot water bottles whisky.'*

The next sensational telegram announced a delay. *'Tyre trouble not so soon later Roothing.'*

Then came: *'Sixish almost certain good fire please Roothing.'*

'It's very good of him,' said Mrs. Plumer, 'to keep me informed like this. But I hope the old gentleman won't be fussy.'

The fire in the downstairs sitting-room was burning brightly at six, there was a kettle on the hob, there were not only tea-things, but whisky, sugar, glasses, and a lemon on the table and a hot-water-bottle in both the beds upstairs when the fugitives arrived. Mrs. Plumer's first feeling at the sight of Sargon were feelings of disappointment. She had allowed her mind to run away with the idea of a warm, comfortable uncle with at most a whisky-drinking cold, an uncle who would be, if not absolutely golden, at least gilt-edged. She had, if anything, exaggerated her memories of Mr. Roothing's geniality. So soon as she held open her door at the roar and toot of the motor bicycle, she saw that her anticipations would have to be modified again. Things were rather indistinct in the deepening twilight, but she could see that Bobby wasn't wearing the full and proper leather costume with gauntlets and goggles complete, that a real young gentleman would have worn on such an occasion and which Mrs. Pringle and Mrs. Mackinder would have respected, and that the shape he was extracting from the side-car was not the shape of a properly-expanded uncle. It looked much more like a large hen taken out of a small basket on market day.

As Sargon came into the light of the living-room, Mrs. Plumer's disillusionment deepened and decreased. She had rarely seen so strange and weatherbeaten an outcast.

His blue eyes stared pitifully out of a pale face; his hair, beneath an unsuitable black felt hat, was greatly disordered. He was clad chiefly in an excessive pair of trousers which he clutched nervously to keep up; very full they were with his dressing-gown tails; his too ample white socks fell like gaiters over his old felt slippers and betrayed his distressful ankles. He looked afraid. He stared at her almost as though he anticipated an unfriendly reaction. And Bobby, too, standing beside him, looked rough and travel-worn and eventful, and not at all the self-effacing young gentleman she had remembered.

When Bobby saw the swift play of Mrs. Plumer's expression he realized that their foothold in this pleasant, restful, firelit apartment was precarious. Happily a reserve lie he had thought of, but not hitherto used, came aptly to his mind.

'Isn't it a shame!' he said. 'They went off with his clothes. Even his socks.'

'They seem to have,' said Mrs. Plumer, 'whoever they were.'

'Pure hold-up. This side of Ashford. My big bag too.'

'And where did the gentleman get the clothes he's wearing?' she asked. Her tone was unpleasantly sceptical.

'They exchanged. I'd gone back along the road to see if I could see anything of the tyre-pump I'd dropped, never thinking anything of the sort was possible on an English high road. (Come and sit by the fire, uncle.) And when I came back they'd gone and there he was – as you see him. Imagine my astonishment!'

'And you never sent a telegram about it!' said Mrs. Plumer.

'Too near home. I'd have got here first, anyhow. Well, we've had adventures enough to-day, anyhow. I've never

338

known such a journey. Thank heaven, we've had our tea. I think the best place for uncle is bed – until we can arrange some clothes for him. What do you think, Mrs. Plumer?'

'After he's had a good wash,' said Mrs. Plumer. She was still doubtful, but a sort of kindliness was struggling to the surface. 'Weren't you afraid when they jumped out on you, sir?' She asked Sargon directly. His blue eyes sought Bobby's for instructions.

'It was a great shock to him,' said Bobby, 'a great shock. He's hardly got over it yet.'

'Hardly got over it yet,' said Sargon in confirmation.

'Took all your clothes off, they did. It's shameful,' said Mrs. Plumer. 'And you with a cold coming on.'

'We'll get him to bed. Of course, if you've got anything for us to eat we might have it first here. Perhaps just a bit of toasted cheese or Welsh Rarebit, or something of that sort, and a good hot grog. Eh, uncle?'

'Don't want much to eat,' said Sargon. 'No.'

'I haven't forgotten that Welsh Rarebit you made for me, Mrs. Plumer, after I got caught in the rain on the way from Hythe.'

'Well, I daresay I could get you a Welsh Rarebit,' said Mrs. Plumer, softening visibly.

'Famous,' said Bobby. 'Make a new man of him. And meanwhile I'll run the old bike round to the shed. If I may put it in the shed? You'll be all right here, uncle?'

'It's safe?'

'Every one's safe with Mrs. Plumer,' said Bobby, and held the door open for her to precede him out of the room.

'I'll tell you about him to-morrow morning,' he said to her confidentially in the passage. 'He's a wonderful man.'

'He's all right?' asked Mrs. Plumer.

'Right as can be.'

'He looks that distraught!'

'He's a poet,' said Bobby, 'besides playing on the violin,' and so satisfied her completely.

But he did not feel that he had brought the wonderful day to a completely successful end until he had got Sargon washed and brushed and tucked up cosily in Mrs. Plumer's bright little best bedroom. 'Now we're anchored,' he said. He went into his own room and sat down for a time to invent things about his uncle in case Mrs. Plumer was desirous of more explicit information when he went downstairs. He decided to say 'He's eccentric,' in an impressive, elucidatory way. 'And very shy.' His uncle, he would explain, was suffering from overwork, due to writing an heroic poem about the Prince of Wales' journey round the world. He wanted a complete rest. And sea air. The more he stayed in bed and indoors the better. He filled in a few useful details of this story, sat for a little while twiddling the toes of his boots, and then got up and went downstairs. He felt sure he could carry it off all right with Mrs. Plumer. He found her waiting for him. The chief difficulty he encountered was her conviction that the police ought to be told of the highway robbery this side of Ashford at once.

'Hm,' said Bobby and for a moment he was at a loss. Then he decided. 'I've done that already,' he said.

'But when?'

'I telephoned from an Automobile Association box. To the Ashford police. It will be in their district you know. Not in Romney Marsh. Sharp fellows, the Ashford police. I had to describe the lost clothes and everything. They don't let much get by them.'

She took it beautifully. After that everything was easy.

§ 9

The next morning found Sargon developing an evil cold in his throat and chest. His chest was painful and he was feverish, red-cheeked, bright-eyed, and short of breath. Bobby did not care to consult a doctor. He believed that all doctors constituted a league for the re-incarceration of escaped lunatics. He imagined secret notices about escapes being circulated throughout the profession. He motored to Hythe and got ammoniated quinine, several sorts of voice jujube, two iodine preparations for the chest, and suchlike trifles that the chemist recommended. When he returned about midday the patient looked better and seemed in less pain. After Bobby had administered quinine and rubbed his chest and made a generally curative fuss, he was able and disposed to talk.

'The pillow all right?' said Bobby.

'Perfect.'

'You ought to doze for a bit now.'

'Yes.'

Sargon thought. 'I shall not have to go back to that Place again?'

'I hope not.'

The flushed face became very earnest. 'Promise me not. Promise me not. I couldn't endure it.'

'No need to be anxious,' said Bobby. 'Here, you are quite safe.'

'And there will be no need to get into that side-car again?'

'None.'

'Never?'

'No.'

'It bumped – horribly. . . . Where is Christina Alberta?'

Bobby did not answer for a moment or so.

'Perhaps I ought to explain. I do not know who Christina Alberta is. I took you out of the asylum because 1 do not believe you are mad. But I know nothing of your family. I know nothing about your circumstances at all. I just couldn't bear the thought of you in an asylum.'

Sargon lay in silence for a little while with his blue eyes on Bobby's face. 'You were sorry for me?'

'I liked you from the very first moment I saw you in Midgard Street.'

'*Liked* me? But you believed I was Sargon, King of Kings?'

'Practically,' said Bobby.

'You didn't. Neither, I suppose, did I.'

The vague blue eyes left Bobby's face and stared out of the window at the sky. 'I have been very much confused in my mind,' said Sargon. 'Even now I am not clear. But I realize I am confused. Christina Alberta is my daughter. The Princess Royal I called her. In Sumeria. She is a very dear, bold girl. She is all I have. I left her and came away from her, and I must have distressed her greatly.'

'Then she may not know where you have been?'

'She may be looking for me.'

'Where is she?'

'I have been trying to remember. It was in a studio somewhere – with peculiar pictures. I never liked those pictures. A studio in a Mew. It had a name but I cannot remember its name. It is stupid of me. Probably Christina Alberta is there with her friends – still wondering what has become of me.'

'At the – at the *Place*, they told me your name was Preemby.'

'Albert Edward Preemby. . . . I wonder.'

He lay reflecting for a time. 'I remember that for a long time I thought I was Albert Edward Preemby, a small creature, a little man living a mean life in a laundry. A

342

laundry with large blue vans. The swastika. You cannot
imagine what a small, insignificant life it was that this
Preemby led. And then suddenly I thought I could not
possibly be Preemby and also an immortal soul. Either
there was no Preemby, I thought, or there was no God.
There could not possibly be both. It perplexed and
worried me very much. Because there I was – Preemby.
I am not good at thinking – all my thinking goes off into a
kind of dreaming. And then when there came evidence
that seemed satisfactory – perhaps I jumped at what I was
told. But Sargon must have been a great king, a very great
king, and I am small and weak and not very intelligent.
When the keepers and attendants bullied me and ill-
treated me I did not behave as a great king should have
behaved, and when I saw them doing evil things to other –
other patients, I did not interfere. Yet all the time I
think I am something different from the Albert Edward
Preemby I used to be, something more and something
better. But it leaves me confused to think who I am, and I
am very tired. Perhaps, when I have rested a day or two, I
may be better able to think about these things.'

The faded voice died away. The blue eyes remained
staring tranquilly at the sky.

Bobby said nothing for a little while. Then he remarked,
'I have seen men ill-treated.'

And then: 'and I am not so slight as you are.'

He said no more. It did not seem as though Sargon had
heard him. Bobby stood up.

'You must rest. You are perfectly safe here. If we can
remain unnoted here for two weeks then it will be impossible ever to send you back to that place again. Are you
comfortable?'

'It is a beautiful bed,' said Sargon.

But beautiful though the bed was it was not sufficient to
arrest the trouble in Sargon's aching chest. He seemed

343

very exhausted that evening. In the night he began coughing; he coughed so distressingly that Bobby went in to him. In the morning he was spiritless and did not want to eat. Bobby sat in the room downstairs working at the pile of Aunt Suzannah correspondence that Billy had sent on to him. He was half-minded to appeal to Tessy to come down and help with the nursing, but there was no bedroom available for her. Mrs. Plumer pressed for a doctor and he put her off. Finally, on her own responsibility, she brought in a young man who was just starting a practice in the place. Bobby had a terrifying interview, but the young doctor betrayed no suspicions. On the whole, he was reassuring. There was congestion of the lungs but nothing worse. Sargon must keep very warm and take this and that. No urgent need for a nurse. Keep him warm and give him his medicine.

Late in the evening Bobby went up to say good-night and found Sargon better and more talkative.

'I have been thinking of Christina Alberta and I should like to see her. I would like to see her and tell her things I have been thinking about her. I have been thinking out all sorts of curious things. Perhaps I am not so much to her as she may think. But chiefly I want to talk to her about a young man I dislike. What was he called? When I was last at Lonsdale Mews, she danced with him.'

'Lonsdale Mews!'

'Yes, yes, of course. I had forgotten. Eight Lonsdale Mews, Lonsdale Road, Chelsea. But my mind is very confused and I do not know what I should say to her even if she came.'

Bobby wrote down the address forthwith.

'And this Christina Alberta is all you have?' he asked.

'All I have.

'Twenty. Quite a child really. I ought never to have left her. But there came a sort of wonder upon me – As

344

though the world was opening. It made everything else
seem very trivial.'

§ 10

*'There came a sort of wonder upon me as though the world
was opening.'*

Bobby wrote that down also. And he sat very late before
the fire in the ground floor room thinking that over and
thinking over the message he would have to send to
Christina Alberta in the morning. To-morrow he would
have to explain himself and his extraordinary intervention
in Preemby affairs. It was by no means plain to himself as
yet, and to-morrow he would have to make plain to a probably very indignant young lady why her father had so
caught his sympathies and fascinated his imagination as
to tempt him to this escapade. He found himself thrown
back on self-analysis. He found himself scrutinizing his
own motives and his own scheme of existence.

He knew and understood that feeling, 'as though the
world was opening' so well. Still better did he know that
feeling of dead emptiness in life out of which it arose. In
his own case he had thought this habitual discontent with
the daily round, this urgency towards something strange
and grandiose, was due to the dislocation of all his expectations of life by the great war; that it was a subjective aspect
of nervous instability; but in the case of this little laundryman it could not have been the war that had sent
him out, a sort of emigrant from himself, to find a fantastic universal kingdom. It must be something more
fundamental than the war accident. It must be a normal
disposition in men towards detachment from safety and
comfort.

He glanced towards the pile of his Aunt Suzannah correspondence on the table and the next sheet of 'copy' for *Wilkins' Weekly* he had distilled therefrom. He rose from his arm-chair and went back to his work with his wisdom refreshed. He wrote: 'So soon as man's elementary needs are satisfied and he is sure of food, clothing and shelter, he comes under the sway of a greater imperative; he goes out to look for trouble. So that I would not discourage "Croydon's" desire to become a missionary in West Africa in spite of his religious doubts and his peculiar feeling about black people. Such a region as Sherborough Island will probably supply him with a good sustained, sustaining, and ennobling system of troubles. A white man who has once challenged the hostility of a West African secret society will have little leisure for morbid introspection. He will hardly have a dull moment. . . .'

He stopped writing. 'Reads a little ironical,' he said. 'And not quite Aunt Suzannah enough.'

He reflected. 'My mind scampers off from me at times. Not in the vein to-day.'

The one thing they must never feel about Aunt Suzannah was that she could be ironical. No! it wouldn't do. He ran his pen through the six sentences he had just written and pushed the sheet away from him. He drew another sheet towards him on which he had been composing with great difficulty a telegram to be sent next morning to 'Preemby, 8 Lonsdale Mews, Chelsea.' He read over various drafts. The current form ran as follows: '*Your father safe but with severe chest cold care of Roothing Maresett Cottage Dymchurch desires see you discretion very necessary return confinement fatal results best station Hythe and cab could meet you Hythe if wire in time but do not know you personally am tallish slender dark Roothing.*'

Properly considered it was all right.

He tried to imagine what sort of girl this Christina Alberta Preemby would be. She would be blue-eyed of

346

course and probably very fair; a little taller and rounder
than her father, soft-voiced and rather dreamy. She would
be timid and affectionate, very kind and gentle and a little
incompetent. Perhaps it would be well to meet her at
Hythe so soon as he knew which train she was coming by.
The cab business might be a strain on her. He would have
to tell her what to do. To a considerable extent now he had
made himself responsible for the fortunes of both these
people. And he liked to think that. He liked to think that
perhaps these might become his own people, more of his
own people than the Malmesburys. Because to be frank
about it with himself he was a little bit of an interpolation
in the Malmesbury household. They liked him; they were
perfect dears to him; but they could do without him.
Even that little devil Susan managed without him; she
liked him and tyrannized over him but he knew he wasn't
indispensable to her. Here at last might be two people
who couldn't do without him, who might to an extraordinary extent become his people.

Of course he would have to put on a little more appearance of strength and determination than was actually his
quality. He owed it to them to keep up their confidence
in him so that he might be able to direct them in their
difficulties.

He would say to her – what would he say to her? 'I have
been hasty, I know, but I know something of the strain
that is put upon the sane patient in an asylum. I thought
that the first thing to do was to get your father out of it.
It didn't occur to me that for a time he might have forgotten your address. Perhaps I ought to have come to you
before I acted. But then how was I to know there *was* a
you? Until he told me of your existence. In so many cases
in these asylums the relatives are hostile to release. It is
dreadful to admit it, but it is so.'

Then rather humorously and quite modestly he would

347

describe the escape. He was already forgetting the uncertainties of the visiting-day conversation and the numerous accidental factors in the meeting by the culvert. But all history has this knack of eliminating unnecessary detail.

So he would make his statement. It did not occur to him that Christina Alberta might be the sort of person who interrupts speeches with elucidatory questions.

He lit a cigarette, strolled about the room, and came to rest standing before the fire and looking down on the glowing coals. He was sure now that Christina Alberta was blue-eyed, fragile, shy – with a deep sweet vein of humorous fantasy hidden away in her. Very probably she concealed a gift for writing. It would be for him perhaps to discover that and cultivate it and bring it out. Together they would protect Sargon, already more than half recovered from the intoxication of his dream. They would have to soften the humiliations of his complete awakening. How fortunate and as it were providential it was that he had been impelled to rescue the little man! – for otherwise he would never have met Christina Alberta, never won her timid wealth of love. . . .

'*Eh!*

'But this is all damned nonsense!' said Bobby violently, and threw his cigarette into the fire. 'This is just fancy! I haven't even *seen* the girl!'

He lit his candle, put out Mrs. Plumer's oil lamp with all the devices and precautions proper to this dangerous survival from the Dark Ages, and went up to bed. He stopped and listened outside Sargon's door. The patient was asleep and breathing rather noisily – ever and again choking with a little cough.

'I wish the weather had kept warmer,' said Bobby.

When he opened his own bedroom door, the flame of his candle writhed and flared horizontally, the curtains streamed into the room and a sheet of paper flapped on the dressing-table. He put down the candle and went to shut the window. The wind was rising and there was a little patter of raindrops on the pane.

The Last Phase

§ 1

IT was part of the general unsatisfactoriness of Bobby's make-up that he was acutely responsive to meteorological conditions. That late Indian summer was over now, and the heavens and the earth and the air between began to push, hustle, wet, chill, darken, distress and bully him. Jumbled grey clouds came hurrying across Dymchurch from Dungeness and the Atlantic, torn, angular, outstretched clouds with malicious expressions like witches and warlocks, emitting fierce squirts of rain. Under their skirts came the waves in long rolling regiments, threatening from afar, breaking into premature handfuls of foam, gathering force at last, towering up for a last culminating thud against the sea-wall and spouting heavenward in white fountains of suddy water.

'Face it, man,' said Bobby. 'Face it. It's only Nature. Brace up to it. Think of this poor girl.'

He forced himself to do a morning's walk along the top of the sea-wall, with his wet trousers flapping against his legs like flags against their staves.

'Glorious wind!' he told Sargon when he went in to see him. 'But I wish there was a gleam of sun.'

'Have you any news from Christina Alberta?' asked Sargon.

'There's hardly time yet for a reply to my wire. But she'll surely come,' said Bobby, and went downstairs to dry his legs at the fire.

He did not expect a summons to Hythe to meet the young lady very much before half-past twelve. Meanwhile he went out to the shed and assured himself that the motor-bicycle and side-car were in perfect order for a hasty

THE LAST PHASE

journey. Half-past twelve came, one, half-past one. He
had some lunch. He became very restless, and rose and
looked out of the window frequently to see if the mes-
senger girl was coming with Christina Alberta's telegram.
About two a large, silent, luxurious-looking, hired Daimler
car appeared outside and stopped at Mrs. Plumer's gate.
A hatless bobbed head appeared at the window and exchanged remarks with the driver, who descended and
opened the door. The car emitted a handsome and determined young woman of advanced appearance, hatless and
short-skirted, and a lean, dark, prosperous-looking man of
thirty-eight or forty in blue serge and a grey felt hat. The
man opened the gate for the girl, and she surveyed the
house as she advanced.

Bobby realized that Christina Alberta had not kept her
promise to be blue-eyed and fragile. She had betrayed
him. Yet for all her treachery he had built up a sense of
personal relationship with her that gripped him still. He
watched her approach with an excitement he found difficult to control. He wondered who the devil the dark man
was. A cousin perhaps. She discovered Bobby watching
her from the window, and their eyes met.

§ 2

Bobby, with an instinct that is given to young people for
such occasions, perceived that he interested Christina
Alberta extremely. He parleyed with her and Devizes in
Mrs. Plumer's little downstairs room. He spoke chiefly
to her. Devizes he treated as a secondary figure, a voice
at her elbow. 'He's got a nasty cold on his chest,' he said.
'He's been asking for Miss Preemby –'
'Christina Alberta,' said Christina Alberta.
'Christina Alberta a lot. But it was only last night I could

351

get the address out of him. He'd forgotten it before. We've been here over a day. He caught the cold coming here.'

'How did you come here?' Devizes threw in.

'Motor-bicycle,' said Bobby. 'But there was a lot of waiting about before we could get away and it was a cold raw morning, and he had just his nightgown and dressing-gown and slippers. So hard to foresee everything.'

'But how did you come to be rescuing him?'

Bobby smiled at Devizes. 'Somebody had to be rescuing him.'

He turned to Christina Alberta again. 'Couldn't bear the thought of his being under lock and key. He took a room, you see, in the place where I lodged, and there was something innocent and – delightful about him. I've a weakness, a sympathy perhaps, with absurdity. . . . You ought to go up to him and see him.'

'Yes, we'd better look at him,' said Devizes.

(Who the devil was this fellow?)

Bobby asserted himself. 'Christina Alberta first, I think.'

He took Christina Alberta up to her daddy and closed the door on a warm embrace. 'And now, Mr. de Vezes, or whatever you are,' he said to himself on the staircase, 'where do *you* come in?' He descended and found Devizes standing very irritatingly upon his hearthrug before his fire. As he stood there a remote resemblance to Christina Alberta was perceptible. Bobby had an incoherent recognition of the fact that in some obscure way Devizes was responsible for Christina Alberta's failure to produce blue eyes. He was a little slow in saying what he intended to say, and Devizes was able to take the initiative. 'Forgive my blunt impertinence,' he said, 'but may I ask who you are?'

'I'm a writer,' said Bobby, refraining from any glance at

352

the accumulation of Aunt Suzannah material upon the side table.

'You've finished lunch?' asked Devizes in a disregarded parenthesis.

'May I ask the same question of you?' said Bobby, 'and how it is you come to be connected with the Preembys?'

'I'm a blood relation,' said Devizes, considering it. 'On the mother's side. A sort of cousin. And I happen to be a nervous and mental specialist. That's why I've been brought in to-day.'

'I see,' said Bobby. 'You've got no intention of – putting him back?'

'None at all. We're not antagonists, Mr. – '

'Roothing.'

'We're on the same side. You did well to get him out. We were trying to do the same things by less original methods. We're very grateful to you. The lunacy laws are rather a clumsy and indiscriminating machine. But, as you probably know, if he keeps clear of them for fourteen days, they'll have to begin with him all over again. He renews his sanity. We're allies in that. We've got to know each other better. Your intervention – most surprising – strikes me as being at once eccentric and courageous. I wish you'd tell me more about it, how you met him, how they got hold of him, and what set you thinking of an escape.'

'Hm,' said Bobby, and came and asserted his right to half the hearthrug. He had thought of the way in which he could tell this story – to Christina Alberta – the original Christina Alberta with the blue eyes. He felt that that version needed considerable revision, indeed, possibly even a complete rearrangement, for the present hearer. He was by no means sure he wanted to tell it to the present hearer. The man was a doctor and a mental specialist and a distant relation, and he was for keeping Sargon out of an asylum,

353

and that was all to the good, but it still lingered in Bobby's mind that he was an interloper. Nevertheless, he made way for Bobby quite civilly on the hearthrug, and his manner was attentive and respectful. Bobby embarked upon a description of Sargon's first appearance in Midgard Street.

Devizes showed himself alert and intelligent. He grasped the significance of Sargon's projected visit to the dome of St. Paul's at once. 'I've no doubt he did it,' said Devizes. 'Neither have I,' said Bobby, 'though I've not asked him about it yet.' They pieced together the probable story of the calling of the disciples before Billy and Bobby had come upon the procession. 'It's touching,' said Devizes, 'and immense.' Bobby approved these words.

'You see how he got me,' said Bobby.

A distinct flavour of friendliness for Devizes crept by imperceptible degrees into Bobby's mind. Difficulties that had seemed to threaten his explanations vanished; this man, he perceived, could understand anything a fellow did. Devizes made him feel that the extraction of Sargon from Cummerdown by a perfect stranger was the most simple and natural thing to do imaginable. Bobby warmed to his story; his sense of humour took heart of grace, and he became frank and amusing about his difficulties on the visiting-day. As he was telling of the foxy-faced deaf-mute, Christina Alberta came back again into the downstairs room.

'He takes me as a matter of course,' she said. 'He seems weak and drowsy and his chest is bad.' She spoke more definitely to Devizes. 'I think you ought to overhaul him.'

'There is a doctor in attendance?' he asked Bobby.

Bobby explained. Devizes considered. Was Sargon dozing? Yes. Then let him doze for a bit. Bobby, working now a little more consciously for effect, went on with his

354

story. Christina Alberta regarded him with manifest approval.

By tea-time Bobby had adjusted his mind to the existence of Devizes and the unexpectedness of Christina Alberta. All that carried over from his state of expectation was the idea that his relations with Christina Alberta were to be very profound and intimate. He still believed that, hidden away in her somewhere, there must be a blue-eyed, yielding, really feminine person, but it was very deeply hidden. Meanwhile the superimposed disguise struck him as agreeable, alert, humorous, and friendly. Devizes too he saw more and more as a strong, capable, understanding personality. He had seen Devizes examining Sargon, and it was clever, confidence-provoking doctoring. Sargon's lungs, he said, were badly congested, especially on the left side; he was on the edge of pneumonia and without much vitality to fight it. He ought to be kept in a warmer, less draughty room with a night-nurse available. Mrs. Plumer had no room for a nurse, and not an hour away by automobile was Paul Lambone's excessively comfortable week-end cottage at Udimore. A little masterly telephoning and telegraphing and the cottage was available, fires were alight in the best bedroom, a trained nurse was on her way to it, and it was all settled for Sargon, warmly wrapped up and fortified with hot-water bottles, to go thither. Bobby found himself a mere accessory in this new system of things; he was to follow next day to Udimore on his motor-bicycle, for there would be room for all of them in Paul Lambone's cottage. Apparently Paul Lambone's conception of a simple cottage in the wilderness involved a housekeeper, several servants, and four or five visitors' rooms.

This fellow Devizes carried out all his arrangements with a smooth competence that gave Bobby no scope for self-assertion. Sargon and Christina Alberta and Devizes

355

would depart at five and get to Udimore by six, by which time the nurse would be installed. Then Devizes would go back to London and get there in time to dress for a dinner he had to attend. On Saturday morning he would be busy in London, and then he would come back to Udimore and see if Sargon was recovered enough for the beginnings of his mental treatment. Perhaps the unknown Paul Lambone would be there too. He was a lazy person, Bobby gathered; he'd have to be brought down by Devizes. Bobby was to stay at Udimore for some days. He made modest protestations. 'No, you're *in* it now,' said Devizes cheerfully and glanced at Christina Alberta. 'You're in for Sargon like the rest of us. Bring your work with you.' 'Yes, do come,' said Christina Alberta.

The only reason Bobby had for resisting the invitation was that it attracted him so much.

§ 3

This 'cottage' at Udimore, which struck Bobby as being a really very pretty and comfortable modern house, and these three people, Christina Alberta, Devizes and Paul Lambone, who now grouped themselves round Sargon, exercised his mind in a quite extraordinary way. They struck him as being novel and definite to a degree he'd never met in anyone before, and even the house was fresh and decisive in its broad white grace, like no house that had ever before held his attention. It made most of the other houses he had ever observed seem accidental and aggregatory and second-hand and wandering in their purpose. But this house was the work of a clever young architect who had considered Paul Lambone intelligently, and its white rough-cast walls sat comfortably on the hill-side and looked with an honest, entirely detached admiration at

356

Rye and across the marsh to Winchelsea and the remote blue sea; and it had seats and arbours and a gazebo for sitting about in, and uphill was a walled garden with broad paths up which you looked from the back of the house through lead-paned windows. You could watch the sunset from a number of excellent points of view, but it did not shine upon any room to weary and blind you. There was a kind wall to shelter hollyhocks and delphiniums from the south-west wind, and to bear a plum or so and a pear and a fig-tree. Downstairs was mainly one great rambling room with a dining recess in one corner and the power of opening itself out into a loggia, and with conversational centres about fire-places or windows as the season might require, but there were several little studies about the house in which one could be shut off and write. Book-shelves grew in convenient corners, and the house was everywhere mysteriously warm from unseen and scarce suspected radiators. The house was so like Paul Lambone, and Paul Lambone so much a part of his house, that he seemed to be really no more than its voice and its eyes.

Paul Lambone was the first successful writer Bobby had ever met. Bobby knew various needy young writers, tadpole writers, insecure writers, but this was the first completely grown-up and established and massively adult writer he had ever known. The man struck Bobby as being stupendously secure and free and prosperous. And the remarkable thing was that he was in no way a great writer, no Dickens nor Scott nor Hardy; his work wasn't, after all, in Bobby's opinion anything so very remotely above Bobby's own efforts. A certain terseness he had at times, a certain penetration: those were the chief differ-ences. In Bobby's imagination the literary and artistic life had hitherto had an unavoidable flavour of casual adventure, glorious achievements, maddening difficulties,

357

wild delights, and tragic unhappinesses. Swift, Savage, Goldsmith, the Carlyles, Balzac, Dumas, Edgar Allan Poe, these had been his types. But this new bright house was as sound and comfortable as any country house, and Lambone sat in it with as safe a dignity as though he was a provincial banker or a mine-owner or the senior member of some widespread firm of solicitors. No fears of losing his 'job' or 'writing himself out' oppressed him. He said and did exactly what he thought proper, and the policeman saluted him as he passed.

If this sort of thing could spring from the *Book of Everyday Wisdom* and Paul's amiable novels, what hitherto unsuspected possibilities of accumulation and ease and security and helpfulness might there not be in Aunt Suzannah's kindly responsiveness? It had never before seemed credible to Bobby that a day might come when he would be secure and his own master, able to refuse limitations himself and to release other people from limitations. All Bobby's life hitherto had been a matter of direction and eminent necessity. He had been *sent* to school and *sent* to college. He had been on the eve of being *put into* the position of agent upon a friendly estate when the Great War had seized upon him and the rest of his generation and drilled him and sent him off to Mesopotamia. And after the war he had had to do something to supplement his diminished inheritance. Life had been so indicated and prescribed for him at every stage, his parents' existence had been so entirely directed by a class tradition, that Bobby's mind was exceptionally well-prepared to be impressed by Paul Lambone's freedoms.

It was curious to note how completely Paul Lambone arose out of the present-day world, and how completely he didn't belong to it. He had all its advantages and so little of its standard obligations. He had escaped from it with most of its gifts. He had to go to no court, follow no

seasons, make no calls, and perform no functions. Was he
exceptional in his circumstances altogether, or were there a
lot of people escaping, as he was escaping, prosperously,
from the old decaying social system? a queer sort of new
people who didn't belong?

Bobby sat on the terrace and looked over the back of his
seat at this extremely new but very sightly and comfortable cottage of Lambone's, with this freshly arrived idea
of a new sort of people getting loose in the world and
living unrelated to the old order of things and shaping out
new ways of living, very active in his mind. This house
seemed to embody that idea; it was new and novel, but not
a bit apologetic nor rebellious. It was just breaking out
like a new fashion. It was just arising like a new century.
He had always assumed that revolutions came from below
through the rage of the excluded and the disinherited. He
had thought every one took that for granted. But suppose
revolutions were merely smashes-up that hadn't very
much to do with real progress either way, and that the
new age dawned anywhere in the social order where
people could get free enough to work out new ideas.

New ideas!

Sargon was new, Paul Lambone was new, Devizes new:
before the war there could not have been any such people.
They had grown out of their own past selves; they were
as different from pre-war people as nineteenth-century
people had been different from eighteenth-century people.
Newest of all was this Christian Alberta who had effaced
her blue-eyed predecessor. She was so direct and free in
her thoughts and talk that she made Bobby feel that his
own mind wore a bonnet and flounces. He had gone for
two walks with her, once to Brede and once to Rye, and he
liked her tremendously. Whether he was in love with her
he didn't yet know. Falling in love with her for anyone
was evidently going to be a quite unconventional, untested,

and difficult series of exercises. Nothing at all like that unborn normal affair with the non-existent blue-eyed girl.

She seemed to like him, and particularly the way his hair grew on his head. She had mentioned it twice and ruffled it once.

A queer aspect of the situation was the riddle of how she and Sargon and himself came to be the guests of Paul Lambone with Devizes in attendance. It was just a part of Paul Lambone's freedom from prescription that he should be able to give sanctuary to Sargon and assemble this odd, unconventional week-end party. But Bobby had a sense of hidden links and missing clues. Devizes was a natural enough visitor, of course; he was manifestly Lambone's close friend. But their interest in Sargon was stronger than Bobby could imagine it ought to be. He was puzzled; he examined all sorts of possibilities in a gingerly fashion. Some impulse like his own, no doubt, but not quite the same, lay at the bottom of this – Sargonism.

Bobby had begun by feeling very hostile to Devizes as an unexpected intruder on a system of relationships sufficiently interesting without him. He was glad that he had to go to London for Friday, and not particularly pleased by his return on Saturday. Then he found his feelings changing to a curious respect, mingled with a defensive element that was almost like fear.

Devizes was more aware of you than Lambone. He looked at you, his mind came at you. It had the habit of coming at people. He was more actively and aggressively interested in things than Lambone and more self-forgetful. Lambone observed enough to make bright comments; Devizes made penetrating observations. Bobby often felt encumbered with himself; most people he thought were encumbered with themselves, but Devizes to a conspicuous degree wasn't. He was a man of science; a man of scientific habits. Bobby had known one or two scientific men before, rather wrapped away from ordinary things, but the interest that wrapped them was something that wrapped them away from oneself; one had been concerned chiefly with stresses in glass and another with the eggs of echinoderms. You always seemed to be looking at the backs of these fellows' heads and smiling at their immense preoccupation. But this man Devizes was wrapped up in the motives and thoughts of people; he didn't look away from you; he looked into you. That grew upon Bobby's consciousness. Devizes' eye lacked delicacy.

He had come down for the week-end chiefly to deal with Sargon. He went up and had long talks to Sargon. He was 'treating' Sargon. He didn't go up and talk to Sargon as man to man, as Bobby would have done. He went up to a sort of mental jiu-jitsu with Sargon to exercise him and push him about into new attitudes. Devizes was formidable enough in himself, but far more formidable as a portent. He had all the appearance of being a precursor, the most vigorous precursor – they were all precursors! – of a new type of human relationships, relationships without delicate reservations, without rich accumulations of feeling behind emotions avoided and things unsaid. So it seemed to Bobby, who didn't for a moment suspect how much these people were avoiding and suppressing. Christina Alberta's thoughts and speech seemed to him to be moving about without a stitch on, like the people in some horrible Utopia by Wells. He compared the vast impalpable network of 'understanding' he and Tessy had woven between each other.

'New people,' he whispered, and looked Paul Lambone's new house in the face. To him they were stupendously new, an immense discovery. The war had overstrained him, he realized, and left him too tired for a time to see new things. He had been one of the vast multitude of those who had come out of the war in the expectation of a trite and obvious old-fashioned millennium, and who expressed their disappointment by declaring that nothing had happened except devastation and impoverishment. They were too jaded at first to observe anything else. But indeed Bobby now realized the European world had been travelling faster and faster since the break-up of the armed peace in 1914; and here were new types, new habits of thought, new ideas, new reactions, new morals, new ways of living. He discovered himself in the advent of a new age, a new age that was coming so fast that there hadn't been time ever to clear the forms and institutions of the old age away. They weren't reversed or abolished, they weren't overthrown, they were just disregarded. Which was just why it was possible to get along for a year or so without noting the tremendous changes everything was undergoing.

'New People.' Did that apply to Sargon? That was Sargon's room: the two long windows between the buttresses. Was Sargon also an escape from the established order of relationships into novel things? What was the real significance of the absurd little man with his preposterous map of the world and his still more preposterous planisphere, who wanted to be Lord of the Earth?

§ 4

When Bobby came to talk it over with Sargon it seemed to him that Devizes had taken the little man completely to pieces and presented him with the disarticulated portions of himself. Devizes went back to London on Monday: he took Christina Alberta with him in his hired car; but Lambone urged Bobby to stay on for a day or so to cheer up the patient. Lambone, so far as he could

THE LAST PHASE

discover his own intentions, meant to stay on at Udimore
for a week or more and work. Bobby saw Christina Alberta
off, meditated on her for an hour, then gave the rest of
the morning to Aunt Suzannah and the afternoon to
Sargon; and Sargon, who was distinctly better, sat propped
up by two pillows and discussed the dissected structure
of himself.

'Not a bit fatigued,' said Sargon. 'I'm having a tonic
now. Every three hours.'

He considered his next remark for some moments before
he made it. 'Who *is* this Mr. Paul Lambone?' he asked.
'It is very hospitable for him to entertain us. Very.
(*H'rrmp*) . . . Is he a friend of yours?'

'He's quite a well-known writer. He's a friend of
Christina Alberta's.'

'She has so many friends. Young people do nowadays.
And what is this Dr. Devizes?'

'He is a nervous specialist, and he was consulted – he was
consulted about the possibilities of getting you away from
that – Place.'

'Nervous specialist. He is a wonderful talker – most
intelligent and (h'rrmp) understanding. I have a curious
feeling that somewhere, somewhen, somehow I have met
him before. In this life – or some other. It is all quite
vague, and he does not seem to have any corresponding
recollection. No. Probably a coincidence of some sort.'

Bobby saw nothing in the coincidence.

Sargon shut his eyes for a second or so.

'We talked of my recent experiences,' he resumed.

'Naturally,' said Bobby, helping.

'There has been a lot of confusion about my personality.
It is a trouble more frequent nowadays than it used to be.
Most of my life I have thought that I was a person called
Albert Edward Preemby, a limited person, a most limited
person. Then I had a light. I began to realize that

nobody could really be such a thing as that Albert Edward Preemby. I began to seek for myself. I had reason – too long to explain – to suppose that I was Sargon the First, the great Sumerian, the founder of the first Empire in the world. Then – then came trouble. You saw something of it. I grasped at the sceptre – one afternoon – in Holborn – rashly. Most painful affair. I was sent to that Place. Yes. It shook me. Humiliations. Hardship. Real – uncleanness. I doubted whether I wasn't after all just that little Preemby. A human rabbit. My faith faltered. I admit it faltered.'

He mused painfully for some moments.

Then he laid his hand reassuringly on Bobby's wrist. 'I *am* Sargon,' he said. 'Talking to your friend Devizes has cleared my mind greatly. I *am* Sargon, but in a rather different sense from what I had imagined. Preemby was, as I had supposed, a mere accidental covering. But –'

The little face puckered with intellectual effort. 'I am not *exclusively* Sargon. You – you perhaps are still unawakened – but you are Sargon too. His blood is in our veins. We are co-heirs. It is fairly easy to understand. Sargon, regal position. Naturally many wives. Political – biological necessity. Offspring numerous. They again – positions of advantage – many children. Next generation, more. Like a vast expanding beam of intellectual and moral force. You can prove it – prove it by mathematics. Dr. Devizes and I – we worked it out on a piece of paper. We are all descended from Sargon, just as we are all descended from Cæsar – just as nearly all English and Americans are descended from William the Conqueror. Few people realize this. A little arithmetic – it is perfectly plain. Long before the Christian era the blood of Sargon was diffused throughout all mankind. His traditions still more so. We all inherit. Not merely from him – from all

364

the great kings, from all the noble conquerors. From all the brave and beautiful women. All the statesmen and inventors and creators. If not directly from them, from their fathers and mothers. All that rich wine from the past is in my veins. And I thought I was just Albert Edward Preemby! And at Woodford Wells I went for a silly little walk nearly every afternoon with sixpence in my pocket to spend and nothing in the world to do! For twenty years. It seems incredible.'

The blue eyes sought confirmation from Bobby, who nodded.

'There was I walking about Epping Forest in a suit of clothes I never really liked – a rather exaggerated golfing suit with baggy knickerbockers that my wife chose for me – they seemed to get baggier every year – and I was quite ignorant that I was the heir of all the ages, and that the whole earth down to the centre and up to the sky was mine. And yours. Ours. I had no sense of duty to it; I hadn't woke up to self-respect. I wasn't only Sargon, but all the men and women who have ever mattered on earth. I was God's Everlasting Servant. Instead of which I was rather timid about horses and strange dogs, and often when I saw people approaching and thought they were observing me and speaking about me, I did not know what to do with my arms and legs, and became quite confused about them.'

He paused to smile at the thought of it.

'It has been interesting to talk to your Dr. Devizes of the absurdity of that contracted blind littleness in which I lived so long. We talked of the Great Man I really was, the Great Men we really were. All the Incorporated Great Men. You and I, the same. Because in the past you and I and he were one, and in the future we may come together again. We have just separated to take hold of things as the hand separates into thumb and fingers.

We talked of the time when the spirit that is in us made the first hut, launched the first ship, rode the first horse. We could not remember those great moments as exact incidents, but we recalled them – generally. We recalled a blazing day when a band of men went out across a sandy desert for the first time, and when a man first stood upon a glacier. It was – slippery. Then I remembered watching my people heap up the earth-walls of my first city. We went out against the robbers of the first herds. Then Dr. Devizes and I stood in imagination on a sort of quarter-deck, and watched our men lugging the great oars of the galley that took us to Iceland and Vinland. We both saw. We planned the Great Walls of China; I counted our lateen sails upon our grand canal. You see, I have built a million wonderful temples and made an innumerable multitude of lovely sculptures, paintings, jewels and decorations. I had forgotten it, but I have. And I have loved a billion loves – I have indeed – to bring me here. We all have. We talked it over, your Dr. Devizes and I. I had not dreamt the millionth part of what I am. When I thought I was Sargon wholly and solely I still did not realize my great inheritance and my enormous destiny. Even now I am only beginning to see that. . . . It is preposterous to think that I who have all this past of efforts and adventures behind me should have been content to run about Woodford Wells in a ridiculous suit of tweeds with plus-four breeches that was extremely heavy and uncomfortable – they tickled me, you know – on hot days. Yet I did. I did. . . . Not realizing. . . . I used to go on until I could endure it no longer, and then I would have to stop and scratch behind my knees. . . .

'Of course, when I called myself Sargon King of Kings and proposed to rule all the world I was – Dr. Devizes called it – *symbolizing*. Of course, everybody is really Sargon King of Kings, and everybody ought to take

366

hold of all the world and save it and rule it just as I have
got to do.'

He had concluded his exposition. He had spread out
his disarticulated parts before Bobby just as Devizes had
returned them to him.

§ 5

'But just what are you going to do?' said Bobby.

'I have been thinking of that.'

For a little while he continued to think.

'It becomes all different,' he said, 'when one realizes
that one is not the *only* Sargon. I thought of being a
great king, a great leader, with the rest of the world just
following me. I doubt if I ever felt quite *up* to a job of
that sort, but I couldn't see any other way of being
Sargon and a king. Now I do. I did my best, but even
when I went to Buckingham Palace I realized that the
thing was going to be too big for me. I was telling Dr.
Devizes – I told him, that since he was Sargon and King
just as much as me and that almost anyone might become
Sargon and King, then it wasn't a case for palaces and
thrones any longer, or for being proclaimed and crowned –
such things were as much out of date as flint implements;
and that the real thing was to be just a kingly person and
work with all the other kingly persons in the world to
make the world worthy of our high descent. Anyone
who wakes up to that becomes a kingly person. We can
be active kings even if we remain kings incognito. One
can be a laundryman like I was when I was just Preemby,
and think of nothing but the profits and needs and vanities
and fears of a little laundryman – and how dull it was! –
or one can be a king, the descendant of ten thousand
kings, the joint heir to the inheritance of all human affairs,

the lord of the generations still unborn – who happens to be living in exile as a laundry-man.'

He paused.

'I agree with most of that,' said Bobby. 'It's – it's attractive.'

'So far it is as plain as can be. But after that the difficulties begin. It isn't enough just to say you are a king. You have to be a king. You have to *do*. You can't be a king and not do kingly things. But it's just there that Dr. Devizes and I – we weren't so clear. There's a lot to be thought out. What is my kingly task? In this frail body – and what I am? I am not clear. Yet the mere fact that I am not clear shows clearly where I have to begin. I have to get clear. I have to get knowledge, find out about my kingdom. That's reasonable. I have to learn more about my great inheritance, our great inheritance, the history of it, the possibilities of it, the ways of the men who misrule it. I have to learn about business and economics and money; and then when I see it all plain I have to exert myself and vote and work, and I have to find out what particular gifts I have and how I may best give them to our kingdom. Each king must glorify his particular reign with his particular gift. We agreed about that.

'So far I do not know my particular gift. Dr. Devizes says that so far as he is concerned he must work out human motives and human relationships; his gift and his natural interest is for mental science. He has his task meted out for him, his kingly task. But for me at present there isn't that much self-knowledge. I have to begin lower down and with broader questions. I have to learn about the universe and about the history of this world-empire of Sargon's, and of all the things I have neglected in my dreams and littleness. I have to go to school again. To learn how to think harder. I don't mind the fatigue.

368

But I am impatient. When I think of all that lies before me, the reading, the inquiries, the visits to museums and such-like places, I want to get up right away and begin. I have lived so unobservant and irresponsible a life that I am puzzled how to account for the years I have spent. I have mooned them away. But I am glad I have awakened to my kingship before it is too late.

'I am quite a young man still. I am a little past forty, but that is nothing. Half of that was childhood and boyhood, and much of the rest inattention. For all I know I may live for another forty years. I'm not half through. And they may be the best years, the full years. I can spend three or four just learning – learning the round world. I shall begin to find out politics, and why men and women are servile and little-minded. I shall begin to realize how I can extend to those others this great liberation that has come to me. I shall begin to have a political life. A man who has no political life is like a rat which lives in a ship rather than like a man who navigates it. Then within that I shall begin to find my own proper life, my particular task. It is premature, I think, but I am very greatly drawn to the riddle of madness and asylums. I do not understand why there is madness. It puzzles and distresses me, and Dr. Devizes agrees with me that when a thing puzzles and distresses the mind the thing to do is to gather all the knowledge and ideas one can about it – scientifically. Presently it ceases to distress; it interests and occupies. And when I was in – that Place, I talked to some of those poor creatures. I was very sorry for them. I made them promises to help them when my kingdom came. And now I begin to see what my kingdom is, and the way in which I must enter in to possess it. Perhaps in good time I shall learn and spread knowledge about asylums, and make things better in them so that they will not simply imprison people but help and cure them.

'It was Dr. Devizes' idea, I think – or we may have worked it out together – that there is a real and important purpose in madness. It is a sort of simplification, a removal of checks and controls, and a sort of natural experiment. The secret things of the mind are laid bare. But then if poor souls are to suffer that sort of thing to yield knowledge for others, they ought to be treated properly; they ought to be cherished and made the utmost use of, and not handed over to such brutes as we had. . . . I can't tell you. Not yet. Brutes they were. . . . And in their sane moments – they all have sane moments, these lunatics – they ought to be comforted and told.'

The queer little round face, with its sprouting moustache and its pale blue eyes, stared at Bobby.

'When first I saw you,' said Sargon, 'I did not realize in the least how things really were between us. I was still wrapped up in vaingloriousness; I thought I was a great prophet and teacher and king, and that all the world had to obey me. I thought you were going to be the first and best and nearest of my disciples. But now I know better about myself. And about other people. They are here not to be my followers and disciples but to be my fellow kings. We have to work together with all the others who are awakened, for our kingdom and the great progress of mankind.'

He went on talking rather to himself than to Bobby.

'I have always wanted to know things, but now I shall have the will really to know them. I shall be different now. It seems incredible that a little while ago I was bothered about what I should do with my time. Now I am only eager to get at things, and however long my time may be I know it will be full. It is astonishing to me that there has been flying in my kingdom for a dozen years, and I have never been in an aeroplane. I must look at the world from an aeroplane. And perhaps I shall need to go to India and China and suchlike strange and wonderful countries, because they, too, are a part of my inheritance. I need to know about them. And jungles and wildernesses that we have to subjugate; I have to see them. The beasts are under us; we have to cherish them or destroy them mercifully as the necessities of our kingdom may require. It is a terrible thing even to be lord of a beast. All the beasts, wild or tame, are under our dominion. And there is science. All the wonderful work men do in laboratories and their marvellous discoveries are our care. If I do not understand I may hinder. How blind I have been to the splendour of my life! When I think of all these things, I can hardly endure to be here in bed; I am so impatient to get on with them. But I suppose I must be patient with these poor wheezing lungs.

'Patient,' he repeated.

He looked at his wrist watch and it had stopped. 'Can you tell me the time? At seven I ought to take some more of that excellent tonic. It is working wonders in me. But no! don't trouble; the nurse will be thinking of it. . . . It puts fresh life into me.'

§ 6

But Sargon did not live forty years more, nor thirty, nor twenty. He lived just a day under seven weeks from that conversation. He stayed in bed for two days after Bobby returned to London; then Lambone also went and he became intractable. As his strength returned he bothered his nurse more and more for books he couldn't name or describe, and for volumes of the *Encyclopædia Britannica*;

and when she declared that seven volumes of that monu-
mental publication were surely as much as any invalid
could need at one time, he got up and put on his rough
little dressing-gown and came paddling downstairs,
h'rrmping resolutely, to the library. After that he got up
for three days running. A fire was made in the most
bookish corner of the downstairs room and screens put
to keep him warm. But his tonic was driving him, perhaps it was too stimulating a tonic, and he would not
stay in his protected corner.

The nurse seems to have been a weak, complaining
character, indisposed to act without authority. She telephoned through to Devizes in London, but she did not
succeed in making clear to him the gravity of Sargon's
misbehaviour. The crowning offence came when he
wouldn't go to bed at seven, but instead slipped out, in
an overcoat and a wrapper indeed but in slippers, upon
the terrace before the house. His bare ankles and legs
were exposed to the cold wind. The slow-moving periodic
beams of light from the lighthouse upon the coast, sweeping across the phantom hills under the clear starlight
had drawn him out, those processional lights, and Sirius
that white splendour, and the steadfast sprawling glory of
Orion. It was a clear November night with frost in the
air. The nurse heard him cough and rushed out to him.
He was looking at Sirius through Lambone's field-glasses,
and she had to drag him in by main force. She lost her
temper; there was an ungracious struggle.

The next day he was in no state to leave his bed. Yet he
tossed about and exposed his inflamed chest in feeble
attempts to read. 'I know nothing,' he complained. For a
while he got better again, and then it is highly probable
that he went to his open window in the night and sat for
a long time wondering at the stars. After that came a
relapse and a week or so of struggle, and then after a

phase of delirium came great weakness, and then one night, death. He was quite alone when he died.

Bobby had not expected the death at all. He heard of it from Christina Alberta with great astonishment. He had been told nothing of Sargon being worse nor of his misbehaviour; he had been thinking of him rather enviously as growing steadily stronger and better and gratifying day by day a happy and expanding curiosity. He had looked forward presently to another talk and another phase in this odd belated adolescence. It was as though an interesting story had come to an abrupt end in the middle, as though all its concluding chapters had been torn out rudely and unreasonably.

This mood of frustrated sympathy lasted over the cremation of Sargon at Golders Green. Bobby went to that queer ceremony. He arrived late with Billy; the coffin that held the little body stood ready to glide into the furnace, the Church of England burial service had already begun. There were very few people in the chapel. Christina Alberta in the black she had worn for her mother was in the front seat, as chief mourner, between Paul Lambone and Devizes. Behind her with an air of earnest support were Harold and Fay Crumb, astonishingly in deep mourning and following the service meticulously in two prayer-books. An unpleasant-looking individual with a very long pock-marked sheep's face, small eyes and habitual-looking blacks turned round and stared at Bobby as he came in. He was accompanied by a very large blonde lady who seemed to have slept in her mourning under a bed. Relations of the deceased? The air of relationship was unmistakable. Behind, a young woman and two detached old ladies seemed to be indulging a simple propensity for funeral services at large. They completed the congregation.

Christina Alberta looked unusually small and overshadowed by her two odd men friends. It was a grey day outside, and the general effect of the gathering was thin and scattered and damp and chilly. The organ was playing as Bobby came in, and he thought he had never heard a less musical organ. The service as it went on sounded more and more trite and theological and insincere. What an old second-hand damp mackintosh the Church of England is, thought Bobby, for a striving soul to wear? But then what can any religion in the world really do in the face of normal death? Theologically one should rejoice when a good man dies, but none of these religions had had the pluck to brazen it out to that extent. None can get rid of the effect of confrontation with a blank amazing interrogation. Was there anything within that coffin there that heard or cared a jot for those sombre mummeries?

Bobby's thoughts converged upon that still thing within the coffin. The little face would be wearing a waxen unaccustomed dignity; the round, preposterously innocent blue eyes would be closed and a little sunken. Where were those thoughts and hopes now, that Bobby had listened to a few weeks since? Sargon had talked of flying, of visiting India and China, of doing noble work in the world. He had said that half his life still lay before him. He had seemed to be opening like a flower on the first sunny morning of a belated spring. And it was all delusion; the door of death that had slammed upon him was already closing then.

Surely those hopes had been life! In them if in anything was something of the life that lives and cannot die. But was it yonder? No. That in the coffin there was no more than a photographic impression, a cast garment, the parings of a nail. There was more of Sargon now in Bobby's brain alone, than in that coffin. But Sargon, where was he? Where were those dreams and desires?

374

Bobby became aware of the voice of the officiating clergyman driving high, like a flying bird, over the welter of his thoughts. '*But some men will say, How are the dead raised up? and with what body do they come? Thou fool, that which thou sowest is not quickened unless it die. And that which thou sowest, thou sowest not the body that shall be, but bare grain, it may chance of wheat or any other grain: But God giveth it a body, as it hath pleased him, but to every seed its own body. . . .*'

'Queer, tortuous, ingenious fellow that Paul,' thought Bobby. Now what exactly was he driving at there? Queer fellow! Bad manners too with his 'Thou fool.' A rather strained analogy this about the seed, 'sown in corruption.' After all a seed was the cleanest, most living bit of vegetable matter you could have; it had to be sown in clean mould. Growing plants you manured perhaps, but not seed-boxes. But there was a queer insistence in the discourse of the 'difference,' the discontinuity, of the new life. What was to come was to be altogether different from what was sown. Bobby had never noted that before, never noted how plainly the apostle insisted that no body, no earthly sort of body, no personality, ever came back.

'*The glory of the celestial is one, and the glory of the terrestrial is another. There is one glory of the sun, and another glory of the moon, and another glory of the stars; for one star differeth from another star in glory.*'

What was the drift of that? Was it translated properly? What had Paul been up against in Corinth? After all, why couldn't the Church speak to one's living needs instead of disinterring this Levantine argument? And that analogy of the seed; was it after all a good one? Whatever comes from a seed must itself die again; it is no more immortal than the plant that came before it. The clergyman was going too fast, too, to follow him closely. Better get a prayer-book at home afterwards and read all this.

'O Grave where is thy sting? O death where is thy victory? The sting of death is sin and the strength of sin is in the law.'

No. There was no following that. It sounded like nonsense. One just missed the implications. It was like listening to some one who was too far off to be heard distinctly but who made eloquent gestures and noises.

The service came to an embarrassed pause. Everyone was motionless, arrested.

'Man that is born of woman hath but a short time to live. . . . He cometh up and is cut down like a flower; he fleeth as it were a shadow. . . .'

Set in motion by unseen hands the coffin went gliding towards the furnace doors which opened to receive it. There was a deep roar, a sound like a mighty rushing wind, an elemental and chaotic sound. . . .

Life is a faint dispersed film upon one little planet, but flames roar like this and great winds rush and whirl, out to the remotest star in the unfathomable depths of space. That deep disorderly tumult is the true voice of lifeless matter, not of dead matter, for what has never lived cannot be dead, but of lifeless matter, outside of and beneath and beyond life.

Everyone in the chapel seemed still and bowed and hushed and dwarfed to minute dimensions until the furnace doors had closed again upon that soulless devouring clamour.

May at Udimore

§ 1

BOBBY forgot that glimpse of the elemental powers
that the furnace doors had given him altogether, for
such things do not remain naturally in the mind. They
inconvenience life. But the voice of the clergyman hust-
ling the arguments of St. Paul along, and the scene in
the Crematorium Chapel with the little coffin waiting
to be launched into eternity and the few still black
mourners dotted among the yellow benches came back to
him very vividly when Paul Lambone began to quote and
twist those familiar sentences about the contrast between
the corruptible and the incorruptible and expand a
fantastic philosophy of his own. Bobby had always
intended to read that funeral service over again slowly
and judicially, but he had never done so and he regretted
it now very much. It left him – and Paul of Tarsus – at
the mercy of Paul Lambone, and he knew that Paul Lambone loved ingenious slight misquotations.

It was a very warm, serenely still May evening, and
Lambone's party sat after dinner in the twilight, some
just inside the house and some on deck-chairs upon the
terrace. They looked out over the marsh and over the
still sea. The sky was like the inside of a deep blue globe
on which an ever increasing multitude of starry midges
was alighting; and Rye and Winchelsea crouched low
beneath it, black low lumps with a street light and a
window or so showing minutely. Receding out to sea was
a liner quite brightly lit. With a swift steadiness the beam
of the nearer lighthouse swept the distant flats, came
near, lit the faces of the talkers, lit the room, called a
church tower and a group of trees into existence and

377

dropped them back into the darkness and forgot about them and passed on. And then presently it was coming again, a thin white streak of light hurrying far away across the levels.

When one's attention wandered from the talk one became aware of an abundance of nightingales. They were nightingales newly come from the south. One or it might be two were in the trees close at hand; others remoter wove a gauze curtain of faint sweet sounds over the visible universe.

Bobby sat on the step between the room and the terrace with his back against a pillar and with his empty coffee-cup beside him. He had put himself there by the feet of Christina Alberta, who was deep in a big arm-chair and very still. Her face was dim except when her cigarette glowed and showed a red-lit unfamiliar face. And yet that afternoon she had been the most familiar thing in the world to him; she had kissed him and pulled his ears and he had kissed her bare shoulders and clasped her in his arms. Devizes too was silent and preoccupied. He sat over against Christina Alberta on the other side of the opening of the room; and he was so much in the twilight that except when the lighthouse beam lit his face, only his shining shoes and socks were clearly visible to Bobby. There had been times when Bobby had thought that Devizes was in love with Christina Alberta, and he had a vague inexplicable feeling that to some extent she was or had been in love with Devizes. He had a sense of unfathomed deeps in their relationship, but he did not know where these deeps lay. If Christina Alberta loved Devizes she would have said so. Bobby knew of no reason why she should not. But to-day she had hugged and kissed Bobby so that it was impossible to believe she loved anyone else.

Yet in the last three or four months she had gone about

with Devizes a lot; Bobby had seen her mind responding and changing with her talks with this man. She used to quote him, and she would say things exactly like the things he said. It had been a great inconvenience and trial to Bobby, this preoccupation. And then suddenly he found Devizes wasn't the lover at all, never could have been a lover. That day she had proved that up to the hilt. And now in a state between pride and servitude Bobby sat at her feet. He sat at her feet and close to her; Devizes in the darkness was remote, a full three yards away.

Except for Lambone's unquenchable flow it had not been a very talkative party. To-night it was less talkative than ever. 'This is too perfect,' Margaret Means had sighed. 'I can't talk. I just thank God I am alive,' and she had nestled into her big deck-chair upon the terrace. This was the girl – it had suddenly become apparent to Bobby a fortnight ago in London – whom Devizes intended to marry. Abruptly she had come upon the scene to destroy the triangle that had obsessed Bobby's imagination. A sweetly pretty fragile thing she was; in the twilight she seemed as faint and fragrant as nightstock, and she was a wonderful pianist. Last night she had played for two hours. Paul's sister, Miss Lambone, had been evoked from somewhere in the west of England to come and be hostess to the engaged couple. Bobby had tried to talk to Christina Alberta about Margaret, but Christina Alberta hadn't wanted to talk about her. 'You see,' said Christina Alberta compactly, 'she has opened the whole world of music to him. That's what brought them together. She's clever; she's very clear and clever.'

'I'd never heard of her – until you mentioned their engagement.'

'They've gone to concerts together and that sort of thing. He's known her much longer than he has known me.'

'When did you first meet Devizes?'

'About the time my Daddy came to Midgard Street. As recently as that. It's hardly six months. Paul Lambone took me to him to get advice about Daddy. But *they* have been going about – for more than a year. I thought it was just music that interested them. They'd seemed to be friends. And I thought he didn't mean to marry again. He just suddenly decided.'

Christina Alberta reflected. 'That's the way with life, Bobby. Things accumulate, and then you suddenly decide.'

'Had she been undecided? Had she made him wait?'

'Not her,' said Christina Alberta with a remarkable hardness in her voice.

'No,' she said. '*He* decided.'

She seemed to feel there was still something to express. 'He just took hold of the situation.'

§ 2

This was Bobby's second visit to Udimore. Paul Lambone had suddenly seen fit to gather this party; apparently on the spur of Devizes' engagement. In the interval Bobby had seen Christina Alberta a number of times and developed an immense sense of relationship to her. It filled his life. He had always been dreaming things about her from the time when he anticipated her with blue eyes and a fragile person, and always she was and did things that tore his dreams to shreds. This made her profoundly interesting. More and more he had become dependent upon her for interest. He wanted to marry her if only to make sure he wouldn't lose the interest of her. She had refused – twice. Without any of the graces proper to the occasion. 'No fear, Bobby,' she said. 'It wouldn't do. I'm not the woman you take me for.'

'You never are,' he said. 'I don't mind that.'

'You're the dearest companion,' she said. 'I like the way your hair grows.'

'Then why not make it yours, and be companions for ever?'

'Nothing more frightful,' she said, and so dismissed the proposal.

They went about together; they spent much of their spare time together except for those distressing occasions when she would suddenly throw him over to go to a theatre or walk with Devizes. Or to go to Devizes to talk. She never hesitated to throw him over for Devizes. Yet Bobby got a lot of her. She didn't know much about theatres or music-halls or restaurants or dancing-places or that sort of thing, and Bobby was discreetly competent in that province. The Malmesburys felt themselves deserted, and Susan was vindictive in her resentment at his frequent absence from her bed-time rituals. Tessy, Bobby declared, remained his dearest friend; but when he tried to tell her all about himself in the old, old fashion – which he did when Christina Alberta was away with Devizes – he naturally had to tell her all about Christina Alberta. But Tessy declined in the most emphatic way to be told about Christina Alberta. It was extremely surprising and disappointing to Bobby to find out how incapable Tessy was of appreciating the endless interestingness and charm of Christina Alberta. It was a blind spot in her mind. She seemed to assume that Christina Alberta was no better than she should be, whereas she was much better. It estranged Bobby and Tessy very much, and it was a great sorrow to Bobby.

Because Christina Alberta *was* good – and interesting – beyond dispute. She was growing with tremendous rapidity mentally and in her knowledge of the world. Every time he met her she seemed more of a person, with richer, fuller, more commanding ideas. She seemed to be living every moment of her time. She was working now at the Royal College of Science under Macbride. She was taking hold of her new studies there with tremendous enthusiasm. She was in love with comparative anatomy. Bobby had always thought that comparative anatomy was dry, pedantic stuff about bones, but she declared it lit up the whole story of life for her. It changed her ideas about the world and about herself profoundly. 'It is the most romantic stuff I have ever read or thought about,' she said. 'It makes human history seem silly.'

She took him three times to the Natural History Museum at South Kensington to show him something of the fine realizations that stirred her mind. She made it clear to him how the bones of a wing or the scratches of a flint could restore the storms and sunlight and passion of ten million years ago.

And then suddenly a week ago Christina Alberta had consented to marry Bobby. She had taken back her two refusals. But the way she did it made it like everything else she did, astonishing and disconcerting. She had a confession to make, and for a time until he could think it over thoroughly that confession seemed to Bobby to explain her refusals completely and to clear up everything about her.

She got him to take her to Hampton Court. But they did not go into the gardens because they saw through the park gates that the chestnuts of Bushey Avenue were in full blossom; they went instead by the pond and up under the riotously flowering branches. A belated spring was coming now in a hurry, warm and brilliant. The trees were glorious. It was as if a bright green sea was splashing up warm creamy foam under a shower of cannon shots. The blue sky hummed with light.

'The spring has come fast now that it has begun to come,' she said.

He felt she had something to say and waited.

'I never know, Bobby – this year less than ever – whether spring is the happiest time in the year or the most miserably restless. Everybody and everything is falling in love.'

'I didn't wait for spring,' said Bobby.

'But what of the frogs that can't find water?' said Christina Alberta.

'There's water where there are frogs,' said Bobby.

'Everybody is marrying and giving in marriage,' she said. 'I thought – I thought – Dr. Devizes at least was an inconsolable widower. But the spring tides have caught even him. They catch everybody.'

'They've caught you?'

'I don't know. I'm miserable, Bobby, and restless and all astir.'

'Then let yourself go.'

'One aches – alone.'

'But are you alone?'

'Fairly.'

'There's me.'

'Bobby dear, what do you want in me?'

'*You.* To be with you. To be always about with you. And to be loved by you.'

'It's kind of you.'

'Oh nonsense! *Kindness!*'

'Listen, Bobby,' she said, and made a long pause.

Her voice when she spoke had adopted the ease of casual conversation. 'Do you believe in chastity, Bobby? Could you love a girl who wasn't – chaste?'

Bobby winced as if she had struck his face with a whip. He went white. 'What do you mean?' he asked.

'Plainly,' she said.

For a time neither of them said a word.

'You have had *your* experiences,' she thrust. 'In France. They all did.'

Bobby made no answer to that.

'Now you know,' she flung at him.

For a little while the light had gone out of Bobby's world.

'Did you love the man?' he asked.

'If I did I don't remember it. It was just – curiosity. And the stir of growing up. And the intolerable sense of being forbidden. No – I think I was almost – cold-blooded. I liked the look of him. And then I disliked him. . . . But there it is, Bobby. That's how things are.'

Bobby weighed his words. 'I'd care if it were any girl but you. You – you're different. I love you. What has or hasn't happened to you doesn't matter. At least – it doesn't matter so much.'

'You're sure it doesn't matter so much?'

'Quite.'

'Sure for good?'

'Yes.'

'From this moment you forget, you begin to forget what I have told you? As I want to forget it?'

'It will go soon enough if you want to forget it. It doesn't matter at all. I see now, it doesn't matter at all.'

'But why on earth do you want to marry me, Bobby? What is there in me? I'm ugly, rude, greedy, inconsiderate. I've no purity, no devotion.'

'You're incessantly interesting. You're straight, swift, and endlessly beautiful.'

'Bobby, truly! Does it look like that to you?'

'Yes. Doesn't my manner – ? Don't you *know*?'

'Yes,' she said gravely; 'I suppose I know.'

She came to a stop in front of him with her arms akimbo.

They stood looking at one another, and Bobby winced as if he was going to cry. Her face was grave and troubled, and then at the sight of his expression her smile broke through. Her gravity vanished. She was a different Christina Alberta. She was suddenly the gayest conceivable thing to him, confident and impudent.

'If you were to kiss me, Bobby, right here and now in Bushey Park, would they lock us up? . . .'

Most wonderful it was to Bobby to take her in his arms. A new Christina Alberta was revealed to Bobby; Christina Alberta seen from a distance of six inches or so, an amazingly beautiful Christina Alberta. One might have thought she had never lived for anything but being loved by Bobby.

'You're learning,' said Christina Alberta after a little while. 'Now do it all over again, Bobby. Nobody seems to be looking. . . .'

§ 3

Neither Lambone nor Devizes had seemed in the least surprised at their engagement. Indeed their attitude of gratified expectation was almost embarrassing. The young couple had come down to Udimore with Devizes and Miss Means under the ample protection of Miss Lambone almost as though they had been appointed for each other from the beginning of things.

But at Udimore there were further surprises and perplexities for Bobby. All day Saturday Christina Alberta seemed to be not so much in love as in a thoroughly bad temper. She seemed far more concerned by the fact that Devizes was going to marry Miss Means than by the generous devotion that Bobby was prepared to lavish upon her. She was inattentive to his various little manœuvres to get isolated with her. The two couples played tennis after tea until it was time to dress for dinner; she was badly out of practice and fundamentally unorthodox, and Margaret played with a smoothness and sweetness that roused her to a pitch of viciousness only too evident to Bobby's fine perceptions. It seemed to Bobby that Devizes also noted her annoyance, but Miss Means was blissfully unobservant of anything in the world but Devizes.

On Sunday morning Christina Alberta carried off Bobby through the distant cheerfulness of church bells for a walk to Brede Castle. And she announced to Bobby that she did not intend to marry him.

Bobby protested. 'You don't love me?'

'Haven't I kissed you? Didn't I hug you? Haven't I ruffled your hair?'

'Then why don't you want to marry me?'

'I do not want to marry anyone. I don't love anybody. Except of course you. But even you, I can't marry. I want to be loved, Bobby, yes. But not to be married.'

'But why? Not the – the old reason?'

'No. I took your word about that. But all the same I don't want to marry you, Bobby. . . . I think it's because I don't want to be bound up with anyone's life. I don't want to be a wife. I want to be my free and independent self. I've got to grow. That's it, Bobby. I want to be free to grow.'

Bobby made protesting noises.

'I don't want some one seeing me grow all the time. You'd always be looking at me, Bobby; I know you would.'

It was useless of Bobby to say he wouldn't. He would.

'I didn't know that things were going to take me like this until I fixed to marry you. I wanted to marry you when I consented – honestly I did. I wanted dreadfully then to

386

get close to some one, as close as possible, and to be kissed and told "There! There!" and to keep there. It was a comfort for me, Bobby. You are a comfort for me. I'd ache to madness without you. But how close we come when we love, Bobby, and how far away we are all the time! How can we know each other when we hardly know ourselves? When we don't *dare* know ourselves?

'You are such a dear, Bobby. You are so warm and kind that it seems ungrateful not to give myself to you with both hands. But I just can't. I'm not a normal woman perhaps. Or something has happened to me unawares. Perhaps life has cheated me out of something. . . . Oh I don't know, Bobby. I want some one dreadfully; I want you dreadfully and I don't want you at all. I'd rather be dead than a female thing like Margaret Means. If *that's* marrying – !'

'But I thought,' said Bobby, 'after all that's happened – '

'No.'

'I'll wait ten years for you,' said Bobby, 'on the chance of your altering your mind.'

'You are the dearest comforter,' said Christina Alberta, and stopped short. . . .

And suddenly she had put her hands upon his shoulders and clung to him and broken into a wild passion of weeping.

'Wetting you instead of wedding you,' she sobbed and laughed. 'Oh my poor Bobby! you dear lover!'

She clung to him for a time. Then she detached herself and stood wiping her eyes, the Christina Alberta he generally knew, except for the traces of her tears. 'If women can't control their emotions better,' she said, 'they'll have to go back to Harems. We can't have it both ways. But I *won't* marry you. There's no man in the world I can marry. I'm going to be a free and independent woman, Bobby. From now on.'

387

'But I don't understand!' said Bobby.

'It's not because I don't want you to love me.'

He was baffled. '*Bobby!*' she whispered, and seemed to glow.

Bobby took her back into his arms and held her, and pressed his cheek and ears against hers, and kissed her and kissed her again, and it seemed to him to mark his own unworthiness that he should think at such a time that there were no such wonderful kisses in the world as kisses flavoured with salt tears.

And yet she wasn't going to marry him! She had snatched herself back from him and nevertheless she was in his arms.

He was enormously perplexed at what was happening, but it was quite clear that the end of his engagement was not to be the end of his love-making. Anyhow here was love. It was so manifestly the time for love. High May ruled the world. About them there were hawthorn trees white with blossom and great bushes of elder just breaking into flower.

§ 4

Bobby sat in the gloaming with his friends and thought of the things that had happened to him that day, thought of Christina Alberta's salt tears and the incessant intriguing strangeness of her ways. He was still immensely puzzled, but now in a large, restful, contented fashion. Christina Alberta and he were not to marry it seemed; nevertheless he had kissed her and embraced her, and he was free to sit at her feet. For a time he was not even to humiliate himself by telling these others he was not to marry her. He said nothing. His thoughts and feelings were beyond words. Christina Alberta too was darkly silent. Everyone indeed seemed preoccupied. Talk about the view and the stars and the coming of the nightingales, and about migratory birds and lighthouses rambled on for a time and died away.

They were all too full for talking. The silence lengthened. He wondered what would happen if nobody spoke any more. He thought of Christina Alberta close behind him and he began to quiver in all his being. The silence was becoming oppressive. He felt as though he could no longer change his attitude. Nobody stirred. But Lambone saved the situation.

'It is exactly six months ago to-night that Sargon died upstairs,' said Lambone. He paused and seemed to answer an unspoken question. 'We don't know when he died exactly. He just faded out in the night.'

'I wish I could have known him,' said Margaret Means after quite a long interval.

Bobby's thoughts came round to Sargon. That still young woman sitting in the darkness behind him ceased to dominate his thoughts. He was moved to speak, and had to cough to clear his throat.

'I hate to think of his being burnt and scattered,' he said.

'It's not so disagreeable,' said Miss Lambone, ' as to think of the body all shut up in the coffin and decaying.'

'Oh, don't!' cried Bobby. 'It's death – any death, that I hate to think of. Now when it is spring time, when the whole world is so full of life, I remember all he was, the hopes he had, and they are scattered and dispersed – . Anyhow they are scattered and dispersed, they are not boxed up and locked up and buried. . . . When I was here last he was like a little boy who has just heard of the world. He was going to fly, going to India and China, going to learn all about everything and then do all sorts of splendid things. And there were the beastly bacteria at work in his lungs and beating his strength down and none of it was

ever to happen. . . . When first I heard he was dead I
could not believe it.'

'*Is* he dead?' said Paul Lambone.

There was no reply to be made to that.

Paul adjusted his shoulder-blades a little more comfortably against the back of the small deep sofa on which he
sat. 'The more I think over Sargon the less dead he seems
to me, and the more important he becomes. I don't agree
with you, Roothing. I don't find anything futile in his life.
I think he was – symbolically – perfect. I have thought
about him endlessly.'

'And talked,' said Devizes, 'endlessly.'

'And given you some very helpful ideas for your treatment. Don't be ungrateful. You think that Sargon is over.
He has only just begun. You are becoming too profes-
sional with success, Devizes. You begin to take up cases
and work them off and drop them out of your mind. You
don't go on with them and learn. You don't sit about and
think about them as I do. I continue to think about Sargon. I go on with him because he is still a living being for
me. I have got a new religion from him, the religion of
Sargonism. I declare him prophet of a new dispensation.
It is my latest new religion. There will always be new
religions, and the new religions will always be the only ones
that matter. Religion is a living thing, and what is alive
must be continually dying and be continually born again –
differently but the same.'

'You believe in immortality, Mr. Lambone,' said Miss
Means. 'I wish that I could. But when I try to imagine it
my wits fail me. Sometimes one seems to *feel* what it
might be. On a night like this perhaps –'

Her pretty clear voice died away in the stillness as the
trail of a falling star dies away.

Paul, a large dark lump on the dim pale sofa, went on
speaking. 'Immortality,' he said, 'is a mystery. One can

only speak of it in dark metaphors. How can we believe that each of our individual commonplace lives is to have an endless commonplace sequel? That is incredible nonsense. Yet we go on living after death nevertheless. When we die we are changed. All wise teachers have insisted upon that. As Roothing said, we are not boxed up and buried and forgotten. Our real death is an escape, and we escape and become – what did you say? – dispersed. Immortal life is endless consequence. Our lives are like lines in a great poem. It is an unfinished and yet it is a perfect poem. The line begins and ends but it has to be there, and once it is there, it is there eternally. Nothing could follow if it was not there. But every star has not the same glory. Some lives, some lines, stand out as more significant than the others. They open a new branch of the subject, they start a new point of view, they express something fresh. They are geniuses, they are prophets, they are major stars. Sargon was the last, the latest of these prophets, and I am his Paul. Not for nothing was I christened Paul.'

'Paul of Tarsus,' said Devizes, 'was a man of energy.'

'There will always be minor differences in such parallels,' said Lambone.

'I will tell you my doctrine,' he said.

He began to talk in that clear miniature voice of his, which was so like a little mouse running out of the mountain of his person, of Sargon and his struggles with his individuality, and of the struggles in every man between his individual life and something greater that is also in him. There was a streak of fantasy in what he was saying, a touch of burlesque in his constant use of theological and religious phrasing, and withal a profound sincerity. In every human being, he declared, the little laundryman battled with the King of Kings. He expanded and amplified this theme. Ever and again Devizes would cut into the monologue and talk for a time, not so much to make objections as to restate and amend and amplify. The others said little. Margaret Means twice made soft sweet sounds suggestive of intellectual sensuousness, and once Christina Alberta said 'But –!' very loudly and then 'Never mind. Go on' and relapsed for a long time into a silence that could be felt. Bobby sat still, sometimes listening intently and sometimes with his mind spreading out like an uncared-for stream into a number of parallel channels. The argument itself was interesting to follow, but moving at the side of that was the question of the talker's sincerity. How much of all this stuff did Lambone mean? How much of what he said was of a piece with the rest of his observant, self-indulgent life, his life as a humorous comment on a universe that was profoundly absurd?

How easily Lambone played with phrases and ideas for which men had lived and died! How widely he had read and thought to bring so many things together! He produced a great effect of erudition. *The Golden Bough* he had at his fingers' ends. He talked of the sacramental mysteries of half a dozen cults, from Mithraism to ritual sacrifices, of varying ideas of personality that had held and swayed human life from Fiji to Yucatan. Now he was in pre-Christian Alexandria, and now among the Chinese philosophers. The 'Superior Person' of Confucius he declared was merely an example of our way of translating all Chinese phrases as ridiculously as possible; it meant really the Higher and Greater Man, the Universal Man, in whom the inferior egotistical man merged himself. It was the salvation of the Revivalist everywhere; it was the Spiritual Man of Pauline Christianity. When the late Mr. Albert Edward Preemby poured out all his little being into the personality of Sargon, King of Kings, he was only doing over again what the saints and mystics, the religious teachers and fanatics, have done throughout the ages. He was just the Master under the Bo Tree translated into the cockney of Woodford Wells.

Presently Devizes was talking. Devizes was a great contrast to Lambone. He talked a different language. He did not seem nearly so clear and clever to Bobby as Lambone did, but he had an effect of sincerity and solidity of conviction that Lambone lacked altogether. His interventions made all that Lambone said seem like a wild and picturesque parody of something that was otherwise inexpressible. Both he and Lambone had an air of casting verbal nets for some truth that still eluded them. And yet this truth so remotely and imperfectly apprehended was for each of them the most important thing in life.

'Stripped of its theological trappings,' Devizes said to Lambone, 'your new religion is simply a statement of this. That our race has reached, and is now receding from, a maximum of *individuation*. That it turns now towards synthesis and co-operation. It will move back towards what you call Sargon, the great ruler, and it will swallow up individual egotistical men in its common aims. As already scientific work swallows them up. Or good administrative work. Or art. That is what you are saying.'

'Exactly,' said Paul Lambone. 'If we *must* talk your language, Devizes, and not mine. Art, science, public service, creative work of every sort, these are parts of what you, I suppose, would call the race mind, parts of the race life. Every man who matters is a fresh thought, a fresh idea. He is himself still, it is true, but his significance is that he comes out of his past and out of his conditions and he flows on to further men. This is the new realization that is changing all the values in human life. It is happening everywhere. Even in the books and reading of to-day you can see the thing happening. History now becomes more important than biography. What made up the whole of life in the romantic past; the love story, the treasure story, the career, getting on, making a fortune, the personal deed and victory, the sacrifices for an individual friend or love or leader; remains no longer the whole of life and sometimes not even the leading interest in life. We are passing into a new way of living, into a new sort of lives, into new relationships. The world which seemed for a time not to be changing any more is changing very swiftly . . . in its mental substance.'

'New sorts of people,' said Bobby softly, and went off from listening to Lambone's lucid little voice into a final recapitulation of the puzzling things Christina Alberta had said and done that day.

§ 5

Bobby was recalled to the matter of the talk by a movement in the chair behind him.

Lambone's smooth voice was explaining: 'So that it does not matter so much what we achieve as what we contribute. That cherished personal life which men and women struggled to round off and make noble and perfect, disappears from the scheme of things. What matters more and more is the work one does. What matters less and less is our personal romance and our personal honour. Or rather our honour will go out of us into our work. Our love affairs, our devotions and private passions for example, will fall more and more definitely into a subordination to our science or whatever our function is. Our romances and our fame and honour will join our vices among the things we suppress. There was a time when men lived for a noble tomb and in order to leave sweet and great memories behind them; soon it will matter nothing to a man and his work to know that he will probably die in a ditch – misunderstood. So long as he gets the work done.'

'With no last Judgment ever to vindicate him,' said Devizes.

'That will not matter in the least to him.'

'I agree. Some of us begin to feel like that even now.'

'Even if one has done nothing worth doing,' said Paul Lambone, and in his voice was that faint quality of the sigh of one who has crowned a rather difficult and uncertain card castle, 'even if Sargon had died unrescued in his Asylum and all the world had thought him mad, all the same he would have escaped, his imagination would have touched the imagination of the greater life.'

Came a pause of edification and then a sigh of satisfaction from Miss Lambone. She never understood in the least what her brother was talking about, but she adored him when he talked. Nobody she thought had ever talked like him, or could possibly talk like him. His voice was so clear and bright, like the best sort of print. Only sometimes you wished you had spectacles.

But now Miss Lambone was to receive a shock. Christina Alberta suddenly came out of the silence in which she had been sitting.

'I don't believe in this,' said Christina Alberta out of the depths of her chair.

Bobby was beginning to know the voice of Christina Alberta very well; and he knew now that she was terrified at having to talk, and at the same time desperately resolved to get something said. He knew too that she was gripping hard at the arms of her chair. He glanced at Devizes and in that instant the lighthouse beam touched his face and Bobby saw it very intent, watching Christina Alberta steadily and as if forgetful of all other things. It was intent and tender and tenderly apprehensive, grave and very pale in that white illumination. When the light had passed away Bobby still seemed to see that face, but now conversely it was a face of ebony.

'I do not believe in *any* of this,' said Christina Alberta. She paused with the effect of marshalling her argument. 'It is theology, I suppose,' she said. 'Or mysticism. It is all an intellectual game that men have played to comfort themselves. Men rather than women. It makes no real difference. Tragedy *is* tragedy, failure *is* failure, death is death.'

'But is there ever complete failure?' asked Lambone.

'Suppose,' said Christina Alberta, 'suppose a man is thrown into prison and misrepresented to all the world, suppose he is taken away presently and made to dig his own grave, and shot at the edge of it and buried and then lied about for a time and forgotten. It isn't a part of the race that is murdered, it isn't a wonderful thing that passes on; it is a man who has been killed and made away with. Your mysticism is just an attempt to dodge the desolation of that. It doesn't. Such things have happened. They happen to-day. In Russia. In America. Everywhere. Men are just wiped out, body and soul, hope and will. That man and his black personal universe are done with and over, and there is an end to his business; he is beaten and wiped out, and all the clever talk upon easy sofas in the warm twilight will not alter that one jot. It is frustration. If I am frustrated I am frustrated, if I have desires and dreams and they are defeated and die, I die. It is playing with words to say I do not die or that they are changed and sublimated and carried on into something better.'

'My dear,' said Miss Lambone to Miss Means. 'You are sure you are not feeling cold?' Her voice conveyed a faint intimation that she would cease to be acutely interested in the talk if this chit of a girl intervened any further in the discussion, and that she would begin to do things with wraps and shawls and break up the meeting.

'I'm perfectly happy, dear,' Miss Means answered. 'All this –! I wish it could go on for ever.'

But Christina Alberta disregarded Miss Lambone's warning. She had something to say and there was some one she wanted to say it to, not too pointedly, not too plainly.

'All this theology, this religion, the new religions that are only the old ones painted over——'

'Reborn,' said Paul.

'Painted over. I don't want them. But that is not what I want to say. What I want to say is that you are wrong about my Daddy, you are quite wrong about him. That I do know. Mr. Lambone has dressed him up to suit his own philosophy. He had that philosophy long before he knew him. And you talked my Daddy over and put Mr. Lambone's ideas into him when he was beaten and broken because they suited his case. They weren't there before. I know him and exactly how he thought. I was brought up on him. He talked to me more than to anyone. And it is all nonsense to talk of him – his exaltation, as being like the great soul coming like the tidal sea into the pool of the little soul. It didn't. When he said he was Lord of the World he wanted to be Lord of the World. He didn't want to incorporate any other people at all – or be incorporated. He was just as exclusively himself when he was Sargon as when he was Albert Edward Preemby. More so. . . . And I believe that is how it is with all of us.'

She went on rather hurriedly, for she knew there were forces there very ready to silence her.

'I want to be myself and nothing else. I want the world – for myself. I want to be a goddess in the world. It does not matter that I am an ugly girl with natural bad manners. It does not matter that it is impossible. That is what I want. That is what I am made to want. One may get moments anyhow. A moment of glory is better than none. . . . I believe that sort of thing is what you all want really. You just persuade yourselves you don't. And you call that religion. I don't believe anyone has ever believed religion from the beginning. Buddhism, Christianity, this fantastic Sargonism, this burlesque religion you invent to make an evening's talk, they are all consolations and patchings-up – bandages and wooden legs. People have tried to believe in such religions no doubt. Broken people. But because we cannot satisfy the desires of our hearts – why should we cry "Sour grapes" at them?

'I don't want to serve – anything or anybody. I may be heading for frustration, the universe may be a system of frustration, but that doesn't alter the fact that this is how I feel about it. I may be defeated; it may be certain that I shall be defeated – but as for bringing a contrite heart out of the mess and starting again as a good little part of something – I *don't* fink. Oh, I know I beat my hands against a wall. It's not my fault. Why don't we take? Oh, why don't we dare?'

Miss Lambone stirred and rustled.

The darkness that was Devizes spoke to Christina Alberta, and Miss Lambone became still.

'We don't take and we don't dare,' he said, 'we don't defy laws and customs because there are other things in our lives, *in* us and not outside us, that are more important to us. That is why. It pleases Paul to dress up his view of these things in old mystical phrasing, but what he says is really an unscientific way of putting psychological fact. You think you are simple, but you are really complex. You are the individual but you are the race also. That is your nature and mine and everyone's. The more our intelligence awakens the more we know that.'

'But it is the difference that is distinctively me, and not the general part. The race in me is no more to me than the ground I walk on. I am Christina Alberta; I am not Woman or Mankind. As Christina Alberta, I want and I want and I want. And when the door is slammed upon my imaginations I cry out against it. Why pretend I give up a

398

thing because I can't have it? Why make a glory of renun-
ciation and letting-go? I hate the idea of self-sacrifice.
What is the good of coming into the world as Christina
Alberta just in order to sacrifice being Christina Alberta?
What is the good of being different if one is not to live a
different life?'

Unexpectedly Miss Lambone intervened. 'The life of a
woman is one long sacrifice,' she said.

There was a pause.

'But we have the vote now?' said Christina Alberta almost
flippantly. 'Why is a woman's life sacrifice?'

'Think of the children we bear,' said Miss Lambone in a
constrained voice.

'*Well!*' said Christina Alberta, and suppressed some scandalous remark.

'The most astonishing thing about us,' she broke out
again, after a pause; 'the most astonishing thing in the
feminine make-up is that hardly any of us *do* seem to want
children. A lot of us anyhow don't. Now that I am beginning to learn something about biology, I realize how marvellous that is. As a race of creatures specialized for children, we ought to be eaten up by the desire for children.
As a matter of fact most modern women will do anything
to avoid having children. We dread them. To me they
seem like a swarm of hidden dwarfs, prepared to come
upon me and eat up my whole existence. It's not simply
I don't want them; I live in fear of them. Love we *may*
want. Many of us do. Intensely. We want to love and be
loved – to get close and near to some one. It's a delusion I
suppose. One of nature's clumsy tricks. It is all a delusion.
He vanishes – he was never there. Under the old conditions it availed; it got the children Nature wanted. But we
don't think of children. We don't want to think about
them. There it is! And anyway children do not take a
woman out of her egotism; they only extend and intensify

it. I have known intelligent girls marry and have children.
and when the baby appeared their minds evaporated,
They became creatures of instinct, messing about with
napkins. I could scream at the thought of it. No, I am an
egoist pure and simple. I am Christina Alberta, and her
only. I am not Sargon. I refuse altogether to mix with
that promiscuous anybody-nobody.'

'After all that may only be a phase in your development,'
said Devizes.

'It is the only one I know.'

'That is evident. But I assure you, Christina Alberta,
that this revolt and distress of yours is a phase. You are
talking rebellion and egoism and anarchism as a healthy
baby screams to get breath into its lungs, and escape from
the stuffiness of old air. The baby doesn't know why it
screams and no doubt finds some dim little grievance in
its brain –'

'Go on,' said Christina Alberta. 'Chastise me and chastise
me.'

It seemed to Bobby that there were tears in her voice.

'No, but you are so young, my dear,' said Devizes.

My dear!

'Not so young. Not so actually young,' cried Christina
Alberta.

'If I live to be eighty,' said Christina Alberta, 'shall I ever
be able to feel more than I am feeling now? Why will you
always treat me like a child nowadays?'

'Feeling isn't the only measure,' said Devizes. 'Even now,
to-night, you are talking below your beliefs. You are not
an egoistic adventurer. You take sides on a score of matters. You insist you are a Communist for example.'

'Oh! just to smash up things,' said Christina Alberta.
'Just to smash up everything.'

'No. You say that to-night, but you have told me differently before. You have a care for the world. You want to

400

help forward the common interest. You develop a passion
for scientific truth. Well – there's no way of fencing in
your individuality from other minds in science or in public
affairs. You're a part by necessity; you can't be a complete
whole. You find already you can't keep away from these
things. They will take you more and more, whether you
like it or not, because it is the spirit of the time. That is
what is happening to us all. You can't escape. Our work,
our part, is the first thing in our lives. To that, pride must
bow now and passion and romance. We have to slam and
lock and bar the door against all personal passion that
might wreck our work. Bar it and put it out of your mind.
As a secondary thing. Work. Give the greater things a
chance to keep you.'

'That's all very well.'

'It's everything.'

'Why *should* they keep me?' came from Christina Alberta,
sullenly and resolutely.

'I know that this is your faith,' she said. 'You told me all
about it. You've always told me about it.' Bobby's quick
ear detected a change in her voice. 'Do you remember our
first talk together? Do you remember our talk in Lonsdale
Mews? When we dined together at that Italian place?
That night. Just after we had found each other.'

Found each other?

'But I did not know then that your faith meant all the
suppressions and sacrifices and discretions it seems to do.
I thought it was something robust and bold. I did not
understand its – qualifications. But since then we have
argued about these things and argued. That day at Kew
Gardens. That day when you took me for that walk over
the downs to Shere. We have threshed things out. Why
should we argue again? I am giving in – what can I do
but give in? – and soon I will be a Sargonite with you and
Paul. But not this summer. Not now. This night – This

wonderful first night of summer. To-night I rebel against any renunciation, any fobbing-off of individuals with second-best things. I am going to be impossible and absurd. For the last time. I want the world from the stars to the bottom of the sea for myself, for my own hungry self. And all between. The precious things between. The love. . . . *There!*'

Vague questions appeared and vanished again on the screen of Bobby's mind. What had Christina Alberta renounced? What was she renouncing? What was anyone renouncing? And had his ears cheated him, or had Devizes called her, 'my dear?' In front of Margaret Means and in face of all the circumstances of the case it seemed to Bobby that Devizes was the last person who ought to call Christina Alberta 'my dear.' And what was this about 'fobbing-off'? Was this really a shameless plainness of speech, an atrocious confession, or something that he misunderstood?

Miss Lambone stirred uneasily.

It was as if an evil spirit possessed Christina Alberta. 'Oh, *damn* renunciation!' she said with bitter gusto.

They seemed to be sitting for some moments in a profound silence, and then the nightingale became very audible.

§ 6

'I think,' said Miss Lambone in the silence, 'that it is getting just a *leetle* chilly.'

'It is so beautiful here,' said Miss Means, who was warm in Miss Lambone's shawl. 'Perfectly beautiful.

'How you can talk of frustration –!' she added, and left her sentence incomplete.

'I think,' said Miss Lambone, 'that I shall go in and light

the candles. It is too wonderful a night for the electric
lights, far too wonderful. We will just light the candles
and the fire. And perhaps you will play us something
beautiful. These are such marvellous fireplaces here that
they blaze up at once. I don't know if you have noticed
them – a new sort. The fire is all on the hearth – no
draught below, but the shape of the back draws it up.

'I love a wood fire,' said Miss Lambone, and sighed and
rose slowly and voluminously.

§ 7

Two days later Bobby came into one of the little studies
on the garden side of Paul Lambone's house. Paul had
found out that Bobby wanted a few days of uninter-
rupted thought in which to begin his novel, and had asked
him to stay on after the other guests had returned to
London. It was a perfect room for a writer of Bobby's
temperament; it had a low writing-table close to the sill of
the casemented window, and on the sill was a silver bowl
of forget-me-nots and white tulips. A little glass-paned
door released one into the garden without one's having to
go back through the house. The writing-table had everything a fastidious writer could desire, a pleasant paper-rack
and wafers, and real quill pens, and plenty of elbow room.
The chair he sat in was an arm-chair, immensely comfortable but not too luxurious; no hint of repose in it but only
a completely loyal support for a working occupant. A
garden path ran uphill from the window, a garden path
skirted by wonderful clusters of pansies. On either side of
the pansies were rose bushes, and though not a rosebud
was showing, yet the fresh green leaves, tinged with ruddy
brown, were very exquisite in the light.

He stood looking up the path for a time and then sat

down and drew the writing-pad towards him. He took one
of those delightful quills, tested the delicious flexibility of
its points, dipped it in the ink and wrote in his very neat
and beautiful handwriting:

UPS AND DOWNS
A Pedestrian Novel
BY ROBERT ROOTHING

CHAPTER THE FIRST
WHICH INTRODUCES OUR HERO

He wrote this very readily because it was very familiar to
him. From first to last he had written it on fair fresh
sheets of paper perhaps half a dozen times.

Then he stopped short and sat quite still with his head on
one side. Then very neatly he corrected 'which introduces'
into 'in which we introduce.'

It was nearly two years now since he had first begun his
novel in this fashion, and he was still quite uncertain about
the details of his hero's introduction. His original intention about the story still floated pleasantly in the sky of
his mind; a promise of a happy succession of fine, various
and delightful adventures, told easily and good-humour-
edly; the fortunes of a kindly, unpretending, not too brave
but brave enough young man, on his way through the
world, to live happily afterwards with a delicious young
woman. 'Picaresque' was the magic word. None of these
adventures had as yet assumed a concrete form in his mind.
He felt they would come to him definitely enough one day.
If one sat and mused one half saw them, and that was
assurance enough for him. And so having rewritten his
title page neatly and prettily, he fell into a day-dream and
was presently thinking round and about his Christina
Alberta as a good hero should.

Bobby was always being puzzled by Christina Alberta, always coming upon something that seemed to clear up everything, and then being puzzled again. But now it seemed to him that he really did know the last fact of importance that was to be known about her. Overnight Paul Lambone had described how he had taken her to Devizes to get advice, and how they had blundered upon the reality of her parentage. He told his story well as a story-writer should; he gave it dramatic point. Evidently he told the tale of set intention, because it was time Bobby knew. Lambone was aware of Christina Alberta's engagement. He did not know and nobody but Bobby knew that she never intended to be married. But this, it seemed to Bobby, made the understanding of her situation possible; explained that watchful tenderness of Devizes' face suddenly betrayed by the light and his inadvertent 'my dear'; explained her position as though she belonged to him and Paul Lambone instead of being a rather un-accountable visitor; excused her vehement jealousy of Margaret Means, because evidently she had become vio-lently possessive of her father and had counted perhaps upon recognition and being very much with him. No doubt Margaret Means stood in the way of that. It was natural for Christina Alberta to want to be with Devizes and work with him, and natural for her to suspect and anticipate and resent an intervening personality. Apart from the magic of kinship it was natural that two such subtle and abundant personalities should attract each other greatly. That Devizes should have decided quite abruptly to marry Margaret Means did not present any difficulties to Bobby; he was not thinking very closely about Devizes. Margaret Means was pretty enough for anyone to want to marry her. There are times, as Bobby knew, when that sweet prettiness can stab one like an arrow. It had evid-ently stabbed and won Devizes. And almost the only thing that gave Bobby a second thought, but no more than a second thought, was Christina Alberta's fluctuation of purpose, why she should have consented to marry him and then have changed her mind so quickly and definitely and yet have retained him as a lover.

That resolution not to marry seemed after all just a part of her immense modernity. Because of all this group of 'new people' in which he found her, she seemed to Bobby to be in every way the newest. She was the boldest enterprise in living he had ever met. Her flare of hungry rebel individuality fascinated him. Where in this world was she going? Would she win out to this free personal life she desired or would she fail to find an objective of work and come upon disappointment and solitude like some creature that has strayed? The world had terrified Bobby in his own person greatly; it terrified him still more when he thought of this valiant little figure going out to challenge it.

Bobby was naturally, inherently, afraid; his instinct was for security, protection, kindliness and help. He clung to his 'Aunt Suzannah' job for safety. He didn't believe Christina Alberta knew one tenth of the dangers she ran of insult, defeat, humiliation, neglect, repulse, fatigue and lonely distress. His imagination presented a tormenting picture of her away there in dark, confused, immense and blundering London, as an excessively fragile figure, light on its feet, shock-head erect, arms akimbo, unaware of monstrous ambushed dangers. Now that he began to understand her, he began to understand a great number of bright-eyed, adventurous, difficult young women he had met in the last few years, and he had his first dim realization of the meaning of the deep wide stir among womankind that had won them votes and a score of unprecedented freedoms.

Many of these younger woman were doing their work and holding their own exactly like men. They were painting and drawing like men, writing criticism like men, writing plays and novels like men, leading movements, doing scientific work, playing a part in politics. Like men? On reflection – not exactly. No. They still kept different. But they didn't do their things in any fashion one could call womanly. Without adding strange new meanings to 'womanly.' The novels they were writing interested him immensely. People like Stella Benson wrote books like – anybody; you could not tell from her work whether she was a man or a woman. All that again was new. George Eliot perhaps was a precursor. Perhaps. The former sort of women's writings,when they were not 'pretty me' books, were 'kindly auntie' books; you heard the petticoats swish in every page.

Sexless, these new ones? Bobby weighed the word. The earlier generation of women who wanted to be emancipated suppressed sex, suppressed it so fiercely that its negative presence became the dominant factor in their lives. They ceased to be positive woman; they became fantastically negative woman. But this newer multitude was not so much repressing as forgetting their sex, making little of it. Christina Alberta had in a way made nothing of her sex, not by struggling against it, but by making it cheap for herself as a man makes it cheap for himself – so that it was a thing of mere intermittent moods and impulses for her – and she could go on to other things.

Going on to other things. His imagination recurred to that little figure resolved to conquer the world for itself in defiance of every tradition.

There was a strong urgency in him to start off to London in pursuit of her, to hover about her, intervene, protect her and carry her off to security. He knew she wouldn't permit that sort of thing to happen anyhow. He'd have to be just a friend and companion to her, be at hand for her, and if she did encounter some disaster, stand by her.

It was a queer thing that he should want to stand by this unsexed young woman. It was just what one would not expect; it was part, perhaps, of the immense biological changes of the time. In the past the species had needed half the race specialized for child-bearing and child-rearing; now plainly it didn't. The tremendous and worshipful dignity of wife and mother was not for all women any longer. That would remain for a certain sort of them to take up if they would. But a vast multitude of women were born now to miss that. Some would become pretty nuisances who would presently cease to be pretty, parasites on love and the respect for motherhood; shams, simulacra. Others would break away to a real individual life – a third sex. Perhaps in the new world there would cease to be two sexes only; there would be recognized varieties and subdivisions. So Bobby speculated. For just as there were women who did not want to bear children, so there were men who did not want to lord it over wife and children.

They would want to love all the same. Every individual of a social species needed love; to fail in that need was to escape out of social life to lonely futility. 'Mutual comfort,' Bobby quoted. In his past Bobby had dreamt of the love of children. Even now he remembered as a fact that he had dreamt particularly of a little girl of his own that he could protect and explore. But now the thought and interest of Christina Alberta had blotted that out. It was extraordinary to him to perceive how possessed he was by her. He could endure no prospect of life just now unless it was to include Christina Alberta as its principal fact. But he'd be no use to her unless she respected him. He couldn't hope to stand subordinate to her, any more than he could hope to be her master. In the latter case she'd rebel, in the former, she'd despise. They would have to stand side by side. And since she was clever, able and resolved to work hard and distinguish herself, he must work hard and also distinguish himself too. He had to be her equal and remain and keep himself her equal. . . .

That, in fact, was why he was going to write a great novel – not just a novel but a great one.

He looked again at the neatly written page. 'Ups and Downs,' he read. 'A Pedestrian Novel.'

It dawned upon him that there was something profoundly wrong about that.

It was to have been a story of wandering about in the world that is; the story of the happy adventures of a well tempered mind in a well understood scheme of things. But Bobby was beginning to realize that there is not, and there never has been, a world that is; there is only a world that has been and a world that is to be. 'New people,' whispered Bobby, and dipped a quill in the ink and made a border of dots round his title. Then suddenly he crossed out those three words 'Ups and Downs' and wrote instead, 'New Country.'

'That might be the title of any novel that matters,' said Bobby.

He mused deeply. Then he altered the sub-title to 'The History of an Explorer.'

He scratched out 'Explorer.'

'Involuntary traveller,' said Bobby.

Finally he put back 'A Pedestrian Novel' as his sub-title. . . .

He became aware of an intermittent dull tapping, and following the sound discovered a thrush trying to break up a snail on the gravel path. But the gravel path was too fine and soft to give a firm anvil for the beating. 'The silly bird ought to find a brick or a potsherd,' said Bobby and reflected. 'I suppose all the flower-pots are shut up in the shed. . . .

'I don't like to see that bird wasting the morning and being disappointed. . . .

'It wouldn't take a minute. . . .'

He got up, let himself out by the little glass door beside the window and went to find a brick. Presently he returned with it.

But he did not go back into the study because while he had been looking for the brick, he had seen a young blackbird which had got under the strawberry netting, and was evidently scared out of its silly wits. So he went back to see about the blackbird. The minutes passed and he did not reappear. Perhaps he had found some other fellow-creature in trouble.

Presently a little breeze blew into the study through the open glass door and lifted the sheet of paper which was to introduce our hero, and wafted it softly and suggestively on to the unlit wood fire upon the hearth. There it lay for a long time.